DOWN THE RIVER

Michael Henry

MICHAEL W. HENRY

DOWN THE RIVER

BOOK 2 OF THE TWO RIVERS TRILOGY

REDEMPTION
P R E S S

DEDICATION

Dedicated to my wife, Shelley,
my best encourager.
And to my children,
who stepped fully into their
own adventures of faith.

THE NIGHT COULD NOT HAVE been more perfect. Broken clouds diminished the light of the full moon. A veil of mist hovered over the water. Cypress trees drooping with Spanish moss stood guard like ghost creatures. Nothing stirred. The abundant life of the Atchafalaya Swamp was held in waiting.

On a night like this, people stayed away. If a fool went in, he never came out. Fear of the swamp, the energy of the full moon, and the cover of mist made it ideal.

La Marque paddled his pirogue through the black water and brought it to rest on a piece of land where five cypress trees formed the outer circle of his temple. His black calf-high boots impressed the thick mud until he entered the sanctuary. Placing a black leather satchel onto a shelf of flat wood lying across two cypress roots, he removed and precisely set and lit ten candles, two at the base of each of the five trees. Ten flames stood at attention, as if fearing to be extinguished and only bowing as their master passed. The shine illuminated the tall gray trunks, giving the appearance of folds in the robes of fallen angels.

The soft but steady light also resurrected a circle in the earth of thirteen round stones the size of human skulls. Twelve were painted white, but the thirteenth stone was shiny black. La Marque had gone to great lengths to acquire the large, polished obsidian energy stone. Larger than the rest, it was positioned at the westernmost point of the circle.

That was where he stood with his legs wide apart. He pulled a polished silver sheath from his belt. Ornately set in the sheath was a cut citrine stone. La Marque admired the orange sparkle as he slid out the dagger, equally ornate and polished, and twisted the blade in the candlelight. The gleam in his eyes matched the unholy reflection off the cutting edge.

"I call upon you, oh Great One. Your servant awaits." The sound of his voice rolled up the temple columns. La Marque raised his left palm and pricked it with the knife. His squeezed his fist until drops of blood fell to the black host stone between his feet. He would wait until the spirit arrived to petition for an assault of revenge. His target was the preacher in Portsmouth who kept setting his captives free, interrupting the greater scheme of infiltrating churches and breaking up the flow of runaway slaves. Killing him would be too easy. La Marque was going to summon all the power at his disposal to make Deacon Abraham a slave of his slaves.

CHAPTER ONE

"TURN HIM LOOSE, HARTMAN, AND we'll let you and the others go," the dirty trapper shouted. "We're going to hang him like he deserves."

Allen Hartman looked at the Arapaho warrior Kicking Lion, on the ground next to him. They lay behind a thick log after getting shot at by four men.

"Not going to happen. Not today," Allen shouted.

"Send him out! He's killed a lot of people, whites and Injuns alike."

Allen looked to his left at his other companions, Two Rivers and Blue Otter. They crouched low beside a mound of dirt, waiting for Allen to decide what to do. Allen regretted leaving the safety of the Arapaho camp. He'd thought they could ride into Fort Laramie for some trading but hadn't anticipated the desire for revenge by some of the trappers. Allen glanced again at Kicking Lion and spoke in Arapaho.

"He's right. You have killed many people."

"Yes. I tried to kill you."

"Hurry up. We ain't going to wait much longer," the trapper said.

"We're going to hang him," a second trapper shouted. "He burned my cabin and stole all my furs."

"He says he's sorry," Allen hollered, hoping to stall.

A shot rang out. The musket ball whizzed over their heads. Allen rolled over and stuck his Hawken .50 through the roots of the log. He could see all four of the trappers' heads and had a clear shot about forty-five yards away.

"Last chance. Send him out." The trapper reloaded.

Lord, what shall I do?

Looking beyond the trappers to the right, he saw that their horses were tied up to one branch. About sixty paces. With the barrel resting on a root, he aimed. Allen squeezed the trigger until the rifle bucked against his shoulder. The branch shattered. The horses flared and bolted.

"What the . . ." One trapper jumped up. "The horses!"

Two Rivers fired a shot, shattering the powder horn that hung at the man's hip and knocking him to the ground.

Allen heard moaning. No more shots were fired.

"We're going to get you for this, Preacher," the dirty trapper shouted.

"Like I said, not today," Allen said. "Your man hurt bad?"

"He ain't bleeding, but he'll be limping for a while." The man glared at the fallen trapper. "You should have stayed down, you fool."

Allen wished he could explain to them that Kicking Lion was a changed man. Try to convince them to give up their notion of hanging him. But he knew it would be wasted words. Kicking Lion had ravaged the white men for many years, and they would have justice. Allen concluded he'd been hasty in thinking that Kicking Lion would be forgiven by the Fort Laramie community just because Allen had forgiven and befriended him. Folks had heard about the strange fight when the warrior had attacked

Allen and by a fluke incident broke his back. But rather than killing him, Allen chose to care for his enemy, and now his broken back was miraculously healing. They couldn't understand why God would have mercy on a murdering thief like him. People wanted justice. Allen could understand their grievances, as he had been under the killer's knife. He'd also been there when the feared chieftain lay helpless in the lodge of his enemies and in a few short weeks began to walk again.

"They go. No fight," Blue Otter said.

Then Two Rivers spoke in Arapaho. "I will return to camp with Kicking Lion. You and Blue Otter go to fort." He reloaded his musket.

Allen nodded his agreement, disappointed that they couldn't continue together. "I was hoping the people at the fort would see that Kicking Lion here is a changed man. And that peace is possible if we give it a chance."

Two Rivers whistled, and in a couple of minutes his roan pony walked in from the trees, followed by the other horses. "It is easier to trust a former enemy when he is unarmed."

Allen caught the wisdom, knowing Kicking Lion did not carry a rifle or a knife but could still be dangerous. He had appreciated the effort Two Rivers, an aging medicine man, had given to allow the chieftain a chance to prove he had turned a new leaf.

The four mounted and parted company. Allen and Blue Otter rode a wide arc to make certain they wouldn't encounter the angry trappers before reaching Fort Laramie.

Tying up their mounts to the hitching rail, they entered the trade store. It took a moment for their eyes to adjust to the dim light permitted by a small window. Mr. Meecer counted out a tally before he looked up.

"Hello, Allen. Blue Otter." He smiled.

"Good day, Mr. Meecer." Allen approached the counter. "How have you been?"

"Just fine. Business has been good." Meecer leaned on one arm. "Is it true that Kicking Lion is walking again?"

"Yes, that is the truth of it. He can walk and ride. It's a miracle story for sure," Allen said. "The fact is, he was riding in with us but got turned around."

"His back start aching?"

"No, he was fine. We got into a bit of a skirmish a few miles out. Four trappers started shooting at us. They wanted to hang Kicking Lion."

"With due respect, Reverend"—the frontiersman rubbed his neck—"it's a fine thing what you've done, sparing his life and getting him healed up. But you got to keep in mind that Kicking Lion has been killing good people around these parts for much longer than you've been here. They ain't going to share your Christian charity with a man like that. Too much hate for him. I'm still thinking I'd prefer to see him hang myself."

Meecer wore a white linen shirt with leather lacing up the front. What little light there was reflected on his mountain-worn face. Allen saw the years of wisdom in his eyes.

"I hear you, sir. I reckon it is too soon to know for sure if he has had a true change of heart. I suppose I've been foolishly hasty. In any case, I believe the people around here will be angry with me. Perhaps I should stay away for a while." Allen stroked a bobcat pelt.

Meecer nodded, then changed the subject. "Blue Otter, you looking for a trade?"

"Want salt, sugar, and kettle."

"I near forgot." Meecer reached under the counter. "These been waiting for you." He handed Allen two letters.

Allen moved to the light of the small window. There was an official-looking letter from the Office of the Secretary of Foreign Missions of the Methodist Church and one from a Mrs. V. Thompson, New York City.

Who is V. Thompson? Allen thought. *Must be a letter to encourage the missionary.*

He opened the store-bought envelope. The letter was dated April 17, 1840, almost five months earlier. About a year from when Allen had left Buffalo with Reverend Bannister's Missionary Band.

Dearest Allen,

It has been a year since I saw you last. I apologize for not seeing you off at the lakeshore. I just couldn't bear to see you go. I received your letters, but I never had the heart to reply. I sat down and wrote many letters, only to throw them into the fireplace. You must think I am terrible after promising to wait for you and then not even writing until now.

The truth, Allen, is that Jonathon Thompson came to call on me. His attentions filled the void in me that formed when you sailed away across Lake Erie. I soon fell in love with him, and we are now married and living in New York City. He is an associate pastor at the Second Methodist Church. I know I am happier here than I would have been in the Oregon wilderness. I hope you can be happy for me.

Pray for us as we lead a large social gathering for all the young businessmen and women of the city.

Yours Sincerely,

Violet

Violet Chamberlain. She'd married Jonathon Thompson and moved to the city. Allen shook his head, disturbed but also strangely relieved. He thought of her golden curls and sky-blue eyes. He remembered how pretty she looked at his commissioning ceremony. She was correct. She never would have been happy in the wilderness. How naïve was he to think she might. *Lord, thank you for protecting us.*

Allen looked at Blue Otter and Meecer standing in the dim, dusty trading post next to a pile of buffalo hides. This was his life now, and he wanted nothing else.

He opened the second letter.

To the Rev. Allen Hartman,

This letter is to inform you that your status as a missionary is under review. You have not complied with our standards or expectations of communication. We have received no report of the number of converts you have made, no report of your expenses, nor an accounting of the funding of your endeavors.

We have been informed by Rev. Reginald Foster that your conduct has been unbecoming a minister of the Methodist Church. It is reported that you have been dressing as one of the natives and living in their primitive camps. That you have not been educating their children in a proper classroom nor inviting the adults to church services at the Mission Station of which you have been left in charge.

We, the Board of Direction of the Foreign Missionary Society, hereby request your presence to complete this review to determine your fitness to remain in the ordained ministry. You must comply by the end of September 1841.

Respectfully,

Horace Macklemore
Secretary of the Foreign Missionary Society

Allen felt sick to his stomach. "Conduct unbecoming a minister?" he said out loud.

Meecer and Blue Otter looked at him.

Allen groaned in exasperation. "This letter says that I am under review for conduct unbecoming a minister. They want me to go back to Baltimore to defend myself."

Blue Otter appeared confused.

"They're saying I should be teaching Indian children in a classroom rather than living with them in their camp."

"That don't make a derned bit of sense," Meecer said. "What Indian boy would sit still in a schoolroom?"

"I'm being held to expectations that are entirely absurd. How in the world can I explain that to people who have no idea what it's like here?" Allen fumed.

"You thinking you'll go?" Meecer asked.

Blue Otter still did not seem to comprehend why his friend was angry at the paper.

"I don't know. I suppose I should, but I don't know what I could say," Allen said.

"Well, you could just tell them that out here in the west, the preachers have to steal horses, have knife fights, and bury witch-doctors in caves." Meecer smiled. "At least the preachers anyone out here would bother listening to."

"I can't imagine they would ever understand what I've been through."

"Write them a letter and tell them to come out to see for themselves," Meecer offered.

"They have formed their opinion based on what Reginald Foster told them. We never saw eye to eye on things." Allen resigned himself to the hard reality of his circumstances.

"Foster. You mean that arrogant spike that strutted around behind Bannister." Meecer folded his arms. "It were easy odds to bet they'd never last out here. Don't put no stake in his opinion."

"Thank you, Mr. Meecer. I appreciate what you're saying. His opinion might not hold up here at Laramie, but he has influence with my overseers." Allen tapped the counter. "I suppose I'll just have to ride back and try to settle things. And clear my name." He shook his head again. The trip would mean being away for a couple of months at least.

Then his eyes brightened. "Maybe I'll go spend some time with my parents."

Meecer nodded. "You're a good man, Allen."

They shook hands.

"Come now, Blue Otter," Allen said. "Let's finish our trading and head back to camp. I'll explain all this to you and Two Rivers."

CHAPTER TWO

TO THE EAST, THE SKY was navy blue. To the west it was a faded royal blue that offered enough light for Allen and Blue Otter to ride into camp. As they came into the clearing, Allen tugged back on the reins and took in the view of fifty-some teepees stretched along the bank of the North Platte River about thirty-five miles northwest of Fort Laramie. These white cone-shaped lodges, some glowing orange from within with firelight, looked like pinnacles pointing from humble earth toward heaven.

"I'm going to miss this. It has become my home." Allen nudged the buckskin forward.

"You will be missed. The whole camp sees you as a leader." Blue Otter spoke with a solemn tone. "Some will miss you more than others. One will miss you more than all."

Allen looked to see if his friend was smiling, but his usual stoic expression held fast. "I do wish I could speak to Moon Cloud tonight, but it is too late. I will see her in the morning. She will not like what I have to tell her."

"Two Rivers will not like that you go to the white fathers. He wants to learn more from the black book. When Dark Wolf was killed and his evil power was broken, Two Rivers was learning the new path of One Who Gives Life. I learn the new path. Many understand there is new way of the Spirit. Kicking Lion watches and learns. When you go, how will we learn?"

"I know . . . I know. It breaks my heart to leave when so many are finding hope in God. When Kicking Lion tried to kill me in the knife fight, I was afraid, but at the same time I had peace in my heart. I knew that he could kill me, but I had faith—I was certain that was not going to be the outcome. When I flipped him and his back broke on the rock, I immediately forgave him. I didn't hate him or want to kill him. I felt compassion in my heart for him that I know had to be One Who Gives Life speaking to me." Allen patted his chest. "Do you understand my words?"

"I do not know all the words, but I understand your heart."

They weaved their way through the teepees until they reached the one they shared. After they unloaded and released the horses, they entered their cone-shaped lodge.

The next day, Allen spent hours explaining his dilemma to Two Rivers.

The holy man's displeasure was evident in his creased brow. "I do not understand why they speak with lying tongues. I see your heart is heavy, and it is good for you to keep your honor and the honor of your father."

Relieved with his mentor's support, Allen sought out Moon Cloud. He found her sitting on a blanket outside her aunt's lodge, sewing beads on a doeskin dress. Squatting by the cookfire, he poked the coals. He explained the situation the best he could with his limited Arapaho but knew the words that expressed his feelings were swept away by the breeze.

Someone cried out, and a horse squealed. A woman called for help from beyond a few teepees. Allen rose, and Moon Cloud set down her work, reached for her medicine satchel, and trotted toward the call of distress. They found a boy holding his arm and a mother with a worried look in her eyes.

Moon Cloud knelt and examined the wound. "Find Two Rivers," she said to Allen over her shoulder.

He trotted away.

When Allen returned, he watched Two Rivers assist Moon Cloud to form a splint of rawhide on what appeared to be a broken arm. The had moved the boy into his lodge, which was filling up with family and concerned neighbors.

How could he possibly leave these people, his home among them, for so long? Allen sighed as he stepped out to organize his belongings for his trip east.

At first light Allen shoved a doeskin bag full of beadwork, flint-blade knives, arrowheads, leather pouches, and small animal skins into his saddlebag. He had traded for common items to sell to pay for his journey and to save some as gifts for friends. It was the last that he needed to pack before taking his first heartbreaking steps away from his village.

He checked the tiedown straps, then paused and looked up. Sensing a presence behind him, he turned and gasped. There stood Moon Cloud. The golden light of morning touched her soft bronzed skin. Her almond-shaped brown eyes, outlined by thick curling lashes, sparkled back at the sunrise. Long black braids wrapped with crisscrossing blue leather thongs fell over her shoulders. Her neck was adorned with a white bone choker with blue glass beads. The elk-skin dress was light tan with lacing along the shallow V neck. Strands of hide lined with white beads dangled at her shoulders. Moon Cloud watched him watching her.

Allen swallowed hard and realized he had been staring with his mouth agape. He swallowed again. Why would she dress like this? Was she trying to lure him into staying? Then he recognized that this was common appearance for her. She was a dressmaker with her aunt. She took pride in her appearance but was never vain.

"Moon Cloud."

Just then Blue Otter walked up leading his horse and Allen's buckskin. He saw the two gazing at each other and backed away.

Allen locked his eyes on her.

"Blue Otter, translate for me." Moon Cloud said.

Allen caught the grimacing expression, as if a log was about to fall on Blue Otter's foot. But he feigned a smile and stood beside the couple as they faced each other.

"Why does White Falcon leave? Why does he go to the white fathers who abandoned him?" Moon Cloud's brow furrowed. "Why does he not stay here with the people who welcome him?"

"He is responsible to the white fathers. He must keep his honor before them," Blue Otter offered, without waiting for Allen.

"We honor White Falcon. He is a hero to our people," she contended. "Dark Wolf is gone, and we are safe from his curses."

As he translated, Blue Otter fidgeted with his hands and side, sneaking glances at his horse.

"I wish I could stay. I want to stay. But the fathers are believing lies about me." Allen held her gaze. "If I do not go to speak for myself, they will not know the truth. They might reject me, and that would bring shame on my own father and family. I cannot let that happen. I will be back before the snow comes."

"We are your family now." Her face softened, and she glanced down. "I am your . . ." Moon Cloud paused and swallowed.

Allen's brow furrowed. He looked at her bowed head and reached for her sagging shoulders. He looked at Blue Otter, whose stoic face revealed nothing but patience.

Moon Cloud slowly put her hand on a beaded leather pendant necklace. Then, like an ember turning to flame, understanding brightened Allen's countenance. Her mother had given her that pendant.

"Moon Cloud." He lifted her chin. "I am sorry." Allen waited for Blue Otter. "I have only been paying attention to my problem. I did not think how painful it would be for you to see me leave. Your parents have been gone for a few months." He recalled the extraordinary day when he'd buried her parents and forty others by cremation after smallpox had swept through the camp. That dreadful day when Allen had thought he was also burying Moon Cloud, only to later learn it had been her sister.

Allen pulled Moon Cloud close and embraced her for a long moment. Then pressing her to arm's length and looking into her sad brown eyes, he smiled. "Blue Otter, please translate this."

Blue Otter shifted on his feet and scratched his ribs. "Yes."

"Moon Cloud, I must go now to respect my elders. I will clear my name and honor my mother and father. I will return here to my new people. I will come back to be with you." He paused for the translation. "You bring joy to my heart. I feel like the birds that bathe at the river."

Blue Otter looked at him and squinted.

"Tell her." Allen waited. "You give me life. Like the early morning sun that chases away the shadows and shines on the flowers and trees. You make me feel like a stream that rises with the melting snow. I will come back to you." Allen nodded to his friend.

Moon Cloud smiled as tears coursed down her cheeks. She carefully lifted the necklace over her head and placed it on Allen. She spoke in a soft but sure tone.

"Go with One Who Gives Life. I will pray for you. I will wait for you," Blue Otter translated.

Allen gripped the medicine pouch at his chest. "I want to spend my life with you. I will be your family. I will be your man." He leaned in and kissed her.

He looked up. Blue Otter had mounted his horse and held the reins of the pack horse. Allen smiled at Moon Cloud and then sprang into the saddle. Nudging the buckskin gelding, he caught up to Blue Otter. "You didn't translate the last part."

"She understand."

"Are you sure? I mean, that was important." Allen took a deep breath. "Wait! I just proposed marriage to her, didn't I?" Throwing up his arm, he caused the pack horse to flinch. "That's not how I expected it to go. Was that proper? Should I go back and explain?"

"She understand. Whole camp understand."

"What?" Allen twisted around to see a cluster of young women around Moon Cloud and dozens of others watching him ride off. "Oh, good Lord!"

Blue Otter smiled his gap-toothed grin and watched Allen. "Your face grows red like the wild strawberry."

Hours later Allen reined in to let Blue Otter come alongside. "What am I doing? Maybe I should go back. I don't need to leave right away. After all, it will take weeks to get to Baltimore. A few more days won't matter." He scowled, pondering his own thoughts. "What do you think?"

"Good idea."

"I know. I could stay for a week and make preparations for Moon Cloud to go with me. I'd love for her to meet my parents. Then she would understand the world I come from." His words came faster. "I know for certain my parents will love her. My mother could sew some dresses for her and teach her to cook my favorite meals. Yes, steak and potatoes and sweet corn. And corn bread with maple syrup. Fried chicken. Oh, I can taste it right now." His hands moved as fast as his words. "I could take her to church, and the people could see her. That would help raise an offering. Just imagine Moon Cloud walking into the big church in Buffalo." Allen motioned at his companion, who watched the trail ahead. "There are so many things I would like to show her.

I could introduce her to some important people." He paused. "Wait. What am I thinking? She's not ready for that. I would be overwhelming the poor girl. And now that I think of it, not many of the church people would see how special she is. In fact, I'm not sure how I will be received now. No, I just need to stay with this course of action. I'll go back to Baltimore, clear my name, and then go see my folks in New York. I can be back in two months, maybe three. What do you think?"

"Good idea."

"Well, my friend, this is where we part ways. Thank you for being my companion." Allen shook Blue Otter's hand. "Maybe I should go to Fort Laramie and buy her a gift. What do you think she would enjoy? Some fabric? Jars? Or a frying pan? What would be the best gift for Moon Cloud?

"You come back soon."

CHAPTER THREE

A T PRECISELY MIDNIGHT, THE LIGHT of a signal fire appeared across the black expanse of the Ohio River.

"Right on time. You gots to help me, Lord, like you always do. We going to get these poor folk onto the free shores of the north." Deacon Abraham stepped into a rowboat and pushed off from shore. It would take him less than a half hour to row more than a quarter mile to the Kentucky side, where his passengers waited. He looked over his shoulder and saw the signal flame disappear.

There was no way to count the number of times he'd made this trip in the darkest hours. Some nights it was necessary to make several trips across. It all depended on the arrivals from the plantations of the south—runaway slaves following the Drinking Gourd every night for however long it took. When they reached the shores of their Jordan River and looked at the Promised Land, it was all they could do to wait just a few more minutes. Those who didn't make the connection with the conductor tried to swim the treacherous cold current only to end their desperate journey floating downstream, back toward the South they had fled.

Deacon Abraham had purchased his own freedom seven years

before from a South Carolina cotton plantation owner. He was ordained as a deacon in the Methodist Episcopal Church and had planted a small church just west of Portsmouth, Ohio. There a community of freed slaves and freeborn Negroes built their life around the church and their parcels of farmland. The church assisted runaway slaves on their way up to Detroit or Canada by giving them food, clothing, and shelter. In some cases, the runaways were nurtured back to health, and all of them got to hear the gospel.

When Deacon Abraham approached the shore, he whistled like a mockingbird. A moment later a matching chirp replied. He rowed until he found a break in the brush and beached. Within a couple of minutes, the dim light of an oil lamp staggered through the trees.

"Here's three passengers for you, brother," a deep voice said. The lamp barely held back the shadows. "You'uns, be careful climbing into that boat."

A man stepped in first and moved past Deacon Abraham to the stern seat. A woman and small boy sat in the bow. "We's mighty grateful to you, sir," the man said.

With a shove from the man on shore, the tiny freedom ferry was back into the dark sweeping stream. Deacon Abraham strained against the oars, pointed them north, and settled into a rhythm. "You're welcome, friend," he said. "But we'll keep quiet till we's safe in the house."

The oars were padded with thick leather where they fit into the oarlocks, making them virtually silent. Just the soft dipping and swooshing of each gentle lunge made noise that could only be heard from a few yards away.

Deacon Abraham skillfully angled the boat upstream, found his landmark trees silhouetted against the stars, and drifted down to a hidden notch in the brush, where he pulled in. The bow struck the muddy bank. The woman and boy filed out, followed by the two men. Hoisting the boat into the brushy hideaway,

Deacon Abraham then led them up a trail through the woods until they finally stopped at a shack. He opened the door and lit a candle. The low light exposed a low bed frame with a straw tick mattress and a woven mat on the floor with folded blankets against the plank wall. A bucket of water sat in the corner, and a burlap sack hung from a hook in the roof beam.

Deacon Abraham put his hand on the sack. "They's johnny cakes and cheese here. You'uns should keep quiet as you can. In the morning, keep to the trail for about an hour. When you sees a barn and a yellow house, ring the bell and wait. The lady will bring you some fresh clothes and fix a nice cooked breakfast. You can trust her, now. She's a good Christian woman. She helps many a traveler along the way."

"Thank you, sir." The woman said, clearly holding back tears.

"God bless you." Deacon Abraham nodded, stepped out, and closed the door.

Turning, he followed a separate trail winding from the secret refuge through dense foliage until it ended at the edge of a clearing. He scanned the familiar cluster of homes, but it was too dark to distinguish anything. Only the usual sounds of the night were evident—a light breeze shaking the leaves, crickets, and frogs.

In his heart something seemed amiss. "Lord Jesus, thank you for bringing your children to the Promise Land," he prayed softly. "Protect them, Lord. Protect all of us." He crossed the road and walked past the little white church and entered the shanty that served as the parsonage. The candle in the window flickered as he pushed open the door.

Back at the edge of the trees, a dark figure struck a match and lit an ivory-bowled pipe. He puffed the tobacco to life and watched his men come from behind the church, rush into the parsonage, and come back out dragging the limp figure of Deacon Abraham.

CHAPTER FOUR

ON THE FIFTEENTH DAY SINCE leaving Two Rivers's camp, Allen rode through the north side of Saint Louis, making his way toward the waterfront. It seemed shockingly unfamiliar to see row after row of tall brick buildings and dirt roads that had been cobblestoned. He had been away from the city for over a year, but this progress overwhelmed his senses. After asking directions to a livery stable, Allen turned east on a street, relying more on his internal compass than what the man had said. Spotting the sign for ALBERT'S LIVERY, BOARDING, AND SALES, he paused for three wagons overflowing with hay to move out of his way.

Tying Caleb and the two pack horses to the rail, Allen stretched his back and shook out his legs. He entered the office and stood waiting for an agent to finish with a client. Through a window, Allen could see that the hay wagons had pulled into the corral. Just then he heard a gruff voice that sparked his memory.

Coming in through a side door was a short, wiry man with a leathery face and a familiar floppy-brimmed hat. He interrupted the agent and handed him a piece of paper. "Here you go, Albert." He glanced to the side, then turned his whole body, blinked twice, and dropped his jaw.

"Well, pop my bubbles! There's a sight for weary eyes. You send out the boy, and back comes the man." He rushed forward to shake hands. "Allen Hartman. Well, I'll be. Or should I say, Reverend Hartman?" He looked over the tall, young man dressed for the wilderness. "You are still a reverend, ain't you? You look more like Jack Burkett."

"Hello, Old Rag. It is sure a joy to see you." Allen grinned from ear to ear.

"What brings you to Saint Louis? Is the rest of them pilgrims with you?" Old Rag looked out to the street for a familiar figure. "Bannister's not here, is he?"

"Hey, Ragsdale," the agent boomed. "You going to put up that hay?"

Taking Allen by the arm, Old Rag led him to the front door. "I'm taking my friend for dinner. The boys will tend to the hay."

They moved out onto the boardwalk. "Sometimes he gets to pushing like he owns the place," Old Rag said.

"Isn't that his name on the sign?" Allen looked above the front door.

"Well, he don't own me." Old Rag looked over the pack horses.

"Should I unload them?"

"No, don't fret on it. I want to take you to the best eatery in this part of town." He nudged Allen. "This way."

They crossed the street and turned a corner.

As the two walked into the restaurant, a large, buxom woman pointed a finger at Old Rag and then at a short hallway. "Don't be coming in here with stable dirt on you. Get to the washroom, then I'll set a table for you." Her stern face never softened.

Old Rag grabbed a small white towel, dipped it in the basin, and rubbed his face and neck. He wrung out the towel into the basin water, leaving a swirl of dirt. He wiped the back of his hands on his shirt and stepped aside for Allen.

After living in an Arapaho camp for most of a year, the dirty water didn't give Allen pause. But he smiled as he rubbed a bar of lye soap that smelled like black licorice over his hands and up his arms, appreciating the luxury of the moment.

Sitting at the table, Allen took in the tablecloth and gingerly touched the silverware and napkin. He looked around at the other diners. They all used their utensils. No one ate with their fingers or sat on the floor.

"Just bring us steak and potatoes with a deep puddle of gravy." Old Rag's eyes twinkled at the matron. "Oh, and some bread with butter and honey."

"Anything else with that? You want the dancing girls to bring out some wine?" She smirked.

"Now, Winifred, don't be teasing that away. I'm hosting the good reverend here to your fine cooking." Old Rag gestured toward Allen.

"Reverend? What would a minister be doing with you, Ferguson Ragsdale?" She raised one eyebrow. "Are you a real reverend? Or is he trying to hornswoggle me?"

"Yes, ma'am. I am a reverend. My name is Allen Hartman, and I'm a Methodist missionary to the Arapaho out west. Mr. Ragsdale was our guide, and I learned a great deal from him."

"Huh. Well, I'll take your word on it. You look honest enough. But you'll need God and a team of draft horses to drag Old Rag into church." Winifred chuckled all the way to the kitchen.

Old Rag's twinkling eyes followed her form. Then he shook his head. "She's a spicy one. So, Arapaho, you say. That mean you didn't go on to Oregon?"

"No. We didn't get past Fort Laramie. Bannister's Band fell apart. I'm the only one left to do the mission work. Well, Virgil Jolifer is still in the area, but he remarried to Polly McMasters," and they live in her cabin." Allen leaned on his elbows.

"I knew Polly, the little red-haired gal. Virgil married her?" He took off his hat and rubbed his head. "What happened to Mrs. Jolifer?" Old Rag looked tempted to spit on the floor.

"She died, Rag. A couple of days after you left us." He leaned in to speak quietly. "We'd had an encounter with Dark Wolf and his bunch. Bannister had us cross over the river again. They came in threatening the wagons, and Mrs. Jolifer squared off with them. One of them tore out a fistful of her hair and gave it to Dark Wolf. The next day she saw Dark Wolf, but no one else did. She threw a rock at him and picked up another, but rattlesnakes bit her six times. She died shortly after. We think Dark Wolf put a curse on her. It was very mysterious."

"That's mighty peculiar, for sure." Old Rag shook his head. "I warned Bannister to stay on the other side of the river. He never did listen to me."

"We made it to Fort Laramie a few days later. We were putting together supplies and hired the Limms to guide us west, but then the Mills and the Herberts decided they'd had enough and turned around for New York." Allen sipped some water. "We finally started west but came across a burned-out caravan. Some trappers had been attacked by Dark Wolf's bunch. Killed them all and took their horses. Jack Burkett and Joaquin Del Castillo were there by chance and led us back to Fort Laramie. I left with Jack and Joaquin to go on a hunt, and they introduced me to Two Rivers. The next day we stole back the horses, and I was invited to spend the winter in Two Rivers's camp." Another sip. "You were right all along, Rag. They weren't cut out for the wilderness. When I came down in the spring, the Bannisters and the Fosters had already returned East. Reverend Bannister is in Baltimore, and the Fosters are working with the relocation of the Federation of Cherokee Nations."

"Well, I'll be." Old Rag leaned back in his chair. "I knew it would be hard on them, but I figured Bannister was stubborn enough to push on through to Oregon." He leaned forward again. "And what about that pretty lass, Gloria? Where'd she end up?"

"That's another one of God's wonders." Allen shook his head in unbelief. "By the time I came out of the hills, she was married too."

"What? You let her slip away?" Old Rag grinned.

"She was just a good friend for me. Still is. But she married a missionary who came up from the South Platte. They fell in love, and she moved down there with him. I rode with them part of the way." Allen's soft smile faded. "After that things got interesting."

"Even more interesting?" He leaned back so Winifred could set down a plate of food.

"On my way back to Fort Laramie, I came across two wagons heading east. They had a woman and daughter with them, sick with smallpox. They told me that they had been up at Two Rivers's village and got chased off. By the time I got up there, I found the camp empty except for forty-seven who had died. I built a big platform to burn the remains." Allen looked at his water glass. "It was the saddest thing I've ever seen."

Old Rag swallowed a bite of bread and stared at Allen.

"Two Rivers and the rest had moved the camp, but I didn't see them until later." He sliced of a piece of steak but didn't put in his mouth. "Then I rode south to go hunting and came upon Jack and Joaquin, as fortune would have it. They gave me some inspiration."

"Yes, I expect so. Did they help you track down Dark Wolf?" the plainsman asked.

"In a way. I encountered Dark Wolf in a cave." Allen paused, deciding whether he should tell the details.

"A cave? Did you kill that devil? He didn't get away, I hope." Old Rag again looked as if he would spit out something bitter.

"Let's just say that God brought justice on him. There was a cave-in when the mountain shook, and it became his grave."

"You mean an earthquake?"

"It was more than that, Rag." Allen looked him in the eye. "I believe it was the answer of prayers to rescue me and bring an end to that reign of terror." Allen wondered if the report would bring out skepticism in his friend.

"Allen." Old Rag's eyes never seemed more sincere. "If anyone else told me about that, I would not believe it for a minute. But I know you are a man of truth, and I believe God did everything you said. As hard as it is to settle in my head, I believe you." He fiddled with his napkin. "I ain't never come out to say this before, but since knowing you, I've started talking to God. And sometimes he talks back."

"It warms my heart to hear you say that."

"Well. I ain't making my way to the church meetings yet, but something feels different in here." He tapped his chest. "I thank you for being true and not like them other preachers what's always telling you what to think. I don't abide by that. I can see your faith, and you let me catch up when I'm good and ready to walk that trail."

"Thank you, Rag."

"Let's get to eating. This steak's going cold." He dug in.

Allen took bites of steak and potatoes. The conversation turned to buying passage on a steamboat for Pittsburgh and how he could sell his trade goods at the emporium. When they had finished their meal, Old Rag helped Allen with the connections he needed. They easily sold the pack horses to Albert, but Rag insisted that he board Caleb for no charge at his place.

"Thank you for everything, Rag." Allen reached out his hand. "I'm very happy our paths crossed."

The weathered frontiersman stepped past Allen's hand and gave him a hug. "God must have made that happen. If you'd come in a minute later, I never would've seen you."

"I'll be back through here in a month, I expect." Allen cherished the unexpected moment.

"I'll be here." Old Rag seemed sad at the parting but proud of the friendship.

Allen received his boarding pass at the depot and carried his new leather satchel with a new suit and shoes to the landing. He spotted the *Pittsburgh Princess* and dodged his way through the stevedores hoisting loads of crates and kegs.

When he reached the gangplank, Allen looked over his shoulder to catch a final glimpse of Old Rag, but the swarm of activity had swept him away. Turning back, Allen gasped. In front of him stood a man whose piercing eyes were darkened in the shadow of his black brimmed hat. He was shorter than Allen and wore a black suit over a high-collared black shirt. Black boots reached his knees, where a silver buckle at the side glistened like a star. He had a dark complexion, but lighter than other Negroes, and was clean shaven except for a small wedge-shaped patch of whiskers beneath his lower lip.

"Don't go down the river," the mystery man said. "Bad things will happen if you go down the river."

Before Allen could say anything, someone bumped him from behind. He sidestepped as a couple with a suitcase pressed past him to use the gangplank.

Allen turned to face the dark stranger. He was gone. Allen looked all around. There was no place for him to hide and several yards of space before the next person in sight. All the people in the vicinity wore colorful clothing, no one in black. He spun in a full circle. Then shaking his head, he walked up the ramp.

An hour later, after getting underway, Allen wandered out of his stateroom to the deck and leaned on the rail to view the water and the shore. To his left he noticed the couple who had brushed past him. He casually approached them. "Pardon me. May I ask if you noticed the man I was talking to on the shore, when you needed to get by me?"

"No, I didn't see anyone there other than yourself." He looked to his wife, who shook her head. "It seemed strange to us that you appeared to be in a conversation by yourself."

"There was a man there wearing a black suit. You didn't see him?"

"No. Sorry, but we didn't see any other person." The man took his wife by the arm, and they moved away.

Allen frowned. "Lord, what was that all about?" He took a deep breath and tried to calm his thoughts. The boat shifted and moved closer to shore. Assuming it was to avoid a sandbar, Allen focused his attention on the brush and trees along the bank as it rushed by. As he looked downstream, he spotted a break in the brush coming up. A glitter of light caught his eye, and he dropped his jaw. There, standing at the edge of the water, was the man in black. His eyes penetrated Allen's, causing him to swallow hard. As they coursed by, the man held out his left hand palm out, as if commanding a halt. He then put both wrists together, as if bound with chains.

The hair on Allen's neck stood up, and a shiver jolted his spine. How in the world could the man in black be there so soon? Not even a racehorse could have gotten so far so fast.

The brush concealed the man from view. Allen grasped the railing and made his way back to the stateroom. His knees wobbled, and his hands shook as he sat on the bed. "Lord, what is this? So profoundly mystifying. It feels like the I'm back in Dark Wolf's cave. What am I to understand?" He reached for his Bible and read Psalm 91 several times through. "I dwell in the shelter of the Most High."

Hours later, popping awake, Allen breathed slowly and deeply. A heavy feeling weighed on his heart, but it also felt physical, as if being restrained by a heavy canvas. He moved his arms and legs and then sat up, just to make sure he could. Sliding on his pants and shirt, Allen left the room to get fresh air. The night was warm and humid, not refreshing. He explored the water with his gaze, listening to the splashing of the wake and the paddle wheel. Closing his eyes, he still felt the heaviness. Then as if some invisible force pushed him, Allen looked up and saw another steamboat heading the other direction, downstream. It made a wide arc to turn south. The *Pittsburgh Princess* curved to the left and slowed slightly. They must be leaving the Mississippi and turning onto the Ohio River. The other boat was heading downriver. He pictured again the man in black and the hand gestures he'd made. Well, Allen was going upriver, so there was nothing to worry about. As the other boat disappeared, so did the heavy feeling.

"Lord, is there something about that boat I'm supposed to know?"

The image of his friend Deacon Abraham came to his mind. "Yes, Lord, bless Deacon Abraham. I am excited to be seeing him soon."

CHAPTER FIVE

Sister Lydia walked briskly across the dirt road, carrying a small black kettle and a basket. Her cheerful blue cotton dress and light-blue head wrap did not reflect her determined scowl as she knocked on the door of the parsonage.

"Deacon Abraham? Is you home?" She knocked again. "Deacon!"

Walking around the side of the faded-white shanty, she called out again, "Deacon!" The outhouse door was ajar. She returned to the front of the house and out to the road. Setting down the kettle and basket, she scanned the area for any sign of a person. No one. Striding to the cabin next to the parsonage, she knocked.

As the door opened, a young woman in a worn-out sack dress with a toddler on her hip and another holding her leg, timidly greeted her. "Morning, sister."

"Good morning, Blessing." Lydia said. "Have you seen the pastor about?"

"No, ma'am. I ain't seen him or heard him. Most days he out singing on his chores by now." Her brow creased.

"He was due for breakfast but never came." Lydia pursed her lips. "Ain't like him to miss the biscuits and ham." She paused. "Well then, if you see him, give him the word."

"Yes, ma'am. God bless you." The young mother closed the door.

Sister Lydia hurried back to the parsonage. She knocked again and opened the door. Her ample figure filled the frame. "Deacon?" Entering, she looked about. Nothing. But the faint smell in the air drew her attention to the melted-down tallow candle on the windowsill. The candle indicated a safe haven for runaway slaves. It also signaled toward Sister Lydia's house for her to be interceding for their safety. Lydia had not seen the flame last night. But now, the candle was nothing more than remains. "He would have snuffed this out had he been here. Oh, Lord Jesus." The startling reality hit her like a slamming door. She fell to her knees. "My Lord Jesus. Oh, oh my Lord Jesus." She sank forward as if a cotton bale was placed on her shoulders.

Gasping with heaving breaths, Lydia cried out to God. "Jesus, Jesus, Jesus. How do you want me to pray, Lord? Guide me with your Spirit. May your Holy Ghost groan through me, Lord, 'cause I ain't got the words. I don't know what this burden means, dear, sweet Jesus. What happened to the pastor? He's your lamb. You gots to save him. Tell me, now. Tell me what I's to do."

She hummed, releasing a soft, slow melody from heaven. Then she stopped. A struggle. In her mind, the image of a struggle appeared. Out of darkness and water, the vague image of Deacon Abraham twisting against the grip of a strong arm. He went silent and drifted away in a dark box. The tree-lined shores of the river took shape as the box became a boat carried away by the black current.

Sister Lydia rose and rubbed her knees. Adjusting her headwrap, she left the parsonage and crossed the yard to the church. Inside the door, she reached for the rope and rang the bell. Louella and Mabel came in first. Within a few minutes, other people scurried in with questioning faces. Blessing, with her two kids, trailed in last.

"What is it, sister?" Louella asked. "Why you ringing the warning bell?"

Not knowing where to begin, Lydia took a deep breath. "Deacon Abraham's gone missing."

Gasps. "How can you be sure?"

"He ain't home. He didn't come for breakfast." She looked at each face. "If you'uns know where he is, say it now."

Silence.

"I called out to him. I went inside his house, and they was no sign he been there. Except for the burned-down candle in the window." She paused. "He crossed the river in the night to bring back some travelers."

"You think he drown in the river?" Mabel leaned into her mama.

"No, child. I's thinking he was kidnapped by the slave catchers." Lydia pursed her lips.

Louella cupped her chin. "Oh Lord, that can't be true."

"What can't be true?" The church door swung open with a thump. "Who rang the bell? I don't see any urgency." Nolia Biss marched in.

Lydia sighed. "Come in, Sister Nolia. We were just about to pray for Deacon Abraham."

"You interrupted my reading for a prayer?" She folded her arms and cocked her hips. "Where is Abraham? Is he sick?"

"He was taken by slave catchers on a boat." Lydia said.

"Slave catchers? And how do you know that? Did you see them?" Nolia planted her fists on her hips. "How do you know he's not out calling on folks?"

"He didn't come for his breakfast this morning. I took some over to his house, but he weren't there. Only a candle was melted all the way down." Lydia held her ground.

"A candle?"

"The signal candle in the window."

"Maybe he shouldn't be going after runaways in the middle of the night. He'll be bringing trouble on all of us." Nolia scowled.

"Everyone here helps the runaways the best we can." Lydia held her gaze. "You came here yourself needing our help."

"I wasn't no runaway. I had my own papers. I was granted freedom because I earned the right." Nolia moved toward the center of the circle. "Deacon Abraham must be in Portsmouth. If no one saw him, we can't jump to conclusions about kidnapping."

"I saw a Holy Ghost vision of him on a boat. It was black water. That means evil carried him away," Sister Lydia confided.

Some of the group nodded.

Seeing the others in agreement, Nolia straightened her shoulders. "Let's pray then. Gracious Lord, we praise your mighty name. You are the Good Shepherd, and we beseech thee to care for Abraham, wherever he may be. If he's buying goods in Portsmouth or if he's caught up in danger, we trust him to your care. Amen." She lifted her chin and walked toward the door. "That's settled. We might as well get back to chores. Who's coming?"

Three women followed her out the door.

Those who remained looked to Sister Lydia. She took a deep breath and blew it out. Her eyes closed, and she shook her head. "You'uns can sit or walk about as you like." Lydia walked in a small circle. "Our precious Lord Jesus. We need you in this hour. Deacon Abraham needs you in this hour." Her voice got louder, and the circle grew larger. "We praise you, Lord. We praise your holy name. We enter your courts with praise and thanksgiving."

The other intercessors interjected. "Amen." "Yes, Lord Jesus." Their prayers increased in volume until the walls throbbed with petitions.

"We plead with you, Lord God, to rescue our brother as you rescued Daniel from the mouth of the lions. Lift him out of the miry clay and set his feet on the rock." Lydia stomped her foot on the wooden plank floor.

They continued for an hour before the shouting dropped to a murmur and then silence. Lydia paced back to the front. "Is all hearts clear? I feel the peace of God in this room. What is the Lord saying to you? Let's see if we be in agreement."

"Well, I didn't see nothing in particular, sister." Brother Dickson, the oldest member of the church, gripped the shirt over his heart. "It was more of a feeling. The more I prayed, the more it seemed like darkness was wrapping itself like a spider binding up a fly. I kept praying, and finally it seemed like a light of hope was shining deep inside that dark ball. But they's hope, and I be trusting the Lord for that hope to grow."

A few others offered similar insights. Sister Lydia nodded her agreement. "Mabel, is the Lord showing you something?"

Mabel looked at the floor. She suppressed her trembling hands. Her chest heaved with anxious breaths. "I seen him." Her eyes darted about and finally rested on Lydia. "I seen him."

"The Lord showed you Deacon Abraham?"

The girl shook her head. "No." Still heaving, she swallowed hard. "I seen La Marque."

Her mother, Louella, gasped. "Sweet Jesus, protect us."

"La Marque?" Lydia asked. "Is he the witch-man who did the voodoo curse on you?"

Mabel nodded, trembling.

Lydia looked around the group. Some had heard the story. "A year ago, when Brother Allen Hartman came through town, we prayed for Mabel. The Lord set her free from demons. Louella and Mabel used the witchcraft for healing down on the plantation before they put their trust in Jesus to be saved. One of the demons said it was from La Marque. Mabel paid him to curse another man who hurt her. La Marque set a demon chain on

Mabel that didn't break until Brother Allen helped her to forgive the man. God's power is greatly to be praised." She looked again at Mabel. "Child, you is set free by the blood of Jesus. Don't be afraid. What did you see?"

"I seen La Marque. He looked like a devil. Like he was making a hurtful plan on Deacon Abraham." She shivered.

"Did you see Deacon Abraham in the vision?"

"No. I didn't see him, but I know he was there. I just know he was chained up, but it's going to turn out fine." Her countenance softened. She fanned the air in front of her chest, as if releasing knowledge. "He got a shackle on him, but he's singing. And angels is coming to rescue him. Like the angel that got Peter out of jail." Her face brightened. "The angels is coming."

"Thank you, Lord Jesus." Lydia lifted her face and hands to heaven. "Thank you for sharing that, Mabel. That fills us with faith."

"Did you see something, sister?" Louella asked Lydia as she hugged Mabel.

"All I know is that the Lord showed us that things turn out all right, but we still have to fight the battle. We gots to keep praying for Deacon Abraham. And I know we gots to be praying for the helper to come. The Lord seemed to be showing me that someone would come along to light the way for us. To light the way to bring Deacon Abraham back home." Lydia looked into each person's face. "We got to keep on praying until the pastor is here at home with us."

Deacon Abraham opened his eyes. Black. Everything was black. He touched his eyelids to make sure they were open. He tried raising himself on an elbow, and like a flash of lightning, sparks of pain shot through his head and neck. He reached back and rubbed the goose egg behind his right ear. It was then he realized what he was lying on was not his bed. Feeling the rough burlap and firm contents, he deduced he was inclining on a pile of flour bags. He forced himself up and reached for another indication of his whereabouts. A crate, a rope, space overhead. Crawling forward, he touched a plank wall. Then a bump jostled him off balance. Moving back to his lumpy pallet, Deacon Abraham heard a splashing sound, the scuffling of feet, and mumbling voices.

"This is a boat. I'm on the river," he said, barely above a whisper.

Then the clinking of metal, a waft of fresh air, and the sudden flare of a match brought everything into perspective. Crouching in the doorway was a burly man. "Get over here, boy."

Deacon Abraham hesitated, taking it all in.

A pistol appeared in the shine of the tiny light. "Move it!"

As Abraham approached the door, the burly man stepped back, revealing another man. Abraham in an instant was flooded with horror at the jangle of shackles. Choking on his own inner panic, he gasped.

"Put your hands out."

Finding strength from somewhere. "Please, sir, I won't cause no trouble. No call for the shackles."

Burly Man grabbed Abraham's left arm in a viselike grip. "Hands out. We'll make sure there ain't no trouble."

In the same moment the iron cuffs clenched his scarred wrists, every part of his being seized. Images of chains, whippings, and bodies hanging from tree limbs burst into his mind. Involuntarily, Deacon Abraham slid into submission. The men forced him to the edge of the boat. His head spinning in unbelief, Abraham vomited. What little remained in his stomach splashed on the gunwale.

"You're lucky that didn't hit me," Burly Man said.

Together the two heaved Deacon Abraham onto the deck of

the steamboat to the feet of another. "There's your slave. Now pay up, Sly."

Burly Man's head jolted back by a swift kick to the jaw.

"Shut up! And never call my name." Sly glared.

Burly Man reached for his percussion cap pistol, but before it cleared his belt, Sly had the long barrel of a Colt Paterson revolver aimed at his face. He held both thugs for a moment at the threshold of death's door. Burly replaced his gun and moved his hand away. Sly raised the barrel and then threw a pouch of silver coins at the feet of the second man. "Go get drunk."

As the boats drifted apart, Sly lifted his captive to his feet and led him into a stateroom at the stern, close to the paddlewheel. At the far side of the stateroom was a door that opened to a large closet. Deacon Abraham was shoved in and the door locked. Thankful the shackles were loose enough for mobility, he felt around the small room. He located a bucket with water and a second bucket, which he knew by the stench would be his latrine. Others had been in this little room, perhaps many at a time.

Deacon Abraham sat on the floor with his back against the wall. He leaned his forehead against his knees and wept. "Lord God, why am I here? Have I offended you? I'm a free man. You set my heart free. You set me free from slavery. Why am I here in irons again?" There was no answer, just the rumble of the paddlewheel.

Jason Sylvester struck a match and puffed his pipe to life.

"What's so special about one slave, Sly?" Captain Denton asked, keeping one hand on the wheel as he guzzled whiskey with the other. "You could buy a half dozen in Memphis for what you're paying me."

"I'm paying you to keep quiet." Sly looked out the pilothouse window at the gray sky above the black river.

"It ain't my business, but it seems a Louisiana plantation owner would make a wiser investment. I pick up fifty or sixty slaves in Memphis that is headed down the river." Denton took another hit from the bottle. "What I'm saying is that a cheap batch of cotton pickers ain't worth all this effort."

"You're right." Sly puffed. "It ain't your business."

Denton squinted, then looked down. Sly saw the shudder of the captain's shoulders. He used the shadow of his low-crown top-hat brim to his advantage. Denton, like most people, was intimidated by the shadows. That was where Sly lived and worked.

"I'm going to get some sleep." Sly eased the tension. "How long before we reach Shawneetown?"

Denton sighed. "About five hours or so. By noon or shortly after, I reckon."

"Send for me before we get there."

Denton spun the steering wheel a half turn. "All right. I just want to be there long enough to meet Nagle and pick up the banner. Those danged river pirates get you coming and going."

The steamboat captain looked over his shoulder. He was alone.

Abraham heard a noise and movement beyond the door. He leaned his ear against the wood. A shuffling sound. "Sir? Sir, if you're out there, would you permit me to change out the bucket?"

"Be quiet."

"Sir, I been in here awhile, and I could use some fresh air and fresh water."

"I said, quiet."

"But, sir, I'm a free man," Abraham pleaded. "You must have made a mistake."

"No mistake. You ain't free no more."

The captive slumped into the door. "You got me in chains. I can't go nowhere. I'm just asking for some fresh water."

The door flung open, and Abraham fell forward. Caught in the arms of the tall, muscular kidnapper, Abraham stood upright and stared into the eyes of evil.

"Grab your buckets."

"Yes, sir." Abraham responded to this simple act of kindness, but he discerned there was no mercy in this man's heart.

The outer room was lit by a dampened lantern. Sly opened the outer door and made sure the passageway was clear. Abraham stepped out and breathed deeply. He quickly lowered the water bucket with the attached rope and brought it up again. Pouring the contents into the latrine bucket, he dumped it over the side. He refilled the water bucket, and his chore was complete. He paused for another moment to take in the night. Suddenly, he opened his eyes, as if a voice spoke from within. Across the river, another steamboat turned up the Ohio as his vessel turned left onto the Mississippi. Abraham smiled. *Thank you, Lord. You are my hope and strength. I don't see it yet, Jesus, but I know help is on the way.*

He lifted the buckets and turned. Leaning in the doorway with his arms folded, Sly watched. Abraham's smile faded from his face. "Thank you, sir." He ducked back into his gloomy cell, and the door closed. He took his position against the wall, and the smile returned.

CHAPTER SIX

The *Pittsburgh Princess* nosed into the landing at Portsmouth in the early afternoon. The sun was bright, and white puffy clouds drifted by, as if admiring the landscape. The soft splashing of the current against the hull, the smell of the mud, and the mild humidity filled Allen with nostalgia. He had only been in Portsmouth a few days, but they'd changed the course of his life. He paused at the bow and looked downstream to the west. "Father God, I give you thanks for this day." Walking down the loading ramp and up the road, Allen saw the brick houses and tall steeple of the church in the town center. He made his way to the Scioto River ferry, then followed the river road west to the small village that he cherished.

Allen walked down the slope toward the cluster of houses, shanties, and the small faded-white Methodist church. He spotted two children running toward a house, and he grinned.

Sister Lydia hurried out to the road, then with a scream of unbelief and exultation, she fell to her knees, crying and shouting praises. "Thank you, Jesus! Thank you, my Lord and my God!"

Rather dazed, Allen trotted the final distance and knelt before her. She clutched him with heaving sobs.

"Thank you, Jesus." Her breathing slowed. "Thank you, Jesus. You heard my prayer."

"My sister, I'm full of joy to see you." He stood and assisted her.

After minutes of silent staring, she said, "Brother Allen, I been praying for help to come, but I never thought it would be you." She hugged him again. "Praise Jesus!"

Others gathered, smiling and welcoming. A squeal of delight caused everyone to turn and watch Mabel run across the churchyard. She stopped against Allen's chest and held him desperately.

"I expected a friendly welcome, but this is remarkable." He smiled at the beaming faces.

"Oh, Brother Allen. You's welcome anytime." Sister Lydia put her hand on his shoulder. Mabel still hugged him. "But you coming right now is an answer to prayer. We needed a miracle, and God sent you. Bless his holy name."

"Amen." Louella raised her hand in the air.

"Miracle?" Allen smiled as he shrugged.

"You is the miracle. Yes, Lord. And now we need us another one," Lydia said. "Let's all go into the church. We can keep praying and tell you the reason."

When they were seated on the benches, Lydia explained. "Two nights ago, Deacon Abraham was kidnapped and taken downriver."

"Kidnapped?"

"Yes. We believe the slave catchers kidnapped him and put him on a boat."

"Slave catchers?" His brow furrowed. "But he's a free man. With papers and legal standing."

"Being a legal free man don't stop them. They grab man or woman and run them south to sell." Lydia paced. "They use us Negro folk like they would a horse or a mule. Buying and selling as long as it makes a profit. They buy more slaves to plow more fields for their cotton and cane."

"And they whips us along the way," Brother Dickson added. "The first time I run away, the master set out the patrol on me. The hound dogs chased me down and nearly ripped my leg off. Then the master whipped me good and hard. I was down for two weeks."

"Did you notify the night watch? Or a lawyer on Deacon Abraham's account?"

"No point to that. They don't come this way unless they looking to arrest someone." Brother Dickson shook his head and frowned.

Allen listened to story after story of horror and injustice. "Brothers and sisters, I am stunned beyond speech. I am both sad and indignant for your sufferings. I have been ignorant of many things. I have believed I had seen hardship before, but nothing of what you have just spoken. I have seen death and conflict among the Arapaho in the west." Allen cleared his throat and swallowed. "And I have seen the Lord God work by powerful displays of his love and justice. I will pray with you and seek the Lord's will."

"We know the Holy Ghost is calling us to pray for a rescue plan." Sister Lydia put her hands on her waist. "We believe you came in time for his recovery."

Allen looked at his folded hands. "The reason I am here now is to make my way back to Baltimore. I stopped by for some brief fellowship. The denominational leaders have accused me of conduct unbecoming of a minister." He was met by blank stares. "They received a report that I was disobeying orders and not accomplishing my work. It is all quite a misunderstanding."

"Brother Allen, you feeling our sorrow." Brother Dickson pointed at Allen's heart and tapped his own chest.

"I must get to Baltimore soon to clear my name," he continued.

"I can contact the denominational leaders regarding Deacon Abraham. I am sure there will be an acceptable legal recourse." He paused, looking at their bewildered faces. "Benefit. A way to help find our pastor and bring him back."

Lydia shook her head. "Brother, even if they agree to help, it would take too long. Pastor will be on a hidden plantation or worse." She looked deeply into Allen's eyes. "We believe he was taken by La Marque."

"La Marque?" His jaw dropped. "The one who put a curse on Mabel?"

"He the one." Mabel nodded.

"Mabel, do you remember enough to describe him?" Allen noted how different the girl looked than at their first meeting. She had added weight, and her countenance was much brighter.

She scowled. "Yes, sir. I remember. He always wore black clothes and has a small beard. Right here." She pointed to her lower lip. "His hair is long and curly. He keep it shiny with oil." Mabel paused and shivered. "His eyes is black like a snake."

"He's mulatto." Louella nodded. "A fair-skinned Negro."

Allen stood and paced. "It sounds like the man I saw. In Saint Louis." He paused. "I don't know if this will make sense to you, but he spoke with me. He said, 'Don't go down the river. Bad things will happen.' Then he disappeared. I saw him an hour later when I was on the steamboat. He was standing at the edge of the river. It would be impossible for him to have traveled so fast. But there he was, as clear as that cross." He pointed to the wooden cross on the wall. "He held out his hand like this, to stop me. And then held his hands like this, as if I would be in chains." He demonstrated the hand gestures. "He wore all black. His boots were tall with a silver buckle at the top. He had the whisker patch under his lip. And the strangest part is that other people did not see him."

There were several gasps. Louella cupped her chin and closed her eyes.

"That's him. I know it is." Mabel tensed her body. "He is a evil one. He done flew out to find you."

"He flew out?" Allen frowned. "I know I can't explain his sudden disappearance, but how can he fly?"

"My cousin used to do the witch power." Lydia, seated on a bench, leaned toward Allen. "She could do some healing. Cast spells on folk three or four counties away. She could tell the future for some people." Lydia looked around at those nodding in agreement. "One day my cousin told me she could sit still and send her soul to flying. She described faraway places and colors that she never seen in this world. Mountains and trees and oceans. She talked about a city of gold where angels taught her the magic and spells. They was so much knowledge that you don't get from a book."

Allen recalled the things he had seen in Dark Wolf's cave and what he had learned from Two Rivers. The Bible mentioned witchcraft as an abomination, but it did not explain what Sister Lydia was describing.

"Did she ever fly like La Marque?"

"No. But she talked about other witches who had the power. They could appear in a place and be spying on people." Lydia shuddered. "She tried to help people with the white witchcraft, but it deceived her. She crossed that line to doing curses. I tried to help her repent and let Jesus set her free, but she moved on with a man she loved. She had put a curse on another man's farm to spoil the crops, but he paid another witch-man who had more power. My cousin's man got sick and weren't good for nothing. She couldn't bring the healing or break the curse. She never would let me pray with her. When we prayed for Mabel to be healed of the demons, La Marque tried to block her. But she repented first and got forgiven. Like you seen, she was set free. Glory to God!"

"There is so much I don't understand about these matters." Allen studied the faces around him. "Have all of you seen these kinds of things?"

They nodded. Brother Dickson stepped forward. "Brother Allen, you gots to know that we believe in Jesus for our salvation. But there was a time when we didn't have the gospel. My granddaddy came on the slaving ship. He come with his beliefs in the voodoo and healing powers. He taught that to my mother, and she taught it to me and my brothers and sisters. We seen some things. We seen powerful evil things. Most of them was dark and give us bad dreams. And shadow people come in the house at night. Make your skin crawl just thinking about it." He rubbed his arms. "I seen the lost souls for my own self. People, slaves mostly but some white folk too, walking about, but they eyes is lost. Looking out but not fixing on anything. They can't hardly keep their mind on the work. Just walking and moaning. Some of them would moan like they was captive in their own body but can't get free. They mind is a slave to darkness." He rubbed his arms again. "Oh, Lord Jesus, protect us from the fear, and protect us from the evil people. Set Deacon Abraham free so's he come back to preach for us again. We love his preaching, Lord Jesus. Shine your light so's the dark ones run and hide. We take refuge in you. In Jesus's name."

The whole room agreed. "Amen."

"I appreciate you telling me this." Allen looked into each face. "I believe I understand. Last year when our missionary band was traveling west, we encountered an Indian witch doctor. An evil sorcerer. By using the hair of one of the women, he cursed her, and she died of rattlesnake bites. After that I was hunting and shot an elk, but it wouldn't die. I was forced into a mountain cave to escape a sudden rainstorm. It was there that I saw captives, like what you described. They seemed insane, almost like living skeletons." Allen swallowed the memory.

Wide eyes waited for more.

"The sorcerer—his name was Dark Wolf—chanted some words, and dozens of rattlesnakes slithered out of the cave walls. Then some powder was blown in my face, and I fainted. I was lost in the cave and had visions of demons trying to attack me, but they were stopped short."

"I seen that, Brother Allen. I seen all of that." Sister Lydia stood and gestured with her hands. "Lord Jesus, you are truly the Savior. Last spring I was awakened in the night to pray for you. I seen rattlesnakes and wolf-men trying to get at you. They was strong demons. But the Lord is mighty. Glory to his name." She paused as the others murmured their agreement. "Jesus sent an army of angels, and they was swinging their swords. Hallelujah!"

"Yes." Allen sighed. "Yes, praise the Lord. I knew you were praying for me. I knew it had to be." He stood and hugged Lydia. "I knew there had to be saints praying for me. There is no other way I could have survived."

"Deacon Abraham was praying that night." She went on. "Louella and others was at the church interceding and praising God. It was a hard battle, but Jesus won the victory."

"I escaped the cave, but Dark Wolf's men trapped me. I had to fight a strong chief with a knife. He came at me and I fell, but when he flipped over me, he broke his back on a rock."

There were many loud gasps as eager faces leaned in.

"Just then my friends rushed in with seventy Arapaho warriors, and they killed all of Dark Wolf's men. I stopped them from killing the chief, Kicking Lion. I felt prompted by God to have mercy." Allen moved about as if drawing a bow and motioning with his arms. "Then a man we call the Prophet Elijah came up. He shouted a declaration of victory at the mountain. And right then a powerful earthquake shook, and the mountain crashed down on the cave while Dark Wolf and the lost souls were inside." He looked from Sister Lydia to Brother Dickson. "It was a mighty act of God. There is no other way to explain it."

"Praise the Lord. Strong and mighty is the name of the Lord," Brother Dickson affirmed.

"The Lord is mighty indeed." Lydia raised her face to heaven. "Brother Allen, this is my assurance that God sent you back for such a time as this. You are the miracle that Deacon Abraham be needing right now. The Lord sent you to rescue him." Her eyes pleaded. "You got to go down the river."

Allen sat down under the weight of it all. Could she be right? He wanted to help. But how? He need to travel to Baltimore. He wanted to get back to Moon Cloud.

The circle watched, waiting for him.

"I want to help. I really do, but I wouldn't know how to go about finding him." Allen's knuckles whitened as he squeezed the bench next to his legs. "I'm supposed to get to Baltimore and clear my name."

"Brother Allen." Lydia stepped forward, arms akimbo. "You just said you come out of a cave full of demons. What makes you think you can't go find Deacon Abraham? You know good and well that God will direct your path." She raised her palm to heaven.

Allen's shoulders sagged, and his head dropped. *Lord, what do I do?*

"Them church elders will wait. You need to clear your name with the judge of heaven," Lydia said.

"Uh-huh. That true." Louella added. "Keep your name clear in heaven."

Lydia put her hand on Allen's shoulder. "You got this to do. We all can see it. Why don't you see it yet?"

"Is you afraid of La Marque?" Mabel stepped up.

"What? No." Allen shook his head. "No, I'm not afraid of . . ."

His thought trailed off at the memory of the man in black at the riverside warning him to stop. He recalled the grip of fear in his stomach when in Dark Wolf's cave, surrounded by rattlesnakes. He held his stomach and breathed deeply. "It might be that I am afraid. His appearance out of nowhere and then disappearing—it's . . . it's hard to understand. I must be afraid of these things I don't understand."

"You done broke his power off me," Mabel said. "He must be afraid of you."

"That the truth," Louella said. "He's going to a lot of trouble to stop you. Must be he's afraid you'll come after him."

"He must know that God is sending you," Brother Dickson said. "His demons see the holy power of the Lord Jesus coming at them."

"When you was captured by the cave-man, was you alone?" Lydia narrowed her eyes at Allen.

"Yes. But I had friends to encourage me and help afterward." Allen scratched his cheek.

"You ain't hearing me." Lydia pointed. "Was you alone?"

Allen shifted on the bench. "I hear what you're saying. I went in by myself, but I was never alone." He nodded his head and straightened his shoulders. "Even at the darkest time, I knew I was being watched over. The demons were held back. And I knew that you were praying for me. And Deacon Abraham. And my parents." He looked into Lydia's eyes. "The Lord was with me the whole time. I was a lamb in trouble, and he came for me."

"And now Deacon Abraham is the lamb in trouble. And you is the friend to help." Lydia's face remained steadfast.

Allen eased into a smile. "You're right. All of you are right. How could I hesitate even for a moment to help our pastor?" He stood. "I will go. The Lord will be my guide."

Shouts of rejoicing filled the church. In turn, each person hugged Allen and praised the Lord.

Mabel clutched him tightly. "I will pray for you every day. And don't be fretting on La Marque. He may bind you, but the victory belongs to the Lord. You will get free, and you will return. Deacon Abraham will come back with you."

Allen's brow wrinkled at the words he did not expect. *Bind me? Get free?* Releasing him, she looked up at his face. "You will have the victory."

"Thank you, Mabel." He smiled, then swallowed.

"Bless you, Brother Allen. My sweet boy." Sister Lydia squeezed him like a mama bear. "Bless you. I knew you would hear the Lord's voice."

She turned to the group. "It's coming on suppertime. Let's fix us some food and bring it back here to eat together. I got some ham. What you'uns bringing?"

"Collards."

"Corn succotash."

"Fresh bread."

"Catfish."

"Very good. Sounds like we got us a feast. Thank you, Lord Jesus," Lydia said. "Go on now."

As the group departed, Lydia took Allen by the arm. "You come over to my house and get you a bag ready for the trip. We got to find you a boat runner."

"Thank you, Sister Lydia. I appreciate all you're doing." Allen covered her hand with his. "I feel the excitement of faith rising in my heart."

"'Be strong. Take courage.' That's what the Lord Almighty said to Joshua. He will be leading you the whole there and back." Lydia faced him. "You got to trust him even in the dark hours. God be sending you because he knows he can trust you. You done this before. It ain't a easy task, but you the one to do it."

Allen used the small bedroom to change out of his new suit

and into travel clothes. He wore woolen pants that once were black and a faded-blue cotton shirt. He put on an elk-skin jacket and low-cut russet boots he'd purchased in Saint Louis. He scuffed them with a charred stick from the fireplace to remove the appearance of newness.

"What you doing messing up them new boots?" Sister Lydia turned from the kitchen table.

"If I'm going down the river looking for a kidnapped man, I may be among some rough company. I think it's better if I look like a worker and not like a preacher." Allen tugged at his sleeves.

"That might be true a year ago. But you done lost that boy. Standing before me is a man who know his business. And I ain't never seen a preacher wear the hunting clothes." She adjusted the skillet on the woodstove. "You a fine-looking man, Brother Allen."

"Thank you. I just don't want to attract unnecessary attention."

"Men on the river is always chastising and picking fights. They a cussing bunch." She shook her head. "It ain't them that fret me. You got to watch out for the womenfolk. They can be dangerous as a coiling snake."

"I'll refrain from their advances." He scooted a rocking chair over. "There's something I haven't told you yet."

She squinted into his eyes. "You got yourself a lady, don't you?"

Allen blushed. How could she guess that? "Yes. A young Arapaho woman named Moon Cloud."

"Moon Cloud." Lydia paused, as if to ponder. "That's a pretty name. She must be pretty to get your interest."

"She's beautiful. She has long black hair that she keeps in braids. Her smile makes the birds sing. She has these brown eyes . . . they sparkle like when the sunshine makes diamonds on the river." He gazed into a memory. "There's a twinkle like she has mischief in mind, but there's also a spark. A spark of life and joy. It's so natural in her. She is joyful in life."

"Did you testify to her about Jesus? Is that what give her the spark of joy?"

"Yes, I have been teaching her and the tribe about the gospel. But I believe she had an understanding of God as Father even before." He leaned on the back of the rocker. "It reminds me of the verse in Ecclesiastes. 'He made everything beautiful in his time and set eternity in their hearts.' Moon Cloud seemed to know God, but not by the name we call him. As I explained the gospel, it made sense to her right away. And not to please me, but genuinely. Her name for God is One Who Gives Life."

"That be a good name for our Lord. That's just who he is." She smiled. "Moon Cloud sounds like a lovely girl. She must be special for God to put you together out yonder."

"There is more I could tell you, but we'd best get this supper together. I'm most happy I could tell you about her. It's important for me that you know. I only wish you could meet her in person." Allen's special bond with Lydia put her in a special category of friendship.

"We'll let the Lord make that reunion happen. Did you teach her to pray?"

"It's a most curious thing. When she prays, she gets serious, then her face will lift and shine with the glory of heaven. And I know that she's before the great throne." He sighed. "It reminds me of how I've seen you pray."

"Well, bless my soul. That makes my heart happy as can be." Lydia beamed. "I'll be praying for Moon Cloud while you're apart."

"Thank you."

"Let's go eat and get you on your way. The sooner you bring

Deacon Abraham back, the sooner you can fix that nonsense in Baltimore, and then you can make your way back to your sweet Moon Cloud." She handed Allen the pan of ham.

As the meal and fellowship were winding down, Sister Lydia's children, Daniel and Esther, came in out of breath.

"Mama." Esther huffed to catch her breath.

"Girl, you slow down. Did you'uns greet Brother Allen?"

Esther smiled at Allen. "Hello."

"Hello," Daniel said.

"I'm pleased to see you both. You've grown so much since the last time." Allen reached into a pocket. "I have these gifts for you from an Arapaho Indian village." He handed Esther a necklace of blue and white glass beads. "And for you . . ." He placed a deer-antler whistle in the boy's hand.

"Thank you," they said together.

"Mama, we went to the ferry man, and he said they ain't no sternwheeler coming in until tomorrow." Esther adjusted the necklace.

"Thank you, doll baby." Lydia touched the necklace. "I guess the Lord will start working miracles right away.

"All right, everybody. Gather round here so's we can pray for Brother Allen."

People gathered around, and some laid hands on his back and shoulders.

"Heavenly Father," Brother Dickson began, "we see you at work, and we praise you for it. May all the glory come to you, Lord. We bless Brother Allen in Jesus's name as he makes this journey, and we don't know where he got to go. Lead him by your Holy Ghost and by your heavenly angels. Protect him. Provide for him. Help him to find Deacon Abraham and bring him back safe. We trust in you, our Lord. Amen."

"Amen," the crowd said in chorus.

"Sister Lydia?" Mabel said. The group looked to her. "Sister Lydia, I seen him. While the brother was praying, the Lord showed me where La Marque is."

"Did you see Deacon Abraham too, child?" Lydia tipped her head to the side.

"No, ma'am. I only seen the old house where we worked for a time." Mabel's eyes seemed fixed on the air in front of Lydia.

"What old house you mean, Mabel?" Louella placed her hand on her daughter's shoulder.

"Do you mean the plantation near Vermilionville?"

"Not that one. Out in the swamp. We was only there for a few weeks. La Marque was building a big barn. And most the workers was sick. Mama, you remember?"

"It was near Bayou Chene. La Marque bought him a farm that had been flooded out. He built a barn, but it didn't make no sense, because they already was a barn. This one was brick down below and wood on top. Only I don't think the barn was for animals or for keeping sugar cane." Louella gazed at the floor, as if lost in a bad memory.

"What do you think it was for, then?" Allen focused on her.

She quaked. "People. Them sick people. Like the ones Brother Dickson talked about. I was sure glad to leave that place."

"Will it be hard to find?" Allen asked.

"You got to know the way in the bayou. It's a swamp in there. With gators and snakes. I can't bear to think of myself going back in there." Louella frowned.

"Louella! Sister, that ain't helping none. Is you trying to strike fear in us? Goodness. You doing the devil's work for him," Sister Lydia interrupted.

"I'm sorry."

"Thank you, Louella and Mabel." Allen stood tall. "Thank you, everyone, for your prayers and fellowship. I will be leaving now, and at least we have a place to start looking. I won't worry about alligators and snakes today. Like Brother Dickson prayed, the Lord will protect me."

As Allen received hugs and blessings from everyone, the church door flung open. In walked a woman with a stormy expression. "I see you all had supper without me. You didn't think it important enough to walk over there and invite me?" She plunked her right fist on her hip. "And who is this?" Her expression changed as she stepped closer to Allen.

Before Allen could speak, Sister Lydia stepped in front of him. "This is Reverend Allen Hartman, our dear friend. He's on his way to search for Deacon Abraham. And we was just talking about how he needs to watch out for snakes."

Allen looked down and bit his lower lip. "Nice to meet you. I was just about to leave. I must go seek my first miracle."

CHAPTER SEVEN

MAKING HIS WAY ALONG THE Portsmouth water-front, Allen searched for someone to direct him to a steam-boat or some vessel to be on his journey. The sun was descending, along with any logical form of hope.

At the wharf there was a row of flatboats, barges, and keel boats tied up, but no one in sight. Upon reaching the end of the boardwalk, he smelled a sweet scent of tobacco. He recalled the pipe smoke of his mountain friend Jack Burkett.

"You looking for something?" A voice drifted in with the smoke.

Allen, caught off guard, saw a young man reclining against the mast of the last keelboat. "Hello. Sorry. I hadn't noticed you." He approached. "As a matter of fact, I was hoping to find some-one who could inform me about the next steamboat landing."

"Steamboat? Might be one along soon. But to my knowledge, the next one will be heading toward West Virginia." He puffed on his pipe. "Which way you wanting to go?"

"I'm going down the river."

"Not till tomorrow, then." The boatman swung his legs around. "You traveling alone or taking some merchandise with you?"

"I just need passage for myself."

"How far down?"

Allen thought for a moment. "I suppose I need to go to Memphis, maybe beyond."

"That's a fair piece. You in a hurry? Is that why you're looking to leave tonight?" He tapped the pipe on his teeth.

"Somewhat of a hurry."

"Hey, is the patrol after you?" He rose and surveyed up and down the bank.

"No. Nothing of the kind." There was something about this man that Allen liked.

"Well, what is it?"

"I'm not sure I want to disclose my business with you."

"I ain't sure I want some suspicious character riding on my boat."

"Are you offering to take me to Memphis?"

"Might be." He leaned back on the cabin. "You need a ride, and I need reason. We'll both be waiting all night otherwise. You can see I'm last in line to pick up cargo. I'll be sitting here until ten o'clock before they get those barges loaded. No cargo, no money."

"A keelboat won't be nearly as fast as a steamboat."

"Tell me this. We can shove off now, and you'll be twelve hours down the river before the next sternwheeler stops here. Or you can wait and let them catch up to me tomorrow night. Only be saving you a few hours the whole way to Memphis."

"But don't you want to take cargo? You'll be losing money."

"I can pick up a load along the way. Cincinnati or Louisville for easy sure."

"In either town there's likely to be more steamboats there, don't you think?"

"Could be."

"How much is the fare to Louisville?"

"Hold on a minute. What if you're up to mischief? I don't want the constables after me."

Allen chuckled. "The truth is, a good friend of mine has been kidnapped and taken downriver. I'm setting out to find him and bring him back."

"Kidnapped, you say?"

"Yes. We believe he was taken two nights ago by slave catchers."

"Wait. You're going after a slave?"

"I'm going after my friend. He's a free man with legal papers. He's been a parson at the little Methodist church on the westside."

"Them slave catchers can be ornery mean. I seen some get into fights, and they don't hold nothing back. It's a fight to the death if you cross one of them."

"My intention is to bring back my friend. No matter what it takes."

"Humm." He tapped his teeth again. "You don't strike me as the fighting type, but I guess you'd hit back if need be."

"So how much will this cost me?"

"Well, seeing how you're a going after a friend who's been kidnapped by possible murdering thieves and you're willing to die trying, let's say twenty dollars."

"Twenty dollars to Louisville?" Allen smirked. "I paid thirty-five all the way from Saint Louis, and I had a bed."

"Twenty dollars will get you to Memphis. We can maybe make some money along the way." He stuck out his hand. "We'll partner up."

"Hold on a minute. How do I know you're an upright boatman and not a river pirate?"

"Ha! Upright boatman? You ain't never going to find an upright boatman." He grinned from ear to ear. "I know some pirates.

But I ain't one. Too much work for the money. And I prefer to be my own boss. I am the master and commander of the SS *Marylou.*" He swept his arm over the deck, as if it were a tall ship. "Name's Dexter Yates." He held out his hand again. "Folks call me Dex."

Allen shook it. "I'm Allen Hartman. Good to make your acquaintance, Commander Dex."

"Welcome aboard, partner." He jumped into action. "Untie the lines. I'll hoist the sail. We got us a good following wind for now. We'll be making about the same speed as a smoker boat at this rate."

Allen swung his satchel onto the deck and released the lines at the stern and bow. Hopping on board, he said to himself, "My first miracle."

Dex skillfully tied off the mainsail line. "Grab that tiller and point it to shore." He leapt onto the dock and shoved the bow away. With two quick steps he was next to Allen. "I'll take that." He took hold of the tiller. "You can toss your kit below." With a few more nimble steps, the boatman snatched up a pole and pushed against the wide barge they were edging past.

He replaced the pole on top of the cabin and returned to the tiller before Allen did.

Allen leaned on the corner of the cabin as Dex worked the rudder as a paddle. The sail filled with the evening breeze, and they moved into the current. Allen twisted to face the final phase of pink clouds becoming gray in the western horizon. Shaking his head, he looked back to his new friend.

"What?" Dex glanced at Allen, then up at the sail.

"Beg your pardon?"

"You was shaking your head. Something wrong?"

"No, it's nothing."

"Come on now. We gonna be partners, or ain't we? It's a long voyage, so you might as well tell me what you're thinking."

"I guess you're right." Allen pressed his back on the cabin wall and propped one foot against it. "The last time I was here leaving Portsmouth on the river, it turned out to be an expedition that changed my life. Now it looks as if it's happening again."

"The river will do that for you, sure enough." Dex let the tiller rest against his hip as he packed tobacco into his pipe. "But what's life if it ain't an adventure?"

Into the night, Allen recounted his past year. Dexter asked questions about Indians, curses, and demons. Allen held nothing back. He explained what he had observed and experienced and referenced the Bible as often as he could.

"So you're a preacher, eh?" Dex said. "I been to the gospel meetings when I was a kid. My ma took me. We'd go hear the circuit riders. A few made sense to me, but most didn't. Telling stories about healings and miracles. I always thought it would be a good trick to walk on water." He chuckled. "That would save me a bit of hassle here and there.

"I guess I didn't mind the preaching, but the way folks carried on is what spun my young head. Shouting. Running up and down the row. And I seen a few people cry out like their stomach was ailing something fierce. They fell down and wobbled around until the preacher shouted, 'Go out! In the name of Jesus.' Then they got up happy and crying and hugging." He shook his head. "Didn't make sense at all back then or since then. But now that you tell me the story of the demons coming out of that young girl and the Dark Wolf curses and such, I guess it's making some things clear now. It's as if the stories in the Bible is still going on." His face turned toward the moon.

Allen was seated on a canvas bundle with his back against the cabin. "The Word of God is quick, and powerful, and sharper than any two-edged sword, piercing even to the dividing asunder of soul and spirit, and of the joints and marrow, and is a discerner of the thoughts and intents of the heart.' That means the Bible is alive and meaningful nowadays like it was back then."

"What's the rest of it mean? Dividing asunder of soul and spirit?"

"It means it's not just any history book. It's inspired. When you pay attention, God helps it make sense deep in your heart as well as your mind. Before I underwent those spiritual encounters, I thought I understood what the living Word of God meant. But now I see that I only believed with my mind until I experienced that same power. The power of the Holy Ghost."

"The Holy Ghost? That's what they said made the people go around shaking hankies. Not sure I'm interested in behaving that away."

"I don't know how to explain that properly." Allen yawned. "I guess it's easiest to say sometimes people get overcome with joy."

"Well, I guess if you're going to play the fool, it might as well be in church. At least you don't wake up with a hangover, like playing the fool at the tavern all night." Dex chuckled. "Why don't you go below and sleep for a while."

"You sure?"

"Yep. Wind's good. Moon's good. I got some things to ponder."

"I'm grateful. At this time yesterday, I was heading upriver. I am feeling tired." He yawned again. "Perhaps in a few hours I can take a turn at the helm if needs be."

"There's a pallet and a blanket in there." Dex nodded at the cabin.

"Do you usually run at night?"

"Depends on what I'm hauling and what strip of river we's on. This here is deep and smooth. Ain't much in the way except another boat maybe. Besides, we're in pursuit of a villain, right?"

"Yes, sir." Allen glanced back before ducking below. "We are pursuing a villain."

The door opened, and Abraham blinked at the light from an oil lamp. He stood up and waited for orders.

"Bring your buckets," Sly said.

"Yes, sir. Coming now, sir." He grabbed his bucket, grateful for a chance to breathe fresh air.

They held to the pattern of stepping out to the passageway in the middle of the night. Abraham dropped the buckets by rope into the water hand over hand and then back up again. He took a moment to splash water on his face and neck. A momentary luxury. He stretched his back and legs. The shoreline was dark. Nothing to identify their location. Somewhere on the Mississippi River, still.

He took another deep breath and smiled at the gift of fresh air. Turning his head, he made eye contact with his captor. His smile dropped at the fierce stare coming back at him. Abraham picked up his cargo and reentered his floating dungeon.

CHAPTER EIGHT

MOON CLOUD STOOD AT THE edge of the North Platte River. She closed her eyes and listened to the rippling flow of the life-giving stream. Reaching into a badger-skin purse, she raised a palm full of dried sage leaves and tipped them into the four directions of the wind. "Great Father, One Who Give Life, as with the water, you provide life to all things. You breathe life into all things. Breathe now, Father, upon White Falcon. Carry him swiftly on your wind. Give him courage and wisdom as he guards the honor of his people. Protect his journey." She let the gentle breeze touch her face and hair. "I am honored by your presence and filled with peace."

The streambed stones clicked beneath her moccasins as she lifted her gather-bag to her shoulder and resumed her search for medicinal herbs and edible root plants. Moon Cloud paused to scan the whole scene—the wind in the trees, distant chirping birds, and the fragrance of the wet dirt. She hummed as she continued, only to pause again upon seeing Blue Otter making his way her direction.

He walked with stooped shoulders, and he bent to examine rocks or driftwood of a peculiar shape. Rising, he held a stone up to the sunlight, then put it into a pouch and back into his larger bag.

"It is a good day, Blue Otter." Moon Cloud smiled.

"It is a good day."

"What have you found? Agates?" She browsed the area around them.

"A small one, but I found this." He searched through his bag and produced a round brown rock the size of a turkey egg.

She raised an eyebrow.

"Watch." He pulled a tomahawk from his belt, knelt, and precisely struck the rock against a larger granite stone. Blue Otter rose. He held before Moon Cloud two pieces of a milky-white inner stone. Moistening his finger, he rubbed the white portion. Then he held it out for her to take.

Looking more closely, Moon Cloud gasped. Within the whiteness she saw dim sparkles of green and orange. "This stone has captured the stars."

"And look at this one." He held the object between his thumb and forefinger. "I found it in the water."

She sucked in a breath. "So blue." Holding out her hand, she received the raw specimen as if it were a sacred stone. "The color of Allen's eyes." She held it up to the sun to get the full impact of the rich blue shine.

"Keep it to remind you of him."

"Here." She handed him a pouch full of breadroot and waved her hand, palm down.

Blue Otter waved his hand. The trade was complete.

Upon arriving at camp, Moon Cloud walked past Two Rivers's lodge. His wife greeted her but did not know where he might be. Moon Cloud continued on her way to her own teepee, when Two Rivers walked by leading his flannel-gray pony.

"Two Rivers, I have lavender and sage. Could I ask you to use it to pray on behalf of White Falcon?" She displayed the plant bundles.

"Meet me on the bluff before the sun is setting." He tightened his grip on the lead rope as the pony nudged him. "We will pray together for White Falcon."

Hours later, Moon Cloud sat on a bear-hide blanket with her aunt, sewing beadwork onto dresses. It was a labor of diligence and precision that satisfied her. She glanced at her aunt, her mother's sister, Waits Long. "Will you have enough red beads to finish that?"

"Yes, I have plenty." She watched her stitching. "This will be a fine ceremony dress."

Moon Cloud watched children run by as their mothers chopped food or scraped fresh hides. Small fires cooked stews or smoked meat on racks. A cluster of men reclined in a circle under a tree. Looking beyond the camp at the hills, she noticed the shadows pointing to the east.

"Niece, you look at the hills, but you have not walked to them for many days." Waits Long looked up from her work. "You do not always need to help me."

"I love working by your side, Aunt. I will go one day soon."

"Your father was wise to teach you to hunt with a bow. Not many women can do that." She adjusted the leather heap on her lap. "I remember when you were little—you would always follow him."

"Hunting was a reason to explore the hills and to provide meat." Moon Cloud picked up loose beads. "My heart does not feel the same without Father. And I wait for White Falcon to return. We will hunt together."

"He's a good man for you."

"It is time for me to meet with Two Rivers." She folded her bundle and wrapped it in a dyed-green hide designated for her work. Setting it among her belongings, she emerged from the teepee with a shoulder bag and red trade blanket.

The trail to the bluff threaded its way up the hillside through brush and ditches. The remains of wildflowers marked the transition of seasons. Deer droppings in various stages of decay lay in random clusters, giving back to the earth. A few yards off the trail, a sage bush that had been blackened by a lightning strike caught Moon Cloud's attention. She sat on her heels to examine the scorched plant. Snapping off a twig, she sniffed it. No scent. It had possibly been years since it happened. Sage was abundant but not a bush touched by heaven—it was marked by power. If the root survived and could be revived, it would perhaps yield a more powerful medicine. She reached for her belt knife to dig at the roots but then held back. No time. Standing and looking around to remember the location, she also saw several pink blazing star flowers scattered across a shallow depression an arrow shot away. More medicine for the aching joints of the elders, for her aunt's fingers. Perhaps tomorrow.

Further up the trail, a few minutes later Moon Cloud paused again. The faint sound of a flute. When she reached the top of the bluff, she saw a low lean-to and fire. Two Rivers was positioned to look over the river valley and the expanse of the pleated landscape.

"That is a beautiful sound."

"It is the flute given to me by my great-uncle, a medicine man who taught me many things." His pensive eyes seemed to envision his ancestors in the space before them. "It is carved from the wing bone of a swan."

Moon Cloud folded her blanket and kneeled, sitting on her heels with her back erect. She inhaled deeply with her eyes closed. As the spiritual leader resumed a melancholy song, it seemed to her he played for the ancient ones, that they might reminisce of their time on earth. Before long the tone transitioned and soared to a greater height, as if presenting an offering of the meager beauty of earth unto the breathtaking glory above.

In her mind's eye she saw what an eagle might see as it caught an upward wind to soar beyond the clouds. There, her thoughts remained until she envisioned an expansive teepee. She saw herself kneeling before a fire, as if in a Lodge of Elders. Across from her, seated cross-legged, wrapped in a blanket whiter than snow, was one like the Great Father. She bowed her head.

The Great Father spoke. "My child."

She did not move.

"My Moon Cloud. You may look at me."

Slowly lifting her face, she looked into his eyes. From his gaze she felt a weight throughout her whole body. As if every cell of her being was embraced in pure love.

She bowed her head again, tears streaming down her cheeks.

"Child of my heart."

She sobbed, her shoulders softly heaving. After moments, she raised her head again. "You are . . ." She caught her breath. "You are the one Allen calls Jesus?"

He smiled and nodded slightly.

"You are One Who Gives Life?"

"I am."

Bowing low again, she held out her hands, palms up.

"My Moon Cloud, I receive your worship." He paused. "What would you ask of me?"

Rising to her upright position, she wiped her cheeks. "I am requesting that you guard and protect Allen on his journey to speak to the fathers of the east."

"I am with White Falcon."

"Will he return to me safely?"

"I have given him another purpose as well. He must enter the darkness once again."

"But why . . ." She stopped herself and bowed her head. "You will be with him even in the darkness."

When she looked up again, she was no longer in the lodge but kneeling beside a stream of water running through a clearing of green grass in a grove of Aspen trees. Beside her stood one of the elders.

"You may rise."

"Do you know? Will Allen return to me safely?"

"The righteousness of heaven kisses the faithfulness of earth."

Her brow furrowed. "I do not understand."

"Your faith and trust in One Who Gives Life will bring heaven to earth."

"My prayer will be fulfilled as long as I believe?"

"Yes." He stared intently at her. "There is much to cause doubt in this world. Many enemies to disrupt your faith. Fear is one. Desires of this world is another. The troubles of people around you. Many things to tempt doubt. You must believe and not doubt."

Moon Cloud pursed her lips. "I don't want to fail White Falcon."

"Trust yourself. You have a true heart. Remain humble. One Who Gives Life is with you also."

She looked down at her feet. "It is all so new to me. I don't feel worthy." Suddenly she felt a light touch on her head, a shiver, and goose bumps covered her. She remained still.

With a growing pulsation, she opened her eyes to see Two Rivers tapping his hand drum. He alternately raised each knee and with a toe-heel step moved to the beat. He chanted a song.

Moon Cloud at times sang her own song. Taking her feather fan from the shoulder bag beside her blanket, she rose and danced. When the time was right, they stopped.

Two Rivers looked at the cold embers of his fire. "I set out the smudge but never got to it." He ignited a new bundle of kindling and small sticks.

"This time did not go as I imagined it would." Moon Cloud wrapped the blanket around her shoulders against the chilling breeze.

With the light of the campfire, the medicine man packed his belongings into two large shoulder bags. He wrapped the deer skull in leather and tucked it in last.

"Two Rivers." She spoke pensively. "Since choosing the path of One Who Gives Life, I have visions much more often. Am I right to do this?"

"Did you have a vision now?"

"Yes." She squatted by the fire. "I was kneeling before him. Before One Who Gives Life and many elders." She motioned with her hand, as if bringing the scene back to life. "He called me by name. I felt love from him more than my own parents."

Two Rivers let the bags drop to the ground and added a handful of sticks to the fire. "I have heard him call my name. In no other spirit vision has my name been called. Creator knows us. Creator loves us as his children." He watched the orange flickering dance of life. "He showed me White Falcon in a big canoe being driven by the wind. The river was taking him into a black cloud. I could see him no more. I had no fear. He will be strong, with the heart of a warrior."

"One Who Gives Life said that White Falcon would enter the darkness, but he would not be alone." Moon Cloud observed the reflection of fire in the old man's eyes. "I was told by an elder that I should believe and not doubt. My heart is searching for peace. When I tell my heart to be calm, it does not last. But the words of One Who Gives Life surrounded me like this blanket. Then I knew peace."

The holy man measured the stations of the stars. "Let us return to our lodges and rest. There is much to consider on this new path. What Allen taught us from the book has not yet been sufficient for clear understanding. We must trust that we hear the same words from the Great Spirit."

CHAPTER NINE

ALAN EMERGED FROM THE CABIN and rubbed his eyes and scratched his scalp. The sun was just clearing the tree line on the Kentucky side.

"Morning."

"Good morning, Dex." Allen stretched. "Are we getting close to Cincinnati?"

"Long past." Dex yawned. "I can't remember ever having a wind like this. Most of the time it blows upstream. We're laying down the miles as quick as you please. I expect we'll be in Louisville before noon."

"That's good news."

"There's a jug of water down there. Just make sure you grab the water and not the whiskey."

Allen ducked back into the dark room. "How do you tell them apart?"

"Well, one will wash down your biscuits. The other will make you spit them back out." He guffawed. "Pull the cork and sniff. You'll figure it out right quick." More chuckles. "There's a sack of apples and a tin box with corn biscuits. Grab us some for breakfast."

Allen came out with a smile and set the jug down next to the bundle seat. He pulled apples out of his pants pockets and handed one to Dex along with a couple of biscuits in a handkerchief. "You made it through the night, I see."

"Just fine and dandy." Dex shoved half of the fist-size hardtack into his mouth. "Like I was saying, this wind made the time pass a fast as the miles."

Biting the apple, Allen studied the vessel. "This is shorter than most of the keelboats I've seen."

Dex packed one cheek with his food. "Thirty-five foot. It's nice and light for heading back upstream. It won't take as much of a load, but I can haul faster than them big lunkers. Up in these northern waters, I can make the run with Louisville bourbon up to Pittsburgh and come back with farm supplies in a couple of weeks. Short runs pay well enough for a small crew."

"How long have you been working on the river?" Allen handed him the water jug.

"My whole life." He took a long swallow. "I was born on a barge, learned to walk on a barge, worked the keelboats since I was big enough to carry my weight. Bought my first boat seven or eight years ago."

Allen studied his friend's face. "How old are you now?"

"I don't think I'm twenty-five yet, but maybe."

"Your folks didn't keep track for you?"

"Ma was young and had to work the barges to get by. She was living in Natchez last I seen her. Set herself up pretty good there. That's where I lived most when we weren't on the river." He flipped the apple core overboard. "I tried school for a while, but being on the boats was more to my liking. As I got older, I'd get some of the men that could, to teach me to read and cipher. At least enough to sign a contract and count the money."

"Your father?"

"My pappy?" His eyes sparkled. "My pappy is none other than Mike Fink. The biggest, toughest, and smartest keelboat captain from Pittsburgh to New Orleans. He could out-fight, out-shoot, out-row, out-cuss, and out-drink any man along the way." Dex's smile faded.

"When I was four or five, he stood above me with his fists on his hips. 'If'n you is my boy, you're gonna have to be a fighter.' He got down low to look me in the eye. 'You think you're tough, boy? Show me how tough you are.' He poked me in the chest." Dex raised his fists like a boxer. "I drew back and popped him as hard as I could right on the nose. It must've surprised him 'cause he fell on his backside and shook his head. His eyes watered up, and his face turned redder than that apple. I thought for sure he was going to smack me across the tavern. Everyone was quiet. I just stood right there with my fists up, waiting. Big old Mike Fink burst out laughing so loud, I didn't know what to think. The whole crowd started laughing and cheering. He scooped me up and held me up to his face. He said, 'I guess you is my boy. I'll claim a tadpole who can punch an old gator in the snout.' He laughed real loud again and held me up for everyone to see. 'This is my boy.' Then he set me down and got on one knee. 'I reckon I could be your pappy. I know your ma, and she's a peach. But I ain't going to be around like a pap should be. I want you to have this here pocketknife to remember me.'" Dex pulled the folding knife out of his pocket and opened the blade. "I've kept it all these years." He handed it over.

Allen examined the well-worn blade. "I see it has MF scored on the heel."

Dex nodded. "Men that was there will testify to what Mike said, but I guess there's no telling for sure that he's my father. He worked up and down the river for decades, and it could be he has a passel of kids he don't even know about. Some say I'm the skinny resemblance. I guess it don't matter much. He took off with the Ashley expedition a few weeks after that day, and he died up there. Ma raised me with whatever boatmen were around. So I learned to fight and gamble and work the boats since I was a tyke."

Allen chewed and swallowed. "I used to read novels about Mike Fink, the king of the keelboaters. He sounded like quite a fellow."

"Most of them tales ain't accurate. He was a ruffian and not much more. He just boasted loud and proud and got to be known for it." Dex yawned. "I guess some of the adventures might be true. You can't be on the river your whole life and not get mixed up in a stir of some kind. He may not have been the tornado they made him out to be, but he was well known. Once in a while I reap the benefits of his reputation." He stretched his arms over his head. "Some fellow might buy me a beer or a steak. Other times a bloke might want to fight the son of the great Mike Fink. Like I said before, what's life if it ain't an adventure."

Allen raised his hand in agreement. "I'm glad to have you with me on this adventure, Dex. Why don't you get some sleep. I reckon I can keep this ship pointed downstream."

"Might just do that." Dex handed over the tiller. "Stay near the middle, but if a big boat comes along, move a bit to the right. There's an island a couple of hours before town. Then when you see houses clustered on the left bank, you'll know we're getting close. That's when you can wake me." He stepped into the cabin, then popped back up. "Don't worry none. She pretty much sails herself."

"Yes, sir." Allen looked up at the full sheet. He felt the wind on the back of his neck and pressure against the rudder. Here he was, steering a keelboat, heading for who knew where. *Lord, thank you for being with me and Dex. May this trip produce a favorable result according to your will.*

True to the estimation, Allen steered the *Marylou* past a long island in the middle of the river, followed by an increasing number of cabins, houses, and more boat traffic.

Dex appeared chomping on an apple and tossed one Allen.

"We'll stop here long enough to get something to eat and find a crew."

"A crew?"

"Once we hit the Mississippi, we'll be needing some rowers and polers. Besides that, they can help us load some kegs of whiskey."

"Whiskey?"

"That's right. Whiskey will turn to silver and gold quicker than anything else along the river. And we might need to pay off the pirates."

"Pirates?"

"You never know. Best to be prepared though." Dex flipped the apple core over his shoulder. "If we time it right, we can get past Cave in Rock before daybreak tomorrow. If this wind holds, we'll make it for sure."

"Cave in Rock?"

"Yep. It's a big cave in the rocky cliff. Pirates been working out of there for years." He took out his pocketknife and used it to pick his teeth. "You ever heard of the Mason gang?"

"Mason gang?"

"Or the Harpe brothers?"

"No." Allen shrugged and shook his head.

"They were the terror of the river and the Trace. As black-hearted as a man can get."

"The Trace?"

"The Natchez Trace. It's a road that runs from Natchez up to Nashville. Merchants use it, travelers, highwaymen, robbers, and sometimes runaway slaves. When we get down that away, we can ask around if anyone seen your friend." Dex checked for other craft. "Still a week before we get there at least. It'll be a long shot, but worth trying."

"Do you want to take over here?" Allen offered the tiller.

"You're doing fine." He bent over to look under the sail. "Just keep her edging over careful like, and we'll find us a place to tie up." Dex untied the line and dropped the sail to half-mast. He folded and fastened the draping sheet to the boom. Then pulling a long pole off the roof of the cabin, the boatman moved to the bow. Plunging the pole into the water, he pressed it to his shoulder and leaned into it. He cat-walked along the side deck toward the stern. After three more similar passes, Dex stopped with his left foot on the prow.

"See that barge with the red stripe down the side?" Dex pointed.

"Yes, the first of three barges."

"Right you are. Come alongside, and don't worry none if you bump it." He laid the pole down, dropped the mainsheet the rest of the way, and secured the boom up against the mast. Lifting the pole to shoulder height, he jabbed the point against the side of the barge to slow their approach. Then setting aside the pole, he grabbed the bowline and flicked a loop over a stanchion on the barge and held fast. Another two loops and he strode to the stern. With similar handiwork he drew the keelboat snug against the barge.

"Grab your money, and we'll go take care of business."

"Will everything be safe?"

"We can lock up your bag in the trunk." Dex produced a key to undo the padlock. "Most of the time I don't need to worry, but like I said before, there ain't any upright boatmen."

Allen nodded. "You going to put on shoes?"

Dex crinkled his nose. "We won't be that long ashore."

The keelboat deck was lower than the barge. Dex boosted

himself up and waited on the flat roof as Allen followed. Together they jumped down to the dock, then up to the street.

"There's an eating house up yonder called Becky's. She fixes a plate of catfish and taters that will make you want to give up the bachelor life." Dex hustled along.

"But you're still a bachelor."

"Ain't for lack of trying. First time I ate there, I asked her to marry me."

"She declined the offer?"

"She said her cooking was the only thing her husband would let her share." He chuckled. "He's a big old brute too. He'd pound a fellow and use him for bait." He pace quickened. "He's the one what keeps the catfish in supply."

"She must be fine and pretty too?" Allen smirked.

"Fine?" He scratched is head. "Well, that ain't the best way to describe her. You remember that barge we tied up to?"

"Oh! Maybe we shouldn't describe her. Sorry I asked."

"She's a good cook. I'll give her that. Maybe she favors the butter and cream a tad too much, and her own pies, but when you take a bite of that catfish, you'll think she's the most beautiful lass in town."

Allen laughed until Dex stopped abruptly. "This is the place. Shhh." Holding a finger to his lips, he moved reverently. As he opened the door, a bell jingled.

Into the dining area stepped a woman looking every bit the way Dex described her. She wiped her hands on a towel.

"Miss Becky, I'm so glad you haven't moved to Frankfort to cook for the governor."

"Oh, go on, Dex, you river fox." She blushed.

"Some catfish and taters for me and my friend, if you please."

"Coming right up. You'uns take a seat."

They sat at the near end of a long dining table with twelve

chairs. When at last the matron brought out the dinner plates, Dex dove in with fork and spoon. He closed his eyes and savored his mouthful.

"This keeps getting better." Dex shoved in another bite and looked at his partner.

Allen, grateful for anything other than apples, smiled. "Ma'am, this is delicious."

"Thank you, hon. I enjoy watching hungry men eat."

"Miss Becky, do you know who's about and looking for work?"

"Hmm." She folded her arms and rubbed her chin. "Just the usual riffraff, I suppose. Jeffrey Berg was in yesterday. Miles Fenwick too. Slappy walked by this morning. I guess you'll find them at the supply store like they always is."

Dex nodded. "I'll go take a look."

"Where you heading?" She folded a dish towel.

"As far as Memphis, maybe more."

"You best get you some men with grit. Them pirates is causing trouble again."

"What have you heard?"

"Bart McMillan put together a gang of roustabouts, and they been robbing barges and steamboats. At first they was just taking money and merchandise, but they's getting bolder and meaner. Got blood on their hands."

"I know McMillan. We worked a barge down to New Orleans a few years ago. Followed the Trace back north. Got into a fight with some brigands around the Buzzard's Roost. He saved my life, then I saved his. If'n he's head of that outfit, then I reckon we'll do just fine." Dex winked at Allen. "Thank you, Miss Becky. I hope your husband brings home some fine flatheads for you."

"You take care now, Dexter."

Down the street, they found a mercantile store and grocer.

After purchasing supplies to feed a crew for a week and armed with used Kentucky rifles and a brace of dueling pistols, Dex sent Allen back to the keelboat while he searched for a crew.

After accommodating the fresh supplies, Allen hopped back to the wharf. The street was wide and bustling with movement. He saw stack after stack of fresh lumber, barrels of pork, and whiskey. The bigger vessels lined up for passage through the Portland Canal. Dozens of horses were being herded onto a barge, and a number of finely dressed people were walking toward a particular building. Curiosity overruled his good sense to wait for Dexter.

Dashing and darting through the congestion, Allen joined the assembly listening to a man calling out instructions. The clusters of people—some businessmen with black silk top hats and suits, some couples with women in fine dresses and bustles that made them appear to float alongside their husbands—diverged and went down smaller alleyways next to the larger brick building. Allen went to the right behind a knot of folks he thought could have been part of the congregation back in Buffalo, New York. As they strolled, the women held delicate handkerchiefs to their noses. Then it struck him—the smell of sweat, urine, and misery. He heard murmuring and shouts to silence those crying out "Buy me, sir." All outbursts were quickly rebuked with a lash as the pen masters worked their way ahead of the shoppers to keep the merchandise in line.

Allen stopped and stared with his mouth agape. "No, it can't be." His remark was overheard by a woman next to him.

"What's the matter?" she said.

"All these people held in cages like animals." Allen looked at her. Could she not see the reality before her? "This is horrible."

"How else would you keep them organized? Otherwise, they might run off like animals." She shook her head, as if he couldn't recognize the practicality. "The horse corrals are down the street.

Is that what you're looking for? Or the hog market." She pointed over her shoulder.

"Ma'am, I have never seen such deplorable conditions for people."

"People? They're just Negroes. Chattel." She waved her hand, as if swatting a fly. "This is a slave market. What did you expect?" She removed a hand fan from her purse and waved it on her face.

Then a man in a gray suit held a ledger before her. "Sign here, Mrs. Johnson."

"Thank you, Robert." She signed. "Now this is for all thirty, correct? Men and women? These two stalls and the one over there."

"Yes, ma'am. All thirty will be loaded within the hour." He tucked the ledger under his arm. "And we will adjust your account according to the agreed-upon price."

"Very well. Always a pleasure." She extended her hand.

The broker shook her hand gently. "See you in a couple of weeks."

The woman turned back to Allen. "And that's how you make eight thousand dollars profit." She brushed passed him, fanning her face.

Allen swallowed the bitter taste rising in his mouth. "Oh, dear Lord. How can this be?" Then he gasped. "No." He scanned down the long alley of cages on both sides. "Abraham!" Quickly searching each barred stall, moving and calling, "Abraham!"

"Here I am." A voice called from inside a cell. "My name is Abraham."

Allen backed up, craning his neck.

"Me, sir." A man much taller than Deacon Abraham pressed up to the bars.

"You're not the man I'm looking for." Allen sagged.

"Please, sir. Please buy me out of here. They took me from my family." He pleaded. "I needs to get back to my wife and children, sir."

"Help me, sir," another man said. Then another.

As the anguish and hopelessness overwhelmed him, Allen turned away. "I'm sorry."

His desperation carried him the length of the narrow passage. Around the building to the left and back up the alley on the other side, which was equally lined with pens crowded with enslaved blacks.

"Abraham!" He shouted as he trotted by each pen, hoping not to miss a reply. Dodging people and glancing into each cell, Allen bumped into the back of a hefty man.

"What the . . ." The man spun, and his eyes glared like daggers.

"I'm sorry. I'm looking for a friend." Allen held up his hands, as if holding back the force of anger. "He may be in one of these stalls."

"You're friends with one of these?" He pointed with a wooden handled whip of leather lashes. "Maybe I'll just throw you in there so you have a closer look."

"I apologize." Stepping backward, Allen hadn't felt such intimidation since he'd faced Kicking Lion in a knife fight.

Turning away, the hefty man whipped at the last slave in the coffle.

Allen noticed the string of men chained together and strode ahead on the right side of the line to avoid the whip and to get a quick look at each face. No Abraham. He backtracked to glimpse into the remaining stalls.

When he got to the end of the row, back out to the street, he looked back. "Lord, is Deacon Abraham among these?"

A sudden jolt to his back forced him to step quickly to keep his balance. Before he could turn, his arms were seized. Two men gripped him while the third, the hefty man, held the blunt wooden handle in Allen's face. "Don't move."

"Is he the one?" A tall man with a top hat peered over the thick shoulder, his thin black mustache curled up at the ends.

"Yeah. He's been running through the market disrupting the clients. He's an agitator."

"What are your intentions here?" The mustache twitched.

"Sir, I'm no agitator. I'm looking for a friend who was kidnapped. A free man. I was looking to see if he is in one of these . . . here."

"These are all slaves on record. Naturally, no free men would be here." The mustache tried to produce a smile. "This is an honest and legal operation."

"How can you sell people with any moral integrity? This is outrageous . . ." Allen was stopped by a solid jab to the sternum.

"What do you want me to do with him?" the brute said.

"Take him to the sergeant at arms."

"Sir, that would take a while. I've still got six strings to get loaded onto them barges."

"All right then. Put him in a room in the stable until we close. Then make sure he understands he is never to come back."

"You can't do this . . . oomph." The wind was knocked out of Allen with a jab to the stomach.

"Shut up." The hefty man nodded, and his comrades yanked Allen around, forcing him toward the back of the large building.

At the end, where Allen had come around the corner, they crossed to an adjacent building that appeared to be a stable. They sidestepped through the exterior door and into a dimly lit corridor. After passing several closed doors, they stopped. The bolt was unlocked, the door opened, and Allen was shoved in and fell to the hay-covered floor. He flinched as the door slammed shut and the bolt was relocked.

He slumped against the wall. "What have I done? How can I find Abraham now?" Once his eyes adjusted to the enclosed room, he pressed his ear against the door. Silence. He pounded on the door. "Is anyone there?" He listened. "Hey. If you let me go, I promise I won't ever come back."

Silence.

He slid his back down the door until he hit the floor, rested his elbows on his knees, and bowed his forehead on his arms. "Lord Jesus, what am I to do? Have I failed you?" He wilted into the exhaustion.

"Allen?" a dim voice called.

Allen raised his head. Was that a person, or was the Lord calling to him? He couldn't tell if he had been there an hour or a few minutes. He blinked several times. High on the back wall was a rectangle of light. He rose to investigate. A boarded-up window, just above the height of his head. He pressed the butt of both palms against it. He tried prying it with his fingertips, but the boards didn't budge. He huffed and leaned on his hand against the wall.

"Allen." The soft voice again. Then a tapping sound. "Allen, you in there?" A bit louder.

"Here. I'm in here." Allen pressed his ear against the wall, straining to hear something more certain.

Whomp! The wooden shutter flew past Allen's head, and a bare foot emerged through the space. Light beamed in.

"Hi." Dex's head popped through. "I doubt you'll find Deacon Abraham in here. We should get back to the boat."

"How'd you find me?"

"I'll tell you that later. Come on. Climb up."

Not seeing anything to step on, Allen jumped and thrust his right arm through the window and anchored his forearm. Prying himself upward and toe-stepping against the wall, he was able to get his head through. Then his shoulders and waist, until he was hanging at the hips.

Dex stood there smiling. "Wiggle on through."

"Can you catch my arms?"

Dex lifted him by the armpits and heaved backward until Allen dropped to the ground.

"Here, carry this on your shoulder." Dex handed him a broken bucket. "Follow me."

They turned away from the stable building in the direction opposite the wharf. After passing rows of brick buildings, they turned left and walked down a street and made a wide sweep back to the docks, avoiding the vicinity of the slave market and main streets.

"When they find out you're gone, he'll send men out to search," Dex explained. "The crew's waiting, but I don't want them mixed up in this."

"How did you find me?"

"When you wasn't at the boat, I began looking, and it seemed a fit that you might try looking for your friend at the slave pens. I was coming up when I saw them grab you." He quickened his pace. "I seen you got dragged to the back, so I followed. I had to wait until it was all clear before I called out to you."

"How did you know which room I was in?"

"The same way I knew you could get out. I been in there once myself." He snickered. "That man, Horace Vaughn, the one with the mustache. He is powerful on this stretch of river. He can do whatever he wants, and no one stops him. He fairly owns this city, or a big part of it. All the slave trading and many of those barges. And he don't tolerate annoyances."

"So he put you in that room before?"

"I guess I annoyed him."

The two leapt aboard the keelboat just as the new crew finished loading the last small keg of whiskey. The cabin was now full of crates of copperware, bales of tobacco, gunpowder, and lead. Everything that was common enough for a fast trade in almost any smaller river port.

"Allen, this is Delbert, Howard, and Lucius. They're top-notch boatmen, and they know how to shoot." Dex positioned himself at the tiller. "Boys, we might have whacked a hornet's nest, so we best shove off now."

The three men jumped into action, and five minutes later they were well away from the wharf, heading out to the main flow of the river. Delbert and Howard rowed while Lucius set the sail.

"Won't we use the canal?" Allen asked.

"Wouldn't be in our best judgment for now." Dex stooped to see beyond the sail. "Mr. Vaughn would have men there. He gets a slice of that pie too."

"What do you mean?"

"Too risky." He smirked. "It means he owns an interest in the canal. Every boat pays a fee for every ton of merchandise that floats the locks. Vaughn gets a percentage. He can stop the movement with a snap of his fingers."

"But now we are heading for the waterfall. Isn't that risky?"

"Let's say it's our better option." As they maneuvered around the tip of the island and jockeyed for a good lineup, Dex barked an order. "Howard, grab a pole. Allen, take his place on the oar. Do whatever Delbert tells you. Lu, drop sail."

The orders were obeyed within a minute. The keelboat caught the swift current.

"Looks like we're aiming at the Indian Shoot." Dex scrutinized the rocks ahead, the channels, and the bend. "We'll be moving fast."

Allen looked at Delbert, who was sitting still. "Am I supposed to do something?"

"Wait for boss to say." He pointed his chin in Dex's direction. "You're port. I'm starboard. Don't row until he tells you. Then pull hard. He'll keep us off the rocks."

"Rocks?" Allen twisted to look ahead, but Delbert bumped him with his elbow.

"Trust the boss," he shouted. "If you turn around, you'll crash us for sure."

The thunderous sound grew to a deafening level. Their speed increased. The rush grew with the tension.

"Get ready!"

Allen could see Lucius and Howard brace their legs and hold their poles at the ready. The cabin blocked his view of Dex. Allen felt his heart pounding and tried to calm his breathing.

"Ready!" Dex shouted. "Port side row! Stop! All row! Stop!"

An abrupt turn to the right, a drop, and the bow plunged against the roiling wave. Water splashed over the bow and showered Delbert and Allen. The jolt snapped the oar out of Allen's hands.

"All row!"

As Allen grasped for the oar handle, the stern kicked to the side, flinging him against the gunwale and oarlock. As he recovered the oar, he looked up to see Howard thrusting maniacally with his pole.

"Row!" Delbert shouted. "We're going into the back eddy."

Allen dipped the blade and heaved over and over, trying to match Delbert's pace. The bow pitched to the right as the stern swung rapidly to the left. The keelboat swung a full circle and stalled.

"Pull hard!"

The boat drifted backward at the whim of the eddy.

"Heave!"

Lucius braced and thrust his pole at a rock, as if he were a knight with a jousting lance. The knob of the pole spiked against the cabin wall, and the force of the boat's movement toward the rock compelled the pole to arc upward, bending it into a rainbow until it shattered with a crack louder than the roar of the falls. The sudden snap pitched Lucius into the water.

Delbert yanked back three rapid strokes, lifted the oar from its lock, and held it out for Lucius to grasp. The boat was still sliding sideways toward the rock with the promise of crushing the swimmer. Getting his right arm wrapped around the blade, Lucius managed to plant his feet against the rock as Delbert leaned back, pressing against the gunwale. It provided an instant lever for Lucius to rise, reach for the side, and nimbly step aboard. Delbert neatly returned the oar to its rightful place and resumed rowing. Allen pulled in rhythm. Lucius found another iron-tipped lance and shoved the rock away.

Dex maneuvered the stern around by pumping the rudder and commanded, "All row! Keep it going! Hard!"

With growing momentum, the bow finally broke into the stream. "Heave!"

The men ground all of their weight into the poles and dug their heels into the deck struts. With that burst of energy, the midsection of the keelboat entered the swift water. They fell onto their backsides but bounced back up to their feet.

"Hooray! Hooray!" Dex shouted. "Well done, lads." He let the speed work for them. "Keep ready! More rocks coming!"

Allen noted that Lucius and Howard were reading the river. He looked to the man at his side. Delbert eyed him and nodded.

The following shoots were fast but smoothly finessed. Allen sighed deeply.

Delbert tucked his oar under the gunwale and slapped Allen on the knee. "I'm thirsty. Let's get us a drink."

The crew gathered at the rear of the cabin near Dex. Howard

lifted a jug and took a big gulp, then handed it to Lucius, who guzzled and passed it to Allen. He lifted the jug and took a drink. One swallow and he spewed out the next mouthful.

A burst of laughter. "What's wrong, Preacher?" Dex grinned.

"Waugh!" Allen gasped. "I assumed by the way you were all gulping that it was water."

They slapped their legs and held their bellies.

Red in the face, Allen laughed too. He caught his breath and offered the jug back to Lucius. "You deserve this more than anyone." He patted the strong, wet shoulder. "Now, where is the water jug?"

CHAPTER TEN

THE DOOR OPENED, AND THREE more filed into the church. Sister Lydia sat on the first bench, braiding Esther's hair. A few candles burned, along with two oil lanterns. Several of the congregation had vowed to meet each evening after work and supper to pray for Deacon Abraham and Allen. They chatted about day-to-day matters until Lydia cleared her throat.

"We might as well start. Sister Savannah, would you lead us in a song so's we can fix our eyes upon the Lord?"

"Before we sing, do you have any news about the pastor?" Savannah limped to the front of the rustic sanctuary.

"No word yet." Lydia frowned. "But, sister, what happened to your leg that you be limping so?"

"Oh, it's nothing." Savannah looked at her ankle. "I was picking greens and stepped over a mound of dirt, and it gave way. I guess I twisted it some."

"We should pray a healing on that," Brother Dickson suggested.

Savannah put her hand to her cheek. "Oh, I don't want to bother. Let's sing first."

"All right, sister. But sit down while you're singing." Lydia adjusted the bench for her.

Just before the final chorus, Nolia Biss emerged into the room along with a young man. Her maroon dress with white collar and bustle were a striking match to his gray suit with black velvet lapels and bow tie. She feigned patience until the song was finished.

"I'm glad I have your attention." Nolia marched forward with the man on her arm, causing several to step aside. "I want to introduce our new pastor, Reverend Chester Stokely. He's visiting from Columbus, where he attended Bexley Hall Episcopal Seminary. I believe it is the Lord's providence that he happens upon us in our time of need."

"We already have us a pastor." Brother Dickson scowled. "And this is a Methodist church, not Episcopal."

Even though the group nodded in agreement, Lydia noticed that everyone appeared confused. She looked over the city Negro in his fine suit. "Sister Nolia, we was fixing to pray for Deacon Abraham's safe return, as we do every night. You're both welcome to join us."

"That's precisely why I brought Chester . . . Reverend Stokely. He will lead us in prayer and the Word. I have apprised him of our dilemma, being without our beloved pastor, and he has agreed to assume responsibility." Nolia put her hand on his shoulder. "Meet Pastor Stokely. Pastor, this is your new congregation."

Lydia stepped forward. "Like the brother said, we already have us a pastor. No offense, Reverend Stokely, but Deacon Abraham will be home before long to resume preaching."

"But you don't know that." Nolia squared off with Lydia. "If it's the Lord's will, he will return. But this might be the Lord's way of removing one pastor to bring in another. A new pastor who is better educated and comes from the city."

"Deacon Abraham don't need an education to show the love of God." Brother Dickson stood in defiance, but his leg pushed the bench over to bang on the floor.

Nolia smirked. "No need to get agitated. Let's give Reverend Stokely an opportunity to prove that he can minister to us." She took his arm, guided him to the front, and positioned the small lectern before him. "There now. Share the Word of the Lord with us, Pastor."

"Thank you, Sister Nolia. Greetings in the name of our Lord." He gripped the stand with both hands. "Believe me when I say, I know what you're going through. I can see that you love Deacon Abraham, and I don't wish to take his place. However, allow me to fill in during his absence. Let me begin by reciting for you the twenty-third Psalm, as it seems most appropriate."

His baritone voice caught Lydia off guard. She listened and was soothed by his lyrical tone. She watched his lips form the words and his eyes express appreciation for the message. She looked down when he made eye contact with her. When her face came up, he glanced back at her and smiled upon finishing the recitation.

"Shall we pray." He pounded the air with his fist as he prayed.

Lydia observed him. It was a prayer that seemed appropriately concerned for this group, and he blessed each person with eloquent words. A faint smile formed on her lips as her eyes moved to the right. She gasped and closed her eyes. Nolia had been watching her.

Upon finishing, amens rose in unison. "Shall we sing another chorus?" the reverend suggested. He glanced at Savannah, who patted her collar.

When she rose to start singing, she abruptly lunged on the pain of her ankle.

"What's this? Are you injured, sister?" Reverend Stokely assisted her to sit on the bench.

"I turned my ankle in the garden." She let him hold her hand.

"Allow me to take a look, please." He waited for her to nod, then held up both legs to examine the ankles side by side. "My goodness, that is swollen." He gently released her right foot, keeping the left one elevated. "Shall we pray?"

The group gathered around to watch. Stokely supported the foot with his right hand and laid his left one over the swelling. "Lord Jesus, you brought forth healing by your word. You healed those who were lame and crippled. Our sister's injury is not so serious, yet it is cumbersome for her. I now command the healing in Jesus's name. I command the pain and swelling to leave in the mighty name of Jesus. Amen."

"Thank you." Savannah smiled.

He stood but leaned over, holding both her hands. Then he tenderly began to sing, "O for a thousand tongues to sing my great redeemer's praise . . ."

The others joined in, and as the volume increased, they clapped in rhythm. The atmosphere shifted to celebration.

Stokely still held her hands, and with the next verse, he raised her to standing. "Ye blind behold your savior come, and leap ye lame for joy."

She stood grinning. As he slowly backstepped, she followed with short, halting steps. The group sang the final chorus, and Stokely raised her arm high and twirled her, as if ballroom dancing.

Savannah squealed and covered her mouth with both hands. "It don't hurt. My foot don't hurt now. I'm healed. Thank you, Jesus." She took bigger and bigger steps, beaming with joy. "I'm healed." She hugged Reverend Stokely. "Thank you. Thank you."

"Hallelujah!" Brother Dickson declared.

Praises popped like fireworks as the group rejoiced and hugged Savannah and shook hands with the pastor.

Stokely made his way around to Lydia and clasped her extended hand with both of his. "Sister Lydia, you have kept this group together in abounding faith. Well done." He smiled.

She swallowed and urged herself to keep eye contact. "Glory. Glory to God. And thank you, Pastor, for that healing prayer and the marvelous song. You have a voice that comforts the soul."

"Why, thank you, sister." He smiled, still holding her hand. "Perhaps we will have a chance to get to know each other better. At least I am hopeful of that proposition."

Lydia blushed and turned her face.

"Thank you, Pastor." Nolia's soft smile turned to a sneer at Lydia. "We should be going now."

"Certainly." He bowed his head toward Lydia.

"Well, Lydia, don't you see now that God has provided Reverend Stokely for us? You couldn't ask for more of a sign than a healing." Her chin lifted. "And they seem to be convinced." She turned, leading Stokely to the door.

After returning to her home, Lydia tucked Daniel and Esther into bed and sat in her rocking chair. As she pondered the day, she could not keep Chester Stokely out of her thoughts. He was pleasant looking, and his voice was smooth as cream. She touched her hand where he had held it and rocked herself slowly.

When finally Lydia lay in bed, her eyes snapped open. "Oh, my Lord. We done forgot to pray for Deacon Abraham and Allen. Forgive me, Lord, and bless them with hope and protection. I promise we'll have the prayer meeting tomorrow."

CHAPTER ELEVEN

BEFORE NOON THE DAY AFTER fleeing Louisville, Allen entered the port agent's office in Evansville, Indiana, to send a letter to his parents in Tonawanda, New York, and one to Sister Lydia in Portsmouth. He stopped by a bakery for fresh loaves and more corn biscuits and rusk, which the crew seemed to favor. As he wandered along the waterfront, Allen noted the resemblance of the town layout to Louisville. The wharf was busy with workers moving trade goods, but there was a distinct lack of slaves, and no slave market. The Ohio River separated states, laws, and philosophies about people's rights and values. How could the nation be divided on the issue of owning people? Was there more to it?

Upon reboarding the *Marylou*, Allen found everyone there but Dex. He passed around a loaf of bread. The men chewed and talked about women they had seen. Minutes later, Dex strode up along with a tall black man wearing a white blousy shirt that could not conceal his broad shoulders, and it formed to his narrow waist by a four-inch-wide leather belt. His black trousers frayed below the knee, and he had low-cut boots.

"Do I have a merry treat for you boys." Dex grinned as he skipped onto the deck. "This is Kinlock Goldsmith. We've done some business before. He'll be a big help on our cruise."

Allen was close enough to shake hands. "I'm Allen Hartman. Pleased to meet you."

"Pleasure's mine." He had a deep voice.

"Well, let's get moving." Dex grabbed the tiller. "As long as we have all the supplies."

The men jumped to action to shove off and row out to the current. The sail was set, and the wind took over.

Allen gave Dex a small loaf and offered one to Kinlock.

"White bread." Dex smiled and bit off a big chunk. "This is merry."

On the second morning, Allen was startled awake by the boom of a gun. He blinked and rubbed his face. He'd slept through the night in the bow of the boat, covered with a blanket. He sat up and set his Bible to the side with the blanket. He noted that they were closer to shore than usual. Kinlock stepped up the side deck to plant the pole, gripped the metal knob, thrust, and walked back to the stern. When he came forward again, he caught Allen's slumbering gaze.

"Morning, Allen Hartman," the shirtless man said. His black skin glistened with sweat.

"Good morning." Allen studied the man's face and taut, muscular form. "And where are Dexter and the others?"

He planted the pole. "Howard's on the tiller, and the rest are ashore hunting." He strolled forward. "From the sound of it, they got something."

"You knew Dexter from before?"

"Yes. We have worked together many times."

Just then Delbert shouted from an opening in the brush on shore. "Hold up there. We're dragging a deer over."

"I guess you were right, Kinlock." Allen stowed his blanket below.

"You can call me Kin." He set the pole on the cabin roof and grabbed a coiled line with a large monkey fist at the end. Twirling the heavy knot at his side, he slung it to land into the brush next to Delbert, who deftly wrapped the line around a stout branch.

The boat lurched to a stop after Howard tossed out a stern anchor. Allen stumbled but quickly recovered. He came to Kin's side as he retrieved line, swinging them closer to the bank.

A few minutes later, Lucius's head and shoulders came into view, then Dex.

"Fresh meat." Dex raised his rifle triumphantly. "Put out the plank."

Kin and Howard unfastened the gangplank from the base-board of the cabin. "Not quite long enough." Howard pointed at the water.

Scrambling down the bank, Dex and Lucius tumbled the deer behind them. Dex analyzed the situation. "Draw her in closer."

Howard gripped the line and heaved with the full bulk of his weight. "Ain't budging, boss."

"Here, let me have a go." Kin took the line, braced his feet against the gunwale, leaned back, and with every band of muscle bulging in his arms, back, and legs, he strained. By inches and then feet, the keelboat moved toward shore. "Now."

Howard swung the plank out, and it touched ground in about six inches of water.

"Close enough." Dex paced up the wide board holding the antlers. Lucius followed, lifting the rear legs.

Dumping the animal on deck at the front of the cabin, Lucius scrambled down to collect the guns and bags. Howard and Allen restowed the plank.

"Untie us, Delbert." Dex slapped Kin on the shoulder, the signal to unlock his grip.

The keelboat swung back in line with the anchor and the

current. The sudden movement yanked Delbert off balance. He spun to get his feet planted in the dirt.

"I can't hold this much longer." He strained against the force of the current.

"Howard, pull up the anchor," Dex ordered.

Howard hesitated, frowning.

"Do it." Dex turned to crewman on shore. "Delbert, you're going to get wet."

Delbert nodded. The anchor broke free, and the craft surged forward. Gripping the monkey fist, the crewman sprang forward, bounded down the bank, and leapt headlong into the river. He kept his face in the water as he skimmed toward the boat while Kin hauled in the line hand over hand. Dex and Lucius reached down and grabbed him by the arms and winched him aboard.

"That were slick and smooth." Dex laughed. "Didn't get a bruise, did you?"

Delbert shook his head and stood to his feet, smiling.

"No bruises, but good thing you got a bath." Lucius slapped him on the back.

"Got a bath, but it cost me my tobaccy." Delbert pulled a cotton pouch from his pocket and dumped the soggy plugs overboard.

"Kin, I swear, but you could cordel this boat from New Orleans to Saint Louis all by yourself." Dex pointed at his bulging biceps. "Well now, I'll take the helm, and Allen, you help Howard cut us some venison steaks. But first we should celebrate our successful hunt with a drink. What say all?"

Delbert produced the whiskey jug and took the first hit. Allen passed it quickly to Kin, who also passed it along. Howard took his big swallow and handed it to Dex, who hoisted it with his elbow and guzzled. "Here's to good hunting."

"And to good fishing." Allen punched Delbert in the arm.

The crew laughed together as the current swept them downstream. Dex steered, and the sail was set again. The jolly mood carried on while Howard lit a charcoal fire in a metal box screwed onto two thick boards on each end. He handed Allen a long-handled frying pan with hooks on the ends. He could see that it perfectly fit in the rectangular box. Howard opened a pottery jar and scooped out grease with a wooden spoon. When that melted, he lay out the slabs of venison and sprinkled salt on them. Allen's mouth watered as the meat sizzled. Howard flipped each steak and sliced them into thick strips. When he deemed them ready, he divided some of the strips onto two wooden plates. Allen handed one to Delbert, who shared with Lucius and Kin. Allen stood near Dex, who bit half the strip and chewed with his eyes closed.

After licking his fingers, Dex moaned. "Now that is fine cooking." He raised his next strip in salute to Howard. "Eat up, boys. We've done lost our wind. We're coming up on the Wabash slough, so get fixed for rowing."

Allen looked at the sagging sail and pursed his lips.

"What you thinking on, Preacher?" Dex said with his cheek full.

"I'm wondering about finding my friend." Allen chewed slowly. A splash distracted him as Howard dumped the coals overboard.

"This here is where the Wabash River meets the Ohio. We'll row for a bit to get back into a good current." Dex swept his arm across the forward horizon. "Ten miles or so, we hit Shawneetown. After that we have to worry about the Cave in Rock gang. I'm hoping Bart McMillan is still in charge. He'll let us through for maybe a keg or two."

Allen swallowed. "Pirates." He scanned down river. "Lord be with us."

"No need to fret. Once we pass that point up on the left, we'll be back in the faster water." Dex bobbed his head.

Allen rested both arms on the roof and closed his eyes. The gentle surging of the oarsmen's work, the splash of the blades dipping and returning, the gurgling of constant motion, and occasional creaking of wood joints were sounds that he thought would calm him. But now the wind was gone, and somehow his sense of favor seemed to have faded with it. *Lord, I know you are guiding me to Deacon Abraham. I trust you are always present. But why do I feel like I've already gone into . . . into a cavern.* He opened his eyes. "Lord what do you want me to know?"

"What's that, Allen?"

Allen began to turn toward Dex, but stopped. He sprang onto the cabin and strode forward to grab hold of the mast. Scanning the tree line on both sides of the river, he pointed toward movement up on the left.

"Look!" He glanced back to see if he had Dex's attention.

"I see it. A skiff." He squinted. "Maybe eight oars."

"Are they pirates?"

"That don't make sense. They never work this far out. We're almost thirty miles from the cave."

"They seem to be moving fast."

"Can't yet tell for sure if they're pirates." He scanned the shoreline in every direction. "Allen, you hop down and go below. Prime the guns and take them up to the men. But keep 'em low and act normal. Then bring me that set of duelers. Easy like. We'll be ready in case they get ornery."

Allen hugged four rifles against his body and calmly lay them on the deck at Kin's and Lucius's feet. He went back to hand Dex the two dueling pistols, which he tucked in his wide leather belt at the small of his back. He loaded another pistol and rifle and slid them beside the poles on the roof.

The skiff closed in fast, headed straight for the *Marylou*.

"Stow your oars," Dex commanded steadily.

The men responded quickly. Each moved a rifle closer.

"Dex!" Allen pointed back to the right. Another skiff burst out of the brush on the right bank and was setting up a pincer movement.

"Steady." Dex glanced around. There was no way to outrun them. The skiffs were propelled by eight rowers each and a man on the tiller. "They got us trapped."

"Hut, hut!" On command the first two oarsmen in each skiff raised their oars, set them upright in their holders, stood, and raised muskets to their shoulders.

"Steady." Dex held the tiller with his left hand. His right hand gripped the butt of a pistol behind his back.

"Hut, hut!" The next two rowers raised their oars.

Before they stood with rifles, Howard raised his.

Boom! A cloud of black smoke erupted from the first skiff, and Howard fell back onto Lucius. His musket splashed into the river.

"Put down your guns and raise your hands," shouted the man at the rudder of the first skiff. "Raise them!"

"Do as he says." Dex raised his hands. "Allen, there's no fight. Put your hands up."

Allen released the pistol and shoved it away. He raised his arms.

Men from both skiffs boarded on each side, while their comrades kept aim. They gathered the guns on the deck and stripped the flints and caps.

The leader boosted himself up, slid a four-barrel pepperbox pistol from his scarlet sash, and pointed at Allen's face, then at Dex. "Who has the say-so here?"

To Allen, he looked like he would shoot to kill and care less.

The cold, brazen glare alone demanded an answer. His presence was commanding, and he seemed to be in control of his every circumstance.

"Me. It's my boat and my crew." Dex did not flinch or look away. "Welcome aboard."

The leader blinked and smirked at the surprising comment. He lowered the gun to waist high and kept it aimed at Dex's belly. "What's in the hold?"

"Not much." Dex remained firm. "I'm running light. Got some whiskey and a few bundles of tobacco. I'll give you a fair price."

The leader chuckled. "A fair price?"

"Well, seeing that you have the gun, it seems reasonable."

"I like you, kid. You've got grit." He signaled for his men to open the hold. "What's your name?"

"Dexter Yates."

"Yates?" He squinted. "Well, Yates, the fair price is that I won't kill you and your crew until later."

His man came up from the cabin. "Whiskey, tobacco, and some fresh venison quarters. Not much else worth taking."

"Is there a lockbox?"

"A chest with a lock on it."

"Break it open."

"I have a key in my pocket." Dex reached in and held out the key.

Another man took the key and handed it down.

"What is your name?" Dex folded his arms. "It's good to know who I'm doing business with."

"Bright Donovan." His chin jutted. "And this is my crew. Right, boys?"

"Hut, hut, hut!" they chanted in unison.

"Impressive, Mr. Donovan. Do you work out of Cave in Rock?"

"That's right."

"Did McMillan send you upriver this far?"

"McMillan?" He smirked and turned to his crew. "Did Mc-Millan send us out, boys?"

"Hut, hut, hut."

"You'll see Bart McMillan when we get to the cave tonight." Donovan's lips smiled, but his eyes sneered.

"May I see to my man?"

Donovan swept his hand. "Go right ahead."

Allen admired Dex's ability to remain calm. It reminded him of the coolness of his mountain-man friend Jack Burkett. Only Dex was much younger. He estimated that Donovan was in his mid-forties, strong but thick around the middle. His black muttonchops were surrounded by scraggly whiskers. His dark eyes were constantly prowling, and the stern set of his jaw made him look like the alpha male of a pack of wild dogs. If he didn't stay alert, even his own men might turn on him. Allen guessed that pirate leadership was a fragile position—either you kept tight control, or you were removed. Donovan, Allen surmised, had a firm grip on this bunch. He must be a good provider of the things rowdy men enjoy, or he was highly feared.

Dex knelt by Howard, whose wound was high in the chest, above his left breast. Blood covered his dirty white shirt and spread onto his trousers. Dex untied the faded red neckerchief from Howard's bulky frame and packed it against the bullet hole.

"I'll say it plain, my friend, but it don't look good." He felt around back to touch the exit wound. "The ball passed on out." He leaned in and spoke barely above a whisper. "Squeeze my hand if you think you can pull through."

Howard grimaced as if in a spasm of pain and squeezed the back of Dex's hand.

"I need another cloth." Dex looked up at the pirate chief.

"By all means."

"Delbert, there's rags inside."

Delbert stepped past two of the pirate's men and caused another to backstep on the narrow side deck. He quickly reached a wad of rags and held it up to the scowling thug. When Delbert turned his back, the man gave him a hard shove. He looked back, as he would in a tavern brawl, squinting at the lout, who shoved him again. Delbert shifted his weight and twisted with the impact. Thrusting his hip out a tad, he made just enough contact to nudge the thug over the side. He looked down at the splash, feigning surprise, and delivered the rags to Dex.

The pirates burst out laughing at their comrade but were immediately silenced by Donovan's hiss. "Get that fool on the skiff." He looked down at Delbert as if he were deciding on instant justice. The brigand pulled his pepperbox and held it to the back of Delbert's head.

"You're going to need him for rowing," Dex said.

Donovan kept the gun in place.

Allen held his breath. He watched the pirate's eyes. "He's right, you know."

"Who are you?" Donovan shifted the gun to inches away from Allen's heart.

"Allen Hartman, sir." He raised his hands, palms forward. Looking into the cold glare, it seemed to Allen that the pirate loved the power of deciding the fate of his victims.

"Donovan, if you kill us all, you'll have a lot more work getting this load to the cave." Dex spoke as if he were an assistant giving advice, firmly but still submissive.

Tucking the gun away, Donovan assessed their position on the river. He aimed a finger at Dex. "You, row with your men. Gunter, you take the rudder of this barge. You two here with me. The rest of you on the skiffs. Run tow lines, and let's get moving."

"Hut, hut, hut."

Smiling at Dex, he added, "I'm hungry for venison and whiskey."

With Dex, Lucius, Kin, and Delbert on the oars, Allen pressed a cloth on the wound to stop Howard's bleeding. Donovan took his men to the stern and spoke quietly to them, and then they returned to the bow. Two leaned at each corner of the cabin while their chief hopped onto the roof and observed his realm. With six oarsmen in each skiff and the four in the keelboat, they made good time. They soon passed the docks of Shawneetown and within an hour were approaching Cave in Rock.

Allen rested his back against the cabin next to Howard, who was breathing steadily. He nodded to Dex, to assure him he thought his mate would recover.

The cluster of boats edged away from shore as a little island with log debris at the point presented an obstacle. Just then Donovan eased himself off his throne.

"Hartman, you ever been in a cave before?" He nudged Allen with his foot.

Allen stood. "As a matter of fact, I have been in a cave." He glanced at Dex, who eyes seemed to light with remembrance of Allen's story from their first night.

"Then you'll love this one." He nodded to his men.

Together the two thugs reached down and grabbed Howard by the arms, lifted him, and tossed him overboard.

"No!" Dex shouted and rose from his seat.

Allen gasped. "What are you doing?"

The two pirates grabbed Allen by the shirt and pinned him to the cabin. Donovan drew his gun swiftly and aimed at Dex. Allen struggled but was immobilized.

"You'll pay for this, Donovan." Dex pointed.

Donovan smiled and flicked his pistol at Dex, a visible command to sit. Dex's oar had shifted with the current when he stood, forcing the handle to the prow. He bent over to regain possession and bumped Delbert's back. Delbert dropped his oar to let it buck against him, and he flailed back, slapping against Lucius, who in turn appeared to lose control of his oar. In that moment of disarray, Kin dove over the side. Donovan snapped a shot but missed. He fired twice into the water. Allen tried to break the grip of the two pirates, but they held fast.

Kin broke the surface, swimming strongly against the current. He reached Howard, who fought to sidestroke on his good side, and pulled him to cover behind the logjam.

The skiffs stopped rowing at the gunshots. The floating convoy drifted forward.

"Want us to go back?" shouted the man at the tiller of the first skiff.

Donovan fumed. In a matter of seconds, he had lost control. He pointed his gun at Allen, then at Dex. "I got one shot left."

Silence.

"Well?" The skiff man shrugged.

"No. Let the river kill them." Donovan lowered the pepperbox to his side. "Row!"

Allen relaxed, and the men let him go. The lunge of the boat brought them back to their pace. He noted that the pirate crew did not respond with a *hut* but rowed in quiet tension. After about a half hour, the tree line on the Illinois shore gave way to a rocky bluff with intermittent sandy beaches. The sun descended toward the edge of the world.

A shot rang out from up on the bluff. A signal? Allen swallowed and tried to slow his breathing. "Lord, not a cave, please."

The boats came around a corner where men could be seen on the beach with their rifles ready.

"Gunter, run us aground just down from the cave. I want

to keep this tub out of sight." Donovan directed forward with a wave.

Allen stood and looked at the great gaping hole. "Oh, that's not so bad." He sighed with relief.

Cave in Rock was just that—a cavern in the face of a flat rocky cliff. The symmetrical opening with a groove cut into the sandstone flat shelf at the bottom looked like a giant keyhole. The trees above the cliff and surrounding it offered some cover, but once you were in front of the cavern, it was obvious. Allen concluded this made a good hideout for pirates to trap unsuspecting boaters.

"I hope you're bringing either women or whiskey," shouted a man on shore. "Eh, Donovan."

The pirate boss didn't acknowledge the comment. They slid past the main beach. The skiffs released the towlines, and the keelboat turned in and ground to a halt. Quickly and quietly the crew stowed their oars. Dex tossed the bowline to a waiting man, then looked at Donovan.

"Skiff one, unload this whiskey and meat. The rest of you come with me, and shoot anyone who tries to run." Donovan leapt to the sand. "Move it."

Dex first, then Allen, Lucius, and Delbert jumped off and followed the pirate leader the fifty yards back to the cave entrance.

Donovan stopped short. "You asked about McMillan, right?"

"Yeah, is he here?" Dex searched up ahead.

"Say hello to your guests, Bart." Donovan pointed up with his arm and laughed. On cue his men laughed with him.

There, hanging dead from a tree limb, was apparently Bart McMillan.

CHAPTER TWELVE

SISTER LYDIA STROLLED FROM TABLE to table at the market. She filled her basket and the one Daniel carried with vegetables and kitchen supplies. Once outside, her daughter, Esther, ran up to her. "Mama, here's your sewing needles."

"Thank you, sweet one." She approved of the purchase and stowed them in her purse. "It's time for us to go on home. We needs to fix supper before the prayer meeting."

"Look, Mama." Esther pointed down the street. "There's the pastor."

"Deacon Abraham? Where?" She searched every face in view.

"No, Mama. Pastor Stokely."

Lydia caught sight of the familiar gray suit striding as if on a mission. She brushed down her dress with her free hand and cleared her throat.

As Stokely came abreast of them, he paused, smiled, and changed course. "Sister Lydia, what a pleasant surprise." He bowed slightly. "And Sister Esther, you are looking sweeter than ever."

"Thank you, Pastor. It's nice to see you in town." Lydia glanced up the street to see if Nolia Biss was in view, since she always seemed be near Pastor Stokely.

"I see you're doing your market shopping. It's such a nice afternoon for it." He pulled a watch from his vest pocket. "My goodness, but it is later than I thought."

"Yes, it is. We was just fixing to head on home." She shifted the weight of her basket to both hands. "I can't miss another night of—"

"Sister Lydia, may I ask you something?" He tucked the watch away and gripped his lapels. "It is perhaps a bit forward on my part, but would you honor me with a sit-down dinner at the Portsmouth Hotel?"

"What?" She folded her arms, then released them. "Dinner? At the hotel? I don't know what to say. I've never been there before."

"Then let me invite you for your first experience. I know you will be delighted." He smiled.

"Well. I just couldn't. Look at how I'm dressed." She glanced down. "I just couldn't."

"Nonsense. You look fine. This is pretty." He held his hands out before her.

"I thank you for the offer, Pastor, but I think another time."

"Please, sister. We're here now. We might not get another chance. And like I said before, I would cherish the opportunity to get to know you better. And here we won't be interrupted."

"But the children?"

"Esther, would you allow me to escort your mother to a nice dinner?" He held her hand. "It would mean a lot to me."

Esther flushed. "All right."

"Here, I'll pay for the ferry." He pulled two pennies out. "You and Daniel can take the ferry by yourselves, can't you?"

"Of course. We've done it lots."

"Thank you, then. I knew you were grown up enough to help your mother." He reached into his pocket again. "And here are two more pennies, one for each of you. You can buy a hard candy on the way home."

"Mama, is that fine by you?" Esther's eyes widened.

"Well, all right. You'uns take these baskets home. You can stop for candy, but don't dawdle." Lydia handed over the basket. "Fry you some eggs."

"Yes, Mama." They ran off toward the mercantile store with the candy jars.

"Thank you, Lydia." Stokely held out his elbow for her to take. "It is my pleasure, indeed."

They strolled past a few buildings, and Lydia stopped at a seamstress shop. There in the window was a lovely white apron with upright ruffles at the shoulders.

"Isn't that lovely?" Stokely gestured with his chin.

"It is so pretty. I don't know how she makes a thing look so fine."

"Let's take a closer look." He guided her toward the door.

"Oh no. I can't go in a shop like that." Lydia pulled back.

"But why on earth would you say such a thing?"

"That's for the rich white folk."

"Nonsense. They will welcome anyone who wants to look." He tugged her forward. "Come along. You'll see."

Lydia's eyes drank in the shelves of fabric bolts and hanging dresses. A large table held patterns and sections of vibrant-colored satin cloth crumpled to the side. The room was brightened by several lamps along a shelf in the back, away from the large windows in front. Two women sat hunched over their handiwork at the back wall.

The seamstress looked up from stitching. "Yes?"

"How do you do?" Stokely bowed. "Such a lovely shop and fine craftsmanship. It was obvious as soon as we stepped in."

"Why, thank you." She stood and approached. "Are you looking for anything in particular?" Her eyes took in Lydia's form, as if measuring her for a fitting.

"As we passed, the pinafore apron in the window caught my friend's attention." Stokely leaned toward the middle-aged proprietress.

"This one?" She took it from its hanger. "Would you like to try it on?"

"Oh, it's too much. I couldn't." Lydia bowed her head.

"Step over here behind the curtain and slip it on."

Stokely prodded Lydia. "It doesn't cost anything to try it on."

Lydia paused for a moment. "Well." She patted her chest and followed the seamstress.

Minutes later, the seamstress came out and held the curtain back. Lydia slowly came out. With her chin down, she looked up at Stokely.

"Now that is truly a lovely item."

Lydia held out the skirt and twisted at the waist. She touched the lace ruffles at her shoulders and put her hands in the pockets.

"And look at the precious pink ribbon. How dainty." His eyes crinkled.

"I didn't see that. Oh my." Lydia held out the apron skirt to admire the colorful detail above the ruffles, which fell below her knees. "I've never worn anything so fancy."

The seamstress smiled.

"We'll take it," Stokely said.

"What?" Lydia gasped. "I could never . . ."

"If it pleases you this much, I must make it a gift." He spoke quietly to the matron, then pulled a wallet from his inner coat pocket.

"Everyone is looking at me." Lydia squeezed his arm as they strolled toward the hotel.

"And why wouldn't they?" Stokely patted her hand. "You're a woman of beauty."

"Not me. I'm just plain."

"Nonsense. Now let's go in here and have a fine dinner." He opened the door for her.

Lydia noticed that heads turned and women in dresses with bustles looked at her. The waiter led them to a table. Stokely held the chair for her. She folded her hands on her lap. The tablecloth and candle, the china plates, the real silverware was so much to admire.

"We should go. I don't belong here with all this finery," she whispered.

"Sister Lydia, please accept this blessing from the Lord. You are a princess of heaven. This is just a small glimpse of what the angels behold for you."

Following the meal, Stokely hired a carriage to get them home. "I trust you've enjoyed the evening, Lydia. I sure have."

"Oh, Pastor Stokely, this has been a day I will never forget. How can I thank you enough?"

He took her hands in his. "You can thank me by letting me call on you again soon."

"Yes, of course. That would be special."

"Good night, then." He leaned forward to kiss her.

Lydia gasped and leaned back.

"I apologize, sister." Stokely pouted. "I was caught up in the romance of the moment. Please forgive me."

"I'm not ready. It's all so much for me. I'm sorry."

"I will still call on you, if that's acceptable."

"Yes, Pastor. Good night."

She went in and closed the door. Leaning against it, she sighed. She looked down at her pinafore. "Thank you for the blessings, Lord Jesus." Stepping past the kitchen table, she bent to blow out a candle and noticed her Bible.

Lydia bolted upright. "No. Lord Jesus, I done missed the prayer meeting. I broke my promise to you."

After being in the dark for so long, Abraham lost track of time. Another man controlled his schedule and his choices. He slept as much as he could and relished the brief moments of stepping out on deck to change his water bucket, breathe fresh air, and see more than darkness.

His thoughts were both his friend and his enemy. From memory he would walk through his ordinary day of visiting the church folk, working his parcel, and repairing what he could at the church or someone's home. Imagining the weeds overtaking his plot and vegetables spoiling on the vine meant lack of food, income, and canned goods for the winter. The frustration was hard to overcome and put to rest. Praying for his congregation one by one and quoting Scripture kept his heart at peace, but even that grew weary. Boredom was an infiltrator that seemed to shut down his desires, his hopes, and his will.

On what he thought was the sixth day, maybe the seventh, Abraham interceded for his friends. "Lord Jesus, I continue to praise you, and I always will. I know you are my rock and my fortress. I stand on you when all my hope is lost. I rest in you." He spoke the words into the dark chamber, knowing they were carried to the throne room of the Merciful One. "Father, I believe you are sending help. I believe you are sending Brother Allen. I knows it in my heart. Give him strength, Lord. Keep him strong, and show him the right path. He'll be facing many obstacles and temptations, and the Enemy will try to steal, kill, and destroy, but you will surround him with wisdom and truth. Thank you, Lord.

"And be with Sister Lydia, Sister Savannah, Brother Dickson, Louella, and young Mabel. I knows they be praying, Lord, but keep them safe and keep them fed. I'm not there to look out for them, so's I trust you to keep them in unity, like the disciples in the book of Acts." He paused, and Lydia came to mind again. Something didn't feel right. "Lord, does Sister Lydia need help? Let your Holy Ghost lead my prayer." He listened and searched within for the word, for the insight that would spark faith and knowledge for his petition.

"Lord, Sister Lydia is your servant, but she is a woman with needs. Protect her heart, and keep her from the foils of the Evil One. Don't let her heart be troubled or dismayed. No, Lord, she done been distracted by temptation." Abraham lifted his hands. "Powerful Jesus, I see it. Someone done took her off the path. Awaken her heart. Call to her, Lord."

Just then, while he was letting the substance of faith flow through his being, an intruding presence caught his attention. The feeling that someone was staring at him caused him to look to the left. In the darkness, there was nothing to see. Yet in his mind, a man wearing black clothes stood there smirking but suddenly seemed startled and disappeared. *La Marque.* The soft impression of the name rose in his thinking. *La Marque must be behind this. He's casting his spells on Sister Lydia.*

"Lord Jesus, in your most holy name, I bind the work of this witchcraft. I expose it to your truth and your holy light. May the angel army come forth and conquer this attack. Send forth your winged servants, O Lord. Send them to Lydia and to Allen and all those who have need of your strength right now. Father God, I can see now by faith. I can see you are bringing light into the darkness. There is nothing hidden from you. I am blind until my faith seeks out your light and your power in every instance. O my Lord and my God, you alone are the victory.

"I bless your holy name. I send a blessing to La Marque. Surround him with the light of your power and your love even for a one so bent on evil. He is the slave. He is the slave of the devil. If there be any way, Lord God, that he can be saved, let it come.

But Lord, if he won't surrender to you, may he be removed so that others can be set free. Set them free, Lord Jesus. Set us all free. Blessed be your name."

Abraham sat again, hugged his knees, and laughed at the darkness.

CHAPTER THIRTEEN

THREE RAVENS PERCHED ON THE highest limb of a dying willow oak, cawing loudly. The tree stood next to the weathered plantation house. Built on five-foot-tall pillars to keep the main floor safely above floodwater levels, the house still suffered water damage every few years. It was for that reason La Marque purchased the property—it was cheap, and neighbors had abandoned the area. Bayou Chene had potential, but the risk of the Atchafalaya River surging devalued the plantation. The white paint was faded and peeling, moss grew in the roof shingles, and the wraparound porch sagged. Across the expansive yard stood a sun-bleached barn with water-level stains along the walls. Adjacent to that was a newer structure, a long shed built on mounded dirt. The clearing was surrounded by tupelo, bald cypress, and sweetgum trees. Beyond them, in another small clearing, was a distilling operation and rows of drying racks for making witch hazel and other medicinal teas and ointments, herbs, and eventually potions.

La Marque had a crew of workers for his legitimate business and a smaller staff that operated the backroom business of supplying those who practiced the dark arts in Vermilionville, Baton Rouge, and New Orleans. He supplied them because no one came into his swamp except those whom he specifically brought in, which were very few. The workers who lived in the long shed didn't leave the property, ever. They were his slaves—some purchased, some procreated—and many were victims of debt or kidnapping. Except for new arrivals, La Marque didn't need to use shackles because they were all held captive by black magic. He began with opium and mushroom intoxication, then torture along with blood curses to numb their minds to the point of minimal function. The slaves' willpower was completely erased. Those who resisted the process for too long were sacrificed in rituals and their remains tossed into an enclosure of alligators.

For years La Marque's goal had been to entice businessmen and their wives, the more respectable the better, by offering them the power to succeed over their competition. Once they paid for his services, he had them for life. A victim would unwittingly enter a debt that cost them their soul, their finances, and at times, their family. Of the hundreds of people he had used and discarded, he kept about two dozen on site at any given time. As long as they served a purpose, they remained to gather crops, cut and carry firewood, or tend to the plantation.

Some slaves had a separate value, and these women, girls, and boys he supplied for entertainment purposes to certain social houses, gambling establishments, and a particular steamboat that ran between the state capital and New Orleans.

La Marque operated his businesses for enormous profits, but the money was just a necessary tool to keep him connected to a growing circle of influential people. It included some government officials who were deeply rooted in the workings of power. He didn't care much for the boisterous politicians, as they came and went. The real power rested in the businessmen who governed from behind the scenes.

A nefarious network controlled the economy of the South, for which slavery was an integral part. Without slaves the progress and production would be minimal, and insignificant profits would follow. With slaves the plantations expanded, land was developed, and and cotton and sugar were harvested and shipped to the North, primarily through New Orleans. The general population benefited from the cycle of trade, and those in control claimed their percentage off the top. And those were the elite people who needed a source of power that remained in the shadows and took care of special concerns.

La Marque had been in the inner chamber of his house for hours. It was only known of and accessible by him, since the men who'd built it for him had ceased to exist. He opened it by way of a secret panel in his bedroom wall. Within the chamber was a high-backed leather chair, a desk, a worktable, a bookcase with a few ancient leather-bound books, and shelving with clay jars of oils and boxes of candles and molding clay. On some shelves and hanging on nails were animal hides, bones, skulls, and feathers of hawk, crow, and blue jay. On other shelves were clay effigies, some with pins in them, others with broken appendages. Candles filled the tall freestanding menorah-style candle holder with the center column bent forward, as if bowing to the other six branches.

Also on the desk was a chess set with gold and silver pieces. At that moment they were placed strategically, depending on whom they represented, and not in the formation of a game. He sat with his head leaning back, his feet on the floor, and his arms on the rests. In his right hand he held a silver pawn that he occasionally rubbed with his thumb. His left hand fingered a raven feather as if it were a writing stylus. From this chair he traveled. He projected his soul to leave his body and pass through a portal to wherever he desired.

On this particular passage he sought Jason Sylvester and

found him in Memphis. He saw quickly that Abraham was still locked in the steamboat, sufficiently bound, but he did not like it that the preacher looked up at him. La Marque had many times visited the councils of the ordained leadership of denominations to watch and to plant messages, but they never looked at him. His soul was invisible, and he took advantage of his ability to see and hear their plans so that he could form his own schemes. But this poor, pathetic black preacher looked right in his eyes. The preacher who kept breaking the demonic strongholds that he had crafted on slaves and assisted runaways to escape to the North.

Abraham was a menace and would pay for disrupting his plans. La Marque had already sent a new messenger to distract the prayer support. But this passage was to give Sly the assignment to capture or kill the white preacher, Allen Hartman. He had warned him in Saint Louis but could sense his presence coming. The river pirates operated under a different host spirit. Perhaps they would be successful in stopping the missionary, but just in case, he would send his shadow man to make sure the job got done.

La Marque saw Sly sitting at a table in a tavern, with his back to the wall. The usual late-afternoon commotion of dock workers drinking and eating had not gotten too boisterous, but they were working on it. The hit man sipped his whiskey and twisted the guild ring on his finger. Then suddenly, as if bumped, he looked to his right, and there on the chair next to him was a silver pawn. He scanned the room to make sure no one was looking in his direction and picked up the piece. He covered it in the palm of his hand, then looked at the near iridescent glow emanating from the token. He closed his eyes.

La Marque could see that understanding registered on the assassin's face. *Order the network in Memphis to detain or kill Allen Hartman. Get the black preacher to Bayou Chene as quickly as possible.*

Once the message was successfully received, La Marque followed his silver cord back through the portal and into his waiting body.

Sly tucked the pawn into a concealed coat pocket and walked across the tavern to where Captain Denton was just being served his dinner plate. The shadow man stood by Denton's shoulder, watching him take an eager bite of steak.

Choking on the meat, Denton coughed. "Dang it, Sly. Why you always sneaking around?"

"Time to go." He sat on the edge of the next chair, leaning in close.

"Sure. Just let me finish this."

"Now."

Denton was about to argue but flinched. He looked down at the tip of a boot dagger piercing his pants and jabbing his thigh. Nodding, he stood, shoved the steak into his coat pocket, and grabbed the bottle of whiskey as he turned to leave.

"Hey. He didn't pay for that," the man at the bar said and reached beneath the counter.

Sly slid a ten-dollar gold piece across the varnished top.

"That'll do." The patron looked away. "I never saw you."

Sly walked out and caught up to Denton, who was dabbing blood off his leg. "Go straight to the boat and make ready to leave immediately."

"But they ain't done loading it yet. I need more time."

"You be ready to leave when I get back, or I'll tie you to the paddle wheel and find another pilot."

Denton swallowed the chunk he was chewing on, nodded, and limped away.

Looking up and down the street, Sly had to choose between

a banker, a merchant, a madam, or a doctor to alert the network of their task. He chose the madam because her parlor was closest. Sly turned down a side street and then an alley to enter through the back door of a three-story brick house. The row of hedges he passed allowed for a client to depart and evade notice by selecting one of three passageways to an innocent location. It was a prime location for men who needed discretion.

Sly went into the familiar salon and was met by a young woman in a burgundy silk dress.

"How may I serve you?" She smiled.

"I want to see Marlette."

"Of course. I believe she is with a client at the moment. Would you like to have a seat?"

A hallway door opened, and in walked Madam Marlette with a gentleman in a charcoal-gray coat with gray striped pants. He held a top hat in his hand. Sly immediately sized him up and noticed something in his favor.

Sly nodded toward the woman in a high-collared black gown that probably came from Paris.

"How do you do, Mr. Sylvester? It's been a long time," she said.

"Ma'am." He touched the brim of his hat.

"Allow me to introduce you to Mr. Hiram Dupont. He's a financier and is establishing a hospital for Memphis." She gestured with her hand. "Mr. Dupont, this is Mr. Sylvester. You won't see him much, but if you ever need someone to take care of, let's say, very contentious matters, you will find him most helpful and very discreet."

Dupont extended his hand. "Good to meet you, Sylvester."

Sly took the opportunity to make himself known by pressing his thumb firmly between the second and third knuckle of the offered hand. The signal was returned.

124

"Oh, a member of the fraternal order, I see," the gentleman said. "Marlette, we have a fellow Freemason here. Now that's just fine."

"That's right." Sly lowered his voice. "I'm asking both of you to spread the word to watch for a man who may show up in Memphis in a few days. His name is Allen Hartman. He's a Methodist preacher, so he probably won't come calling here, Marlette, but get some ears on the streets."

"You might be surprised at how many men of the cloth have stopped by for a visit." She smirked.

"Why are you interested in this preacher, may I ask?" Dupont tapped his hat.

"He'll be asking around for a Negro named Abraham. He's one of them that helps runaway slaves get to the North. I'm returning him to my employer near Baton Rouge to pay for the trouble he caused."

"I see." Dupont said. "And what does this Hartman want with him?"

"They're friends."

"Is he an abolitionist?" Marlette folded her arms.

"I reckon. The point is, we want him stopped. I'm taking the Black down river as quick as I can."

Dupont rubbed his chin. "When you say stopped, you mean . . ."

"He's worth more captured alive, but putting an end to his journey, with proof, would also be rewarded."

"Humm. An interesting challenge."

"I'll tell the girls down at my waterfront inn to pay attention." The madam nodded.

"May I ask who your employer is? Perhaps also one of the brotherhood?" Dupont kept his voice low.

Sly paused to make sure this businessman understood that revealing the name was a weighty burden. "La Marque."

"La Marque. I believe my wife has had her fortune told a few times by a man named La Marque. He held a séance in our home a few years ago. A Creole man, if he's the same one."

"Likely the same." Dupont seemed to be intrigued.

"What's so special about this Negro? La Marque could have slaves aplenty without going to so much trouble."

"Like I said, he's helping runaways. He needs to pay for it."

"Very well. I will let our people know to be on the lookout for a preacher named Allen Hartman."

"Just let Marlette know if you hear anything." Sly turned to leave.

"Mr. Sylvester, wouldn't you like to stay for a drink and relax?" Marlette's business was pleasure.

"I need to get back to the boat."

"Cynthia will take care of you. How long is up to you." Marlette drew the younger woman forward.

Sly moved toward the door but hesitated. Cynthia looked elegant, much cleaner than most of his opportunities. He nodded at the madam and followed Cynthia through the door. "Denton probably ain't ready anyway," he mumbled.

By the time Sly reached the *Pegasus*, Denton was fuming. "What's the rush to leave? I have to cut my order short. I'm losing a lot of money."

"You ain't losing that much, and you'll be compensated. Besides, you'll have to sell off everything in Natchez. You'll have to run light on the Atchafalaya."

"What? I ain't taking this boat down there. It's too risky." Denton pounded the railing.

"Then you better hope I find someone who can get me down there faster." Sly scanned the waterfront. "I'm heading below."

Sly stretched out on his stateroom bed and took the pawn from the inner pocket. The iridescent glow had faded, and he examined the polished silver piece. How could they appear and disappear? How did it speak to him? He closed his eyes and held it again, but no message emanated to his mind. He had seen La Marque do incredible things, move objects across a table with his mind, talk with spirits, and cause a man to choke to death from across the room. He had been in a room full of people in black robes surrounded by candles and chanting. Other times men would take turns raping women, or women would willingly be used in the bizarre rituals. Some women were used by men until they became pregnant. When the baby was born, it was taken away from the aggrieved mother to be set before the altar of an idol or to be raised for other reprehensible purposes.

It didn't all make sense. Sly stayed because of the power he had to work in the shadows. He had done remarkable things beyond his own proficient skill as a burglar. There was a time when a pawn directed him into a mansion to kill a man in his sleep. The occasion that most remained in his memory was sneaking past armed guards into a military compound to execute a colonel who had insulted one of La Marque's clients. Power generated power, and lust for power propelled the evil wheels that turned other wheels. Fear influenced the wheels, and that was where Sly was masterful. He kept the wheels moving that La Marque wanted to move.

Slavery was a machine. When the wheels got jammed because a part was missing, it messed up the works down the line. Runaway slaves caused other slaves to seek freedom. A captured slave, beaten or hung, kept the wheels turning with fear. Those who prospered needed the fear intact and perpetuated. A run-of-the-mill slave catcher worked by brute force and intimidation. Sly had advanced his reputation to an elite status by murdering, or in the case of Abraham, capturing within the shadows. He was a living legend along the Natchez Trace—and anywhere that runaways looked for an avenue of escape—because he worked like a ghost. He owed the reputation and almost supernatural skill to his allegiance with La Marque.

Sly set the pawn on the table. Abraham was just another kidnap job. It would be over soon enough, Sly would be paid, and he would wait for his next orders. The preacher was an easy capture. He wasn't making trouble, but in some way, he was different than other victims. It was as if he were sorry for Sly and that he would offer help if Sly needed it.

"I got all the help I need." Sly blinked and scowled. Why had he just spoken that out loud?

CHAPTER FOURTEEN

TWILIGHT FADED AT THE CAVE opening, and the two campfires struggled to fill the vacant space with light in the deepest part of the cavern. Allen watched the smoke rise fifty feet and escape through a hole in the ceiling that looked like the slash from a giant blade stabbed into the earth. He sat on sand and leaned against the rough limestone wall next to Dex, Lucius, and Delbert. Some twenty brigands lounged on blankets wherever they could. Two were roasting the venison that Dex had shot earlier that day. Others were pouring whiskey from a small keg taken off the keelboat.

"Since we've provided your dinner, how about passing some over this way?" Dex held up his hands bound at the wrists with rotting hemp rope.

"Sure." One of the pirates cut off a chunk that was more gristle than meat and tossed it at Dex's feet. It bounced in the sand.

"You're not cooking it right." Delbert shook his head. "Move it from the flames and keep it over the coals."

The other pirate glared over his shoulder. "Shut up."

"You're ruining a great piece of strap steak . . . I'm telling you."

"I said shut up." The ruffian shook a Bowie knife at him.

Delbert raised his bound hands in surrender. "I can help if you want."

The man threw a stick of firewood, but it hit Lucius.

"Hey!"

Allen thought the man was embarrassed enough to apologize, but he didn't. Just when he turned back to the meat, Lucius threw the stick with both hands in a chopping motion and struck his hip. The man jolted around, enraged, but stepped on a fire-ring stone, lost his balance, and knocked over the spit, dropping the chunks of meat into the fire.

"Idiot!" The other cook whacked him with a leg bone.

Punches were thrown both ways while the meat crackled in the blaze. Donovan came up and shouted for them to stop.

"That's my dinner you're burning."

"Sorry, Boss." They both scrambled to recover the charred remains.

"You, get a fresh roast. And you, feed this to our guests." Donovan pointed at the burned meat.

"Yes, sir." The pirate picked up the skewer and handed it to Delbert, who gave him a disgusted look.

"The rest of you lay off that whiskey until we eat something." Donovan swept his pointed finger at all of them. Then he stooped over to pick up the long knife and stood in front of the clumsy scoundrel. "It was a mistake I know you won't make again."

The man shook his head.

Striking like a rattlesnake, Donovan thrust the knife into the man's gut at an upward angle to reach under the ribs. The man bent over the jab, grasping for the handle, but the hand that held it was too tight. He sank to his knees.

Allen gasped, and bile rose in his stomach.

The brigand boss yanked the blade out and wiped it and his

bloody hand on the back of the dead man's coat. He rose and appraised the knife in the firelight. He knelt again and raised the bottom of the coat to find the sheath. He slit the belt and removed the sheath, then stood again as he tucked the knife into the sheath and then his pants.

"Finster, get some help, and get this guy out of our kitchen. Go feed the turtles with him." He squatted in front of Dex. "I apologize for his bad manners. That's no way to behave in front of guests, is it?"

"You're a true gentleman, Donovan. I appreciate your hospitality." Dex tipped his head toward the meat skewer. "Could you pass us the salt tin?"

Donovan chuckled. "I like you, Yates." He called over his shoulder. "One of you bring the salt."

"Thank you."

"You saw what I'll do to a man who makes mistakes." The pirate scratched his sideburns. "It would be a mistake for any of you to cause trouble or try to escape. Now, enjoy your dinner."

Delbert took a pinch of salt from the small tin box and sprinkled it around the lump of charred meat and wolfed off a mouthful. He passed it to Dex, who did the same.

"Allen, you're going to need some food. This might be all we get for a while, so take a few bites," Dex said.

Allen nodded. He bit into it and tugged until it tore loose. He recalled eating fresh venison and elk in the Arapaho camp, but it was never burned. At least the meat underneath was fine. They passed the provision back and forth until it was gone. Delbert gnawed on the stick for the final morsels. He then tucked the sharpened skewer between his side and Lucius.

A pirate, the one Delbert had nudged into the river, now sat across from them to the left of the fire, some fifteen feet away. He reclined on the low ledge with an elbow on his knee and a pistol tucked into his waist belt for an easy cross draw. He leered at them, mostly at Delbert, with a partially open-mouthed smirk, as if waiting for a chance to repay his humiliation.

"How about some water?" Dex asked, as if speaking to a waiter.

"I'd prefer a glass of wine." Delbert flashed a smile.

The man shifted on his perch and looked about. He slowly rose, and when he returned, he dropped a gourd canteen at Dex's feet. He resumed his guard position.

Dex prodded the canteen closer with his heel until he could lift it and remove the stopper. He handed it to Allen, who drank, took a few gulps for himself, and passed it to Lucius. Delbert took a drink and corked it. Before he could ask for his wine again, Lucius elbowed him. They were being watched by another pirate back to the right. This one seemed poised to strike at the slightest provocation. Delbert gently placed the gourd beside him.

Allen caught a movement to his left and watched Donovan materialize in the cut in the middle of the cavern floor. The orange glow barely clarified his features as he loomed over the prisoners.

"So what are you going to do with us?" Dex asked.

"I'm not sure yet." The brigand chief took a knee and rested his elbow on it with his hands folded. "It would be easier for me to dump you in the river. But I'm still pondering what value you might have. You know, I can always use some good men. Why don't you join me and my company? There'd be money and plenty of it."

"Well, let me think on that." Dex pursed his lips. "I'll give you an answer in the morning after I talk over the prospects with my associates."

Donovan laughed. "Dexter Yates, you're a sharp blade, aren't you. I'd like you as my second-in-command." His eyebrows arched as he smiled. Just as quickly, the smile faded. "But then, maybe you're too sharp. You ever heard what the Harpe brothers used to do to people they robbed?"

"Yeah." Dex returned the glare. "They gut open their victims, filled the insides with rocks, and dumped them in the river so they'd never be found."

Allen swallowed the bile that rose in his throat at the gruesome history.

"Right you are. And that's one option, or you could join the gang." Donovan rose and put his fists on his hips.

From Allen's angle, the ruffian was silhouetted against the firelight, forming the visage of a demon. He was flesh and bone, but a menacing presence caused the hair to rise on the back of Allen's neck.

"Perhaps your man here could usher us out to relieve ourselves," Dex suggested. "We wouldn't want to disrupt the atmosphere of your fine lodgings with unpleasantness."

Donovan chuckled and shook his head. "You two, grab lanterns and take them out. Finster, get a couple more men to keep watch." He kicked Dex's bare foot. "Just so you know, there are more men up on the bluff. There ain't no way out unless you want to become turtle food."

When they returned from their brief reprieve, Allen noted that each of his comrades seemed to assess the number of men, guns, knives, and other possible weapons, as he did himself. He realized he needed to be ready to act in accord with them. Delbert seemed particularly clever at causing instant chaos. If Allen delayed, it might cause an injury or the death of one his mates, and he couldn't live with that. Howard and Kin might already be dead—the probability seemed high—and that thought brought a crushing weight onto his shoulders. The best thing was to make his own assessment and plan for escape in case he got away alone. Dex had been so cool headed and calculating that being without his guidance seemed daunting. But he had done it before, gone into the cave and come out again. He would get out of this, the Lord being his helper.

Allen leaned close and whispered. "Dex, we have to get out of here. I need to find Deacon Abraham."

"I'm glad you're thinking that way." Dex's eyes darted about. "We'll have to wait for the right chance. Too risky tonight. These fellas are on edge, like they're waiting for it. It's best we get rest and let them stay awake to worry." He slid down to prone and tucked his hands behind his head.

Delbert was already snoring. Lucius was breathing steadily. Allen breathed deeply and whispered Psalm 91. He focused his attention on the low fire. "Lord, help me to be ready for the right timing for all of us to get out of here."

Moon Cloud sat on a sandy bank by the river. Pulling the blue stone out of the pouch around her neck, she held it up to the sun and closed one eye. Rolling it between her thumb and forefinger, she cherished the indigo sparkle that was so much like the twinkle in Allen's eyes when he smiled.

Upon lowering the charm, she noticed Two Rivers upstream offering a token to the wind and the water. She stepped carefully across the stream, which reached midcalf.

"Uncle, may I join your prayer?"

He handed her a parfleche, from which she poured dried and ground sage, yarrow, bitterroot, and kinnikinnick into her palm. The holy man took some as well, and together they faced the east, raised the offering, and sprinkled it into the wind as they turned to the south, west, and north.

"Great Father, you have given life to the earth, and we send these sacred herbs back to you in thanksgiving. Thank you for the life plants and the wind that carries their seeds. Thank you for the earth and the water, which unite to bring forth the provision of food, medicine, and beauty. You called them to give us life, as you are the Life Giving One." Two Rivers paused, then softly sang and raised his arms over the stream. His voice faded to silence.

"Moon Cloud, you look weary." He gestured for her to sit on a fallen tree, and he leaned on a stout branch.

"I do not sleep well." She removed her wet moccasins and rubbed her feet on a clump of green grass. "I am tormented by dreams. When I wake, my thoughts are of White Falcon, but I do not see him in the dream. I see only a black storm cloud that hurls people to their death."

"Are the people in the sky?"

"No. The cloud is over a great river and the ground. I do not see any escape. I see no one clearly. The storm cloud destroys many, but there are others who sit together weeping. They are pushed down by the great cloud. They are people of skin the color of the elk's neck." She shrugged her shoulders. "I do not understand. It only makes me afraid that I am watching the death of many souls."

"I am having trouble seeing White Falcon. I saw him many days ago in a big canoe with a great wing. But now his canoe went into the cloud of the storm. The Spirit does not show me more, even when I am fasting." He clutched his shirt at his chest. "I feel that my heart is being clenched like the squirrel caught by the owl. Before when I saw the great cloud, I did not feel fear. But now it grips me, and I do not understand."

"I no longer feel the peace I had before. Have I done something wrong? Do I love Allen too much that he is being taken from me?" Moon Cloud held back the tears. "It is so hard to understand the ways of the spirits." She opened her hand to reveal the gem and stared as if she could see past the rough edges to bring clarity.

"What do you have?"

"It is a stone that Blue Otter gave me. When I hold it to the sun, the color is like the eyes of White Falcon." She held it out to Two Rivers.

He twisted to hold it up to the sun and turned it, admiring each new shimmer of azure light. The medicine man frowned as he studied the ancient creation that now, of all times, was provided for a purpose. "Umm." He laughed and placed the medicine stone back into her palm. "It looks dark here, but even the darkness cannot hold back the light."

Moon Cloud furrowed her eyebrows. "Yes?"

"Do you not see the meaning of the light in the stone?" His eyes held a tender smile. "One Who Gives Life is the light. When you look close enough at the darkness, the light shines through. It shines in the color of White Falcon's eyes to tell you that Great Spirit is with him."

She gasped. "We do not fear what we cannot see because the Spirit's light can be found in the darkness." She stood, squeezing the stone in her hand against her cheek. "I will not fear for Allen." She squealed with delight and opened her arms to the sky.

CHAPTER FIFTEEN

TILLING THE GROUND AND PULLING weeds were necessary chores, but for Sister Lydia the garden was one more place of prayer. It made the mundane task a time to be in the throne room of her blessed Lord. Of an evening, she would sit in her rocking chair by the fire. Or she would be at the prayer meeting. She leaned on her hoe and gazed at the glimpses of sunlight flashing from the river through the trees.

"Lord, thank you for all of this. And thank you for sending Pastor Stokely while Deacon Abraham is away. Keep him and Brother Allen safe on this journey." She paused at her own words. "Lord, you must have them safe, 'cause I don't feel any particular burden for Abraham and Allen. Is that the case?" She shrugged her shoulders and went back to hoeing and humming a medley of hymns.

"Mama, I gots the chicken plucked, and the bread's done baking." Esther skipped to the garden.

"Thank you, precious." Lydia looked over her work. "Pick you some snap peas whilst I go wash up."

"Yes, Mama. But why you baking so much bread?"

"I was fixing to invite the pastor for supper and want to have enough." She looked over her daughter's head to see Nolia Biss tapping on the parsonage door and entering. "Well, what she doing, going in there?"

Lydia scurried to wash her hands and put on her clean new pinafore. She wrapped a loaf of bread in a towel and carried it with her in a basket. She walked quickly to the church but found it empty. "Now where could Pastor be?"

Reluctant to raise the question to Nolia, it seemed like a good pretext to find out why she had gone into Deacon Abraham's home. Carefully circling the shanty, she came by the window and peeked through the curtain. There was Nolia, wearing a different dress.

"What? We'll just see about this."

Lydia tapped twice and opened the door. Nolia turned and gasped, covering her front with her arms up against her chest. She wasn't wearing a different dress but standing in her undergarments while her dress lay on the floor.

"What on earth are you doing . . ." Lydia started but then gasped and covered her mouth. Right then Nolia turned, and Chester Stokely sat up in bed shirtless. "Oh . . . oh my."

"Sister, it's not what it looks like." Stokely grabbed for his shirt. "Nothing happened. We were tempted, but I put a stop to it just before you came in."

"Pastor, I don't know what to think." Lydia held her cheeks and shook her head.

"Trust me. We stopped before the sin was committed." He buttoned his fine white shirt.

Nolia Biss picked up her dress and held it against her. It seemed that her startled look became a gleam in her eyes and a light sneer on her lips.

"I have to go." Lydia stumbled out the door and hustled home as tears streamed down her cheeks.

She shut the door to her bedroom and flopped onto the bed. "No, no, no. It can't be." Her face pressed into the pillow. "Why?" She gasped for air and groaned. "Why is Nolia Biss always interfering in my business? She disrupts church. She always putting on like she special, wearing a fine dress during the day. She makes me so angry, Lord. Why don't she just act like the poor woman that she is, like the rest of us? Why don't she stop trying to act like she's something special in your eyes?" Lydia scrunched the pillow and screamed into it.

"Oh, what am I saying, Father God? What am I doing? I'm angry 'cause I must be jealous. Forgive me, Father God. She is special in your eyes, and you keep working in her heart just like you're working in my heart. I'm sorry.

"Lord Jesus, have I been deceived? Deceived by a man of the cloth? Forgive me, Jesus. Forgive me. I done missed the prayer times 'cause I was letting my heart go to that man. I thought you was blessing me with a man to care for me. To be a husband, maybe. I longs for a man, Lord, but I done put him before you and got distracted."

"Mama, are you all right?" Esther called through the door and then opened it. Daniel's worried eyes looked in over her shoulder.

"Yes, precious. I'll be all right. Just a spell of aggravation I had to give to Jesus." She sat up. "You'uns come here." She opened her arms and hugged them both. "Mama be just fine."

"Is Pastor Stokely coming for supper?" Esther asked as they moved to the kitchen.

"No, child. If he knows what's good for him, he won't be coming."

Several minutes later, when the table was set, there was a knock on the door. Esther opened it.

"Pastor Stokely." Esther beamed.

"My, but you look pretty this afternoon, Esther." He touched her cheek. "Your mother invited me for supper."

"Esther, you run over and pick us some tomatoes, please." Lydia patted the girl's back and grabbed the doorknob. "I'm sorry, but there is no place for you at my table. After what I seen, I'm surprised you would come by."

"Sister Lydia, if I may explain. I admit I am a man like any other. Temptation befalls every one of us."

"Umm-huh." She still held the door.

"Sister Nolia washed my shirt for me and was bringing it by. I thought it would be better to meet at the parsonage rather than the church. When I turned to put on the shirt, she began removing her dress. And I admit, I was tempted, but I was just telling her that I couldn't, when you came in. I believe the good Lord sent you in time to disrupt her lustful snare. She was going to take advantage of me."

"I seen your trousers on the floor. Did she wash those too?"

"Lydia, please. My true interest of any of the women around here is you. I believe you are the one God is intending for me. And now that I have passed the test—with your help, I might add—it is certain to my heart, my whole heart, that you are the woman I need to keep me strong. We can be good together."

Lydia sighed and looked down. "If what you say is true, then you got to come clean to the church folk. You got to ask their forgiveness."

"But that would be humiliating. I shouldn't have to make such a public declaration. It was only you that is aware of my indiscretion. Let me ask your forgiveness." He shifted on his feet and glanced around.

"We a close group, like a family. You hurt one of us, they all going to know and feel the hurt." She put her hand on her hip.

"It's too much to ask."

"It ain't too much. You got to make this right."

"Are you going to hold me to it?"

"Yes."

He took a half step back and smiled. "I see you're wearing the pretty pinafore apron I gave you. It does look lovely."

Lydia swallowed. "You better go now."

"You're going to dismiss me without supper?" He frowned.

She disappeared from the doorway for a moment and then handed him a round loaf of bread. "Good night."

Lydia closed the door and exhaled. She untied the ruffled white apron. Laying it on the back of a chair, Lydia noticed Stokely out the window, handing something to Esther, who grinned and hugged him. She then ran toward the house with a small sack of tomatoes.

"Mama, look." Esther held out her hand. "Look what the pastor gave me."

Picking up the round pewter brooch, engraved with flowers and an amethyst in the center, Lydia held it to the remaining daylight at the window to look at the facets. "It's lovely." She moved to put it back into the waiting palm but examined it again. Even in the diminishing light, tiny flashes of purple beckoned her to see more. *You are beautiful.* Lydia blinked and gazed, gathering more of its soft illumination. "Valuable," she whispered.

"It's mine." Esther snatched the brooch from her mother's hand.

"Esther." Lydia gasped and clutched the front of her dress. "Girl, what are you doing?"

"He gave it to me." She held her arm back out of her mother's reach.

"I'm sure he intended to give it to me." Lydia took a half step forward. "Didn't he tell you to give it me?"

"No. He gave it to me and said I was pretty. He wanted me to have something as pretty as I am." The daughter stepped back. "He didn't say it was for you. You sent him away."

"Esther." The mother sighed. "Esther, he's a grown man, and you're still a girl. He wouldn't give you something this valuable to play with. His intentions are for me. Don't you understand?" She smiled softly. "Please give it back to me."

"No, he gave it to me." The girl moved behind a chair. "You sent him away. Maybe he wants to marry me now."

"Esther." Her hand covered her mouth. "What are you saying?"

"He gave it to me." She burst into tears and ran up the stairs to her bedroom.

Lydia eased herself into the arms of the rocking chair. "Lord Jesus, what just happened?" She rested her head in her hand and heaved a breath of anguish.

"Mama." Daniel burst through the front door. "Is it time to eat?" He leaned on her shoulder.

"Oh, darling child." She rocked forward to rise from the chair. "It ain't quite ready. Grab you some bread for now. I'll get this chicken to frying."

She lit a fire in the stove and cut the chicken into pieces and dipped them in flour. After the sizzling began, she slid the pan to the back of the stove and stared at the upstairs door. Finally, Lydia went up the creaking steps and tapped on the door.

"Esther, honey? I'm sorry we fought. Come on down to eat."

"I ain't hungry."

"Please come. You can put the brooch in your box. I won't ask for it again. The chicken's almost ready."

Silence.

Lydia returned to the stove and tried to hum a song, but it wouldn't come. When she and Daniel were almost finished eating, Esther crept down the stairs. Without saying anything, she took her place, bowed her head for a moment, then took a bite of chicken thigh. The conversation was meager. Exhausted from her emotional turmoil, Lydia put her children and herself to bed.

The next morning, their routine seemed normal. Esther bounced down the stairs, singing "Skip, skip, skip to my Lou." Lydia glanced up to heaven and smiled her thanksgiving.

"Morning, Mama."

"Morning, precious." She set a plate on the table. "I warmed up the chicken from last night and toasted the bread."

"Is Daniel going to eat?"

"I think he done ate his breakfast. He took his pole down to the river." Lydia gave thanks, and they partook of the meal.

Esther finished and set her plate in the washtub.

"Child, after you finish chores, what will you do today?"

"Sister Dickson said she'd pay me to help with her work today."

"Oh, that's just fine. She can use your help."

Later that afternoon, Lydia looked up from her garden to see Daniel coming up from the river, walking alongside Brother and Sister Dickson. The brother had a pole resting on his shoulder and a stringer of catfish in his other hand. Daniel swung his catfish back and forth.

"Afternoon, sister. The Lord done blessed us good." The elder man smiled and raised his stringer. "And Mr. Daniel got the big one today."

"Thank the Lord. They look mighty fine." Lydia stepped out of the garden.

"Yes, ma'am. Catfish is good eating."

"Sister Dickson, was you down there a fishing too?" Lydia put her hand on Daniel's shoulder.

"I just went down the last little bit."

"Was Esther still doing some work for you?"

"No, she finished up a while ago. Didn't she come right home?" The elder couple looked at each other.

"I just figured she was still a working with you." Lydia scanned past them. "Well, she'll show up by and by."

"If we sees her, we'll send her on home." Brother Dickson switched the fish to his other hand. "Enjoy your fish supper."

As the couple left, Lydia and Daniel strolled toward the house. "Where do you think she could be?" Her brow furrowed. "Son, let me take the fish, and you run up to Louella's to borrow some cornmeal."

"Yes, Mama." He handed her the stringer and trotted away.

Lydia set the fish next to the washtub. She dipped her hands in the water and wiped them on a rag towel. "Esther, is you upstairs?" Staring at the upper door, she tied on her old apron. "Esther?"

The corner of her eye caught a color that drew her attention a few feet away. The pinafore rested on the back of a chair with a soft white gleam that stood out from the plainness around it. She pursed her lips and swallowed. Removing the old apron, she put on the pinafore, adjusted it, and climbed the stairs. Lydia tapped lightly on the door and entered. She looked in Esther's box, under the pillow, and fondled through the drawer of clothes. She checked under the pillow again and felt down the blanket, then under the tick mattress. Not bothering to check through Daniel's bed or drawers, she struck a match to light a candle, and in the moment of the flare, a twinkle caught her eye. There, tucked behind the candle and partially covered by a folded handkerchief, was the brooch.

Lydia raised the amethyst to the flame and let the purple shine caress her eyes. She pinned the jewel to the pinafore above her left breast and admired the beautiful gift. She held out the skirt and twisted from side to side. "I needs the mirror."

Partway down the stairs, she gasped. Daniel abruptly came through the front door.

"Louella bringing the cornmeal." He stopped short. "Mama, what you wearing?"

144

"Oh this? It's just a new apron." She passed her hands along her waist. "Do you like it?"

"No, I mean that." He pointed to the brooch.

"Pastor Stokely gave it to me as a gift." Her fingers stroked the edge of the pewter. "It's nothing really."

Daniel drew close, to within inches, to see it. "May I have it?"

"What? No." She jerked her shoulder back. "Why you saying that?"

"You said it was nothing." He scowled. "I want it."

"No." She swatted at his hand, but he pulled away. "This is for a lady, not a boy."

Just then a voice called out, "Sister Lydia? I gots the flour."

Lydia brushed past her son and opened the door. "Thank you, Louella."

"My, my." The slender woman touched her throat. "Ain't you looking like a lady of the big house."

"Oh this." She fingered the ruffles at her shoulders and stepped back to be admired.

Louella hesitated to cross the threshold. Mabel, her daughter, pushed her in to behold the sight. Upon seeing the brooch, she froze. The teenage girl hugged herself and rubbed her arms. "Aagh," she cried and gasped for breath. She stepped back until she bumped the wall next to the door.

"Girl, what is wrong with you?" Lydia frowned.

Louella stood stunned, embracing her stomach.

Mabel's eyes darted from the brooch to the far corner of the room, near the bottom of the stairs. She pointed. "It's him."

"What? Who?" Lydia looked back.

"It's him. He gave it to you." Mabel grabbed her mother and pulled her out the door.

"What is you saying?"

"Take it off." Mabel blocked her eyes with the back of her hand.

"Girl?" Lydia covered the purple eye with her left hand. "What?" Then she untied the pinafore and wadded it up with the brooch deep inside. She tossed it back to the table.

"What are you seeing, Mabel?"

The girl heaved her breaths. Clutching her mother's arm, she leaned to peek back into the room. "It's him. La Marque."

Lydia gasped and looked back. "You saw him here?"

She nodded. "I saw him. He was a shadow, but I know it was him. I could feel him." Mabel shivered as her mother held on to her.

Louella hugged her daughter close. "Where did you get that thing?"

"Pastor Stokely gave it to me." Lydia slumped against the doorframe. "He gave me the white apron too."

"Stokely." The mother released her girl and squared her shoulders. "He come by the other day sweet talking on Mabel. Trying to give her gifts." She shook her head. "He don't feel right to me. Uh-uhn. A man don't talk to a girl like that unless he wanting something in return. Uh-uhn. I sent him away, and he got mad."

"He did that to you?" Lydia looked at Mabel.

She nodded her head. "He made me think of the store man that used to hurt me."

"You mean the one back in Louisiana who took advantage of you?" Lydia swallowed hard. "Oh Jesus, what have I done?"

"Ever since he come with Nolia, we been having trouble around here. People fighting each other. No prayer meetings." Louella folded her arms.

"You think La Marque sent Stokely to break apart our church?" Lydia spread her feet apart and put her fists on her hips.

"He the one who kidnapped Deacon Abraham, and then come Stokely to take his place." Mabel pointed toward the river.

"Oh Lord Jesus. And we ain't been praying." Lydia rubbed her chin. "It do make sense."

"It's a wily scheme of the devil," Louella agreed.

"Esther. We gots to find Esther right now. Stokely was being sweet on her too." She grabbed the pinafore bundle. "Daniel, you come with. And bring that hammer."

Hustling across the dirt road, Lydia pointed. "You'uns go look in the church. I'll see to the parsonage."

A minute later they regrouped.

"Church is empty," Louella reported.

"Here too."

"Mama, look." Daniel pointed beyond the church.

Brother and Sister Dickson walked up with Esther.

"Girl, where you been? Is you all right?" Lydia reached for her.

Esther pulled back. "I'm fine. What's the bother?"

"I didn't know where you was."

Sister Dickson held Esther's shoulders. "We found her with Jane, snapping peas."

"After I done the work, I saw Jane and helped her and her mother." Esther frowned. "They's fixing to put up the peas."

Lydia explained the story of the pinafore, and Mabel added her awareness. The Dicksons shook their heads as discernment lined up. Then Lydia exposed the brooch.

"That's mine." Esther reached for it, but Mabel slapped her hand.

"It belong to the witch-man."

"But he gave it to me." Esther pouted.

"Esther, don't you see all the trouble it's bringing? You fighting with your mother," Brother Dickson said. "It ain't worth it. It comes with a hex on it."

"That be true," Luella agreed as Sister Dickson bobbed her head.

"We ought to destroy it now." Brother Dickson looked around.

"I gots a hammer." Daniel held it up.

"No," Esther cried.

"They's a anvil back of the parsonage." The elder led the way.

Lydia set the pewter brooch on the anvil. "Go ahead."

Daniel raised the hammer and struck right on the gemstone. It bounced back so fast it almost hit his forehead.

Brother Dickson reached for the hammer. "Let me see that."

Just then Chester Stokely stepped out of Blessings's cabin in plain view of the group. Blessing lurked behind him, but upon seeing the others, she ducked back inside.

"What have we here?" He adjusted his tie as he approached. He smiled at Lydia.

"It's good that you see this." Brother Dickson raised the hammer.

Stokely flinched upon seeing the brooch.

The hammer clacked on the stone but bounced back up. Another strike and a third with the same results. Not a chip or dent on the ornament. Brother Dickson stepped back, huffing.

Stokely laughed. "You all need to learn about the deeper power." He strolled away laughing. "I'll be seeing you."

"I can't believe it. I hit that hard and true." The brother looked at the hammerhead.

"It's a devil stone." Mabel pointed with her chin.

"Lord Jesus." Lydia looked to the sky. "Forgive me, Lord, for bringing these things into my home. Forgive me for putting trust in a man that aimed to do us harm. How do we break the power of this devil stone?"

They listened.

"The river," Mabel said.

At the same moment, Esther spoke. "We gots to throw it in the river. They took Deacon Abraham down the river, so we throw it in and let the water wash it away."

Lydia tipped her head back and stared at her daughter. "I agree." She wrapped the brooch in the apron again.

When the cluster of saints reached the shore, Lydia pulled out the brooch and looked at each face. She drew back her arm.

"Mama, wait!" Esther reached out. "Let me throw it. I'm the one who took it in the first place."

Lydia nodded and pressed it into her palm.

Esther gazed at the purple stone and touched it with her fingers. She sighed. "Lord Jesus, take this away from us." She leaned back and flung the curse as far as she could. It barely made a splash and was gone.

"Thank you, Lord Jesus, for the power of your blood." Brother Dickson raised his hands.

"Amen," they said together.

After watching the river flow by, the group turned to leave.

"Mama."

"Yes, lamb."

Esther looked at the pinafore.

"But this don't have a curse on it." Lydia looked for reassurance.

Each one held her gaze, unmoved.

"But . . ." Her lips worked for a smile. "Oh, you'uns is right. I never had something so fine before. It pains me to let it go."

Daniel picked up a rock as big as two fists and set it on the clean white pinafore. Lydia slowly folded the ruffled apron around the rock and grimaced at the mud smears. When it was bound, she raised it with both hands over her head and flung it into the river. The rock dropped out, but the white cotton floated just under the surface, drifting downstream like a ghost. "Lord Jesus, wash it away. Forgive me." Her chest heaved. "I forgive Mr. Stokely. I'm done with him. We all done with him. Send him away from us. Thank you, Lord Jesus."

"Amen."

"We should go to the church for a prayer meeting," Luella offered.

"That's just what we'll do." Lydia led the march back up the slope.

As they reached the step of the church, Mabel shouted. "Look."

In the distance, Chester Stokely, carrying a bag, walked away from Nolia's house. When he saw the group looking his way, he broke into a run and was soon out of sight.

Laughing together, they entered the church. Daniel rang the bell for meeting time. Within a few minutes, more than a dozen people gathered, including Blessing and her kids. They hugged one another and started singing a praise chorus and clapping.

As the song ended, the door opened and Nolia Biss shuffled in, sniffling with slumped shoulders and disheveled hair. She paused before reaching the circle. "I don't deserve to be here." She clutched her shawl. "I done you wrong. I'm sorry." She sobbed and wobbled.

Sister Lydia sustained her as Brother Dickson pulled over a bench. "You did hurt us. But he hurt us more. He was a deceiver, but he's gone now, and we're stronger." Lydia spoke for the group. "We forgive you. Forgive us for gossiping on you."

Nolia leaned into the comforting shoulder and trembled. "Thank you."

"Sister Savannah, you got us a song?" Lydia held Nolia's head.

"And can it be, that I should gain." She burst into the familiar hymn with an upbeat pace. "An interest in my Savior's blood."

"Hallelujah!" Brother Dickson shouted as he marched with his hands raised.

Mabel, bending low at the waist, elbows out, rocked her arms. "Died he for me who caused his pain."

Esther matched Mabel in her own form.

"For me, who him to death pursued," Lydia sang softly near Nolia's ear.

The syncopation of feet stomping and hands clapping lifted the contrite woman to her feet. "Amazing love, how can it be, that thou my God shouldst die for me."

"Glory!" Lydia shook her hands in the air. "Amazing love, how can it be, that thou my God shouldst die for me."

CHAPTER SIXTEEN

TO ALLEN, IT SEEMED HE had only slept for a few minutes when Dex squeezed his arm. He had lain awake most of the night swatting sand fleas, twisting around lumps, and drowning out the ensemble of snores.

"Yeah?" He opened his left eye.

"It's morning." Dex thrust his chin toward the gaping entrance.

"Already?" Allen rolled to face the overcast light. "I just barely fell asleep."

"You'll have to shake off that disappointment. We got to be alert for any chance to get away. Hopefully without too big a fight." Dex counted the men close by.

"I don't see Donovan." Allen squinted into the shadows.

"I reckon he's outside, maybe with those camped up above." The river fox seemed to be calculating all the risks.

Lucius shifted his position and tested his strength against the bindings. He looked at Dex and shook his head. He leaned to his right and prodded his companion. "Delbert, what do you want for breakfast?"

Delbert sat up and rubbed the sleep from his eyes. Just then

Finster knelt to coax the cook fire to life. "Hey, will we be enjoying more burnt venison for breakfast?" Delbert raised his eyebrows, as if it was a pleasant idea.

"Shut up."

"Well, a man gets hungry sitting in a cave."

"Seems you're always hungry." Finster sparked a flint and steel into the tinder.

"I thought we should eat a good meal if we're going to help with the chores. You know, carrying in more firewood." Delbert smirked. "Or taking out the rubbish."

"Shut up, I said." Finster shook a stick at him. "You keep pestering me, I'll cut out your belly. Then you won't be hungry so much."

"That's disgusting. Here I offered to help, friendly like, and you get rude." Delbert shook his head.

Allen covered his grin and looked away to not laugh out loud. He cleared his throat when he saw the familiar silhouette of Bright Donovan advancing, fortunately for Delbert, as Finster appeared ready to give him a boot.

"I trust you rested well." Donovan paused before the fire.

"We was in a good mood until Finster here spoiled it," Delbert reported.

"Why, Mr. Finster, have you been impolite to our guests?" Donovan tipped a gracious hand to the captives.

"He keeps provoking." Finster pouted. "Why don't we kill them and be done with it?"

"I believe they might be useful to us yet." Donovan squared off with his man. "Get some men to bring in firewood and roast what's left of the venison."

"We offered to do just that—bring in firewood," Delbert said. "And I'd be happy to cook your breakfast, sir. I guarantee it won't be burnt."

"Shut up." Finster scowled.

"That's a fine idea," Donovan agreed. "Finster, these men can carry extra firewood. Get your men on it. That will free up the rest for my morning venture."

Finster's scowl turned to his leader, then subsided. "Aye."

Donovan tapped Dex's foot. "You better keep your fella in line. Finster don't tolerate fuss, and he might strike before I can intervene."

"I understand." Dex nodded. "Delbert gets fussy when he's hungry."

Donovan left, and a minute later Finster returned with six men, four with guns and two with axes. "On your feet." His folded his arms and positioned himself so that his pistol pointed at Delbert.

They filed out of the cave to the right and made their way up a steep trail to the top of the bluff. Two large canvas tents were pitched in a clearing, with two more tents in the trees beyond. Their line of travel veered left and followed a deer trail deep into the woods. Allen noted the sparsity of wood on the ground, and a few downed trees were trimmed clean of usable branches. They were heading out to where the firewood hadn't already been scavenged. These pirates had been living here long enough to clean out the forest. After five more minutes of steady walking, Allen added up the firearms. They had four guns, five counting Finster's pistol. Were they being led to be executed?

When they finally stopped, Dex sidled up to Allen and whispered, "Ain't no point trying to overtake them out here. But be ready."

"You don't think they'll just shoot us here?"

"No. Donovan would want to make a show of it, something amusing."

"Amusing?"

"You seen how crazy he is."

"Quit your talking," Finster shouted over his shoulder. He had been giving orders to his men. The riflemen spread out, and the axmen began chopping arm-sized branches off a fallen oak tree. "You two." Finster pointed at Allen and Dex. "Pick up firewood."

"What about us?" Delbert asked.

"Just stand there and keep your mouth shut."

"Let me chop wood. He obviously doesn't know how," Delbert offered. "Even with my hands tied, I can do better."

The woodcutter raised the axe. "I'll chop off your leg if you don't shut up."

Delbert smiled out of the side of his mouth. His eyes caught Dex's look of caution, and he leaned his shoulder on a tree.

A half hour later, when there were armloads of sticks and branches for the keelboat men, Finster told his men to finish up.

"It's about time," Delbert mumbled, but only clear enough for the axman to hear as he raised his arms for another blow.

The ruffian turned his head midchop. The ax-head angled slightly, glanced off the branch, and hit his shin. He cried out, fell to the ground holding his leg, and cussed the world.

"You danged fool!" Finster bent and poked the bleeding wound. "It ain't broke." He glared at Delbert, even though he likely hadn't heard the comment. "Grover, give me your gun and help him get back to the cave. The rest of you move out."

When Allen calculated they were halfway, he was sweating profusely, and his muscles ached. It was hot and humid, and biting flies buzzed around his eyes and ears. When he stepped over a log, he glanced back to see his friends also sweating.

"May we stop for a minute of rest?" Dex called out. "These flies are pestering us something fierce. And my arms are about to give out."

Finster swatted at the flies around his face. "Three minutes."

Allen dropped his load and wiped his forehead with his sleeve. He scratched at the bites for a moment of relief and opened two shirt buttons.

Finster walked forward and spoke quietly to the lead guard. As he circled back, he shouted, "Pick up your loads."

Allen bent to scoop up the wood, and Finster stopped. "What's that?"

Rising and cradling the load against his chest, Allen looked at the pirate, puzzled. Finster reached inside Allen's collar and pulled out the leather cord that held the large gold nugget that Blue Otter had given him months ago. The pirate tugged the cord.

"Please, just take it over my head."

Finster tugged again, but it only yanked on Allen's neck. Finster finally lifted it over and admired his prize. "What else you hiding?" He pulled out the other lacing, to which hung the medicine pouch that Moon Cloud had given Allen. Finster squeezed the small leather bag. "Humph."

"We going or ain't we?" the brigand at the rear hollered.

Finster gleamed at the bumpy thumbnail-sized nugget with a natural hole through which the leather thong was looped. "Yep, let's go." He dropped it down the front of his gray shirt and chuckled as the line moved ahead.

At the cave, after they dumped the firewood in the pile and returned to their seats, Dex leaned in to Allen. "What was that he took from you? It looked like gold."

"It was. A good-size piece that my Arapaho friend gave me. I don't care about it for the money value—it's what it means coming from my friend." Allen frowned.

"Money is all it means to that lout," Dex reasoned. "Why'd the Indian fellow give it to you?"

"Blue Otter." Allen patted his chest, where the nugget had rested. "When I moved up to their camp, he was my translator. He taught me how to live with them and not make a fool of myself. I learned a lot from him. He found it years ago in a stream. A French trapper tried to take it from him, and Blue Otter had to kill him or be killed. That made him a man in the eyes of his people. It's a symbol of courage and respect, not money. When I was moving away from the camp, he gave it to me as a sign of friendship and esteem." Allen watched the fire as if it were the screen of his memory.

"We'll get it back. Don't worry on it none," Dex promised. "Somehow, we'll get it back for you. It don't belong to that scoundrel."

"Thanks." Allen tried to smile.

One of the pirates squatted by the fire and dipped a gourd full of stew from a hanging pot. He tried a bite of meat but quickly spit it back into the vessel and inhaled rapidly. Setting his stew aside, he eventually rose and passed out chunks of cold leftover meat and bread to the hostages.

"This bread is moldy," Delbert griped.

The pirate took his gourd and walked away.

Allen and the crew ate what they could of the meat and tossed the remains at the fire. He startled at the sound of a woman's scream. Dex stood up to look, but a guard appeared with his musket raised. "Down."

Dex sat with a worried expression on his face. Allen whispered a prayer as the squeals continued.

Then Donovan strutted in and pointed for the guard to dish him up some stew. "Well, I must say my morning venture was productive. How about yours?" He glowered over his captives. "Oh wait. I see a large pile of firewood that wasn't here before. You've been productive as well."

157

"What are they doing to the woman?" Dex asked.

"The Lord's ways are mysterious, aren't they. He gives to some and takes from others." The pirate boss chortled. "We came across a flatboat with a family on their way to Saint Louis. But they decided to set up residency here for a while. A man with a wife and daughter. Two other men were with them, but they decided to keep heading downriver. Facedown." He guffawed and ate a spoonful of stew.

Just then a man's voice commanded, "Stop. Leave her alone." A burst of laughter followed. "Stop. We gave you everything we . . ." His shout was cut off by a thud.

"Sit him down and make him watch," a growling voice said.

The sounds of screaming and crying continued.

"Hurry it up. I want a turn with the young one."

Allen choked down the sourness in his throat. "In God's name, stop this evil." He glared at Donovan.

"They're men with needs, enjoying the spoils of the river." He slurped off the spoon. "Like I said, the Lord giveth, and we take whatever we want."

A file of thugs came carrying armloads of goods from the family's flatboat. The one named Gunter organized the scavenging. Food and supply items, like tools and household utensils, were set aside. He showed a chair to Donovan, who nodded his approval, and it was set among his portion of the take.

Allen couldn't watch. He kept his head down on his forearms, which were resting on his knees. "Lord, you have to intervene. You must help this poor family."

Boom! A gunshot. The woman screamed, and the daughter cried out for her daddy.

"Put them together and tie their feet. We'll let them have a rest until tonight."

Allen recognized Finster's voice. The bitter taste flowed in his mouth again. He looked at Dex. "Can't we do anything?"

Dex narrowed his eyes at his bindings. "I don't know what yet, but we'll get a chance for justice. Just keep praying on it, I guess. See if God will help us out."

"This is so disturbing. I don't know what to pray." Allen shook his head.

"I remember a couple of brothers named Joshua and Caleb. Said they were named after heroes in the Bible." Dex spoke barely above a whisper. "Maybe that's what you can pray about. Getting us a couple of heroes."

"True." Allen stretched his legs out. "We need a couple of heroes like Joshua and Caleb. When other soldiers were afraid of overwhelming odds, they'd kept the faith that God would intervene, and that's just what happened." He chuckled.

"What makes you laugh?"

"God always surprises me by inspiring my faith from sources I did not expect." Allen narrowed his eyes. "We will get through this. But I am afraid for those women."

"We'll have to take them if we can. Hopefully, they will be able to run, but that don't seem likely." Dex seemed to be pondering a plan.

"You think you can escape?" Donovan appeared before them. "If you were to cut those ropes and get past the men in here, you wouldn't have no place to go. As you've seen, there are guards all around, and one gunshot would signal the men above to circle around. No place to go but dead, and I'm just fine sending you there."

"I admit you got the upper hand. But the life of a pirate ain't a long and happy one." Dex folded his hands and rested them on his bent knees. "Even if you kill us, someone will put an end to your treachery."

"Maybe so. But not today." Donovan stood, arms akimbo. "Today I'm king of the river."

"Well, Your Highness, can we help carry in the goods from the flatboat?" Delbert offered.

Allen's brow furrowed as he glanced at Delbert. He was getting to know this shrewd crewman but was still caught off guard by his apparent nonchalant nature.

"Very well. Gunter, these men will help unload that boat. They can carry the load up to the tents." Donovan gestured with an upward swing of his arm, then strolled to his new chair and sat.

"Yes, Boss." Gunter pointed at four men to grab rifles.

Allen fell in line behind Gunter and one rifleman. The others followed them to the sandstone ledge and the view of Kentucky across the river. Allen kept glancing to his left until he finally saw the two beaten women huddled together against a tree that grew out of the sandstone ledge. The teenage girl leaned on her mother's chest, and their faces were bruised and their dresses torn. The girl cringed as more men looked at her. The mother seemed to be unconscious. Allen glanced over his shoulder at Dex, who imperceptibly nodded his awareness.

"Keep moving," Gunter called.

They turned right and walked down the beach to where goods were stacked and the family's flatboat was tied to a rock. One wooden crate was open, revealing kitchenware and barrels of salt pork. Sacks of flour and sugar waited beside the crate.

"It would help if you cut off these ropes." Delbert lifted his lashings. "Lucius can carry two sacks of flour at a time if his hands are free."

Gunter smirked. "I ain't cutting no ropes. Figure it out."

"He's right." Dex pointed at the crate. "Bound up like this, it will take all four of us to carry that box, and the trail is too narrow. Two men could handle it if their hands were free."

"And what about the barrels?" Allen added. "Too heavy to move up there."

Delbert and Lucius moved together and started lifting the crate, letting it sway, as if out of control. When they finally steadied it, they took a few steps, Lucius walking backward. They were fine for a few paces, but then the crate tipped and fell, spilling out some frying pans.

"You have guns on us." Dex held out his bindings.

Gunter huffed, pulled out a knife, and sliced through the ropes on each man. "Mind yourselves."

The two restored the crate and lifted it with hands positioned at the corners and made their way smoothly up the trail and over to the first tent. Setting it down, they casually assessed the area. Dex and Allen dropped sacks of flour beside the wooden box.

"Take one of those sacks to that other tent." Gunter pointed to a tent back in the trees.

Allen hoisted the sack and moved it, but just before he set it down, a tapping sound caught his attention. He looked down and saw an acorn rolling. He took another step, and an acorn hit his chest. He glanced up and searched the brush and tree trunks. A face appeared and disappeared. Then it leaned out for a moment. *Kinlock.* He ducked away. Allen dropped the sack and returned before he drew notice. The crew filed to the beach for another load, and back for a third. All that remained was the three-hundred-pound barrel of pork.

"Wouldn't it be wiser to put the meat into smaller containers to take up?" Dex looked at Gunter, who watched Donovan come forward.

"Yes, that would be easier, but not as amusing as watching the four of you work." The boss folded his arms. "Besides, if you're tuckered out, you'll sleep better."

"That's thoughtful of you." Dex half smiled. "May we use poles from the flatboat to make a litter?"

Donovan pushed out his lower lip. "Clever idea." He turned to his associate. "See, Gunter, that's what I like—clear thinking and solving problems. Go ahead, Dexter Yates."

Lucius and Delbert grabbed two poles and a rope, with which they lashed the barrel in place. The four heaved the load and shuffled their way up the steep incline. Just as quickly they untied the burden and headed back for the beach.

"Mind if we wash up?" Dex sniffed his armpits.

"By all means." The pirate chieftain smiled, then pointed at Gunter to get the rifles spread around.

The hostages stripped to their drawers and waded into the water, causing muddy swirls to rise. They dipped and rubbed themselves down with sand. They came out one by one to air-dry for a moment before dressing, being retied, and returning to the cave.

Allen waited for when the pirates were distracted and the closest guard was looking away. "I saw Kinlock." He leaned over to whisper in Dex's ear. "When I took the sack of flour to the other tent, he was back in the trees."

"You sure?"

"He hit me with an acorn. I saw him clearly for an instant, then he ducked away." Allen stopped as the guard looked back at them.

Dex inclined his head. After a few minutes, he whispered to Lucius and then back to Allen. "Be ready."

Looking around at the position of the men, potential weapons, and placement of cover, Allen formed a strategy of options. There was only one way out, and with so many men milling around, it would require a fight and maybe killing. He had been in tight spots before and knew that if forced to, he would fight and defend his life and the lives of his comrades. And he would fight to rescue the women.

It grew dark, and the fires were lit. The pirates seemed to be especially rambunctious, picking fights with each other, playing poker, laughing, cussing, and shouting. Allen surmised that the women and the loot had invigorated their proclivity for indulging the lusts of the flesh. The cavern became a raucous tavern.

Donovan strolled in behind Finster, who fired off a small pistol to get attention. "Who's responsible for all this carousing?"

"Donovan." The pirates cheered.

"Who keeps you full of whiskey and women?"

"Donovan."

The celebrity put a smile on the brigand's face, and two men carried a chair over for him. Donovan perched on his throne and aimed a finger in the direction of his captives. "Feed them some hardtack and meat." He slapped his knee and laughed, then raised a fist in the air. "And open another keg."

"Hooray!"

Allen observed Delbert and Lucius tucking hardtack in their shirts and snatching more from the burlap bag. Allen and Dex took a handful each and a slab of pork from the platter. Hunger had loomed for hours, and the keelboat crew satiated their longing as quickly as they could.

Some of the pirates seemed drunk, and now more whiskey was poured around. They'd lost interest in the captives, except for the one guard who seemed bent on getting revenge on Delbert for bumping him off the boat. He waved off the drinks until another convinced him that the bound men weren't going anywhere and he should join the party. He threw back two shots and laughed at the actions around him.

One pirate sat down next to Donovan and played lively tunes on a concertina. Six or seven tried to sing but made up their own words. Several went out for a chance at the women.

It was so loud in the cave that Allen couldn't hear any cries of desperation. "I'm worried for the women." He nudged Dex.

"We'll save them if we can, but they been hurt bad by now. It's a sad truth, partner, but we might have to leave them." Dex bumped Allen's knee with his fist.

He frowned at the grim reality and rested his forehead on

his knees. Trying to block out the noise, he prayed, "Lord, please keep the women alive and give us an escape route."

Dex elbowed Allen. "There's more men in here than I saw before. I count twenty-two. Can't be too many outside. Even with them being drunk, the odds don't favor us. I'm hoping Kin comes up with a good plan soon."

Scanning the position of men and weapons again, Allen sighed and resumed his prayer. "Father, as you rescued me out of Dark Wolf's cave and as you saved Two Rivers's camp from the death cloud, so you can rescue us now from this army of pirates." Allen paused, listening to his own words. "Of course you will rescue us. You've sent me to find Deacon Abraham and take him home safely. I will clear my name before the denomination, see my parents, and return to Moon Cloud." He took a deep breath. "Yes, Lord, I know you will rescue us from this snare of the Enemy. But how?"

A few minutes later, sensing movement and a brightness that prompted him to look up, Allen saw Gunter adding wood to the fire and picking through the food.

"Hey, Gunter, could you pass us some hardtack?" Dex asked, as if he were included in the party.

Gunter looked over, dull faced from wine and whiskey, and bobbed his head. "Sure, why not." He brought the burlap sack over.

"Thanks." Dex took a couple of biscuits and let Lucius take the sack. "Gunter, you've been decent with us. We can see you're a leader."

The pirate crouched and scratched his head. "What do you mean?"

"When tasks need to be done, you get them done, and the men seem to respect you." Dex watched the man's eyes registering the compliment. "I think you're a better leader than Finster."

"Finster." He spat.

"What's your name—your given name?"

"Joe." He knelt on both knees to keep from wobbling.

"Joe, like Joseph?"

"No." The pirate burped. "Like Jehoshaphat."

Allen looked at the man. "That's it."

"What?"

"Jehoshaphat was a king in the Bible." Allen subdued his epiphany. "You're a leader like King Jehoshaphat."

"Jehoshaphat Gunter," Delbert piped in. "It's true—you should be sitting in that chair with men at your feet, not Donovan or Finster."

As the flattery sank in, Gunter peered over his shoulder right when Donovan tipped back a bottle of wine with two men sitting on the ground. He grumbled under his breath.

"Do you share equally in all the loot?" Allen inquired.

"Yeah." He slurred. "Donovan gets the boss's cut, but the rest of us split the remains."

"What about Finster? Does he get more?"

"No, same as me."

"What about the gold nugget he stole from me? How will he share that?" Allen prodded.

"What gold?"

"He took it off my neck. But maybe he's going to give it to Donovan as a favor. Or maybe he'll keep it for himself. Either way, it's his advantage. He's got it tucked in his shirt." Allen flipped his lapel and pointed down his shirt.

Dex held out the bread bag. "You should be the king, Gunter."

He took the bag and staggered away and sat across from Finster, glaring at him.

"Good play, Allen," Dex said. "But what's this about King Jehoshaphat?"

"He was the king of Israel, and three armies were coming for war. They were outnumbered, so he called the nation to fast and pray. Then the enemy armies fought each other until they were all dead. And Israel just watched and then collected all their spoils."

Dex seemed to ponder it for moment. "I like the part about them killing each other, but there ain't much here that I care to take for spoils, except a few guns. And this don't seem like the place for a prayer meeting."

Allen chuckled. "It gives me faith that we'll get out of here. Tonight or tomorrow, I don't know, but we will."

"It will take a miracle for sure." Dex stretched out his legs.

Amidst the carousing, loud bragging, outbursts of accusations, and scuffles and laughter, Allen measured the opposition against their potential for escape. He noted that Lucius continually stretched his wrist bindings. Delbert nibbled at a biscuit.

Allen caught sight of Finster bending over to speak into Donovan's ear. Gunter, apparently stewing in jealousy, marched over to them.

"Hey, Finster. I want to see that gold nugget." Gunter grabbed a fistful of Finster's gray blouse.

Finster slapped the hand away. "What are you talking about?"

Gunter pointed to Allen. "The gold you took off that bloke."

Donovan rose from his chair and put a hand on his belt pistol. "That true, Finster? You have gold you're keeping for yourself?"

"I was waiting to show you . . ." He tipped his head to indicate the crowd. The men nearby were leering their way.

"He's holding out." Gunter tugged at the shirt.

"Let's see it." Donovan beckoned with his hand.

Allen strained to hear over the raucous din but observed that Finster's face grew redder as he reached into his shirt and pulled out the necklace. The leather cord was wrapped through his fingers as he dangled the shiny stone before Donovan's covetous eyes.

The cavern's hollow echo stopped suddenly.

"I told you." Gunter grabbed at it before Donovan could reach the nugget.

Finster slammed his shoulder into Gunter, knocking him back a step. "It's mine."

They both pulled knives, but Finster's flashed forward, piercing deeply into his opponent's belly. With another rapid motion, he slashed across Gunter's face, causing him to cry out and fall to the ground. Finster, apparently satisfied with the damage, turned from his foe to look into the four barrels of Donovan's pepperbox.

In the palpable tension, a shout rolled from the cave entrance. "Where are the women? We want our time with them," one of the four men shouted as they stomped toward the fire.

"And more whiskey," another yelled.

Clusters of men pressed forward toward Donovan. "Show us the gold."

It seemed that time froze, except for a crouching shadow that appeared before him. "Kinlock."

"We gots to hurry." Kin grabbed Allen's arm and slit the cords with a dagger and moved to Dex.

Just as Allen was about to rise, the guard who had been watching them held his pistol at Kin, cocking the hammer with his other hand. Allen kicked him in the knee, and he fell back, firing off the round. The ball burst out of the muzzle, through the smoke, passed between two pirates, and struck Donovan above the right ear.

Chaos broke out as twenty drunken river pirates rushed for the gold.

"Move it." Dex pushed Allen and grabbed the pistol from the downed guard.

Kin cut the last strands of rope and followed Dex, with Lucius right behind him. Delbert paused at the guard, cocked back his arm, and slammed him in the jaw, knocking him unconscious.

Allen stopped as they reached the beach. "Where are the women?"

"This way." Kin motioned ahead. "Keep moving."

The crew ran down the beach trail as muffled gunfire and screaming sounded from the cave. They reached the *Marylou* and leaped aboard as Lucius untied the line and helped Kin shove the keelboat away from the sand. Once on deck, they grabbed poles. As Delbert and Allen rowed, Dex rocked the tiller back and forth.

"Look." Lucius gasped at the sound of thundering hooves and riders holding torches. The mob rode on the shore toward the cave.

"They ain't looking for us," Dex said. "Heave on."

Moments later shouts sounded in the distance, followed by gunfire. Then quiet, except for the splashing of oars and the footsteps of the polers.

"Did you see what happened to the women?" Allen pulled on his oar.

"I'll explain up ahead." Kin pressed into the pole, surging the boat forward.

CHAPTER SEVENTEEN

TRAVELING BY RIVER AT NIGHT took the skill of an experienced pilot to feel the current and recognize signs of potential hazards. Allen appreciated that his friend and partner, Dexter Yates, had that skill, even at his relatively young age. He seemed to know by intuition how to avoid hidden logs and, perhaps more treacherous for their escape vessel, the sandbars.

Allen kept pace with Delbert, but the muscles of his back and arms burned with fatigue. Then he felt a shift in direction as they moved closer to shore.

"Up ahead. The light," Kin said as he reached his poling point.

"I see," Dex said. After a few minutes more of propelling the boat ahead of the current, he steered them in close. "Hold up. Keep quiet."

Allen stowed his oar and stretched out his arms as he looked to see what was coming. They drifted to a dock, where Kin stepped off and tied the bowline while Dex tied the stern.

"Give us a hand," Kin urged the crew.

A stack of small crates, canvas bundles, and food sacks were ready to be loaded. A man held a lantern up, bringing his face into the light.

"Howard," Allen blurted and then covered his mouth.

The wounded friend smiled. His eyes looked sunken, and his left arm rested in a sling.

The men loaded the goods in minutes, and Kin appeared cradling several muskets, which he passed off to Lucius. Beside Kin stood a woman. "Dex, this is Miss Nelly. She and her husband run the Rose Hotel. That's where the women are being cared for."

Allen guessed that Miss Nelly was in her sixties. She wore a flannel housecoat and big unlaced boots. She held a lantern in one hand and a double-barrel shotgun in the crook of her arm.

"You boys take this food, ya hear." Her voice sounded scratchy but determined.

Dex picked up the bundle at her feet. "Thank you, ma'am. We appreciate it more than you know."

"I heard you was in that pirate cave—that's enough to know. Once I seen the condition of them women, we called a patrol of men together to go clean out the cave. They left a couple of hours ago, and I don't expect them back till morning. So, you'uns best be getting along."

"God bless you, ma'am." Allen waved.

"God bless you." She returned the wave.

Within a few minutes, the crew settled into the rhythm of the river. Howard sat with his back against the cabin and seemed happy to be with his buddies again. Dex steered them into deep water. He tied off the tiller and then came forward with a loaf of bread to share. Kin and Lucius put their poles up while Allen and Delbert stroked just enough to keep their line straight.

"Allen, I guess your prayers paid off." Dex perched on the cabin roof. "I can't call it anything but a miracle that we made it out alive."

"Amen." Delbert laughed. "It was the miracle of Jehoshaphat."

"Agreed." Dex chewed a mouthful of bread. "Kin showed up at the perfect moment."

"He was the answer to that prayer." Allen balanced a chunk of bread on his thigh. "But how did Howard get clear down here?"

"Kin showed up for me at the nick of time," Howard began. "Them fellows chucked me overboard, and I was having a hard time keeping my head above water. Kin grabbed on to me and pulled me behind the logjam when they was shooting. I'm sure glad they didn't send a skiff back, 'cause we were sitting ducks.

"When we figured you'uns were far enough away, Kin dragged me off that little island to shore. We scrambled through some brush until he had a chance to patch me up. We rested a mite, then started humping them hills. It were rough going, so Kin shouldered me until we was close to the cave. He tucked me in a pile of leaves and let me sleep."

Dex looked at Kin. "How'd you get a fix on the cave? There's a lot of ground from where you got left."

"I knew there's a big bend in the river, so we cut across the hills. Got close enough to smell the camp." Kin leaned on the corner of the cabin. "I waited till the morning and snuck around to get a good look at their tents. Stole us some food and rested a few hours. Then I climbed down the bluff on the other side of the cave, where there ain't no trail. That's when I seen them women getting tossed about.

"Then I watched you boys carrying the boxes up the hill, so I climbed back up to follow and flicked the acorns at Allen. Them pirates would move about, so I kept hid away. When it came to dark, I put Howard on the flatboat. I choked a fellow to get his guns, and that were enough to persuade him and two others to row down to Elizabethtown. But first I snatched them women and put them on the boat with Howard. Those men agreed to get the women to the Rose. They said they was done with pirating and would be happy to oblige.

"Then I acted like I was a pirate and told them other four to go into the cave for the women and more whiskey. They was just drunk enough to believe me. I snuck on in behind them to cut you loose, but I weren't expecting the brawling the way I seen it. Why would they fight among themselves that away? Then Allen saved me by kicking that guard. You know the rest." He bit his piece of bread.

"Yep." Howard sipped from a canteen, then set it down. "Them boys was too scared to do anything but help. I had a pistol on them, but they could've taken me anytime, being so weak. We docked, and they each carried a woman. One helped me all the way to the hotel. Miss Nelly put the ladies to bed and patched me up.

"Her husband loaded up his guns and got a troop together. They rode off to the cave to hang them pirates. Said 'enough was enough.' She fed those three and told them to repent of their wicked ways. I'm supposing they drifted off on the flatboat. It weren't all that long before you showed up."

"It's mighty fine that we're all together again." Dex hopped down. "You ought to get some sleep, Howard. You look plumb done in. Delbert and Lucius can row for a piece, while Kin and Allen can sleep and take over in a couple of hours. We should hit Paducah by sunup, and we'll get Howard to a doctor."

Allen stayed with Dex, who took the tiller. "Hey, partner, reach into the food sack there. Miss Nelly threw in some apples."

He handed Dex one and took a bite of his own. "A few days ago, I was tired of eating apples, but right now it tastes like a deluxe meal."

"True enough. Nothing but fine dining on the good ship *Marylou*." He bit off a crisp snap. "You know, I seen many a strange thing along the river, but what happened back at Cave in Rock has got me wondering."

"You mean how Kin showed up just as the fight was breaking out?"

"More than that though." He bit the core in half. "We was sailing with the wind at our back the whole way, then right when it dies away, them pirates jumped us. Then everything changed, like we was caught up in a whirlpool.

"We was sitting in that cave for hours with nothing to do, but looking back, it seems like a dash of time. And you was talking about King Jehoshaphat, and just then Kin comes in, and we popped out of the whirlpool."

Allen chewed slowly. "I knew in my heart I had to get out of there to find Abraham. I kept clinging to that purpose."

"Well, now you can pray us up a good wind." Dex chuckled.

Allen laughed and boosted himself onto the roof. "I'm going to stretch out here. And I want to tell you, Dex, that being with you in that cave kept my courage up. I'm not sure what I would have done if I'd been alone."

"You made it out of that Indian cave, which sounded worse to me. I figure God's on your side, so he'll get you out of any cave you find yourself in."

"Truly spoken." Allen leaned on his elbow. "He's on your side too, Dex."

Dex shivered, as if a cool breeze gave him gooseflesh. "Truly spoken."

Six hours later, the crew of the *Marylou* tied up at the wharf in Paducah. Delbert went in search of a doctor. Lucius dug into the food bag and set out a molasses cake, smoked ham wrapped in oilcloth, and a wedge of cheese.

"That Miss Nelly, bless her heart." Lucius sliced up portions with a small knife he found in the bag. "Dig in, boys."

Delbert skipped aboard with a jug. "I found the doctor's house about a half mile out. He was up early to pull a black tooth out of some old codger. Said to come back in an hour and gave me a jug of his wife's fresh apple cider."

"Pass it around. We'll see if it's fresh cider or fresh cider." Dex winked at Allen. He uncorked and hoisted the jug. "Ahh. You're in luck, Preacher. It's just your style."

Howard nibbled at a piece of cheese. His face looked ashen as he propped himself against the cabin. "Help me with a swallow of that, would you?"

"Let's hire a wagon and get you to the doctor," Dex said. "It's too far to walk."

"I can make it." He pressed away from his support.

"I'm sure you'd try, but there ain't no point in pushing our luck. You'll go in a wagon." Dex shoved in the last of his cake. "Kin, you best stay put."

"Aye." He tipped his slice of ham in agreement.

Within minutes Delbert and Lucius parked a borrowed freight wagon beside the boat. They loaded up and clattered over the cobblestone street to the doctor's yellow house. The doctor took one look at Howard and sent him to bed. "He'll be here for more than a week."

Dex huddled the crew outside. "We can use this wagon to un-load the goods Miss Nelly sent along. Trade for what she needed and see what we come out with on the other end." He paused. "I'm thinking one of you might need to stay here with Howard until he's fit."

"He hates being fussed over." Delbert climbed into the wagon seat. "Let's do the trading and then decide."

Paducah was a small enough town they could move about easily. The new construction was away from the river. The wa-terfront street had the stores and businesses to make easy trading and selling. Within an hour they were back at the *Marylou*. Dex came last with a box of food and a jug.

"Well, my friends, this has been a productive morning." Dex set down the box and passed around a napkin bundle. "I stopped at a bakery to get bread, and this pretty Dutch gal gave me a batch of these oat cookies to try."

Lucius nibbled on one and nodded. "She must be drumming up more business."

"Or she's sweet on you, Dex." Kin had most of one in his mouth.

"Now that's tasty," Delbert agreed. "Let's save a couple for Howard."

Dex straightened, and his smile faded. "He needs to rest for at least a week, the doc said. And we need to get these new goods back to Miss Nelly. But Allen's needing to get down the river." He paused while each man acknowledged him. "I talked with the gent selling tickets on that side-wheeler. Since we're short on cash, he said he could get me and Allen on as deckhands. You fellows would have time to make the run to Elizabethtown and get back here to pick up Howard."

"I see that." Delbert cleared his throat. "But if you'uns is downriver, then what?"

"I'm thinking you four can work the run upriver and meet us in Portsmouth in a few weeks." He leaned an elbow on the cabin roof and clasped his hands together. "You ought to make some money on the way."

Lucius stopped chewing. "We was figuring on helping Allen find his friend too."

"I know. That were a good idea until Howard got shot." Dex frowned. "Now we got to take care of him, and the best way is on this boat with friends, not heading off into an uncertain task. He might need more doctoring by the time you get to Cincinnati. And Kin might have challenges downstream. You all know that to be true."

"I'd risk it," Kin threw in. "I been down there before."

"You proved yourself over and over, Kin, for sure. But we're after a free man that's been kidnapped. If we head into that territory, you put a risk on us all."

Kin conceded. "What Dex says rings true. But Allen, say the word, and I'll help find your friend and carry him back on my shoulder."

Allen swallowed. "Thank you, Kin. Thanks all of you. I'm touched by your loyalty and willingness to risk your lives for me. And for my friend that you haven't even met." He swallowed again. "I am blessed to know you, I am. If I only knew Abraham's whereabouts, it might be different. But I'm going in the dark."

"You're going by faith, Allen," Delbert piped in. "You can say it 'cause we all know this is a mission from God. I guess we done our part this far. Now we'll nurse Howard back to Portsmouth and meet you there. You can't plan a journey like this—you go when the signs are given. That steamboat will make up for the time we lost in the cave. That's a sign."

Each crewman agreed, and Lucius raised the jug. "It's settled then. Let's have a drink. Allen, you first." He bit out the cork and handed it over.

Allen received the jug with a sniff and shuddered. "That's not apple cider. Oh well. This is for Howard." He took a swig. His face turned red, but he swallowed and held back the cough.

"Hooray!" Dex shouted, and they all laughed. "What a fine thing it is that we can enjoy living. The river gave us an adventure, and it seems this chapter's come to an end."

"Them pirates didn't take all our goods. There's a box of clothes down below." Kin thumped the cabin with his fist. "But if you want to say goodbye to Howard, you best be moving."

Allen found his bag that contained a clean shirt, trousers, and his buckskin overshirt. He tied them in a bundle and declared himself ready. Dex found a pouch of tobacco and his pipe and was equally prepared for departure.

The crew walked quickly to the doctor's house, only to find Howard deep in a morphine slumber. They returned just as quickly to the wharf to bid each other farewell.

Dex handed Delbert a purse of silver coins. "Hopefully, this will help you get a start on some trade goods. You can offer a consignment load since you'll be back in a few days."

"That package there holds some dresses, fabric, and sweaters for the ladies. Threw in a knit sweater for Miss Nelly too. It reduced our profit a mite, but I figured you'uns wouldn't mind a gift of kindness since those gals didn't fare so well in this escapade."

"We'll make sure they get the gifts." Delbert stretched out his hand. "You go find your friend."

Allen and Dex shook hands all around and departed for the steamboat. Upon reaching the gangplank, they encountered two men, one in a suit and the other in worker's clothes, examining a ledger. The closest man turned to them, while the other continued studying the page. "You the new hands?"

"Yes, sir. I'm Dexter Yates, and this is Allen Hartman." Dex offered his hand, but it was not received.

Allen noticed the man in the suit glance up when his name was mentioned. He then turned and approached another suited man, whispered in his ear, and pointed back in Allen's direction. It seemed odd but significant.

"Can you tie a Tom Fool's knot?" The man folded his arms.

"Yes, sir," Dex said.

Allen nodded.

"Good. We're bringing on a dozen Berkshire hogs. Tie them up so they don't cause no trouble. You'll find rope in the animal stalls." He pointed with his thumb over his shoulder. "Then keep busy in the steam room."

"We're jumping to the task." Dex waved for Allen to follow.

"Dex, I don't know what a Tom Fool's knot is, and I've never tied up a hog before." Allen hurried behind.

"We hobble their back hooves. You'll catch on quick." Dex found the empty stable and opened the gate just when the herder brought in the lead pig.

Allen stared at the string of black hogs with distinct white legs. "They're enormous."

The herder kicked them into place. He was a wiry black man wearing clothes that looked more like rags.

"These your hogs?" Dex leaned back against the pen railing.

"They belong to Master."

"You must know a smart way to tie them." He held up the rope.

The slave took the two-foot-long cord, made two loops, pressed his knee against the closest one, lifted the hind legs, slapped the loop on, wrapped twice through the hooves, and stood up.

"Smart and fast." Dex nodded.

Allen imitated what he had just seen and was quickly knocked backward by the bucking sow. He rose and brushed the seat of his pants. Dex leaned his knee on one but was bumped off balance. He reacted by lunging on the pig's back, but instead of tackling the alarmed beast, he was carried around the pen, banging into the other pigs until he let go.

Allen looked at the herder, who stood watching in the center as his workers held back laughter outside the small corral. "I'll pay you a dollar if you help us bind them."

Three minutes later all the hogs were bound, and the herder took the silver coin and stepped over the rail.

"I guess we know who the real master is." Dex rubbed his shoulder.

"I ain't no master." The hog handler pointed with his lips in Allen's direction.

Allen leaned on the back rail of the pigpen and furrowed his brow. He glanced over his shoulder, dropped his jaw, and flinched away from the rail. There were four rows of six men, each sitting with his back against the knees of the one behind. Their space was smaller than the pigpen. He looked back at the herder, who locked eyes for a long moment, then turned to leave.

Dex came next to Allen and peered into the shadow at the sullen faces. "Dang."

Just then another crewman came near. "Here's the pig food." He handed Allen a sack of leftover bread, fruit, and meat, probably from a restaurant.

"What about food and water for them?" Allen pointed to the slaves.

"Give them some if you want. But this is owner's orders."

"You're saying the swine get better treatment than these people?"

"I don't know. Maybe the pigs is worth more." The man walked away.

Dex looked at Allen. "Look, I know what you're thinking, but we can't cause trouble. Just feed the pigs now, and maybe we can bring something down later for them."

As they walked along the lower deck toward the steam room, Allen paused at the rail. "I can't stand it, Dex. It riles me to the core to see people treated like that. To be held captive at the whim of another man. I . . . I just can't comprehend it."

"What do you mean? Just yesterday we was captives to another man's whim." Dex paused and tapped the railing.

Allen shook his head, as if recalling a nightmare. "But we're free men. We had hope of escaping. If they escape, they're still slaves and have to live under that shadow of fear until somehow they become free. We must have a change in this nation. It just can't go on."

Dex looked up and down the deck. "Listen, I hear what you're saying. But we have to get back to work. If someone hears you talking like that, we could get tossed off this boat. And I mean right into the river. We're heading deep into slave country, and you'll have to keep your feelings tucked away. It's painful, but you ain't gonna help Abraham if you get into trouble."

"You're right." Allen exhaled deeply. "Let's go."

Dex put his hand on Allen's shoulder. "You have a big heart, Preacher Man. But we ain't going to change the world today."

Allen forced a smile. "Maybe not the whole thing." He ducked through the doorway. "Should we try to get them some food?"

"If we wait a couple of hours, there should be more scraps available in the galley. After more passengers eat."

Allen pursed his lips. "What do we do in the steam room anyway?"

"Mostly we move firewood around and chuck it in the boiler furnace."

"That doesn't sound too difficult." Allen rolled up his sleeves.

"In about an hour, you'll understand why I like having my own boat."

An hour later, Allen wiped sweat off his forehead. "I understand."

Dex smiled. "Just remember that you're a free man and this is paying our passage. Them two do this every day just to get food."

Allen glanced at the two Negroes working alongside them. "You mean they're . . ." He caught himself. "I assumed they were working off their passage like us."

Picking up another armload of wood, Dex moved it to the pile closer to the furnace and got the slaves' attention. "We're getting low over here. Do you get more, or do we?"

"We stays."

"All right. We'll keep it coming." Dex turned and waved to Allen to follow him. "Let's get more wood from the hold. Then someone should spell us, and we can get some food."

A deckhand came in with two fresh slaves. The sweaty ones, along with Allen and Dex, were relieved of duty and ate fried catfish and cornbread in the workers' mess.

"Ain't you going to finish your cornbread?" Dex forked the last bite of fish into his mouth.

"I thought I would save it to give to the folks in the hold," Allen whispered.

"You eat that piece. We can get scraps from the cook for them." Dex stepped out from the bench.

Allen followed Dex into the galley, where the cook wiped his hands on a greasy apron.

"Howdy. We're here to get some food scraps for the hogs."

"Them buckets there." He pointed with a wooden spoon.

"Any other bread or meat you looking to get rid of?"

"Here. This bread from last night is going hard. Might take that too." He turned back to the frying fish.

"Thank you kindly."

They carried the buckets and bread along the deck and turned into the hold. "Why did you say it was for the hogs?" Allen set his bucket down.

"Too risky to say it was for them slaves." Dex opened the stall gate. "You got to understand, Allen, that if we get caught, it'll be trouble. And we're on a mission."

Allen frowned.

"It's dangerous business messing with a man's property." Dex lit the candle lamp hanging on a post and tossed some slop to the hogs. "Pass out the bread and then pick out the better chunks of fish as quick as you can."

Breaking portions of the stale loaf, he handed it down to the men closest to him. Each one passed it over his shoulder to the man behind. The shackles jangled as they shared the meal. Thinking there wouldn't be enough for all twenty-four, Allen grimaced as he grabbed the last meaningful-size piece of fish. *Lord, let there be enough, please.* Then Dex tapped him on the shoulder. "Here's another loaf."

"Where did that come from?" Allen took it and passed it along. "I thought I had all the bread."

"Well, it looks like they all get some." Dex shrugged.

"God bless you, sir," said the shackled man closest to Allen. Several others nodded as they chewed quickly.

"Let's go before someone comes around." Dex turned to leave.

"Thank you for helping me feed them. It's not much, but I guess it will have to do for now. Some of them looked like they haven't eaten in a week." Allen leaned on the rail, looking at the water. "Doesn't it pain your heart to see people treated that way?"

"Allen, I've been around the black folk my whole life. In the South, it's just the way it is. Some are slaves and some are free. I guess I don't think of it as a heartache." He scratched his head. "I'm glad I ain't one of them, but I don't see what I can do about it.

"I got friends, like Kinlock, and others. I don't know. I guess it's just the way of the world. I don't see how to make things different. Right or wrong, it's just the way things are."

"A man shouldn't be able to own another man."

"Up North, where the Negroes is free, you can think that way. But down here, they got slaves to do the hard work. It's been that way for generations."

"Don't you think that all men should be free?"

"I'd be happy if all men were free, sure. It don't make much difference to me. I just want to sail the river and make money. I don't know if I'll ever come into riches, but as long as I'm on the river, I'm a happy man. I guess I don't think as big as you do."

"Could you own another man? Could you be a slave owner?"

"That question ain't never been put to me in such a serious consideration." Dex faced Allen and leaned his elbow on the rail. "I reckon not. Seems it would make me as much a slave to keep someone working all the time. No, I guess it's not my way. I hire a crew, pay a fair wage, and they share in the profit. That's the way I like to do business."

"I'm glad to hear that. I agree that's a better way to do business."

"Well, our business now is finding your friend and getting him home. We can take care of the rest of the world's problems after that." Dex's right cheek creased in a smile.

"I can't wait for you to meet Deacon Abraham."

"For now, let's go find a place to sleep until we get called back to the steam room."

Near the bow, Dex shoved around several small bales of cotton to make a space for them to lay down out of the wind. "Here now, this ain't too bad. Soft cotton to stretch out on, and we shouldn't smell them pigs from here." Within minutes, he was purring.

Allen adjusted his position to look at the sky. As the steamboat turned a bend on an east-facing stretch of river, the half-moon slipped out from behind a cloud. "Perfect." He reached into his shirt to take out the medicine pouch. "Moon Cloud." He closed his eyes to picture her smile.

"Ahh. When will I see you again?"

"Hmm? What's that?" Dex rolled to his side.

"Nothing."

"You thinking about your Indian gal?"

"I sure am. I wish I could see her, but at the same time I'm glad she's not here. At least not in these circumstances. You know what I mean?" Allen paused for a response but only heard the easy snoring.

"Lord, I know you're watching over Moon Cloud and Two Rivers and Blue Otter and even Kicking Lion. Show yourself to them, Father, as you did to Elisha and his servant. Be with them as you were with Shadrach, Meshach, and Abednego. Be with them, Lord, so they understand your voice even though I'm not there to read your Word to them. Bless them with safety. And be with Deacon Abraham. Deliver him from evil. Direct my path to find him." Allen stood and moved to the bow. "Please raise up a new Moses for this generation to release your children from slavery, Lord. Break the grip of this pharaoh curse from our land." His right hand grasped the stanchion at the prow. He dropped to his knees, sobbing. "Set them free, Lord, please."

His shoulders slumped, as if a wooden yoke were laid across his shoulders. Bowing low, he gasped. "Oh, Lord. Sister Lydia and the congregation. The slave markets. These here by the pigpen." The breath went out of him. "Lord Jesus, I'm being crushed. Help them."

Sly's captive sat blindfolded in the middle of a pirogue. Paddling in the bow was a man he'd found in a tavern across the river from Baton Rouge. The tavern was a ramshackle shed made of weathered, uneven cypress planks. Gaps in the planks permitted dim lantern light to seep out, but whatever was spoken, whatever deals were made, remained inside. The fur trappers and alligator hunters drank whiskey with outlaws who sought safe passage through the Atchafalaya Swamp to run west. Sly didn't need a guide. He just wanted another paddler for time's sake. A couple more hours and this prisoner will be La Marque's problem.

They made their way through the channels formed by flooding and the merging of rivers in the lowlands, occasionally portaging over patches of ground.

"Sir, I would be most happy to help if you have another paddle." Abraham lifted his bound hands.

"Quiet."

"Is the blindfold necessary, sir? Even if I could remember the way, I'm mostly thinking that Mr. La Marque will want to keep me close by." He spoke over his shoulder.

"What did you say?" Sly missed a couple of strokes. "Who? How?" He swallowed. "What makes you think he's got something to do with this?"

"You just now did, sir."

Sly grabbed Abraham's collar and yanked him back and pressed the flat side of his knife against his throat. "I ain't never spoke his name. Tell me now who you heard it from."

"Your reaction says what I know'd for a few days now." Abraham shifted his weight.

"Who told you?" The knife pressed down.

"The Lord Jesus told me the other night when I was praying. I seen a man dressed in black, and the Lord says he was La Marque."

"You never saw him. It could have been anyone wearing black." Sly pulled the blindfold off to look for truth in his captive's eyes. "Wait. The only person you seen was me. What are you talking about?"

"Sir, the truth is that I was praying whilst I was sitting in the dark room. I felt like I was being watched, so I looks over my shoulder and seen a man wearing black. How I seen that in a dark room is a mystery. I knew then it was a revelation from the Lord Jesus, and he said it was La Marque."

"Don't tell me about no vision from Jesus." Sly shoved him forward.

Abraham adjusted his shirt. "You know about visions. You seen things that ain't there to touch, but they seems real enough."

"Shut up!" Sly dug his paddle into the water. "Put that blindfold on."

Abraham adjusted the blindfold and turned his face back to prove it was in place. "You seen dark visions. A voice that tells you to do evil."

"Shut up, I said."

"You hear La Marque's voice. You carry out his evil work. Like a slave shackled to his master."

Sly grabbed Abraham's collar again and yanked him back, pulling off the blindfold. Who did this preacher think he was? "I ain't got no shackles on me. My hands are free, see?"

"Your hands is free." Abraham nodded. "But your heart is wrapped in chains."

The shadow man swallowed. "No. I do as I please." He released his grip.

Pulling himself upright, Abraham slipped the blindfold in place. "Call out to Jesus. He'll forgive you and set your heart free."

"Be quiet." Sly hit him on the back with the paddle handle. He pulled several strokes. "I'm beyond saving. There ain't no hope for me."

"The love of God is deeper than your sin. Only he can save you, and he will."

Using his paddle as a rudder, Sly maneuvered the pirogue around a stump. "There ain't no point preaching at me. You can't even save yourself. This swamp is the gateway to hell."

CHAPTER EIGHTEEN

THE STERNWHEELER LANDED ALONG THE sandy shore in Memphis. Allen stayed close to Dex as they helped position gangplanks and ramps for unloading cargo.

"Listen." Dex tapped Allen's shoulder. "You stay here and shove these barrels around to look busy. Whatever you do, don't take anything down the ramp, or they'll keep you working all day long."

"What are you going to do?" Allen pinched at a splinter in hand.

"I'm going to see if I can grab some food, and we'll slip away before that foreman tries to keep us working." Dex picked up a rope and coiled it over his shoulder as he walked away.

Allen shifted barrels toward the ramp until he heard chains rattling. The men he had fed filed past with their hands shackled. Each wore an iron collar with a chain that bound them together. He watched their downcast faces stare blankly at the space before them. Only one made eye contact, which seemed to be a sign of gratitude for a momentary kindness in his dreary existence.

As the last slave shuffled down the ramp, Allen turned back to his task and was startled to see the man in the suit coming toward him.

"You're Allen Hartman, correct?"

"Yes, I am."

"I understand you're looking for a particular slave."

"No, I'm looking for a friend, a free man." Allen's brow furrowed. "How would you know that?"

"That doesn't matter." He leaned in. "You should find Hiram Dupont. He can help you."

Just then Dex arrived, chewing a piece of bread. The man left abruptly and walked down the ramp.

"Who was that?" Dex offered Allen a bite.

"I don't know. He didn't say." He tore off a chunk. "He told me to look for Hiram Dupont. Said he could help me find Deacon Abraham."

"How in the world does he know about that?"

"No idea. Have you heard of Hiram Dupont?"

"No. But I know where we can find out. Let's go."

A half hour later they walked out of the merchandise broker's office. The cobblestone street was loud with horses and wagons and a rush of people generating the life of the city. Allen stood on his toes to see as far as he could over the crowd.

"I'm thinking you ought to try Dupont's office before you go to his home." Dex pointed north. "I want to ask around some more. I'm getting a peculiar feeling in my gut about this."

"Is that your way of saying you got a hankering for some fried catfish?" Allen grinned.

"Now that you mention it, catfish do sound mighty fine right now. But the problem is we're very low on cash, and we'll need more to buy back Deacon Abraham or to get further on down the river."

"Or to buy a catfish dinner."

"You bet."

"Are you going to borrow money from someone you know?"

"No. I'm fixing to get lucky at the card table."

"Gambling? You're going to risk what little we have gambling?"

"Maybe you should pray for me to win."

"Pray for gambling winnings? That wouldn't be right. I can't do . . ."

"Relax. I'm teasing on you." Dex's eyes twinkled. "I know how to make my own luck. Besides, it's a good place to get information."

"You had me going there." Allen grinned. "Where should we meet up then?"

"Chances are I'll need most of the night to collect the money we need. But if I learn something sooner, I'll write a message on the wall right here. You do the same. That all right?" Dex tapped the wall.

"Sounds fine. Does the place you're going have a name?"

"The River Inn. But it ain't the pleasant side of town." Dex folded his arms. "Sorry. There's not enough money for you to get a hotel."

Allen pursed his lips. "How far is the nearest cave, you suppose?"

Dex burst out laughing. "That's the spirit. You'll be fine for the night."

"You won't have to worry."

"You might have to ask again, but you'll find Dupont's office on Madison Street. I hope he can help. But I got a bad feeling. Can't put a fix on it, but be careful." Dex disappeared into the bustling stream.

Allen stepped off the boardwalk onto the cobblestone street. "Well, Lord, please open the door of revelation to know your truth, and direct me to find my friend."

After several blocks he reached the part of the city with tall brick buildings, banks, and a courthouse, and the people were more finely dressed.

Allen approached a man coming out of an office building. "Excuse me, sir. Could you direct me to the office of a Mr. Hiram Dupont?"

After apparently assessing Allen's appearance, the man pointed up the street. "His office is in the next block. But at this hour, you're more likely to find him at the French restaurant."

"Thank you." Allen strolled up the street until he found the restaurant.

He paused to make a plan, when he overheard the doorman. "It's a pleasure to see you again, Mr. and Mrs. Dupont. Come again soon." The couple walked arm in arm toward him. The man wore striped slacks and a black coat with long tails. The wife wore a dark-green dress buttoned to her neck. The narrow sleeves became puffy gathers at the shoulders. Her broad-brimmed hat was adorned with flowers and feathers.

"Pardon me, sir, ma'am. I'm looking for Mr. Hiram Dupont, and I overheard the doorman mention your name."

"Yes, I am Hiram Dupont. And who are you?" His top hat made him look tall.

"My name is Allen Hartman. I'm searching for a friend, and I was told that you might be able to help me." Allen noticed that the wife clutched her husband's arm.

"How could I possibly know your friend?"

"He is a free Negro who has been kidnapped by a slave catcher and brought downriver."

"And who told you I would know something about slave catchers? That is not my business, nor is kidnapping." He scowled.

"I apologize. I'm not saying you're involved, but I was told you may be able to direct me to people who may be in the slave market who may have heard of Abraham." Allen saw what he thought was compassion in the eyes of the woman.

"The slave agents I know only deal in legal business."

"Darling." The woman smiled at Allen. "You could ask some of your acquaintances on Mr. Hartman's behalf. It's a long shot, but he has come so far. Perhaps you could mention the situation to Marlette, for a start."

He winked at his wife. "Of course, dear. That is a good suggestion. I'll head over there straightaway. Allen, this is my wife, Vivian. She will accompany you to our home until I get the information you desire."

"Thank you. Thank you very much." Allen shook Dupont's hand. "I appreciate you going out of your way on my behalf. Especially being a stranger."

"Oh, nonsense." Mrs. Dupont took Allen's arm. "We are happy to help if there has been an injustice. I'll have the doorman signal for a carriage. Our home is not far away, and I'll make sure you're comfortable until my husband returns."

As they climbed into the carriage, she insisted that Allen sit beside her rather than across. She held his left arm gently with both hands.

"Mrs. Dupont, I don't want the appearance of any impropriety if people are to see us."

"You are a gentleman. I appreciate your concern, Allen. May I call you Allen?"

He nodded.

"There are always rumors and gossip about me and my husband. It's the price you pay for being successful in a small city. I've learned to ignore the comments. And please, call me Vivian. I want us to be friends, even though our time together may be short." She patted his arm.

"Now tell me where you're from and how you got involved in this quest."

Allen took a deep breath. "I'm from a town near Buffalo,

New York, but for the past year I have been living out west, in Indian country."

"Indian country." She leaned back to look in his eyes. "My goodness. How thrilling that must be. And dangerous, I suppose."

"I live with a clan of the Arapaho. They have received me and treat me as one of their own. I have grown accustomed to their ways, but yes, there has been some danger. But by the grace of God, I remain intact."

"Yes, of course, by the grace of God." She sat taller to keep the brim of her hat from touching Allen's face. "I apologize for my hat. Now tell me about your friend."

"Deacon Abraham." His eyes fixed on his memories. "He is a remarkable man. He was a slave but purchased his own freedom. Now he is the pastor of a small Methodist church in Portsmouth, Ohio. That's where I met him in a brief visit. I assisted him in comforting some members of his congregation."

"Why stop in Portsmouth in the first place?"

"It was on the way. I am also a Methodist pastor, and I was traveling with a group of missionaries to the Oregon Territory to establish a mission."

"I see. How noble of you." She patted his arm again. "We are members of the Congregational church. My good friend is the wife of the Methodist parson. He's a lovely man. But why on earth are you here in Memphis? How did you know your friend was kidnapped?"

"I received a letter from my denominational leaders calling me back to Baltimore. Along the way, I stopped in Portsmouth to greet my friends, when I learned he had been taken. So I began my pursuit to bring him back."

"Oh my. Again, such a noble undertaking. But are you sure it's worth risking your life for a Negro? You don't know what dangers you will face down in the swamp."

Negro? Before Allen could answer, the carriage rolled to a stop.

"Ma'am." The driver held the door open.

They stepped out before an opulent brick house surrounded by a manicured garden and a wrought iron fence. Tall columns welcomed guests into a formal and orderly household. Vivian opened the front door and was promptly greeted by two women dressed in matching pinafore aprons. One was portly and mature, and the other young and slender.

"Constance, Jenny, this is Mr. Hartman. He will be our guest. Please see to it that he gets food, and draw him a hot-water bath. He can use the Blue Room to rest.

"Allen, please excuse me from joining you, but we did just come from the restaurant. They will get you whatever you would like. You can freshen up in the room, and I'll see that you get some clean clothes."

"Thank you, but you don't need to go to any trouble for me."

"What kind of hostess would I be if I didn't provide for my gallant knight on his noble quest? Certainly the good Lord brought you here to be cared for. Please don't deny me my blessing by refusing our hospitality." Her lips pouted.

"Of course. I am grateful."

"Very good. Jenny, lead Mr. Hartman to the kitchen."

The portly woman nodded and walked from the entryway past a long, finely crafted dining table and through a swinging door into a kitchen with long counters and two stoves.

"Have a seat there." She pointed at the oak table. "What would you like?"

"I suppose some bread and cheese would be fine."

"You look like you need more than that. I can fix you a beefsteak and potatoes, bacon, and corn."

"Bacon? Yes, bacon and potatoes would be exceptional."

"I'll fry some green tomatoes with it. How would that be?"

"Thank you."

Her hands were busy cutting and slicing. "If you don't mind me saying, sir, you don't sound like you're from around here. You don't dress like most of the businessmen that come to visit."

"I am from New York. I'm not a businessman." Allen studied her face. "I'm actually on a special kind of business, which is how I came to meet Mr. and Mrs. Dupont."

"What kind of special business brings you into my kitchen?"

He roll-tapped his fingers on the table. "A friend of mine was kidnapped by a slave catcher and taken down the river. He's a free man, but he was taken nonetheless. My business is to find him and take him back home to Ohio."

Jenny stopped stirring and looked out the window.

"I was told that Mr. Dupont may know some slave traders, and perhaps one will have a record of my friend."

She served him bread and cheese on a pewter plate. Allen could hear the bacon sizzling. Constance passed through the kitchen with a waste bin and out the back door. She came back through, as if in a hurry.

When Jenny brought another plate with bacon, fried potatoes, and tomatoes slices, she was silent.

"Thank you. It looks and smells delicious."

She pumped water into the basin. "When I was a young'un, my father and brothers run away from the farm we was at. They was looking to go north and make a home, and then they would send for us. But the slave catchers caught my daddy and killed him." Tears rolled down her cheeks. "He was hung in the tree so's we all could see." She sobbed.

"I'm sorry. I didn't mean to upset you."

She shook her head. "My brothers sent us a letter from Detroit, saying they would come back for us as soon as they could. Shortly after that me and mama was sold to the Duponts, and

I been here ever since. Living in a big house with nice clothes and good food." Her head dropped and shoulders sagged. "Never heard from my brothers again. But that letter said they crossed the Ohio River and was given help by a church in Portsmouth."

"That's where my friend is from. Did they mention a name?"

"I don't recall a name." She wiped her eyes with a dish towel. "Is you thinking it might be your friend that helped them?"

"It's hard to say, but if they went through Portsmouth, it seems possible. His name is Deacon Abraham. Have you heard any news of him?"

"No, sir. I can't say I did. The Duponts talk about business but not about slaves." She rose and began washing utensils. "I fear your friend has been taken down the river. They'd take him deep."

"Do you mean the cotton fields?"

"No, sir. My fear is that they took him to the swamp. If that be the case, you won't find him. He'd be as good as dead. Sorry to say it, but you got to know the peril he's facing. Slave owners will punish a man who helps the runaways. The swamps is worse than death."

"I have to hope for the best and pray that I find him before he's taken into a swamp. That's why I'm here. I hope Mr. Dupont may find some good news."

Jenny looked out the window again. "Don't put your hope in Mr. Dupont."

Allen bit a piece of bacon off his fork but paused to glance at her. More words of caution about Hiram Dupont. *Lord, make your way clear.*

"You . . . you will be wrong to trust him." She wiped her hands and walked out the back door.

Allen ate a few more bites, then put his plate in the basin. Looking out the window, he could see Jenny leaning on a garden bench, weeping. He returned to the entryway and found Constance coming down the stairs.

"Your bath is ready, sir. This way." She climbed the long stairway.

The room was painted blue, and the four-poster bed had an inviting blue comforter. She showed him the copper tub in an adjacent bathroom. He touched the hot water.

Constance offered him a towel. "Mrs. Dupont said you should put on these clothes, and we will wash yours. Would you like for me to assist you?"

"No. That won't be necessary." He looked at her eyes, as if they would reveal the motivation of her offer.

She looked away. "Leave your dirty clothes outside the door."

"Thank you."

After the door closed, Allen appraised the room, which was designed for comfort. A small wood-burning stove warmed the space and heated water. Several oil lamps and scented candles brightened the room in place of the fading daylight coming through the leaded-glass window.

"Lord, I've never seen such opulence. How can I enjoy this luxury while my friend may be captive in a swamp?" He recalled his last bath, dipping in the Ohio River outside a pirate cave. "I guess I could use a good scrubbing, along with the clothes."

After dressing in the borrowed black slacks and white shirt, Allen looked in the mirror of the vanity table. "Thank you, Lord. I hadn't realized how refreshed I would feel. And look at that bath water—it's as muddy as the Mississippi."

He returned downstairs in search of Mrs. Dupont and found her in a sitting room, reading. "Pardon me, ma'am. I don't want to interrupt, if you'd prefer to be alone."

"Allen, I've already told you to call me Vivian. I am a hostess who will not ignore her guest. Please come and sit with me." She placed her book on the small table beside her.

"Thank you." He sat on a small cushioned couch across from

her. "I do appreciate the hospitality. And the bath was pleasant and much more necessary than I realized. You're very gracious to have allowed me into your home."

"Never mind that. You're welcome here. I'm pleased to see the clothes fit you. You look handsome."

He shifted in his seat. "Any word from your husband?"

"As a matter of fact, he sent a messenger saying he is following a lead to someone who on occasion works with slave catchers. He would also be aware of, let's say, the darker deals. Hiram may have to enter the more disreputable area of town."

"I am sorry to bring risk upon him."

"Don't you worry. He can take care of himself. However, he may well be a couple more hours. We really won't need to wait up for him." She sat forward with her hands on her lap. "Would you care for a cup of tea, or perhaps a glass of wine or brandy?"

"No, thank you. I believe I'll go to my room."

"Very well. I will turn in as well." She stood. "It's been delightful to get acquainted. Rest well."

"Good night, Vivian."

Allen climbed the stairs and found his clothes clean and folded on the bed. He quickly removed the borrowed clothes and fitted himself in his undergarment and wool trousers. He slid on his shirt but left it unbuttoned. He tucked the buckskin jacket into his bag and stretched out on the bed, hands behind his head. "Lord, thank you for this home and hospitality. It's admirable, but to be honest, I miss my teepee. Keep your watchful eye on Moon Cloud so that she knows your peace instead of worry. And Lord, be with Dexter, wherever he may be. And I can't believe I'm making this request of you, but help him win the money we need at poker. Lord, I suppose I should ask that it be provided in a more respectable way, but you keep surprising me. Father, how shall I pray for Deacon Abraham? Will Mr. Dupont have helpful information? Why did Jenny seem so concerned? How can I find Deacon Abraham if he gets to the swamp?"

Allen sat up. "How did Vivian know that he was going to the swamp?" Just then he heard a voice in the hall. He opened the door to see Constance descending the stairs.

"I apologize if we disturbed you, Allen." Vivian's voice drew his attention toward her bedroom. She wrapped her robe quickly to cover her chemise.

"I don't want to disturb you, but I did have a question."

"Pardon me, but I'm not hearing you clearly. Please come this way." She motioned with her hand, as if wafting him forward.

When he reached her door, she stepped back to draw him in. Allen stopped at the threshold. She reached for his hand and pulled him in far enough to close the door.

"I shouldn't be alone in your room." He reached back for the knob.

"We don't need the help overhearing us. Now what did you want to ask?" She looked at the length of his body and fixed on his eyes.

"Earlier, just before we got out of the carriage, you asked if it was worth the risk for a Negro and that I would face danger in the swamp. How did you know that Abraham is being taken to the swamp?"

"Oh. I don't recall saying that." She shifted her weight. "Perhaps I was just making the assumption, as many runaways are taken down to the plantations in the delta swamps. I certainly wasn't implying that I know the whereabouts of your friend. I'm surprised that you would hold me in suspicion, Allen."

He swallowed. "I'm sorry. I suppose this journey is wearing on my emotions. Of course you wouldn't know anything."

"You poor man, doing such a valiant undertaking for a friend. Naturally, it would be a burden to your soul." She moved closer.

"You must be under a great deal of pressure. No doubt you'll feel better after a good night's sleep." She reached for his arm. "I hope you find him. I really do. My heart goes out to you, Allen. Let me give you a hug of reassurance."

He put his hands on her arms to ease her away, but she squeezed him tighter. The thumping sounds of footsteps coming up the stairs alerted Allen. He pushed her shoulders away from him.

"Vivian?" A shout from the hall.

She fell back, dropping to the floor with a scream. "Hiram, help!"

The door burst open, and Dupont pointed a pistol at Allen. Other men barged in, clutching his arms.

"What is this?" Allen struggled.

"You came just in time, Hiram. He tried to take advantage of me." She sat on the bed, holding her head.

"How dare you. We welcomed you into our home, and you repay kindness with this disgusting act of evil." Dupont thrust the gun close to Allen's face. "I could take justice in my own hands this very moment, and no one would blame me."

"It's not true, any of this. I did not take advantage of your wife—"

Dupont slapped him across the cheek. "Enough. I don't care to hear what you have to say. I can see for myself that you are not dressed and in my wife's bedroom. Don't be a fool. Take him out."

The men dragged Allen backward down the stairs and outside. Dupont followed but stopped at the front door. "You know what to do. Go over to that oak tree and finish it. Jergens, you'll find a rope in the garden shed around back. Be quick." He went back inside and closed the door.

Allen gasped for air. A tall man pinned him against the trunk with a forearm at his throat. "You stinking abolitionist, you're going to hang." The other man, shorter, held back Allen's left arm.

199

"What's taking Jergens so long?"

"There he is."

Allen twisted, trying to break free. The short man punched him hard in the ribs.

"I ain't got time to tie a hangman's noose."

"Just throw a loop around his neck."

Jergens tossed the rope over a branch and tightened the loop over Allen's head and set up a crate. Three times Allen kicked over the crate.

"Hoist him up, then he'll stand on it."

Allen clawed at the noose as they raised him off the ground. A man hugged his legs together so his feet stood on the crate.

"There. Tie it off quick."

Jergens wrapped the rope around the trunk and secured it with a knot. Allen choked and wheezed while balancing on his toes. He blinked back the fading vision as blood was cut off.

The clatter of horse's hooves and wagon wheels resounded on the cobblestone. "Hey!"

"Who is it?"

Allen coughed. "Help."

"Kick the box, and let's get out of here."

Just as Jergens turned to kick, there was a loud thunk, and Allen fell to the ground. From behind the tree, Jenny came out holding an axe up high.

The horse and wagon skidded to a stop, almost hitting the two men, who scrambled away. Dex leaped from the seat and hit Jergens in the jaw before he could pull his pistol. Jenny swung the axe down on Jergens, who stopped the blow with his arm. He ran.

Dex reached Allen and pulled the loop over his head but then quickly leaned back with his hands raised. Jenny held the axe up and glared at him.

"I'm helping," Dex shouted.

"Jenny. He's my friend." Allen rose before her. "This is Dexter. He's here to help."

"Yes, ma'am. I'm here to help." He stood behind Allen.

She huffed and lowered the weapon. "What you fixing to do now?"

"Let's get out of here." Dex climbed onto the wagon.

"Here, Allen. I brought your clothes." She grabbed two satchels from behind the tree.

"Thank you, Jenny. But that one's not mine."

"No, it belongs to me." She lifted the bag. "I can't stay here no more."

"What will you do?"

"I'll go see my brothers in Detroit."

"Allen, we got to scramble." Dex held the reins.

"Come with us now." Allen took her bag and tossed it into the wagon. He offered his hand to help her up, but she hoisted her portly form up onto the bench seat.

Dex slapped the reins. "Get on up. Get up." The wagon bucked forward, racing toward the next corner, where they leaned almost to tipping over. Their dash ended on a small street two blocks from the waterfront.

"Are you leading us back to the tavern?" Allen gave Jenny a hand down.

"No. It ain't safe there." Dex tied the reins and jumped down. "A heap of money is being offered to find you. I heard those men talking that tried to string you up. I followed them and stole, er, borrowed the wagon, and came a running."

"Money? For me? How would anyone in Memphis know I was here?" Allen scowled.

"Beats the sense out of me." Dex picked up the pace. "Now they're looking for both of us. And her, I reckon."

"After what I done, I know for sure the Duponts out to get me." Jenny panted.

"Do you think Mr. Dupont will give you a beating?" Allen read her eyes.

"I knows for a fact that Miss Vivian will do the beating. Then she'll hang me from that same tree. Teach the others to behave like a good slave ought." She shuddered. "The only thing to keep me alive is run away the best I can."

CHAPTER NINETEEN

DEX LED ALLEN AND JENNY into a storage shed. "Any idea how you're going to run?"

"No, nary a one." She remained by the door.

Feeling his way around, Allen found a candle lantern and matches on a post. He sparked a match to light it and have a look around the shed. "Jenny, come sit on this stack of lumber." He and Dex made a quick search for anything useful but found nothing among the stray lumber and old harnesses.

"We need to get on the river and be gone. Once word gets out, there will be people hunting for us. This ain't much of a hiding place," Dex said. "Jenny, do you have money?"

"Yes. I have fifteen dollars that I been saving."

"That won't get you far. Here, take this. It's eighty dollars in paper money and silver coins." Dex counted out the money into her hands. "This should get you to Cincinnati, maybe Portsmouth. We'll find someone to hide you on the steamboat. And you must stay hidden. People will be looking for you."

"I don't know what to say." She gripped the money to her chest. "I trust the good Lord to get me though. He sent you two angels to get me out of prison, just like Saint Peter. Bless you. Bless you both."

"Dex, let's go to the wharf. I have a feeling we'll find her the right boat if we go now." Allen extinguished the tiny flame.

Pausing at the corner of a building on the waterfront, they could make out the line of steamboats and barges waiting for daylight. A short distance beyond, some men were moving in the light of two lanterns.

"They must be loading firewood," Dex whispered. "Wait here while I take a closer look."

Allen and Jenny watched Dex slink in the deep shadows until he disappeared. The minutes dragged on, like waiting for tea water to boil.

"Listen, if you do make it to Portsmouth, when you get off the boat, ask for the ferry to take you across the Scioto River. Then follow the road to the west and ask for Sister Lydia. Everyone knows her. Tell her that Allen sent you, and she'll take care of you. They'll see you on your way to Detroit."

"Sister Lydia in Portsmouth." Jenny clutched his arm. "Thank you. You are an angel sent by God. When you told me about Deacon Abraham, my heart broke open. I knew I had to leave. I was living in a lie by serving those people. Living in the big house like it was my own. Miss Vivian always reminding me I was a slave. She read us the Bible stories after she come back from church on Sundays, but the rest of the week she would beat us if she had a mind. Sometimes she would have men come to visit. Then she would beat us so we wouldn't ever speak of it. She's as wicked as a Jezebel woman."

Dex trotted up to them. "Come along. I think your 'feeling' has produced a way for us."

The lanterns were gone except for one on the small stern-wheeler. They stepped aboard and found the captain beside a stack of cotton bales.

"This your valuable cargo?" He made a quick study of the trio.

"Yes, sir. And here's the fifty dollars I promised." Dex held out a wad of paper bills. "We good?"

"Keep the money. I ain't hauling passengers, only crew and freight. If she can cook, she'll be one of the crew." The captain turned to Jenny. "I pay twenty-five cents a day."

"Yes, sir. I can cook just fine. Thank you, sir." Jenny smiled.

"We're leaving right away. You best be off." The captain moved to untie the stern line.

"Jenny, God be with you." Allen touched her shoulder.

She embraced him tightly. "And God be with you." Turning to Dex, she hugged him. "You're a special kind of angel. Thank you."

Allen and Dex hopped onto the dock as the paddlewheel began churning the water. The next vessel in the line was a barge with a long, flat roof. Dex hopped on top to see from a higher point of view. Allen joined him.

Dex pointed down the length of the waterfront street. "That looks like trouble."

A mob of a dozen men carrying lanterns and torches were making their way up the wharf. A light or two would break off into a side street or beside a building before returning to the mob.

"You think they're looking for us?" Allen squeezed the shoulder strap of his satchel.

"More than likely." Dex stepped to the far side of the barge. "Listen. Do you hear snoring?"

Cat-walking forward, they searched for the source of the sound. "Look." Dex pointed to a twenty-foot skiff with a mast tied to the barge. "That's our chariot of fire."

"You going to steal it?"

"No, never. We'll just borrow it. Keep an eye on that fellow while I take a look." Dex swung down into the skiff. "It has everything we need," he whispered. "Let's go. Grab the bowline."

Allen lowered himself onto the smaller boat and released the line. When he tried pulling it free, he discovered the other end was tied to the sleeping man's ankle. The guard stirred and cleared his throat.

"Dexter." Allen shrugged.

Dex nimbly came forward. "I'll get it." He boosted himself onto the barge deck and untied the rope.

"Hey. What's this?" The man grabbed for Dex's arm but wasn't quick enough.

"Is this your skiff?"

"No. Smith's paying me to guard it. Who are you?" He burped.

"I just want to borrow it. I'll have it back soon."

"No. Can't do that."

"Here, I'll pay you five dollars just for the time I use it."

"What?" He rubbed his face.

"Give the money to Smith. It will be fine. And this is for your trouble." Dex pulled a silver flask from his pocket and let the man take a drink.

"That's fine whiskey." He took another gulp.

"It's a deal then? You keep the flask, and I'll use the boat for a short time." Dex shook his limp hand.

"No. Smith said to watch it."

"Give me the whiskey back then." Dex held out his hand.

The drunk looked at the silver flask. "I guess you can take it as long as you come back in the morning."

"Good choice." Dex unwrapped the line from the man's leg. He was snoring again as they pushed off from the barge.

"Grab an oar, and let's get away from them lights." Dex settled on the seat next to Allen. They pulled swiftly and felt the current aiding their escape just as the torches reached the area of the barge. "That were close enough, I guess."

206

Several minutes later, when they were enveloped by the darkness of night on the river, they stopped rowing.

"It feels like the wind is in our favor. I'll set the sail." Dex rose and unlashed the bindings.

Allen twisted on his seat. "Where did you get so much money? You gave Jenny eighty dollars and offered the captain another fifty. And you gave the guard five."

"I told you I make my own luck at gambling." He moved astern to set the rudder. "I was aiming for two hundred but got interrupted when I heard those men talking about you. That Hiram Dupont was offering money for your capture. I left the game early with only a hundred and fifty-five dollars and the silver whiskey flask."

"That means we have seventy dollars now, when yesterday we had nothing? That's astounding." Allen stroked the rope burn on his neck. "Wait. You gambled honestly, didn't you?"

"Sure. Fair and square." Dex tapped his knuckles on the seat. "Look, the men in those places are dead serious about poker. I mean dead serious. They catch you cheating, they'd shoot you right then and there and then go back to playing. And no one would bat an eye."

"And that's the kind of people you spend your time with?"

"Them's the people I grew up with," Dex said. "I feel comfortable in that crowd. It's folks like the Duponts that makes me nervous. Wearing fine clothes, living in a big house, going to church, and then they smile while they hang you from a tree." He pushed the tiller to keep wind in the sails. "Not that all churchgoing folks is bad. I met one or two that seems all right."

"I trust you're smiling. It's too dark to see." Allen tucked the oar away.

"I'm smiling." Dex sat quiet for a moment. "Why don't you sleep a spell. I got some pondering that'll keep me awake."

"I can try, I guess." Allen slid off the board seat. "A couple of hours ago, I had a rope around my neck. That's not the most pleasant thought to fall asleep on."

"Sorry I ain't got a pillow for you," Dex mused. "I sure miss the *Marylou* about now. And I'm missing my pipe."

After a few minutes, Allen fidgeted and adjusted his position. "We should have stolen a softer boat."

"How long before we strike Natchez?" Allen assessed the keel-boat they were passing.

"I reckon on three days, maybe more at this pace." Dex steered away from a log. "What we need is for one of them small side-wheelers to come by so we can hitch on. That will improve our state considerable."

"You mean to go aboard or to tie on and get towed?"

"Hitching a tow rope is risky." Dex stood and managed the tiller between his knees. "You got to pitch a line at just the right time and not get tossed by the churning. But that ain't the real risky part. You got to hope there ain't some cranky old coot with a shotgun to chase off the freeloaders." He scanned the river up-stream. "If we could get on board, well, that would be peaches and cream."

"Is that risky too?"

"At this part of the river, they ain't going to slow down to take on passengers. They might slow for a sandbar or a logjam, but that requires a piece of luck. If so, we'll try to come alongside and jump aboard. We got some money, so they might let us stay. But we need to hope—no, you need to be praying—that they ain't heard about us from Memphis." Dex thought for a minute. "Let's you and me row for a bit. If we find a sandbar or a tight bend, we might take a shot."

The skiff was wide enough for two to sit side by side and long enough for six oarsmen to row. Dex braced the tiller and took his place. When two hours had passed, they paused to rest their backs.

"We ought to be seeing other boats soon." Dex rose to study the stream. He stepped forward onto the gunwales at the bow, folded up the sail, and wrapped his arm around the mast. As the skiff drifted around a bend, he noted the flow turned west and in the distance a touch to the north.

"Look, a cabin." He pointed on the right bank. "Let's hit that sandbar and see if breakfast is ready."

Allen stood and squinted. "Do you believe someone is there?"

"Let's drop in and say howdy." Dex held his oar ready. "If nobody's home, maybe we can find us a fishing pole or something useful."

They pitched the boat into the sandbar and approached the shack. "Hello in the cabin," Dex hollered. He glanced down the sides of the one-room structure. The boards were uneven and dried, and the flat roof angled to the back. He knocked on the door, and hearing nothing, opened it. The faint smell of decayed fish greeted them. Mice had nested in the corner of a table built into the wall. On the left side was a cot.

"Fisherman's cabin. Guess they ain't been here for spell." Dex moved so Allen could see inside. "I'll look around back."

Allen closed and latched the door. Walking out onto the sandbar, he evaluated the river.

"Nothing out back." Dex let his bare toes touch the water and sink into the sand.

"If a steamboat comes along, they'd have to slow down on the bend and miss this sandbar." Allen motioned with his extended hand.

"I see your point. It does go shallow, but they may swing wide," Dex calculated. "See down there at the big sandbar? I bet the river splits and makes an island. They'll stay in the main course, but we can wait out there and be closer. Might get us a chance. Let's try."

Jumping back into the skiff, they rowed until they were adjacent to the island. "Now we drift until our ride comes along." Dex tucked his oar and coiled the bowline. "I hope you're having one of those feelings you get."

"I feel like one of those pirates back at Cave in Rock." Allen massaged his lower back.

"Hut, hut, hut." Dex chuckled. "Looks like the river is giving us another adventure. Here she comes."

Allen saw a large white steamboat coming around the bend the skiff had been at an hour before. He took a deep breath.

"We'll start rowing to get on her line and catch on to the side. Row hard, jump quick, and hope they're friendly." Dex measured the speed and distance. "She's a sternwheeler, and she's slowing down. Let's get in front of her."

Even running at a slow speed, the steamboat loomed large and powerful. "Hard and steady. Try to match her pace." Dex guided the skiff to a favorable line. "It's going to jostle us a bit. We'll catch her about midway back."

Allen breathed hard and pulled his oar to match Dex. His muscles screamed for relief. The boat towered above them like a monster with smokestack horns. The thundering splash of the wheel crushed what had been silent minutes before. The wake of the bow bucked them sideways.

"Heave. Hard." Dex bent his oar three fast strokes, then jumped to throw the rope around a stanchion. The first one missed. He coiled quickly and tossed again. The big loop scored. He braced his feet against the gunwale as the slack tightened. "Jump."

Allen dropped his oar, reached for the low deck rail, and sprung aboard. He pulled himself onto the deck. But his jump

caused the skiff to dip, and Dex lost his footing. He held the
rope in one hand and the rail with the other. His lower legs were
dragging in the water, and the skiff bounced back to slam him
against the big boat. Allen grabbed his forearm and pulled. Dex
dropped his grip on the rope and raised his right foot to block the
side of the skiff. He pushed, leveraged himself up, got his right
arm against the rail, and with Allen's help, lunged onto the deck.

He caught his breath and looked at Allen, smiling. But Allen's
eyes looked past him.

"Don't move," a voice commanded.

Dex turned to stare into the eyes of a double-barrel shotgun.
The man holding the gun looked anxious to use it. The man behind him slapped a wooden club against his palm.

"Erskine!" Dex grinned.

"Dex, is that you?" The man with the club tapped the gunman on the arm, who lowered the muzzle and stepped aside. "I
swear, Dex. I'm surprised to see you." He shook his head. "But
then again, I ain't."

"I'm mighty glad to see you." Dex hugged him and slapped
his back. "This is my friend, Allen. Allen, this is my second cousin, Erskine."

They shook hands. The shotgun man walked away.

"You aiming to keep that boat?" Erskine pointed with his
chin.

"No. We borrowed it. I'll turn her loose so she can make her
way back to Memphis." Dex lifted the loop and dropped it overboard. "Is Uncle Randall on the wheel?"

"Course." Waving his hand, Erskine led them along the deck.
"It's certain he'll want to talk to you. We'll go to my bunk and
wait."

They climbed two flights of stairs to reach the crew's quarters.
Erskine left them in his small room with wooden bunk beds and

climbed the ladder to the pilothouse on the roof. A few minutes later, an older man appeared with bushy gray muttonchops and sharp blue eyes. His navy-blue coat was lined with two rows of brass buttons, and his flat-crowned hat with a short, curved brim showed signs of wear.

"Uncle Randall." Dex embraced the husky frame. "I'm happy to see you."

"When's the last time you ate, Dexter? You look like a broomstick."

"A couple of days ago, I guess. Uncle Randall, this is my good friend Allen Hartman."

"How do you do?" He shook hands. "I've heard your name. Didn't expect to run into you though."

Dex's brow furrowed. "You heard of him? Back in Memphis?"

"Yes. They say you attacked a woman, and they're putting up a reward for your capture. Three hundred dollars." He folded his arms and leaned on the wall. "They say you took their slave woman, maybe killed her."

"What?" Allen gasped.

"Any truth in that?" He looked into Dex's eyes.

"No truth at all." Dex returned the steady gaze.

"No sir, absolutely no truth to that." Allen squared his shoulders. "They tried to kill me, but Jenny, the slave woman, intervened. We helped her get on a steamboat heading north. I would never hurt her. Why would they lie like that?"

"I told you I don't trust them rich folk." Dex shook his head. "They mentioned his name—did they mention me as well?"

"Yep. Your name was thrown in there." Uncle Randall nodded. "You're worth two hundred dollars."

Dex beamed. "What you fixing to do from here?"

"I'll send for some food, and you both are going to tell me the whole story."

Allen exhaled. "Are you going to turn us in for the reward?"

Dex patted him on the shoulder and sat on the lower bunk.

"Dexter's kin. Ain't no amount of money cuts that tie. Nor is there a problem so big that we won't help one another." He nodded at Allen. "You're my friend now. We'll help as we can."

With that, he abruptly went out the door and returned several minutes later with food and water. The captain sat on the one chair in the room and lit his pipe. "Now tell me from the start."

For more than an hour, they explained the search for Deacon Abraham from Portsmouth to Memphis.

Uncle Randall listened as he puffed smoke. "That Dupont fellow and his wife seemed to know you was coming. It sounds like a big conniving scheme to keep you away from the swamps. There's some malicious intent that makes me think someone is fearful of you coming. Else they wouldn't go to so much trouble."

"That's what I been thinking." Dex lay on the bed, with one knee up and the other leg crossing it. He puffed on a borrowed pipe. "Word will be down to Natchez by the time we get there."

"Whoever told Dupont likely has others looking for you clear down to Baton Rouge." Randall uncrossed his legs and leaned his elbows on his knees. "Maybe that secret society, since they're putting up so much money."

"What secret society?" Allen, seated on the bed next to Dex, extended his legs and folded his arms.

"The fraternal order of the Freemasons." The captain sat upright. "Most are good folks, but some use their connections for underhanded business. They wear a ring with a symbol on it. I was invited to join a few years ago, but declined. I wasn't interested, and besides, I'm away most of the time."

"Dupont had a ring like that. I noticed because I saw a similar one back in Louisville." Allen rubbed his finger. "Perhaps La Marque is behind the scheme."

"Could be." Randall tapped the pipe ashes into a tin box. "I reckon we shall bypass Vicksburg and make the run straight to Natchez."

"I'm sorry to interfere with your business."

"Have no worries, young man. You are my business now." Uncle Randall patted Allen's knee.

Dex smiled slyly. "Besides, we have a secret society of our own, you might say."

"That's true. There might be some at Under the Hill that could be tempted by the money, but they'd be set straight in short order." The elder man stood and rubbed his backside. "Ask your ma about seeing a woman named Judith. You might get some helpful information."

Dex leaned forward on his elbow. "Judith? You mean Judith the witch lady?"

Uncle Randall opened the door. "Ask your ma." He stepped out and closed the door, but it reopened right away. "And stay here on this level or up in the pilothouse. It ain't wise to go below." He shut the door.

Allen turned to his partner. "Is there something I should know about Judith the witch?"

"Other than she's a crazy old bird, not much. If I recollect, she came from Ireland and brought her magic powers with her." Dex yawned. "She walks in the forest and sings to the trees and birds. She comes back and says they talked to her. Ma says she's very wise and has a gift from God. Maybe you can figure it out."

"It sounds like a form of divination. I might be interested to talk about her beliefs, but we need to keep on Abraham's trail as soon as possible." Allen stopped when he heard Dex snoring.

Going out to the railing, Allen filled his lungs in the wind made by the fast-moving vessel. The shoreline streamed by in a rush compared to the drifting skiff. The sky had more clouds than blue, and sunbeams occasionally shone on patches of trees.

As they came around a bend, another steamboat made its way upriver. Both blasted a signal horn and rang bells. When they passed, Allen could see passengers on the decks. Two men wearing black stood out to him. At that moment, one of them pointed in his direction, causing him to gulp and shudder. He watched them sail by, and the men seemed to move to keep watching him.

"How could they know it was me?" He spoke aloud to make the grip of intimidation subside. "Calm down. They could have been pointing at anything. It wasn't La Marque. They were just two fellows heading north." He took another deep breath and exhaled slowly. *But Uncle Randall said they could already know about the reward as far as Natchez.*

"Oh Lord, you are my fortress and my refuge."

"What's that you say?" Erskine came up the stairs and stood beside Allen.

"Just saying a short prayer. My nerves are on edge knowing that there's a reward out for me."

"You should be safe while we're moving." The lanky cousin sipped from a flask and offered it to Allen, who shook his head. "Will come by Vicksburg about this time tomorrow. Not much between here and there. A bloke would have to be fair desperate to board a moving smoker."

"We did. I guess we were fair desperate."

"You was with Dex. That's more like normal activity for him." Erskine chuckled and swigged.

"What about your friend with the shotgun?"

"Birk? He's not really a friend, just a good deckhand. He seems to enjoy keeping the freeloaders at bay. But he knows the way of things when it comes to kinfolk. We've known him for some years."

"He won't be tempted by the money?"

"Might be. That's a year's wages. But I doubt it." He squeezed Allen's shoulder. "We'll be to Natchez by late tomorrow night. You're good until then. But that's when you'll need to make a longer prayer."

CHAPTER TWENTY

"BROTHER DICKSON, WOULD YOU BRING the blessing for us." Sister Lydia got everyone's attention.

Following a brief prayer of thanksgiving, a chorus of amens and hallelujahs echoed in the church building. Two rows of plank tables had been arranged and more benches made to allow for sixty people, and others could sit along the walls for an evening meal.

"Let's commence to eating." Brother Dickson raised his hands toward heaven. "And then we'll get to praying. Amen."

"Amen." Many agreed.

"You'uns help yourself to them vittles whilst they hot." Lydia pushed a bowl of mashed potatoes aside. "And this here is Sister Nolia's sweet corn succotash. May the Lord cause it to multiply."

Lydia stepped back to take in all the activity. She found joy in the chatting, and laughter filled the air along with the aroma of fried ham, catfish, collard greens, okra, and corn bread. Wooden bowls and platters were passed until they were empty.

"Lord Jesus, I give you all the thanks and praise," she said with one hand raised. Since the encounter with Chester Stokely, the prayer group had begun meeting every evening, and the habit soon became a shared meal. The gathering included most of the community and a few people from outlying farms.

Children left the table, and adults continued in conversation. Sister Savannah crossed the room to join three other women who were standing quietly in a corner. They began singing a praise chorus, which cued others to move the tables against the walls. The men, women, and children left whatever had their attention and came closer. Rhythmic clapping and alternate stomping of feet invigorated the repeating phrase "Jesus broke those chains—I can raise my hands." Clapping turned to movement and dancing.

When the songs faded, Brother Dickson shared a word of encouragement. "Brothers and sisters, while we was praising, the Lord spoke to my heart. I heard him say he is most pleased with our offering of song. He saying that our prayers is being heard. We be making petitions like sons and daughters of the inheritance. We ain't beggars. We ain't slaves no more. We live in the inheritance. Pray like sons and daughters who own the land."

"Thank you, Jesus."

"Glory to God."

He was about to lead the intercession when the door burst open and two big white men came in. Every person looked their way. Children hid behind their mothers. Men stepped forward.

Brother Dickson came forward. "How can we help you?"

"We's looking for a man called Deacon Abraham." The stout man looked over the crowd. "You him?"

"No, sir." Brother Dickson rubbed his hands together. "He's not here now."

The man's lower lip pushed up. He shifted his weight. "My grandson is sick. Doctor can't do nothing." His eyes watered, and he waved his hand. Two other young men came in supporting a boy by the arms over their shoulders. "I heard that Deacon Abraham prays to heal folk. We're all out of hope. Came here for a prayer."

"Friends, bring the boy." Brother Dickson indicated with open arms. "We can pray for him."

They cleared a space and set two benches side by side for him to lie down. Lydia stood near the boy's head. "Is he in pain or a broke bone?"

"Mostly weakness. Fever comes and goes. Don't eat nothing," the grandfather offered. "Been that way for a few weeks now."

She folded her arms and pressed a finger to her lips. "Guess we'll get to praying and ask the Lord for direction." She began, and the room filled with her loud prayers. "Lord God Almighty, this is why you sent your Son, Jesus, so's we can pray in his name. We praying now, Lord, for the power of his stripes to bring a healing on this boy."

The grandfather and other men watched with eyes wide. The young men who had carried in the boy stared with their mouths open.

When Lydia paused, Brother Dickson picked up the prayer. After several minutes, as quickly as it started, the intercession faded to a close. The brother looked at Lydia. "I seen a spirit of infirmity. Like a dark shadow clinging to him."

"Anyone else?" Lydia glanced at the faces around her.

Mabel stepped forward. "It seems like an old vine wrapped around him coming from deep roots."

Lydia looked at the grandfather, who held his hat in both hands, squeezing the brim. "This kind of sickness run in the family?"

The grandfather snapped back like he'd been struck. "Humph. I ain't thought of that in years, but my mother suffered that way. I was a young'un, and she suffered a long time, and then it took her. Now that you mention it, seems like the same kind of thing." He choked back a gasp and then sobbed. His companions stared at him.

"Brother, you seen the spirit, so you do the praying. Then Mabel." Lydia swept her hands above the boy and murmured her petition.

Brother Dickson paced at the side of the boy, whose eyes followed his movement. He made chopping gestures in the air. He commanded the spirit of infirmity to the feet of Jesus.

Lydia knelt by the boy, waving her arms out, as if pushing layers of coverings off him. The boy breathed deeply and quivered.

Mabel raised both hands in surrender. "Mister, when your mama passed, was you the same age as him?"

"Yes, more or less."

"When your mama passed, did you curse God for taking her away?"

The man's chest heaved, and he fell to his knees. "Aagh. I did. I cursed God. The preacher said the Lord gives and he takes away." He leaned on the boy's legs, weeping. "I was angry that he took Ma when I needed her. I cursed God. Oh, what have I done?" He pulled a hanky and blew his nose. "What do I do now?"

Lydia touched his arm. "You got to ask forgiveness and break your hard heart."

"Oh, oh, it hurts. My heart hurts. I been angry my whole life. Why did God take her?" He clenched his fists.

Brother Dickson touched his shoulder. "You done wrapped yourself in a chain of bitterness, hating God. You done made yourself a slave to anger."

He nodded his head up and down. "I want my ma back." His back rose and fell. His head dropped between his arms. "Aagh. God, I hated you. I hated you for taking Ma from me. Aagh." He sobbed again. "God for . . . for . . . forgive me. Jesus, help me. I'm so, so sorry. Forgive me." Falling to the floor, his body trembled and heaved in deep breaths.

The young men with him stood stunned, watching their patriarch crying and broken on the floor.

Sister Lydia put her hand on the sick boy's forehead. "Leave him. Leave him now, you spirit of infirmity. The blood of Jesus heals him, and it be washing clean the sickness of the generations. And the curse is broken in Jesus's name."

Mabel raised her arms high above her head. "The curse is broken in Jesus's name."

"Amen," the group shouted in unison.

The boy quivered and coughed. His body quivered again. He took a deep breath and sat up. He looked at Lydia, shook his head, and then searched for his grandfather. Seeing the man lying on the floor, he rose and stepped over the benches and knelt. "Grandpa? Grandpa?" He patted the strong shoulder.

The man lifted his head and blinked. "What . . . You . . ." He grabbed his grandson and held him tightly. "You're healed. You're healed." He squeezed the boy again. "Thank God, you're healed."

"We give God the glory." Brother Dickson raised his arms. "Glory."

Shouts of praise and hallelujah resonated. Many shed tears of joy.

Sister Lydia raised her hand to still them. "You boys have seen a miracle of God to heal this child. You seen this man break open his heart before the Lord of mercy."

They nodded.

"Do you'uns want to kneel down and repent like your grandfather?"

"I do," the oldest one said.

"Me too," the second said. "What do I do?"

Lydia looked at the third and raised an eyebrow.

He nodded and knelt beside his grandfather. The other two joined him. Brother Dickson told them how to pray in repentance and invite the Savior into their hearts.

When they finished and stood together, the grandfather wrapped his arms around all of them, with the healed boy in the middle of the cluster. They laughed together.

The grandfather turned to face the congregation. "Thank you. I was desperate, and you helped me. You helped my boy. I'm grateful." He paused and swallowed hard. "I ain't always been good to you people. In fact, I been downright mean at times. Maybe not to you in specific, but to your kind. I let that hatred grow in my heart for no good reason." He sighed. "I want to ask your forgiveness as well. I didn't think I could ever be a neighbor to you people, but now I want you to be friends, if you'll let me. I truly hope you can find it in your heart to forgive me and my family."

Brother Dickson came before him. "We all been hurt by the white folk. Each one of us got reason to hate back for the hate you give us." He displayed the shackle scars on his wrists. "But Jesus set us free from the chains of slavery from our hands. And glory be to God, Jesus broke the chains of hate from our hearts. He paid our debt like he paid for yours." He glanced around. "I forgive you. We all do. We'll be friends with you."

The man caught his breath, and his shoulders sagged as tears rolled down his whiskered cheeks. "Thank you. Thank you. Thank you, all." He extended his hand but then pulled Brother Dickson into a hug.

Gasps and tears of reconciliation flowed in the church. Louella put her arm around Mabel, and Esther came to lean into them.

"Is you'uns hungry? We got plenty of food here," Lydia offered.

"Thank you kindly, ma'am. I need to take this boy home to his ma. She's going to want to see that her prayers was answered." The grandfather waved and led his family out.

Sister Savannah began rhythmic clapping. "Yes, Lord." She bent at the waist and moved with the beat. "Jesus broke those chains—I can raise my hands."

Lydia joined with her own expression of praise, as did the

others. Brother Dickson shouted a hallelujah.

Lydia paused her dance to catch her breath. She wiped sweat from her temples with her apron. "Lord, Lord. You done gave us a gift tonight. We give you this gift of praise. Thank you, Jesus." She smiled at the dancers. "I see the bright light of your glory upon us. Send this light to Deacon Abraham, Lord. Surround him with your light. Surround Brother Allen with your light."

Two girls reached Moon Cloud at the top of the rise. Several yards behind, the third pressed her hands on her knees to leverage her chubby body up the slope. Upon reaching them, she breathed heavily. Moon Cloud always enjoyed teaching children, especially the preteen girls, who needed so much guidance. After the devastation of the village by small pox, so many were affected and wondering about the vulnerability of life.

"Why do you come out so far?" the first one asked. "There are roots to gather closer to the village."

"The mothers should be the ones to gather close to their lodges." Moon Cloud pulled a digging tool, made from a deer shoulder blade, from her satchel. "What do you see here?"

"Cockleburs," the chubby girl ventured.

"Let's look closer." Moon Cloud held the stem of the silver puff ball. "Bear Cub, this is burdock. It is different than a cocklebur. The root has healing power for stomach problems, and it can be used to give smooth skin. It is called the bear plant, like you, because the bear eats the root for healing. And it is fuzzy like the bear cub."

The girls giggled. "What about that one?" Hopping Bird touched a yellow flower. "Does it have medicine?"

"This is called mule's ear. You can eat the seeds. The leaves make a poultice to reduce swelling to injuries," Moon Cloud explained.

"The pointed leaf looks like a long ear." Bear Cub held it to her ear and then by Hopping Bird's ear.

The third girl, Dares to Run with Boys, plucked the yellow flower and gave it to Moon Cloud. "Why do some plants have medicine and others don't?"

"Just as people are different and animals are different, so are plants." She tucked the flower stem into her braid. "Creator makes all things to work together. Sun and rain come from the sky to touch the earth. Plants and trees rise from earth to feed and shelter the animals and people. We must understand their purpose to give them respect and be thankful to Creator. We use what is provided and don't take more than we need. Others, even animals, may need roots and seeds, so we will leave some for them. Here, there is plenty of burdock that we can take—enough for us and to share with the elders. We will leave some for the bear."

"I will dig this one." Hopping Bird picked up a sturdy stick.

Bear Cub and Dares to Run found rocks and began digging to expose the roots. Moon Cloud used a knife to break up the hard surface soil and scraped away the clods with her tool. When the holes were deep enough to cut out the roots, she called the girls over. "What do you notice about the dirt beneath the root?"

"It is wet." Hopping Bird rubbed dirt between her fingertips.

"Rain soaks into the ground. The roots reach for the water because it gives life." She pinched the moist dirt and rubbed her fingertips together. "Another name of Creator is One Who Gives Life. He gives life to the roots from the water. He gives life to our bodies from the water and roots. And he gives life to our spirit when we honor him and pray to him."

"Is that what you learned from White Falcon?" Bear Cub dangled a root over her gather-bag.

"Yes. I did not know the name One Who Gives Life before. The Great Spirit made a sacrifice so that we can know him as

Father." Moon Cloud spoke as she dug.

"When will White Falcon return to our village?" Dares to Run leaned on her left arm.

"I do not know." She tapped her tool on the dirt. "When I pray to One Who Gives Life, I have seen a vision of him as a small flame shining in a great darkness."

"Are you afraid for him?" Bear Cub tilted her head.

"No, I am not afraid. My heart rests in knowing One Who Gives Life is greater than the darkness."

CHAPTER TWENTY-ONE

ABRAHAM RUBBED THE BLINDFOLD DOWN
with his shoulder and examined his surroundings.

Slicing through the bright-green duckweed and surface scum, Sly poled the pirogue until it lodged in black mud. He placed his foot onto a sunken log beside him and leaped to dry ground. "Wait here. Keep him over the water till I get back."

Up ahead, where his captor disappeared beyond the cypress trunks and briars, Abraham made out a narrow trail and enough overcast sky to indicate a clearing. The deceitful green-and-black swamp water hid sinking mud, broken branches, snakes, and other monsters that Abraham had heard about in his childhood. He studied the logs in the vicinity of the boat.

The hired man appeared impatient as he held the bow between his knees. His eyes darted around the muck and mire, and he frequently looked over his shoulder.

"That log there seem to have eyes fixed on you." Abraham pointed with his chin. "Like it's a moving real slow. But it's dark enough I can't see for sure."

"Where? What log?"

"Over there about twenty feet." He tipped his head to his left.

"Aww. That ain't nothing. You just trying to scare me." He shifted the pole that Sly had handed him to his right side.

He was a short, wiry man with dark wavy hair and stubble whiskers. He wore a dark-gray blouse wrapped at the waist with a black sash, from which Abraham could see the butt of a pistol protruding and a knife sheath on the other side.

"I think it's a gator." Abraham pried at his bindings. "Pull me up so we both can get to high ground."

The hired man shook his head. "You just trying to get away."

"Well, throw a stick out there and see what happens."

"Be quiet. There ain't nothing there." Just then a bullfrog croaked, and the man flinched. "See there. You likely just seeing a bullfrog. Making it out to be something it ain't."

"It ain't a frog, sir. But I don't see it now. It's gone behind that snaggle brush." Abraham kept searching. "Please, sir. Pull me up. This boat ain't big enough."

"Quiet, I said. You ain't moving. You just sit there and be—" He gasped and jumped back.

A sudden splash and shuffle sounded when the alligator rushed forward with his jaws wide. The man fell on his back and poked at the monster with the pole while pedaling his feet at the slippery dirt.

Abraham gasped and stared at the surreal scene, unable to move or help.

The gator snapped down on the lower calf of the man's right leg, and he screamed. The beast yanked him with a tug of its scaly head and dragged him toward the water.

Boom, boom. Two shots rang out. The gator roared and released the leg and vanished into the black water. Abraham stared as Sly ran to grab the man's arm and pull him back. The big man scanned the water and brush for another attack. Then he examined the leg wound. "These bites are deep. You're spilling a lot of blood into the dirt."

"I need help," Abraham called. The pirogue had drifted out when the alligator splashed in escape. "You left me tied. I can't paddle."

Sly cussed. He removed his coat and dropped it. Holding the pistol at the ready in his right hand, he waded in, probing with the pole, watching the surface for movement.

Abraham rose as tall as he could on his knees to keep guard. Sly stepped in, and he abruptly dropped from knee deep to his arm pits. He lost balance and splashed to keep his head up. The pistol dipped under water, soaking the powder and rendering it useless. He pressed his weight onto the pole to keep upright, coughed, and spit water.

The wounded man lay on the ground helplessly. Abraham saw his captor struggling and leaned over the gunwale to paddle with cupped hands. He changed sides and kept splashing forward. When he drew near enough, he clutched Sly's wrist and took the pistol, dropping it in the boat, and tugged his hand until Sly grasped the side. Abraham leaned back as water spilled in. Sly pulled himself closer, let go of the pole, and gripped with both hands. As he strained, he grunted and kicked his legs free of the mud.

"Look out!" the man on shore shouted.

Abraham looked to the side just as the alligator rose with teeth bared. Its mouth opened and snapped as he lunged back, causing the pirogue to pitch violently under Sly's weight. Water rushed in.

"Hurry!" Abraham shouted.

Sly hoisted himself up to his waist and then swung his legs in. The gator's tail slapped the side of the boat. Sly found his pistol, cocked, and pulled the trigger. The hammer snapped, and he dropped the gun.

"Where's a paddle?" He dove toward the bow to grab the paddle that had been secured in place for portaging. He chopped down and struck the gator on the head. It recoiled. The pirogue pitched again.

Abraham bailed by the scoop as fast as he could. Sly paddled rapidly until they bumped into the mud. He hopped out and yanked it forward.

With the boat stable, he waved for his captive to step out. Sly slumped to the ground.

Abraham went to look at the wounded leg in the fading light. "He bleeding something fierce. We gots to tie that up quick as we can."

"I was lucky you came back when you did, Sly." The man groaned.

Sly spit. "I should've let him take you. Then at least one of us would've been happy." He dug through his coat pocket to produce a small powder horn and began the process of cleaning the revolver and reloading. "Give him your waist sash or tear off a sleeve or something. And hurry. If that gator comes back, he can have you."

Abraham used the sash to wrap the wounds as tightly as he could with tied hands. "That should slow the bleeding a mite. If it don't get clean soon, you'll get the infection."

The hired man nodded. "What now, Sly?"

"Up to the manor." The gunman pointed at the trail with the barrel. "You, shoulder him." He glared at Abraham.

They came into a clearing where a house on stilts was alit with candle lanterns. A silhouetted figure stood on the porch. "What took so long?"

"Gator bit." Sly pointed. "Maybe Wanda can see to him."

A man came and relieved Abraham and assisted the wounded one to the porch of a bunkhouse.

Abraham rolled his shoulders to wear off the fatigue. He looked at the dark figure high on the porch. It was too far to be sure, but that must be La Marque.

"Take him to his room," the silhouette said.

"Let's go." Sly guided Abraham across the yard to the barn.

He opened the big door, lit a candle, and pointed to a closed-in stall. "Hands." He slipped a rope through the bindings and passed it over a rail and tied it out of reach.

There was enough slack for Abraham to sit and lean on the boards, but he had to keep his arms up in a posture of pleading. "The good Lord kept you from drowning in that swamp. And he protected us from the alligator. I believe God has a plan for you, sir."

"I didn't see no God in that swamp." Sly secured the stall door with a lock. "You was the one . . ." He balked. "Don't be telling me about God."

The shadows moved as a lantern drifted into the barn, exposing a man dressed in black. Sly stepped aside.

"I finally have you. You have been setting slaves free, and now you're my slave. You will pay a price for what you've done." He adjusted the lantern to shine through the space between boards onto Abraham's face. "Do you know who I am?"

"Whoever you is, you need to understand that I's a willing bond slave of the Lord Jesus Christ. I don't serve two masters." Abraham searched the dimness for his eyes. He noted that the lantern jostled slightly at the mention of the name of Jesus. And there was a soft shuffle sound by the barn door.

"My name is La Marque." He waited for a reaction. "I know you've heard of me. You've been stealing my property, my slaves."

"No man can own a child of God. I set them free from a lie." Abraham stood and presented his wrists. "Bind my hands, but you can't bind my heart. And you isn't La Marque." The lamp moved again. "He's hiding behind the door."

"What?" This man swallowed hard. "I am La Marque. You are my slave. Tomorrow you will see how much of a slave you really are." He turned to leave. "No food, no water."

Sly followed him out but left the candle burning. Abraham peered into the dark corners of the barn as much as he could.

"Anyone here?" He listened. "Anybody in this barn with me?" Nothing. "I guess it's just you and me, Jesus. You been with me in the dark before. I knows you going to rescue me when I done my work here. I serves only you."

The barn door creaked as Sly entered. "Take this." He slipped a large flask through the gap in the sideboards, then a piece of bread and a fistful of peanuts wrapped in paper. "It's water. Keep it out of sight."

"Sir?"

"For your help in the swamp."

"Obliged." Abraham could see the gunman's eyes through the boards. "God will repay the kindness."

But the eyes were gone, and the door creaked again.

CHAPTER TWENTY-TWO

ALLEN FOLLOWED DEX AND ERSKINE up Silver Street along the row of two-story brick buildings—some with balconies—and log warehouses. Dusk was upon them, and lanterns cast an orange hue within the buildings. Dex had described his hometown to Allen on the boat, and now Allen was finally there.

According to Dex, Natchez Under the Hill was home to inns and taverns right on the river. People who lived in Natchez, the town on the bluff, preferred not to interact with the Under the Hill crowd unless it was absolutely necessary. The waterfront folk didn't care. They worked hard, played hard, and welcomed anyone who shared their robust and rebellious ways. The reputation as the den of iniquity on the Mississippi was a source of pride, and anyone who claimed Under the Hill as home held a measure of respect, and disdain, among boatmen.

Dex waved at people and shook hands like he was the mayor. "Allen, we're going in here to ask where to find my mother. I want you to wait outside, maybe by that tree across the road. This is the kind of place you don't want to see."

"Could it be worse than the pirate cave?"

"Might be. But that's not the reason. To be square, you're a kind of a target for trouble."

"What do you mean?" Allen frowned.

"I know you seen some things and you can handle yourself. But besides the bounty on your head now, you rather shine of goodness." Dex glanced at Erskine, who nodded.

"What if I change my clothes?"

"That won't make the difference. These people will see that you're a good man. Good enough to make them feel nervous or even guilty, and then maybe try to get you out of the way or corrupt you." The river fox lifted a hand, as if revealing the truth. "Nice folk come down from town and get robbed and killed. They're just unaware of the danger, or they think they can make friends. These cutthroats might see you that way, but they're also going to see the goodness that they hate."

"Well, no sense tempting a provocation." Allen resigned himself. "I'll wait by the tree."

Working women waved at him from the balcony and made invitations. A man staggered by and asked for money. Allen hoped they wouldn't have to stay here long. Deacon Abraham was captive somewhere, maybe in shackles, maybe suffering. It took what seemed like a half hour before Dex came out. He smelled of cigar smoke and liquor.

"Whew." Allen waved a hand under his nose. "Did you have yourself a smoke in there?"

"No, I just talked to some friends." Dex sniffed his shirt. "Mom's staying up the street."

Partway up the hill, they found a small house next to a new construction. The sign read CATFISH CASINO, OPEN SOON. Dex watched his feet on the creaking porch and tapped on the door.

As it opened, a squeal of joy pierced Allen's ears. The woman jumped to wrap her arms around Dex's neck. "Dexter. You're here."

Marylou Yates appeared to be too young to be Dex's mother. Her sandy-blond hair was bound in a bundle on top of her head, and a few strands fell loose about her face and neck. She wore a cream-and-tan-striped dress that was unbuttoned from the collar down a few inches.

Dex lifted his mother and stepped over the threshold. "I'm here, Ma." He received five kisses on each cheek. He lowered her feet to the floor and waved Allen in. "It's just a short visit, sorry to say." He hugged her shoulder. "This is my friend Allen."

"Hello. I'd say you're welcome here, but I know you're both in trouble." She offered a smile. "It's true then?"

"I apologize for that, Ma. That's why we won't be staying long."

"I am sorry, ma'am. I don't mean to bring trouble on you." Allen gripped the shoulder strap of his bag.

"Don't you worry. You'll both be safe here while you're in Natchez." She squeezed Dex. "Ain't the first time he's brought trouble through the door. I hear they put a bounty on you, but you can lay low right here."

"How long you been in this house?" Dex appraised the living room. "It looks nice enough."

"It belongs to Larson McDill. He's a gambler, and he's building the place next door." She folded a blanket to lay on the back of a flowery settee. "Larson takes care of me now. And I'll have a good job in the casino."

"That's a fine turn of affairs for you, Ma. Glad to hear it." Dex leaned on the settee. "We're hunting down a friend of Allen's that was kidnapped, and we think they're heading for the swamps down west of Baton Rouge."

"In the Atchafalaya?" Her brow creased. "I only hear terrible stories coming out of there."

Allen noted her reaction. It wasn't what he wanted to hear.

"Have you ever heard the name of La Marque? As a fortune-teller or sorcerer?"

"No, I can't recall that name. If he's running slaves, he most likely did business above. The rich folk don't come down the hill." Her hands were on her hips. "Hey, are y'all hungry?"

"Thanks, Ma, but Uncle Randall fed us on the boat." Dex folded his arms. "He told me to ask you about Judith, the witch lady, thinking she might know something."

"Oh, Dexter. She's not a witch. Or if she is, she's a white witch. She has a place north of town."

"Mrs. Yates, the main information we're seeking is if she would know where he lives."

"You're sweet, Allen, but please call me Marylou."

He nodded. "Marylou, we don't want to search in the swamp if he's somewhere else."

"That makes perfect sense. We'll go find her first thing in the morning." She took Dex's hand. "Now let me find you some food."

Allen and Dex followed Marylou up the path to a log cabin with ivy crawling up the walls and moss covering the shingle roof. The cabin fit so tightly in the midst of the locust and magnolia trees that it could have been easily missed if it weren't for the variety of wind chimes and colorful ribbons that hung in every available space from the porch beam.

Lord, you use strange messengers sometimes.

"Madam Judith," Marylou called. "Are you here?"

Before she called again, Dex tapped her shoulder while looking at Allen. "Listen. Do you hear that?"

Allen nodded, gazing into the trees. "It sounds like a hummingbird. A big one."

"It's a wind wand. Follow me." Marylou scurried around the cabin into the forest.

Pursuing the sound, they came upon a woman wearing a dark-green skirt and white blouse wrapped with a white shawl. She had multiple strands of colored bead necklaces and a maroon paisley scarf keeping her long, wavy gray hair under control. She stood barefoot with her left foot in the grass and her right in the sand of a small creek. In her right hand she held a triangular device made of wood slats connected by leather cords with a handle that allowed it to spin and make a whirring vibration sound while she sang a variety of high-pitched notes that created a song without a melody.

Dex nudged Allen with his elbow. "Do they sing that one in your church?"

Allen raised his eyebrows and shook his head. He listened to the discernment of his heart. This witchcraft seemed different from what he had sensed in Dark Wolf's cave.

"Madam Judith." Marylou was clearly hesitant to interrupt. "I apologize, I truly do, but this young man would like to ask you some questions. Would that be all right?"

"Of course, my darlings." She stepped forward and hugged Marylou. But when her gaze fixed on Allen, she gasped. "Men like you don't come to seek my advice. Usually you come to condemn me."

"What do you mean?" Allen's brow creased. "I'm not here to condemn you."

"Men of the church refuse to accept me or my gifts. They call me a witch and tell me I will burn in hell if I don't repent and do as they say." Madam Judith continued to examine his face.

"How did you know he was a preacher?" Dex looked from one to the other.

"I see it on him, but his aura is different than others. There is the white light of goodness that I call the gospel light. But in others the white light is shrouded with a dark cloud of pride and anger where there should be the shine of love. But you do shine of valiant love and peace."

"What about me—do I shine?" Dex stepped beside Allen.

"Silver and green." She smiled at him. "Let's go have a cup of tea, shall we?" Her Irish brogue registered with Allen. *Lord, please make sense of this for me.*

Allen, Dex, and Marylou sat at a small hickory table while the hostess stoked the stove and set on the kettle. The beams and walls were covered with herbs and dried plants.

She put a three-candle stand in the center of the table and pulled up her chair. "How can I help?"

"I'm searching for a friend who was kidnapped, I believe by a man named La Marque, and taken down the river, probably into the—"

"Swamp." The odd woman finished the sentence. "The Atchafalaya. You'll find your friend at the plantation in Bayou Chene. It's dark and dangerous. Dark with evil. An evil that empowers and enrages the animals." She reached for Allen's hand, closed her eyes, and drew breath. "You've seen him, haven't you? La Marque."

He nodded.

"How will we know when we're at Bayou Chene? It all looks the same in there." Dex rubbed his hands together.

Judith paused, scowling. "I dare not look further. I risk too much telling you this."

Marylou reached behind her neck and removed a silver chain with a single pearl pendant and laid it before Madam Judith.

"That's lovely." She studied it, then dropped it into a pocket in her skirt. "When the peril seems greatest, you will be there. You will find your friend in the light."

Dex turned his head and rolled his eyes. His mother bumped his knee with hers. He sniffed and rubbed his nose.

Allen looked into Judith's emerald eyes, surrounded by smile lines and mild cheek wrinkles, but she was not haggard by any means. "By light, do mean lanterns or a spiritual glow?"

Madam Judith smiled.

"When I'm praying, it's easy to see him shining in a dark place," Allen said.

"Yes, look for that light. Be sure not to be deceived by a will-o'-the-wisp." She pressed herself up from the table. "My spirit guides won't go into that part of the swamp. There is a very strong evil presence there. Many souls are crying out from the darkness." She blew out the candles on the table. "My primary guide is named Verdance. Do you know your spirit's name?"

Allen paused. "Holy. His name is Holy."

Marylou gave Judith a thank-you kiss on the cheek and asked to buy some lavender tea sprigs as Dex and Allen departed. When she caught up with them at the wagon, Judith was behind, calling up the path, "Take a warrior with you into the swamp."

Dex waved and slapped the reins. "This is her advice? Take a warrior into a dark swamp and follow a spirit to the light." He shook his head. "Ma, why did you give her that nice pearl? Seems like we should have got better advice."

"Dexter, now don't go mocking her. She's been around a long time, and you don't know that it won't turn out true. And don't worry about the pearl. I can always get another."

"Fine. I'll let it be. But Ma, we're going to leave straightaway. It's a good hundred miles down to that swamp, and the Atchafalaya don't run as swift as the Mississippi. And we've yet to find us a boat."

"And a warrior." Allen chuckled. *I don't know what you're planning, Lord, but I keep my trust in you. Please send us the warrior to lead us in the battle ahead.*

After dropping them at the gaming house under the hill, Marylou squeezed her son and Allen goodbye. Dex and Allen found Uncle Randall eating fried eggs and grilled bread and explained their need to find a guide who could leave right away for the Atchafalaya.

"I'll be pulling out soon myself, heading for Baton Rouge." The captain pushed his plate away. "Let's find Danny. He knows that stretch of river better than most."

Within a few minutes, while checking into each inn along the way, they bumped into Danny coming down the outside staircase of a boardinghouse. Two hours later they dropped into his modified pirogue, wider than most, and untied from the steamboat at the branch of the Atchafalaya River. Danny and Dex rowed as Allen sat on the stern bench. He noted the guide's features, which contrasted against his white cotton shirt. He had a square jaw and high cheekbones, black eyes, and black hair that reached his shoulders beneath a black felt hat with a broad brim. Around his neck was a leather cord with a long white triangular bone. At first it seemed to Allen that it might be a bear's tooth.

"Who are your people?" Allen ventured.

"Huh? My people?"

"Your tribe?"

"My father's is Cherokee, and my mother's Choctaw."

"They live near Natchez?"

"No. They were taken on what we call the Trail of Tears, but they did not finish the journey. I was raised by a white woman outside of Natchez. My uncle started bringing me down here to fish and trap when I got old enough."

Allen nodded. "Is Danny from Daniel?"

"Danuwoa."

"What's it mean, if you don't mind me asking?"

"It's Cherokee for *warrior*."

Allen shook his head and looked at the sky. *Your ways are a mystery.*

Dex's right oar splashed as he lost his grip. "Wait. Your name is Warrior? Aha." He guffawed. "So the witch was right after all. I don't believe it."

"Witch?" Danny twisted around. "What are you getting me into?"

"Not to worry, now. She said we needed to go into the swamp with a warrior. It's all dandy as five-cent candy." Dex couldn't stop chuckling.

Danny resumed rowing. "You don't look like one who seeks advice from witches."

"I'm not. I trust in the Christian God." Allen leaned his elbows on his knees.

"He's a Bible-thumping preacher," Dex threw in.

"You don't look like one of them either." The guide assessed Allen.

He reached into his shirt and pulled up the medicine bag that Moon Cloud had given him.

Danny studied it and returned his focus to Allen's eyes. Allen tucked it away. "I've been living with the Arapaho up the Platte. Their holy man has taught me many things about their view of spirits. That is why I listened to what the witch had to say, but my trust remains in God and his Word. The man we're searching for also taught me to understand matters of prayer and listening to God's voice. I believe God is directing us on this rescue mission. But I didn't know to look for you until the witch somehow mentioned a warrior."

Danny listened, then scoffed. "You saying that God picked me to help you?"

"Yes. I believe he cares about you."

"If he cares so much, why did he take my parents when I was so young?"

After a long pause, Allen held his hands out. "I don't have an answer for you. I only know that whatever the hardship, he'll be with you if you keep the faith."

"Not sure I want a god with me who'd take a little boy's mother away." He rowed steadily.

"Danny, I'm sorry about your folks, but Allen's got a point." Dex scratched his bare foot. "I seen things I can't explain but to call it a miracle. We should have been dead three times over by now, but here we are, live as can be and with a bounty on our heads. I'm going to keep the faith. You should too."

For several minutes it was silent except for the splash of the oars. Danny winked at Allen. "How much is the bounty?"

Allen turned his head to hide his smile. Dex stopped rowing, then burst into laughter. The low wooden boat rocked with the hilarity until a bat swooped past Dex's face. "Yikes."

"Easy. It's a bat eating skeeters." Danny steadied the boat.

Dex slapped his neck. "Well, he ain't eating fast enough." He slapped again.

The bat swooped past his ear and then past Allen. He threw up his arms.

"There's a good camp up ahead a piece. Keep rowing—we get there quicker." The guide picked up the pace.

Allen caught Danny's eye and tipped his forehead toward the bow. Danny looked over his shoulder and chortled. Dex had grabbed the only thing in reach, a yellow cloth, and wrapped it around his head and neck, shrouding his face. A bat flapped by, then another. "They must be attracted to yellow."

"Like catfish to a worm." Danny steered toward a sandbar and beached the craft.

After securing the pirogue, they climbed a six-foot bank and found a cleared area with a lean-to and fire circle. Dex followed Danny, looking for firewood, while Allen struck sparks into a bundle of dry moss and covered it with twigs. He kept the little fire going until Danny returned with an armload of sticks. The blaze grew and sizzled. Then at the sound of a crack, they both looked into the dark beyond the trees.

Danny stepped away from the fire. "Dex shouldn't be way over there. He ought to see the fire." He pulled a pistol out of his belt. "I'll have a look. You keep that burning bright."

For much longer than seemed safe, Allen waited. Just when he was about to give a shout, he heard movement, and Dex appeared with an armload of branches. Shortly after, Danny brought in another load and a bundle of greenery. He dropped a wad on the flames. "This'll keep the skeeters at bay."

A thick cloud of white smoke billowed, and Dex moved into it. "I ain't usually bothered by skeeters so bad, but this is crazy." He was still wrapped in the yellow cloth.

Danny produced bread and smoked venison and handed a parfleche to Dex. "Rub this on your face and neck."

"What is it?" He sniffed at the pouch and grimaced.

"Possum fat."

"No thanks. I'll stick to my method." Dex adjusted his turban. "Those derned bats ain't doing their job."

Allen dipped two fingers into the grease and smeared it on his cheeks and neck. "How far back did you go in there?"

"Not so far at first." Dex gnawed on his jerky. "Then I saw a light. I thought it was a lantern at first, but I couldn't say if it was near or far. I tried to get a look, but I couldn't catch up. Then I thought how it looked more blue than yellow, like a lantern ought to be, so I turned myself around. I couldn't see the fire and was stumbling my way back when Danny found me."

"What do you suppose it was?" Allen bit into the bread.

"*Asgina*." Danny stared at the undulating flames. "Ghost light."

"Ghost light?" Dex packed a wad of jerky into his cheek. "The will-o'-the-wisp. Ha, just like the witch lady said. I swear, I always thought that was an old wives' tale. Now I seen one."

Allen studied the guide's forlorn look. "Is there more to it, Danny?"

"The light moves and lures people into a hole or quicksand. Many have died. Many children. Some hear the light call their name, and they go into the swamp but never come out.'"

"Do you believe it to be a ghost?" Allen knelt to poke the embers.

"Not a ghost." He glanced over both shoulders. "*Asgina* can also mean demon."

Dex stood up and sidestepped around the fire to be close to Allen. "I'll take care of the boats, and you take care of the demons." He shuddered. "Dang, I feel like ants is crawling up my back."

"What other things do we need to watch for?"

"Snakes, copperhead, and the cottonmouth. More south, gators," Danny said.

"And bats." Dex shuddered and pulled the yellow cloth snug against his neck.

Danny tapped a stick in the dirt. "I ain't seen a panther in years, but I seen a wolf."

"Ugh. Not a big black one, I hope." Allen spit into the fire. He related his encounters with Dark Wolf and the demonic figures of men with wolf heads he had envisioned while held captive in the sorcerer's cave.

The guide nodded but remained silent for a few moments. "Sounds like a rougarou. A wolf-man."

"I've heard of them when I was down in New Orleans," Dex said. "Seen a drunk beggar outside a gaming house, but I'm telling you he was dead-dog ugly. They said he was bit by a rougarou.

You never seen one, have you, for yourself?" He shifted on his feet. "I'd rather see one of them than another bat."

Allen side-smiled at the comment as he gazed at the embers. Danny dropped another fist wad of green moss to smolder. A choir of cicadas reached their crescendo, and a horned owl made his presence known. Allen noted that Danny stroked his medicine pouch, then raised a crucifix and kissed it.

"Umm. You ain't seen one, true, Danny?" Dex blinked the smoke out of his eyes.

"Yep, I seen one, true on, Dex, true on." He made eye contact with both. "Two, two and a half years ago, down south of here. I was poling down a channel to mind my traps, and I seen the wolf's head in the brush. I was still a piece away and lost sight for some trees, but when I come up, I seen him again, just staring at me. I was fixing to take my rifle and shoot, but he rose up to man height and run off on two legs."

"Did you take the shot?"

"No. It was gone too fast. I found tracks but not fair enough to follow. I set in my boat for an hour, then checked my traps. They was empty, and I didn't see any critters for two days after." Danny took long deep breaths. "Oddity of the swamp is all I can say."

"What do you think, Allen?" Dex moved to the canvas ground cloth under the lean-to.

What can it be? "I've heard people describe demons like that, but a real creature?" Allen shrugged. "An oddity of the swamp."

Danny found his space on the canvas. "We'll get moving as soon as we got good light."

The morning mist hovered over the water, as if it were hiding something. As daylight increased, the mist seemed to get thicker.

Danny removed his shirt, knelt, and splashed water over his arms, chest, then face. He rose, kissed the crucifix, and pulled his shirt on. "There's good light, but before we get in the boat, I want to follow Dex's tracks from last night."

They weaved their way through the brush and trees until the guide stopped. "This about where you seen the light?"

"Yes, I think so." Dex pointed. "I went off that way." He walked in the direction but was soon off his tracks.

"This way." The guide pointed to a line through the low brush, then stepped over a log.

"It can't be right. I don't recollect stepping over that big log." Dex scratched his head.

"Tracks go here." He continued weaving until he halted and held his arms out.

"Lord almighty." Dex gulped.

They peered into a murky pit with a snarl of sharp, broken branches. Danny studied the ground. "This is where you turned when I called you." He led them swiftly back to the riverbank.

"Gosh, I would've been hurt for sure. Might be you saved my life, Danny. I owe you."

"Might be. But let's get on the water." Reaching the camp, he passed around a bag of hardtack.

"Can you see where we're going?" Dex sat at the forward oars. "I may run us into a snag. This fog is thick as buttermilk."

"I'll row. You eat. I want to get away from here." Danny pulled smoothly on his oars.

"Something making you nervous?" Allen bit his hardtack.

"You heard the owl last night? He must have conjured the mist."

"How can an owl do that? He was just a hooting." Dex kept chewing.

"It was a witch or a witchdoctor using the owl. Called in the mist to block your journey. It ain't a regular mist, too thick. Tastes like a bad egg."

Dex sniffed the air and breathed through his mouth, shook his head, shrugged, and popped a bite of the biscuit into his mouth. "What do you think, Allen? Seen the likes of this before?"

"Can't say that I have." He peered from side to side. "I can smell the air, but I can't make out the shore on either side. It can't be but twenty feet."

Danny rowed cautiously several strokes, then drifted. He closed his eyes and made three strokes with only his right hand. Then a sudden bump on the port side jolted them. A log brushed past. Dex put out his oars and stroked in time with Danny. Suddenly the boat rocked as Dex's left side tangled in brush.

"Stow the oars." Danny pulled a few more times until his right-hand oar tangled. They lurched to a halt. "We got into a back channel." He tucked the blades away and crouched past Dex, pulled a pole from beneath the seats, and pried them out of the jam. He backed the pirogue until they finally reached the river. "We lost some time, and this mist ain't lifting." He resumed rowing.

"So, Reverend Hartman, how do we keep the faith in this witch's brew?" Dex leaned over to make eye contact.

Allen squared his shoulders. "God is our refuge and strength, a very present help in trouble." He quoted Psalm 46 as his prayer. "There is a river, the streams whereof shall make glad the city of God." He let his voice grow louder as he noted that Danny picked up the pace. "The Lord Jesus went to the cross and came out of the grave to overturn the works of evil. As he overturned the tables in the temple, I proclaim in his holy name that this curse is overturned."

After several minutes, Danny told Dex to row. With the fresh surge they came around a bend, where the mist broke apart. Around another bend and they were in the clear light of day.

When a solid hour had gone by, Allen and Dex exchanged

places. They maintained a quick pace for another hour, then Danny steered onto a sandbar for a brief recess.

"I calculate we're just a few hours away from Bayou Chene." Danny scanned the brush. "The river changes and floods after a hard rain. We'll navigate through a batch of them backwater channels until we come to a wide lake. Then we got to pick the right lane to wherever your friend is. We got to hope and pray that we find it before dark."

"You ain't thinking there's more bats, is you?" Dex spotted his yellow cloth in the bow.

"If it's only bats, it'll be butter on the bacon." Danny stretched his back.

Allen folded his arms. "Do you have any notion of where to look first?"

"Years ago my uncle took me in there, and we found an abandoned plantation. They got flooded out. I figure we start there. If it's still idle, at least we'll have a place to sleep. If there's someone there, then it might be what we're looking for."

"You have any apples in that food bag?" Dex patted his stomach.

"Just the jerky and hardtack. Help yourself, and let's get moving." Danny took his place at the rear oars.

For the next hour, Allen studied the surroundings as they worked their way through a flooded expanse broken up by small islands and fingers of dry land covered with the brush and trees that made overland navigation nearly impossible. The high overcast evened out the daylight, not forming shadows and not offering the optimism of sunshine. The guide skillfully located the only remnant of a current and followed it into a channel directing them southward and eventually back to the mainstream of the river.

About 150 yards downstream, Allen spotted a figure on a low mud bank on the right. "Up ahead. Might be a man squatting on the right." Allen squinted.

Danny continued rowing steadily and spoke softly. "Dex, stow the oars and get the rifle close, but don't raise it."

"It ain't a wolf-man, is it?" He slid the gun to his side.

Danny watched Allen's eyes. "Does he have a gun?"

"Not that I can see. Maybe he's fishing."

"Tell me when we're a stone's throw away."

"Now." He gripped the gunwales.

Danny ceased rowing, put his right hand on the butt of his pistol, and looked over his shoulder. He stroked the left-hand oar and turned the boat to face the man, who now stood. Danny raised a hand and spoke a native language. The man—Allen estimated at just over five feet tall—wore a loincloth, and his buckskin shirt hung loosely off his shoulders, leaving his chest fully exposed. There was a short bow and quiver on the ground. Allen tried a greeting in sign language that he'd learned from Blue Otter.

Suddenly the man began chattering, and Danny replied. Allen tried to distinguish words. After some back and forth, Danny pulled the pirogue to the bank. The little man pulled a stringer with four large catfish out of the water, dropped it into the pirogue, grabbed his bow, and hopped in.

"Hey now, that's just dandy." Dex admired the catch. "Ask if he's got some taters."

Danny and the man exchanged words again. The man pointed south, then gestured to the west while making a sign that Allen assumed to mean a marker tree.

"No taters then?" Dex started rowing.

"What did he say?" Allen glanced between the little man and Danny. "Is that Cherokee?"

"He's Chitimacha. They know the swamps better than anyone. Speaking a mix, type of trade language, I guess. He was afraid of you until you signed. He thought you were going to fly off with him." Danny paused, grinning.

"What?"

"He asked me why a Cherokee warrior was in a boat with a silver fox and a white falcon."

"That's what the Arapaho call me." Allen smirked. "I'm glad I signed correctly."

"You said, 'It is a good day, Father, to speak together in peace.' It was very respectful."

"Are we taking him home?"

"He knows the way to the plantation. Says people live there, blacks and whites." Danny's brow furrowed. "But he says they walk like an owl with no wings."

Allen looked toward the water, as if picturing such a sight.

"Hey." Dex leaned over. "What's the sign language for taters?"

CHAPTER TWENTY-THREE

ABRAHAM SHOOK HIS LEGS AND leaned against the stall to let blood circulate in his arms. Stretching, he took several deep breaths. Morning light peeked through gaps in the barn walls and the two small windows. He had been grateful for the bread and peanuts from the night before, but his stomach growled for more. Straining against the wrist bindings, he sighed. "Lord, I thank you for the new day. How might I serve you?"

An undistinguishable shout followed by murmuring alerted Abraham to the activity of the compound. After several more minutes, the door opened with a burst of light.

"Good morning, sir." He greeted Sly as the stall gate swung open.

"Hands." With one stroke of his long knife, Sly cut the bindings. He then took a coil of rope from his armpit and placed a loop over the captive's head and snugged the slip knot. "It ain't what you're thinking. Go on out."

There were a few people milling about the yard, but Sly led him around to the back of the barn. "Relieve yourself."

As they returned to the front, Sly stopped at a barrel that held a plate of grits and bread. He pointed with his chin. Abraham took the cue, lifted the plate to his chin, and scooped the grits with the morsel of bread. He paused his chewing when the man in black approached carrying a pewter mug in both hands. He set it on the barrel head.

"Welcome to your new home, Abraham." He swept his arm. "If you cooperate, I'll let you be with the labor crew. Otherwise you'll remain in the animal stall. And when you've proven yourself, you can be free to roam as you please, like these here."

Abraham could see in the distance, beyond the bunkhouse and into the next clearing, a line of men carrying firewood to a distillery. But the slaves close by wandered aimlessly. If one moved in their direction, a foreman would shove them back, and rather than resist, they slumped off. "What's wrong with these people? They all gots that unnatural look in they eyes."

"They dared to challenge my power." The phony La Marque snickered. "I put a spell on them that only I can remove. I will hex you in the same way if you refuse to obey me. You're my slave now."

"You can bind my hands, but my soul belongs to the Lord Jesus."

"Don't say that name." His face reddened. "Never utter that name again." He held out a leather strap. "Now finish your meal. And drink the tea."

Abraham lifted the mug to his lips but paused. His nose crinkled as he sniffed.

"You must drink it for energy." The counterfeit raised his eyebrows.

After a long, deep breath with his eyes closed, Abraham squared his shoulders, glared at the deceiver, and raised the mug. Just before taking a drink, he turned toward the manor, and staring at a gap in the persianas, he lifted the mug in salute, then drank several big gulps. He set the mug down and cringed at the bitter flavor. The persianas snapped shut.

Counterfeit Man beamed, as if he'd won a contest. "Soon you will feel the energy of jimson tea and my special mushrooms." He tipped his head at Sly. "Put him to work."

La Marque paced in the front room of the manor, slapping his thigh with a rosary made of black ebony-wood beads with an inverted crucifix. When he heard footsteps on the porch, he cleared his throat. A knock on the door caused him to jump.

"Enter." He slipped the beads through his thumb and forefinger.

His look-alike crossed the threshold and shut the door.

"Well, Trahan? What did he say? What did you tell him?"

"I told him the tea would give him energy." He held out the mug. "He drank most of it. Half that much would put down a man as big as Sly."

"Are you sure it's the right mix? We must be sure." La Marque tugged on his black vest and adjusted the collar of his black shirt.

"Of course I'm sure." Trahan scowled. "Look, we can grab a worker and make him drink this much. Then you'll see how potent it is."

"Yes, find one quickly."

A few minutes later, Trahan brought in a man larger than Abraham, who fidgeted with his shirttail. "Here, drink this." He watched the man tip back the mug. "Now wait on the veranda."

"Do you think Abraham is buying our ruse?" La Marque peered through the louvers.

"It won't matter an hour from now." Trahan poured himself a shot of whiskey. "He won't tell us apart. Tonight he'll be begging for more tea."

"He suspects. He looked right at me when he drank."

"Why does that worry you?"

"Something about him is different. It's as if he has a power I've never seen before." La Marque gazed at the rosary.

"But you've captured other priests. His blood will run just like theirs. And he'll cry for mercy just like them too."

"Fine. When will you check on him?"

"I told Sly to bring him in an hour." There was a loud thump against the wall. Trahan opened the door. "But it won't take an hour. Look."

La Marque stepped out and gleamed. The man was rolling on the porch boards, holding his head. A minute later he pulled himself up, then leaned over and retched.

"See that. It was a potent brew." Trahan pulled the man's arm and nudged him down the stairs. "Abraham drank three times that at least."

"Very good." He watched the man shuffle away, pinching at the air. "Call me when Abraham goes under." He entered his house and closed the door.

Abraham estimated that he had been carrying firewood for about an hour. Not much work was being done, as most of the slaves looked too sick to be of much use. He counted over twenty that he figured were slaves. Maybe eight were hired hands who kept the slaves moving or lounged in the shade. There was an out-building where several women lingered, and occasionally a man would enter.

He dropped his load of branches on the pile next to the tarnished copper distillery.

"Don't look at the women," a man said, barely above a whisper. He fed wood into the fire box beneath the boiler pot. "They'll lash you if look that way. Best to keep moving."

253

Abraham stacked branches that had strewn about. "You don't look like a slave."

"Not a slave. More like a prisoner. They hired me in Vermilionville to haul a load of supplies. Now they won't let me leave." He pulled a cloth from his pocket and wiped his brow. "I know how to keep the stills running, so they let me be for the most part."

"How long you been here?" Abraham sized up the middle-aged white man with a scruffy beard.

"Over three months. They bring new people every week. But no one leaves unless they're dead. The ones with whips and guns are the only ones who go out, but they always come back. See them women? But don't stare. The one on the right with the dark hair. I did business with her husband in town. They both came here owing money to the master, but he's been gone a month. He put up a fight when they put his wife in there, you know, to be with the men that goes in. They beat him and fed him to the alligators." He shook his head and spit. "The women drink the laudanum like it's water, and men smoke opium at night. That's why they seem so dull."

Abraham nodded as matters were becoming clear. "What about them others what walk about like they're blind, but their eyes is wide open?"

"They're given something worse than opium. And the master does some ritual on them. I fear it's some kind of devil worship."

"When you say 'master,' does you mean La M—"

"Hush." He held up his hand. "Don't ever mention his name. And whatever you do, don't drink the tea he offers. It steals the soul." He turned abruptly and stepped behind the still.

"Hey, what you doing there?" a man with a whip barked. "Go fetch more wood."

Abraham moved to pass, when Sly stopped him. "I'll take this one."

The whip man cowered away like a pup before the alpha dog. Sly grabbed Abraham's chin and looked into his eyes. "How you feel?" He squinted.

"Fine, sir, but I could take some water."

"You don't have a headache or a bellyache?" When Abraham shook his head, Sly pursed the corner of his mouth. "Go."

Coming around the bunkhouse, Abraham saw the counterfeit man standing on the porch of the big house. He rubbed his hands together and rushed down the steps, but as he drew closer, his expression pinched.

"It didn't take." Sly held Abraham's elbow.

"But that's impossible. We saw it take effect on the other." He scanned the area. "There, that one. Look." He pointed at the man scuffling back and forth between two trees. "This has never happened before." He glared at the captive. "What did you do?"

"Sir, you tried to poison me, but God is protecting my soul, just like he protected the apostle Paul from the viper."

"Stop it. Don't talk about God." His fists clenched, and the veins in his neck bulged. "Put him back in the stall." He stormed up the steps and pounded on the door.

Abraham entered the barn behind Sly. "Funny how a man knocks on the door of his own house."

Sly faced away before he smirked. Opening the stall, he tipped his head, entered, and held up his wrists. Sly went out and secured the door. "I ain't never seen him so perplexed. I don't know what'll happen next, but it won't be good."

For the next several hours, Abraham used the time to pray, recite Scripture, and sing hymns. "My Lord, I don't worry for myself, but I pray for these folks being held captive. It ain't right for them to be oppressed by this man of the dark. You gots to bring the light. The light of truth and freedom."

The barn door swung open, and two lanterns illuminated the

space. Sly put the noose on Abraham's neck and directed him to follow the other man, who held a shotgun. They marched along a trail through the forest until Abraham could see the glow of a bonfire, where a cluster of people seemed to be coaxing someone. Sly pointed to the low-hanging branch of a sprawling live oak. Abraham scrambled up for a better view of the horrifying activity. Several people wore their ordinary clothes, but three figures wore black shrouds with hoods, and five women, dressed in white garments, held a young woman down while a man seemed forced to violate her. The man was then spread on the ground, covered with a black cloth, and stabbed with a dagger. The crowd shouted words, not cheering, but it sounded like a name repeatedly called out.

Abraham could see the guard with the shotgun craning his neck. Sly leaned on the trunk of the oak, not watching the ritual but keeping his eye on his prisoner's reaction.

Jumping down, Abraham stood beside Sly and swallowed the bile and saliva that preceded vomit. "I seen slaves whipped to death and lynched. It's all horrible, but nothing as revolting and wicked as this."

Sly said nothing.

"He wanted me to see this." Abraham turned his head from the ensuing debauchery. "Is that the end he has planned for me?"

"Don't know." Sly turned to leave and flipped the noose rope.

When Abraham was again tied in place in the stall, a candle lantern burned as his only comfort. "Lord, wash my eyes and my mind clean of the vile things I seen. It upsets my heart so. It must break your heart for the lawlessness to prevail when you went to the cross on their behalf."

"Are you praying to a god that can't help you? It's a fool's faith." A man's voice came from under the black hood that blended into the barn shadows. "As you saw today, my power is extensive. Even that foolish priest thought he could come to the rescue. It only took three days for him to lose faith in your powerless god. He frequented the women's quarters so often, we had to lock him away. He took advantage of the nuns that we brought in just to see how easily they could be corrupted. Now they'll do anything to satiate their cravings for a sip of laudanum or to smoke the opium pipe. Anything. Shed their own blood or sacrifice another on the altar of Belial." The hooded voice paused, waiting for a reaction, a sign of fear. "But I have special plans for you, Abraham. I went to great lengths to bring you here where no one can find you, to make you my slave. I could have had you killed at any time, but I'm going to make you pay for what you took from me. You helped slaves run away. I'm going to keep you alive and watch you turn your back on this god of yours. Then I will own your soul."

"Mr. La Marque, if I be your slave, then why you need the hood? Is you afraid of being seen?"

The black figure shook. "I am not afraid. Ha, certainly not." He shifted his feet and cleared his throat. "Tomorrow I will show you the meaning of fear. Rest well tonight, for by the end of tomorrow, you will be kissing my feet." He looked over his shoulder when the light shifted.

A young black woman came in holding a lantern and a plate with bread and a pewter mug. She waited for La Marque to wave her to his side. "I feel like being generous, so I give you a meal. A last supper, if you will." He laughed. "And I'm willing to leave her here to keep you company. Young and tender." He caressed her cheek and shoulder. She smiled softly at him and then at Abraham. "You'd be a fool not to accept."

Abraham looked away. "Good night, Mr. La Marque."

After waiting a moment, he shook his head. "At least eat the food. Show him."

The woman took a bite of bread. When she lifted the mug, she looked first at the darkness of the hood. He tapped her elbow, and she drank. "See, it's safe." After setting the plate on the ground, she smiled again.

Abraham moved forward to see her eyes in the dim orange glow. She held his gaze with a soft smile until she shuddered, blinked, and her eyes glazed.

"Come now." La Marque took her arm and led her out. Before they reached the door, she staggered, and he caught her by the waist and grabbed the lantern from her hand.

Sitting down, Abraham watched the candle flame. "Lord, I believe you protected me from that poison. Please save that poor girl before her soul gets lost for good. If La Marque won't ever turn his heart to you, Lord, then strike him down before his evil ways hurt more folk. And turn Mr. Sly's heart to you. He seem to be considering your truth. May the Holy Ghost work to save his soul. Be with Allen, Lord. I believe he's a coming. Help him to follow your light." He sighed.

Two rats came to nibble on the meal, and one tipped over the mug of tea, which saturated the bread. They continued eating until a few minutes later when, one at a time, they shook, twisted, rolled in the dirt, and finally tottered away. The candle flickered out.

The door burst open with light of the new day. "Morning, Mr. Sly. I was just praying for you."

"Quiet."

A moment later the look-alike walked in. "Well, I see you drank your tea last night." He picked up the empty mug. "Did you have interesting dreams?"

Sly put the loop over Abraham's head. "Where do you want him?"

"Take him and find some others to get rid of the bodies." But he halted Abraham as he stepped into the daylight. Counterfeit Man grabbed Abraham's chin and stared into his eyes. "Go."

Sly led Abraham in a loop past the distillery, collecting four more men and ending at the ash pile where the ritual killing had taken place. The naked man's body was there looking gray and bloated. Three other men and a woman also lay dead. One of the helpers vomited.

"You two, take them to the hog pen." Sly pointed at two bodies at the edge of the clearing. "The rest of you take these here and dump them in the swamp. Down that trail." He pointed with his chin. "Make sure they get clear into the water." He removed the noose.

Abraham partnered with the man from the distillery to drag the naked body. When they were down the trail and out of earshot of the others, the man dropped the arm to catch his breath. "This man was the priest I told you about." He huffed. "It's a terrible and shameful thing for him to die this way, drugged and disgusting."

"Come now." Abraham pulled on the arm. Sly was leading the other pair toward them.

The trail ended at a dock that reached over the water some twenty feet. Tied at the end was a flat-bottom rowboat. The surface of the water was black, and cypress stumps and green vines made a labyrinth that crowded the channel that led to the river.

"Dump him off the end. Hustle it up. You, dump her too." Sly then pointed at Abraham and his partner. "Go back to the distillery and keep it active. You stay there till I come." He pointed at Abraham's face. As they turned to leave, Sly ordered the other pair to get the last body.

Then a loud shout and splashing caused them to look back. "Alligators." The distillery man shuddered and trotted toward the security of his still. After igniting the fire and loading the copper boiler with herbs, he sat down and pointed to a log.

Abraham sat, leaning forward on his elbows. "That happen often? That you dump bodies like that?"

"Too often." He shook his head. "Several people each week."

"Ain't they afraid of running out of workers?"

"More come in all the time, paying a debt, kidnapped, promise of a paying job. No one leaves alive to warn folks in town."

"You ever try to get away?"

"I thought about it the first few days, but I seen too many get killed trying. Or else they end up like those lost souls, the mindless ones." He leaned back to check the fire. "My name is Leroy Rinker. In case you do make it out, you can get word to my wife at the Rinker Store in Vermilionville."

"I'm Abraham. I pray you see your wife soon. God can't let this go on."

"I hope so. But God didn't help the priest."

"Hey, let's go." Sly marched up and flipped his hand.

Abraham rose, stepped over the log, and whispered. "God bless you, Leroy."

They walked out of the production clearing and came into the yard between the manor and the barn, and Sly stopped. "What's this?" He looped the noose over Abraham's head, wrapped his wrists, and tied him off to a post that held up the porch roof of the bunkhouse. Abraham watched Sly run and drag one man off another. The fallen man leaped up and, uttering a hideous scream, lunged at Sly. With a swift blow to the chest and another to the crazed man's jaw, Sly knocked him down and turned to eyeball the other. Three more shadow people shuffled toward the bigger, clear-minded man, touching their open mouths as if begging for food. Sly pulled his pistol and aimed from one to the other, but they kept coming.

Abraham stared at these people who were so desperate they would risk getting shot. Finally, another guard came to help Sly. He slammed a man with the butt of his shotgun. They both kept backing up and shoving the closest ones. "Must be the drug wore off."

"Trahan," Sly shouted toward the house. "Trahan, get out here."

A large woman stepped onto the porch of the bunkhouse, saw what was happening, and jumped back in before Abraham could ask for help. Two drugged women came along the porch toward him. Their clothing was dirty and shredded, their hair tangled and mouths agape. "Tea. Want . . ." They came closer, reaching for Abraham. One pulled at his sleeve. "More tea." She gagged.

The more Abraham pulled away, the tighter the noose got. The other woman, screeching, pulled the rope to draw him closer. He struggled, choking. Boom! Over the woman's head, Abraham caught a glimpse of smoke from the shotgun. The women continued clutching at him until Sly clobbered the one pulling the rope on the head with the butt of his pistol. She dropped to the ground, holding her head and moaning. Sly loosened the noose.

"Here." A voice called out. "Over here. Tea and bread."

Sly shoved the women. "Go on." He herded the other addicts toward the manor. "Trahan, you're late."

"Here you go. Enough for everybody." He glared at Sly. "Here you go." Handing out cups of tea and chunks of bread, he smiled as if he were a benevolent host.

Abraham watched Counterfeit Man pass out the soul-binding poison. "Lord, what . . . what . . ."

When the last one stumbled away, Trahan came toward Abraham with a cup in hand.

"It's your turn." He punched Abraham in the stomach and gripped him in a choke hold. "You're going to drink this now." Pinching his jaw and forcing back his lips, Trahan poured the tea into Abraham's mouth until he gasped and had to swallow. "There now. I'm going to leave you tied up until you're ready to go play with your new friends." He pointed the cup in the direction of the wanderers. He cackled as he returned to the manor.

CHAPTER TWENTY-FOUR

ALLEN STRETCHED, TWISTED, AND SAT tall on the wooden seat. He watched a heron snatch up a little fish. It might be another long day.

"Hey, Danny." Dex stopped rowing and massaged his palms. "Does Catfish Man here have a name? Want to ask him why we're going in circles? I seen that cypress stump before."

"It ain't the same one."

Just then Catfish Man spoke and continued for more than a minute. Danny twisted around to look, then resumed rowing.

"What's he jabbering about?" Dex leaned forward.

Danny winked at Allen. "He said turn right."

"Oh." Dex rowed, then stopped. "Wait. He had to say more than that."

"Yes, he said turn right by the tree." Danny kept a straight face, but Allen chuckled.

Catfish Man spoke again in a softer voice.

"Well? What was that? Turn left now?" Dex shook his head.

"Now he said the silver fox should stop barking—we're getting close." Danny pressed his left oar and pulled the right, causing a sharp turn.

"Stop barking? Now that's rich." Dex turned to look at the little man but pinched his face upon seeing only what the loincloth didn't cover.

"Dex, stay sharp. Only row as I say." Danny spoke just above a whisper. They eased their way through the green swamp grass, cutting a black lane. "Hold." Dex stopped.

Catfish Man uttered softly and tapped the port side with an arrow. "*Amouskositte.*" He held his bow ready.

"Dex, stow your oars. Keep an eye on the water and one in the brush." Danny nodded at Allen to do the same. "He calls it *death water*. Keep the rifle close, Dex, but don't shoot unless I say."

Dex replied by spinning around on his seat to face forward.

Danny pointed with his chin at the water. Allen glanced to see a black snake weaving past his right side. He snatched his hand from the gunwale. Danny slid them along silently. After several minutes, he stowed his oars, pulled out the pole, and swapped places with Allen. The Chitimacha guide directed the path through what Allen thought would lodge them in mud or bump them into roots. Light from the late-afternoon sky struggled to penetrate the canopy of foliage to touch the murky water, as if the water wanted to keep its secrets.

Catfish Man drew his bow and held it steady. Following the line of his aim, the men spotted a gator slipping from black mud into the black water. Dex glanced back over his shoulder and made eye contact with Allen. A wedge of ripples on the surface went away from them. Danny lunged on the pole and ducked beneath a low-hanging branch and then brushed Spanish moss off his shoulders.

The guide threw up his hand, aimed the bow, but quickly set it down. Dex pointed forward left. An alligator came steadily toward them.

"Two more off the right bow," Danny said and braced his feet. Dex pointed at a third on the right side.

Allen spotted all four positioned as if they were intentionally blocking the path. He watched the guide, waiting for him to arrow the one moving in. He white-knuckled the seat.

Dex shifted the musket to his lap.

The big gator splashed its tail in a thrust to raise his head, opened his mouth, and bit down on the boat. Catfish Man tossed a fish into the white gaping row of jagged teeth. The gator snapped down, splashed, and submerged. He tossed two more catfish to the right side, drawing the other three monsters out of their path. Holding the last fish ready, he flagged Danny forward. With several quick thrusts, they cleared the area and glided to a halt at a beach next to a smaller pirogue. Catfish Man hopped out and held the bow.

Boom. At the sound of a gunshot, they all ducked. "That weren't aimed at us. Get out and keep low." Danny tucked the pole under the bench and climbed out. He tied the boat to a root and crouched with the others behind a briar patch.

Catfish Man duckwalked around the area, studying the dirt. He joined them and reported. Danny translated. "He says three days ago that boat came. One man was attacked by a gator. Two others helped him up this trail."

Speaking the trade language, Danny told the Chitimacha to lead the way. They were looking for a black man who would seem new. The four found a vantage point in the brush at the edge of the clearing. Men with guns kept watch over more than a dozen haggard people, some of whom were drinking from cups as others wandered about.

"The owl people," Danny interpreted.

"Makes sense now." Dex squinted. "That ain't no ordinary drunk walk. Any sign of Abraham?"

"No, I don't see him. The barn is blocking too much of my view." Allen peeked around the trunk of a locust. He hoped Abraham was in that barn and not in one of those buildings farther back. They heard a shout of aggravation, and a man yelled orders.

Catfish Man made a clicking noise with his tongue, then crawled on his elbows and knees to the left for a better view of the yard. A man wearing all black stomped toward the house and struck an owl man for no apparent reason. He turned at the top of the steps and yelled at the men with guns. Some scrambled away, but others strolled about the yard as if on guard. A big man emerged from the barn and strode to the house.

Danny grunted. "Sylvester." He glanced at his two collaborators. "They call him Sly. He's an assassin and a slave catcher. Very dangerous."

"Do you recognize the man in black?" Dex brushed a bug off his arm.

"No." Danny scanned the area. "Looks like more people back yonder." He pointed beyond the bunkhouse.

The hair on Allen's neck stood up, and his skin crawled as the front door opened and another man dressed in black stepped out. "La Marque."

"What? Him?" Dex squinted at the men on the porch. "How can you be sure? They both look the same."

"I know it's him." Allen swallowed. "Abraham has to be here."

"We best move." Danny nudged Dex.

Just then La Marque turned his head, as if staring into Allen's eyes. He pointed his finger, and Sly and two other gunmen walked their way.

"Get moving," Danny urged.

The four crawled quickly in the fading light back to the trail. Crouching low, they made their way to the boat. Danny climbed in. "You two go hide. Stay away from the water. But go deep as you can and hide. We're going to hide the boat. Meet back here in two hours. Go."

Catfish Man jumped aboard, and they faded into the swamp as lanterns flickered in the trees at the top of the trail.

Allen and Dex took long strides at the edge of the low bank to skirt a briar patch, using every trick they could think of to conceal tracks and sound. Their progress slowed as darkness enclosed the Atchafalaya Swamp.

Dex climbed a tree just high enough to examine their back-trail. "No lights," he whispered. "Climb up."

Allen hoisted himself up to the thick branch that Dex claimed for a perch. "Let's roost here. Doubt they would look up if they come this far. And we'll be out of reach of other critters." Dex leaned his back against the trunk. "I doubt that even a rougarou would look up here."

"Good thinking." Allen shifted to get comfortable. "What about bats?"

"Now why'd you have to go and say that? I don't have my yellow scarf." Dex tried to cover his neck with his hands without losing his balance. "Hey, what do you make of them owl people? They give the creepers. I'm guessing they got their brains fried or something."

"I don't know what to think. I just hope we find Deacon Abraham before they put the drugs in him." Allen kept his voice low. "No telling what La Marque might do."

"That must be him all right. I swear he looked right at you. Like he knew you was there." Dex scratched his neck. "Do you think he saw the aura like Madam Judith did?"

"Can't say for sure, but it must be something like that. Maybe he saw it in his mind's eye or something. It must be a kind of discernment." Allen's skin crawled as he recalled a similar feeling in Dark Wolf's cave. I *know the Lord will see me through another encounter, but I'd rather not have to.* "The only sure thing is that I'm sitting in a tree in the middle of a swamp."

"Yup, life's an adventure."

The crickets chirped, bullfrogs croaked, and an occasional night bird whistled, and then the sounds stopped. Allen tapped Dex's arm, and he sat up. A different bird called, and the rest of the sounds resumed. A couple of minutes later, the new bird whistled again. They strained their ears for noise of a predator or hunter. Allen gasped when Catfish Man tapped his knee and waved them to follow. They climbed out of the tree and stayed close behind the guide, who seemed to have night vision. In half the time it took to find the tree, they were back at their post and next to Danny, spying across the compound.

Danny spoke in Cherokee, and Catfish Man vanished into the shadows. "You can see lamplight at the house and the bunkhouse. People are walking into the woods yonder, where they're starting a fire. See?" Danny rose to his knees. "I don't see guards. Our little friend went to have a look."

"Look at the barn window. What kind of lantern puts off such a white light?" Dex pointed.

"It is different than the other ones. Some kind of candle?" Danny mused.

Allen stood bent with his hands on his knees. "That's Abraham, not a candle. It's Abraham praying. It must be. Follow the light."

"Follow the light." Dex put his hand on Allen's shoulder. "Let's go get him."

"We wait for Catfish Man." Danny scrutinized the yard. "I don't want to fall into some trap."

"Maybe we'll see an angel in there." Dex looked at the tree beside them. "I might shimmy up this tree for a better angle."

When Catfish Man appeared, he conferred with Danny,

pointed in various directions, paused to listen, then as quickly as he'd appeared, he disappeared.

"He says many people stand at the fire, and they knifed a woman, an owl woman. He thinks they will kill more. They are drunk for more blood." Danny stroked his chin. "I sent him to check for guards around the barn."

The guide trotted straight for them across the open ground. He chattered while pointing back at the barn. Danny calmed him and made him repeat his report. "He says there is a guard, but it is not a man. He heard singing of many voices."

"That don't make no sense." Dex's fists were on his hips.

"I say we go now," Allen declared. "I'll go in and call to him."

The four ran, hunched over. Allen stopped at the door to listen, grinned, and nodded. He cracked open the door so they could all hear.

Abraham sang, "My chains fell off. My heart was free."

Allen walked in, singing, "I rose, went forth, and followed thee." The three rescuers entered, staring at the shine coming from the stall.

"Oh, Lord of mercy." Abraham gasped. "Brother Allen, is that really you? Or am I seeing another angel?"

The stall door opened, and Allen embraced his friend. "It's me." He sobbed.

"Thank you, Lord Jesus. Thank you."

"We should go." Danny pulled a knife to cut the ropes. Dex stood staring. Catfish Man stayed by the door, as if ready to escape the mysterious man.

Allen clutched Abraham's arm. "You up to running a bit?"

"Lead the way." Abraham paused at the door and pointed at the fire through the trees.

Allen looked back to see Danny, Dex, and Catfish Man delay for a moment to watch the brightness in the stall dissipate.

They crouched and ran toward the trail. Upon reaching the landing, Danny turned off, pulled a rope, and his boat slid forward, covered with branches. Catfish Man tapped Dex to help untie and shove the other pirogue out to deeper water. Allen and Abraham climbed in at the stern and took seats, though Catfish Man stood at the bow. Danny pushed off and began poling. The quarter moon offered scant light to the mossy labyrinth. If not for their guide's intuitive skill of a life in the swamp, they would have bumped into every stump and mud bar. After a few more minutes, Danny paused at the faint but distinct sound of gunfire. He stowed the pole. "Dex, let's row."

Trahan lifted his shroud to produce a flask and guzzled. He gratified his lust of the flesh, but now the lust for power overwhelmed him. He found Sly at the edge of the firelight, leaning on a tree. "Come with me."

"Where to?"

Pulling down the hood, he glared at the bigger man. "To wherever I order you."

Sly returned the stare. "Well?"

Trahan grabbed a torch and marched straight to the barn. He barged in, but upon seeing the stall door open, he halted. Sly studied the tracks in the dirt and squatted in the stall, picking up the rope. "Someone cut him loose."

"Who? How can that be?" Trahan huffed. "Arrg. This is your fault, you fool." He swung the torch down to strike, but by reflex, Sly raised his arm to block. The flaming club glanced off his shoulder but hit the side of his face.

Sly fell back and twisted. "You dirty . . ." He drew his revolver, cocked, and fired. The bullet caught Trahan in the chest, knocking him back against the doorpost. The torch flipped back to a pile of straw. He fired again. Trahan was dead before he dropped to the ground.

Sly flinched when he touched the burned welt on his cheek and right ear. The straw ignited, and he tried to stomp it out, but it was spreading too fast. He grabbed the torch and went out, shouting. "Fire!" Only one man with a lantern ran toward him. The rest either didn't hear or were too intoxicated to respond. The flames in the barn were almost eye level. "Never mind that. Come with me." Sly trotted down the trail to the landing, raised his torch, and squinted into the dark channel. "Look over there for my pirogue."

"Nothing here."

Sly went over, holding the torch low, then high. He shielded his eyes from the bright flame with his palm. "Is that my boat or a log?"

"Where? I can't tell."

Sly cursed, stomped, and hustled up the trail to watch the barn burn around Trahan.

Tension was high in the crowded pirogue, as pursuit was expected. Allen kept his eyes peeled for movement on the water where they had been. Danny and Dex rowed hard and fast for an hour straight across the wide lake before Catfish Man directed them to a cove with a wide, sandy beach. Within minutes he had the last catfish cut open and roasting on spits over a fire between two logs. Even though the midnight air was warm and humid, the group gathered near the fire for the light and comfort it provided. Any boat hunting them would not see the firelight until they were right in the sheltered cove.

"My friends." Allen kept his voice low. "This is Deacon Abraham. I want you to meet him officially, since you've risked your lives for him. And I can't thank you all enough . . ." His lip quivered, and he paused to wipe his eyes.

"Deacon Abraham, it's good to meet you. I'm Dex, this here's Danny, and we call our cook Catfish Man."

Abraham put his arm across Allen's back. "Lord bless you all. I'm grateful for your kindness. I knew that the Lord would send men of valor. I'm truly honored."

The men were quiet while Allen sobbed. The guide passed around the spits with the browned filets dripping with juices. They blew on the meat, picked off chunks to eat, and licked fingers and wiped chins on sleeves.

"Dang, that were good eating." Dex burped. "We named you proper, Catfish Man, and I forgive you for leaving out the taters."

Allen laughed and tossed his spit in the fire. "What should we do from here, Danny?"

"Hard to say if Sly and his boys will try coming after us in the dark. I expect they'll wait for daylight. Don't know if they have more boats." Danny scraped sand with his spit. "We have an advantage as long as our guide stays with us. Baton Rouge is not more than twenty miles northeast as the crow flies. But we got some nasty swamp to work between here and there." He looked over at Abraham. "How did you come to be here?"

"Yes, sir, it was like you said, hard work. We rowed when we could and dragged the boat when we had to." He nodded. "Mr. Sly said many times that the bayous change with every rain."

Catfish Man waved his hand and made a shooshing sound with his lips. Squatting down, he pointed up into the dark sky. "*Tsigili.*"

"He heard an owl," Danny explained. "It's the same word for witch."

"We should be leaving and get some more miles behind us. If this owl is a watcher, then maybe Sly's on the move already."

Allen kicked sand on the fire. They'd come this far—surely they wouldn't be overtaken.

Dex helped. "I'm all for leaving, but which way do we go? Making our way in the dark is going to be tough." He chucked a rock at the owl and hit a branch just below it.

Abraham watched the owl fly away. "I have a strong nudging in my heart that we should go south. That make sense to you'uns?"

Danny interpreted the question and answer. "There is a bayou to the south that runs toward the Mississippi. But it has been low water and may not be passable. Even if it has water, it's a long way round to get to Baton Rouge."

"I believe we got to try. The Lord made dry land for them Israelites. We'll trust he fill in the water for us." Abraham moved toward the boat.

"It's a big risk. Sly and his boys could catch us stuck in the mud." Danny shoved the bow around.

"I'm for it." Allen cast his vote.

"Me too." Dex agreed. "We got to keep the faith."

"All right then, let's go." Danny shoved them off. "At the bottom of this wide lake, there's a finger that runs a couple more miles south. If we get there before Sylvester spots us, we'll have a fighting chance."

They took shifts rowing through the night as the Chitimacha guide kept his place in the bow. When he wasn't rowing, Allen tried to sleep, but nerves and the cramped space made it difficult. A keelboat would feel luxurious compared to this.

As gray rose in the east and the water was distinguishable from humps of land, Catfish Man waved them over. Allen held a stump as he watched the Indian hop out of the boat. He pulled up plants by the dozens and dropped them into the bow. When he seemed satisfied, he jumped back in and waved them forward. Pulling out a small knife, he cut off the root bulbs and tossed the stems back into the water. He held a bulb up, slit it open, and ate it. "*Nunv.*"

Danny burst out laughing so hard he held his belly. They passed handfuls of bulbs around. When Danny caught his breath, he held one up to Dex. "Potato. This is a swamp potato."

As they shared the laugh, Dex looked back at Catfish Man, who grinned with his mouthful. "Ain't you the sharp chisel, boy howdy."

The pirogue weaved through the cypress trunks like a toddler running through a crowd of women wearing pleated skirts. Catfish Man picked his teeth with one hand and pointed with an arrow in the other hand. He urged them forward between two long mounds of land. They came into an east–west cut about twenty-five-feet wide and as long as the eye could see in both directions.

"None too soon. Look." Danny pointed behind them. Some two hundred yards or more, three pirogues moved through the trees. "I guess Sly had some boats hid away."

"How'd they know to look for us this away?" Dex stalled his oars. "That derned owl must have told him which way we came. I should have pegged it when I had the chance."

"It looks like maybe two foot deep." Danny gave instructions to Catfish Man to alert them to shallow water.

Catfish Man replied.

"He says there shouldn't be this much water here." Danny moved into a fast-paced rhythm. "This cut was made years ago when the big river flooded, like it was trying to start a new little river." He rowed hard for several minutes until the hull dragged across a mud bar. Catfish Man swerved them to the left and then back to the right. After thirty yards, they were back in the deeper water. "Allen, grab that rifle, and keep an eye on them coming."

Abraham passed the musket and powder horn to Allen, who was on the stern seat. He checked the cap and held the long gun across his lap. A moment later, the three pirogues turned into the narrow bayou. They were lighter and moving fast.

Danny strained at the oars. "They're sitting high and won't drag like we did." He huffed. "If they get within a hundred and fifty yards, you shoot at the lead boat."

Catfish Man called out shallow water. They looked over the side at the muddy bottom. Both oarsmen were flicking mud. "Oh no. Lord help us," Danny cried out. "If we bog down here, they'll catch us for sure."

Allen sat tall and took aim. He cocked, drew the set trigger, and covered the firing trigger. The movement of the strokes kept his sights wavering off target. He took a deep breath and let out half. As he was about to touch the trigger when the front pin drifted down on the cluster of men, he paused and then raised the muzzle.

The forward pirogue lunged and pitched to the side. The next in line rammed it and capsized as the third turned but ran into the brush. The men were out and standing in ankle-deep water. They began dragging their boats through the mud, seeking the deeper water. Allen could see Sly throwing up his arms.

"We're out of the shallows," Dex called out. "Let's make some time."

As they coursed around a bend, losing sight of their pursuers, Danny punched the air. "I think we done beat them. That must've been a powerful prayer you sent up."

"Hallelujah." Deacon Abraham beamed. "Brother, I reckon it was your prayer done brought us through. You saw how we skimmed over the bottom when we should've been grounded."

"That's right, Danny." Dex kept rowing. "Keeping the faith."

"Well, I don't know. At least we're getting away."

"I'm inclined to agree with Dex," Allen added.

Hours later they broke out of the brush to a wide clearing. Dex stood up and scanned as much as he could see. "You know what? We ain't far from the river. I bet we're close to Plaquemine. Maybe we'll find us a smoker boat heading north."

Catfish Man pointed and urged them to shore. When they beached, the crew followed the guide through the brush into a wide field. A quarter mile across stood a cluster of small huts with tall conical thatched roofs. He waved them toward the village.

"This is a village of his people," Danny explained. "He has family here, and we'll be fed."

They ducked into an *asi* and sat cross-legged. Within an hour roasted turkey, venison, and boiled squash was set before them. Colorful woven baskets and pottery bowls were used as utensils and for storage. Catfish Man introduced other men as chiefs and spiritual leaders, who nodded and murmured when he pointed to Allen and then to Abraham. Danny interpreted what he understood. "He says that you are on a long journey to rescue your friend. They are surprised that a white man would risk his life for a black man, but they say you have a warrior's heart. And Abraham sings with spirits and has joy in his eyes. They know of the evil work of La Marque, and you did not become his slave. There is great power in your heart because you do not keep hate for your enemies."

Danny conveyed their need to leave, but then the people brought baskets with food, bead necklaces with alligator teeth, and knives.

"Let's go before they offer us a wife or something." Dex smiled and nodded at the robust-figured woman staring at him.

Allen used sign language to express gratitude and affirm the bravery of Catfish Man. Abraham spoke a blessing over the village. They returned to the pirogue and made their way to Plaquemine.

"You two best keep out of sight," Dex said to Allen and Abraham. "Danny and me will hit the wharf."

They were back within a half hour. Dex pranced into the boat. "You won't believe it. Well, maybe you two will, but Uncle Randall is here. Said there was damage to the boiler, and this was the only place to fix it. He's ready to go. We'll be in Natchez by morning."

Danny's pirogue was loaded onto the cargo deck. They shared staterooms on the second level and watched the shoreline whiz by like lightning compared to rowing in the swamp. Allen and Abraham lounged on one bunk, Danny and Dex on another, and they recounted their journeys.

Allen leaned in with a furrowed brow. "What happened to make those slaves act so unnatural, wandering about?"

"Their minds are lost in the darkness between dying and death." Abraham slowly shook his head. "La Marque makes a concoction he called a tea. Made from the jimson weed and some kind of mushrooms that makes the mind see things that ain't there. People get a spell of visions, but they also get a somber feeling they keep on craving. They goes near crazy if they don't get the next drink of tea when it wears off. Gets agitated, then angry, like they'd choke you."

"Have you seen anything like it before?" Allen sought to learn all he could. Spiritual battles were strange enough, and the use of narcotics complicated the healing process.

"Not like this. Lord bless them with hope." Abraham yawned. "That La Marque did the devil ritual on them too. Drunken orgies and then sacrificing people to an altar of Belial."

"The idol of lawlessness. That explains some things." Allen gazed across the room. "When we were in Cave in Rock, the pirates boasted in their lawless behavior."

"Rebelliousness is as the sin of witchcraft," Abraham quoted. "And the Lord will remove them both."

Dex had been paying attention to the mysteries while smoking his pipe. "Maybe we can talk about something more cheerful. Tell us about Moon Cloud, Allen."

"Deacon Abraham, you haven't heard about her yet." Allen leaned his elbows on his knees.

Abraham shook his head.

"I was invited to live in an Arapaho camp. One day she walked by leading a group of small kids. She was telling them stories about their people's history. I could see right away she was pretty, but there was something else about her that made her special. We went hunting together. You should see her shoot a bow and arrow. She can pick a flying quail out of the air. We went on walks along the river, and it's nothing like the Mississippi. It's smaller and faster and so clear you can see every rock on the bottom. She taught me to speak Arapaho words, and I'm teaching her English.

"She picks berries and roots and gives them to the old women. She organizes dances for the camp and makes the most beautiful beadwork." He paused, gazing into the air. He recalled how she looked in her white doeskin dress when she watched the sunset.

"She sounds like a real sweet gal," Dex said. "What's she look like?"

Allen sighed. "Moon Cloud has long black hair that she keeps in braids most of the time. Most women do. And she'll put beads in there or dangle beads off a strip of leather. She wears buckskin dresses that have beadwork all across the front or down the arms." He motioned with his hands. "They're all just decorations, but . . ."

"Yeah." Dex prompted with a hand gesture.

"Well, they prove that she takes care of herself, but, I guess, it just makes her face shine and her eyes get bright. I mean, she doesn't need the dress to look good—she has the prettiest . . ." He was interrupted by a burst of laughter. "What?"

Dex guffawed and slapped his leg. "You said she didn't need a dress to look good." He grinned.

Abraham chuckled, and Danny laughed.

Allen finally caught on. "Wait. That's not what I meant. I mean she's pretty without a dress." Another burst of laughter. "Oh no."

Danny pointed at Allen. "Look at your face. And they call me red man." He folded over, holding his stomach. Dex laughed so hard he leaned back and bumped his head on the wall.

"Go on, Brother." Abraham patted Allen on the back. "We know what you was saying."

Allen took a deep breath to stop chuckling. "I was trying to say her eyes are the prettiest brown you've ever seen. They sparkle when she smiles, and they're as comforting as . . . as . . ."

"As a cup of coffee on a cold morning?" Dex intervened.

Allen nodded and sighed.

"Well, it's easy to see you're smitten. We're going to have to get you up the Trace as fast as we can so you can get back to that girl. She sounds like a real peach," Dex said.

"One step at a time." Allen smiled at his friends. "That is my wish and my prayer—to get back to her as soon as I can. But the next step is to get Abraham safely home, and then I go to Baltimore to meet with my overseers and clear my name."

"Brother Allen, I'll go with you to Baltimore to testify how you lay down your life for your brothers," Abraham said.

Allen believed Abraham's concern linked all their hearts.

"I'll go too if you need a witness. I'll tell those stuffed shirts how you been taken prisoner by pirates and slave runners just to rescue one lost sheep." Dex poked the air with his pipe stem.

"Thank you, friends. I appreciate your support. But like I said, let's take one step at a time." Allen yawned and moved to his bunk. "We'll make our way back to Portsmouth on the Trace, and perhaps start tomorrow."

"The Natchez Trace." Abraham lay out on the soft bed. "It has its own dangers."

CHAPTER TWENTY-FIVE

ALLEN STOPPED THE ROCKING CHAIR and studied Uncle Randall's stern face while Dex puffed on his pipe, sitting on the back-porch railing at his mother's house. Deacon Abraham and Danny listened intently.

"The river ain't safe at all. You're going to have to make your way up the Trace. No doubt about it." Randall propped himself on the rail, with his arms folded. "I'll run my steamer up north, see if anyone follows. I'll lay low in Saint Louis for a week or so."

"Sorry to put you at risk." Allen shook his head.

"Like I said before, you're with Dex, so I'll treat you like family. Goes for you too, Abraham," Randall said, as if he'd already drawn a line in the sand.

"Rightly obliged, sir." Abraham nodded.

"All right then, if we's going up the Trace for eight hundred miles, I guess we'll be needing horses." Dex looked in the distance. "That'd be three or four hundred dollars we ain't got."

Danny stood up to lean against the house. "Horse races start in a couple of hours. I'll go see who's riding."

"Good idea." Dex tapped out his pipe. "I'll head down to the inn to see about a game."

"I'll go with you, Dex," Uncle Randall offered. "Might be we can work something out."

"What should we do?" Allen wanted to be useful.

"Stay put," all three said at the same time. Then Dex added perspective. "You've got a price on your head, and Abraham might too by now. Best you stay here and keep out of sight. I know how to blend in around here and can move quicker on my own. We're fixing to leave in the morning as early as possible."

Marylou came out. "No one's going anywhere until you been fed proper. I got a ham roasting and fresh bread. Ya'll get cleaned up."

After the group of men had eaten to Marylou's satisfaction, they rose from the table. The three went off on their fundraising endeavors while Allen and Abraham helped wash the dishes.

"Dex says he makes his own luck at the poker table. I don't know what that means exactly, but he came back with enough to get us this far and help out a woman in need." Allen wiped the last plate and placed it in the cupboard. "I feel a bit guilty praying for him to win at gambling, but I don't know what else to do."

"The Lord works in mysterious ways." Abraham dried his hands. "This ain't normal circumstances, and we can't judge those the Lord sends our way to help. Maybe he's leading up to something we can't see just yet."

"Would you men care for a cup of tea here in the parlor?" Marylou called from the front room.

"Yes, ma'am, that would be nice." Allen led the way to the settee.

After sipping from delicate cups, the hostess rocked slowly. "All my life has been on the river. I've seen all kinds of violence, greed, corruption, and there are times I've seen the goodness in people. When a man steps in to protect someone who's helpless or to be generous. The way I figure, we have to do all the good we can to make the world a better place." She paused a moment. "I done my best to raise Dexter to be one of the good ones. I hope you don't hold it against him to go off gambling."

"Ma'am, Dex has saved my life several times since I met him. He has been generous and taking care of people along the way. My only course to raise money is to ask the church for a special offering, but considering our situation, that doesn't seem like a wise thing to do." Allen set his teacup down. "I believe God made our paths to cross, and that's been confirmed over and over. So I won't hold anything against Dex. He's come to be a very special friend."

"Thank you for saying that, Allen." Marylou blinked, clearly holding back tears. "I'm grateful that you two met. I know you're a good influence on him. The way you went to such lengths to rescue Abraham and talking about God the way you do, like you really believe."

"Thank you. I've learned some good things from him."

"And, Abraham, I only just met you, but I feel so calm and peaceful with you." She placed her hand over her heart. "I heard about that terrible man that held you prisoner. It must have been horrifying."

"Yes, ma'am, thank you. There were times when I fell to fear and discouragement. But the Lord is faithful to bring me the strength I needed to carry on. I know that the witchcraft that was formed against me would be broken, just like the prophets Isaiah and Micah said."

"Do you believe that all witchcraft is evil?"

"Yes, ma'am, I do. We must call on the name of the Lord for our strength and direction, not to the work of other powers."

"Even if it's helpful and does good?"

Allen interjected. "You took us to see Madam Judith, and some of the things she said were helpful, like finding Danny and seeing a light. I can't say I understand it all, but I do know that witchcraft that seems good can draw you in deeper and deeper. Like Abraham says, we must put trust in the Lord for our strength."

"I know what you're saying, and it moves my heart, it truly does, but I tried calling out to the Lord for help. Even to take me away from the taverns and what I had to do to survive. May God forgive me, but the church people judged me and cast me out. I found Madam Judith, and she gave me medicine that cured me, and she told a fortune that gave me hope, and it came true. I believe I'm alive today on account of what she done for me. How can that be a sin?"

"Miss Marylou." Abraham gripped his shirt at his chest with both hands. "I'm sorry, and I beg your forgiveness. Us church folk have failed you. You been judged and rejected when you should have been loved and welcomed. It breaks my heart something fierce to see it happen. You trying hard to find your peace with God. Forgive us."

She sniffed and nodded as tears rolled down her cheeks.

Allen leaned forward. "I've been out west with the Arapaho and learned things I don't think I ever would have known. I saw a man as evil as La Marque trying to control people's lives and grow in power. And a good-hearted medicine man who seems to hear from the Lord even though he had never heard the name of Jesus. All I can figure out on my own is that God is at work calling people to draw close to him from wherever they stand in life."

Abraham had been listening with his eyes closed. "Miss Marylou, if you'll allow me, I'll share a word of hope from the Lord."

She nodded.

"You been hurt by men all your life. They done taken advantage of you and left you. So many men that you can't remember. All you done is survive this hard life."

Tears streamed down her cheeks.

"Your mama done her best, but she passed on when you was young."

She sniffled. "How do you know that?"

"Your father left to find work, and when he come back, you was living with another family. And the man treated you wrong. And your father tried to get you, but the man chased him off."

"How can you know all that?" She stared at him. "I've never told anyone."

"What that man done hurt you bad, deep in your heart."

Her shoulders moved with the sobs as she nodded.

"What hurting you deeper is that your father didn't fight for you—he just left."

Marylou fell to her knees, holding her stomach. "Papa, why did you leave me?" she wailed. "Why didn't you care? Papa, why didn't you love me?"

Allen found a handkerchief and knelt to place it in her hand. When her groans and gasps paused, he helped her back into the chair. He noted the firm compassion in his friend's eyes. There was so much to learn about this deep emotional healing.

Abraham held her gaze. "God is tugging at your heart, but you're holding back because he's called 'Father.' Deep in your soul you don't want to risk that he will leave you too. Child, you've got to trust him. Let him prove that he loves you and will always be with you. He won't disappoint you like people do."

"How can I be sure?"

"You have to listen to your heart. Is it pounding right now?"

She nodded.

"You pray and ask the Lord for forgiveness and to make your heart clean with his Holy Spirit."

Just then Danny walked in the front door. "I have some good news. I've lined up four horses for a bargain. We'll still have to buy saddles and gear, but that should be easy doings."

Allen stood with his hands on his hips. "That is good news."

"Dex?" Danny looked toward the kitchen.

Marylou wiped her eyes. "Not here. I imagine he'll be a couple more hours. Y'all should get some rest. Not much can be done until morning anyway."

Just then in walked Dex with a big grin. "Don't know if it was a particularly lucky night or if your prayers was working, but I came home with the money we need." He smiled and tossed Danny a felt pouch full of coins. "That's for your guide service in the swamp."

Danny bounced the black bag in his palm and nodded his approval. "I got lucky at the Pharsalia racetrack too. We got four horses on hold for us."

"It's peaches and cream then." Dex pulled a larger pouch out of his shirt. "That'll save us good bit of time. Did you place a bet?"

Danny shook his head. "No. I was about to put down ten dollars when I came across Ben Shirkland, who owed me money. He'd been on a losing streak and was miserable worried. I offered to buy his retired horses for ten dollars each plus cancel the debt. He agreed, and I gave him my ten to seal the deal. He bet on the next race and won twenty-five and felt like I brought him good luck."

"We'll have plenty of cash then. Good." Dex reached into the pouch. "Allen, I have a special gift for you. This is one of them things that helps me keep the faith." He held out a black leather cord on which hung the lost gold nugget.

"Hey." Allen took the gift. "I can't believe it. How?"

"I remember saying back at Cave in Rock that no scoundrel deserved to keep it. But believe this—Finster was at the gaming table. Don't know how he escaped the cave, but I sat across from him. He looked surprised at first but then got cussed ornery. Some of the boys didn't like him calling me names and threatened to toss him out. I challenged him to poker, and he laughed like

284

he was the devil. I cleaned him out in twelve hands. Last thing he laid down was that nugget. When I won, he pulled a knife and shouted that I was cheating. Uncle Randall knocked him on the head with a spittoon, and he dropped like a sack of beans. They dragged him out, and that's the last I seen of him."

"This is just astounding. I don't know what to say but thank you." Allen put the nugget around his neck.

Danny listened as Dex recounted the story of Allen's nugget from Blue Otter. Danny grinned. "So did you cheat?"

Dex shook his head. "Didn't need to. I didn't cheat, didn't bluff. I was dealt a winning hand every time. Never seen that before. That's when I figured you was back here having a prayer meeting."

As laughter broke out, Allen saw Abraham smile softly at Marylou, who acknowledged with a slight tip of her head.

Dex slapped Allen on the shoulder. "Guess we better turn in. Can't wait to see what happens tomorrow."

"I'm anxious to get up the road. I can't wait to see Sister Lydia's face when we walk in the church." Allen beamed with anticipation.

Abraham followed Allen out the back door to take a turn in the outhouse. When they had finished, they stopped to look up at the stars.

"The Lord is good." Allen breathed deeply the fresh air. "I thank him for showing me the way to find you. And now he's worked in Marylou's heart. What marvel will he show us next, Abraham?" He turned to his silent friend. "Abraham?"

A truncheon struck him on the back of his head. Looking up from the ground, Allen saw two dark figures leaning over him. "Who . . ."

Everything went black.

Dex stepped off the back porch in the direction of the out-house. "Allen? Abraham? You out here?" He walked out to the front of the house. Nothing. Hustling back in, he found Danny. "Hey, come out, would you? They're not here."

Danny squatted to touch the ground. "Bring a candle."

When Dex got there with the candle, it confirmed what he had already concluded.

"Two big men in boots, maybe more. Dragged off Allen," Danny said. "Might be they just carried Abraham over their shoulder. They was hiding in them trees, watching the house."

"What we going to do?" Dex looked up and down the street for a shadow or silhouette against the far lights of the taverns. "We best check down to the water, see if they took them in a boat."

An hour later Dex met Danny at the bottom of Silver Street. "See anything?" Danny asked.

"Nothing." Dex swung his arm in the direction of some river boats. "I asked in the tavern, but no one knew anything. They ain't even hiding information."

"Maybe they were taken up to town." Danny started walking up the street. "We'll have to ask around in the morning. Someone has to know something."

When they reached the house, Dex paused again where the scuffle took place. "I got a bad feeling deep in my belly." He spit in the brush.

An owl screeched and then swooped past their heads.

Dex threw his arms up. "Oh no. Oh God. God, you have to help Abraham and Allen."

Sister Lydia bolted awake, gasping for air. In her dream, she was walking down a narrow road through a dark forest. She had to step over fallen logs and twist around broken branches, and each one tried to trip or scratch her. The road was muddy and slippery, but she could move forward steadily. Then the owl flew up and screeched in her face.

She slipped on her oversized shoes and wrapped herself in a crocheted afghan. "I rebuke you, witchcraft spirit. I rebuke you in the name of Jesus. You will not intimidate me. I am a child of God." Lydia moved out to the front room, lit candles, and paced. "Lord Jesus, I praise you tonight. How do you want me to intercede? This witch owl must be threatening Deacon Abraham and Brother Allen. Lord, direct me now."

For three hours Lydia set her beloved brothers before the altar of the Lord. Finally, she knelt and leaned her elbows on a chair. "I thank you, my Father. Send the angel band, Lord. Send the angel band. In thy precious name. Amen."

In the teepee of Waits Long, the fire had gone out, but the buffalo-hide blanket was warm. Moon Cloud pulled back the blanket, which suddenly felt heavy, as if it were suffocating her. She sat up and breathed in deeply. Scraping sparks into a wad of tinder, she blew until a flame flared, and she added twigs. The night light was enough to see her aunt and cousin still sleeping. She pulled the blue stone from its pouch around her neck and held it to the light. Seeing the comforting shades of azure glow, she smiled, but then frowned as the pressure of the weighty blanket seemed to be pressing on her heart. She added more kindling, slipped on moccasins and her three-point trade coat, and exited the lodge.

Moon Cloud made her way to the river, where she found Two Rivers singing softly. She knelt and sipped water from her cupped hands, filled her palms again, and rose to let the cold, life-giving stream fall and return to its source. "Great Father, give me an understanding mind and hearing heart."

When the hours had passed and the weight finally lifted, Moon Cloud remained poised in thanksgiving. With her eyes closed, her mind could picture Two Rivers standing there and a man of brilliant white standing behind him. She opened her eyes and saw only the aging medicine man. "White Falcon has been captured as a slave but will walk free. He will return to me, to us."

Two Rivers looked at the stars. "Yes, One Who Give Life fights for him."

CHAPTER TWENTY-SIX

ALLEN OPENED HIS EYES TO a dimly lit room that swirled around and around. *Where? How did I get here?* He touched the goose egg on the back of his head and flinched. Deacon Abraham lay asleep a few feet away on a cold brick floor. There were no windows, only a door slot covered by a metal slide hatch. At least he wasn't shackled. He stood and steadied himself against the wall. A light dizziness accompanied the throbbing lump.

He squatted next to Abraham and touched his shoulder. "Abraham, Abraham, you awake?"

"Oh, Allen, that you?" He rubbed his eyes and examined his arms and legs with his hands. "This looks like a dungeon room."

"I think it is. It doesn't seem to be an ordinary jail." Allen held Abraham's arm as he tried to rise. "Did you see who grabbed us?"

"No. They whopped me on the head while you was talking, and that's all I know."

"Do you suppose it was Sly? Maybe he caught up to us."

"Who else could it be? Mr. Sly or his workers." Abraham leaned back on the wall.

"If that's the case, he might hold us until La Marque comes."

Allen swallowed at the worrisome thought. "It was past midnight, maybe one o'clock, when Dex came in. Hard to say how long we've been here.

"I believe the Lord will be our refuge and strength. He will rescue us from the mouth of the lion." Deacon Abraham spoke out his faith. "As long as we have breath, we must praise his holy name."

In the following hours, they quoted psalms and sang hymns, turning the damp dungeon room into a sanctuary.

Dex lay awake on his bed. "I hate not knowing where they are. I hate waiting like this."

Danny lay on a blanket on the floor. "Ain't no sleeping tonight. Sun be coming up in an hour or so."

"Where do you think they could be?"

"No idea." Danny rolled and settled on his elbow. "How you supposed to keep the faith like this?"

"I don't know. It seems hopeless." Dex sat up. "I guess I can try a prayer."

"If you think you know how."

Dex took a breath, then let it out and shifted his legs. He took another deep breath. "Lord . . . Hey, Danny, do you think I ought to be standing, or kneeling maybe? Should I read the Bible or something?"

"From what I seen of Allen and Abraham, it don't seem to make a difference."

"Yeah, right. It don't make a difference. Abraham prayed in the barn stall." Dex shifted again and inhaled. "All right, here goes. Don't laugh."

"Just go already."

Dex cleared his throat and squeezed his eyes shut. "Oh Lord.

Um, God. I don't know how to pray like Allen or Abraham. Um, forgive me for that. Um, we need your help. Again. You been helping us with the wind and in the cave and such. You done got us out that swamp. But how you going to help us now? We need one of them miracles. Like them fellows Joshua and Caleb. Send us someone who ain't afraid of the giants around them." He paused. "Um, that's it."

"Say amen."

"Right. Amen, Lord. God Almighty. Um, and thanks for the help. Jesus, God."

"You done?"

"I guess. I can't think of nothing more to throw in there."

Dex rolled back to his pondering position. For the next half hour, the room was silent except for soft breathing and the squeak of the bed with Dex's slight movements. Abruptly, he sat up. "I can't wait no longer. We got to go find them."

"Me too. But where do we look?"

"I don't know yet. But it's time to go. I got a feeling." Dex jumped off the bed and went to the door to his mother's bedroom. "Ma, wake up. Ma, get up. It's important."

"What is it, Dexter?"

"Does Larson McDill have another place up in town?"

"Yes, the back of the land surveyor's office. Why?" Marylou peeked through the opened door.

"Collect our bags and go wait up there. It won't be safe here until we can get out of town." Dex leaned in. "We're fixing to get Allen and Abraham and skedaddle up the Trace. They might press you to talk, or worse, hold you until we surrender. Do you understand?"

"Yes. I'll go right away and wait for you to come."

"All right then. Sorry, Ma."

"Don't worry about me none, Dexter. You go find your friends."

Dex and Danny slipped out of the house and stayed to the shadows as the sky turned a lighter shade of gray. They reached the business center of Natchez and paused to catch their breath and listen.

"You don't think they would be held at the courthouse, do you?" Dex tapped Danny's elbow.

"No. But I think close by. My guess is that the kidnappers got connections with the big-caliber businessmen." They continued up State Street, and as they passed a two-story brick building, Danny stopped. "Listen."

"What?"

"Singing." Danny held his hand up to still all movement.

"I don't hear nothing."

"Let's keep moving. I feel like we're being watched." Danny faked a sneeze, and they walked on.

At the next corner, they turned left, then left again to double back down an alley.

As they approached the brick building, Dex touched his ear and nodded. "It's got to be them." They faded into the deeper grayness under a tree and behind the corner of the carriage shed on the right. "They ain't on the first floor. There must be an underground room."

"Look up there. An open window." Danny pointed with his chin to a second-floor window in the middle of the building.

"Should a brought a ladder, I guess."

Danny described his plan. "See how the brick is offset at the corner? We can shimmy up there to the roof, cross over, then dangle down to the windowsill and slip in."

Dex blew a silent whistle. "If I had an apple pie, I'd knock on the front door. But lacking that, I guess we climb. Lead on, Warrior."

The bricks at the corner extended out to make a decorative outline, enough for a solid handhold, and the mortar gaps were deep enough for a foot grip. By opposing pressure and foot friction, Dex scaled the wall and pulled up onto the roof, Danny right behind him. At the point above the window, Danny lowered himself to rest his right foot on the wide sill. Dex dropped next to him, his bare feet feeling for solid placement. They each hooked a foot under the open gap and raised the window as high as it would go. Shifting his right hand to the shutter and his left to the frame, Danny hung his body lower and let both legs swing into the room. His hand grabbed the window and rotated all the way in. He patted Dex's calf. Dex smoothly followed and lowered the window to its original position.

The pair crept through the small office, peeked into an empty hallway, and sidestepped down the stairs, with their backs close to the wall. The hall of the main floor was lined with closed doors, except for one at the end. Dex let Danny lead and watched him edge his way until he could glance in the room. Dex peered over his shoulder. A watchman sat in the corner, looking out the window where they had been a few minutes earlier. Too risky to try overcoming him, Dex figured.

Danny slowly pulled the door, reached around to find a key under the knob, and slid it out. He gently closed the door with the softest possible click and turned the key, locking the unaware watchman inside.

Danny and Dex crept to another set of stairs that led down into a large, cool cellar. They could hear the singing clearly now. At the far side, lit by an oil lamp on the floor, were two doors with slide hatches and bolts. A guard dozed on a chair that reclined steeply against the wall, a pistol tucked in his waist belt. Danny moved swiftly, pulled the gun, and stuck the muzzle in the man's face as he rocked forward. Grabbing him by the collar, Danny lifted him to his feet, twisted him into a choke hold, and whispered "Quiet" in his ear.

Dex held the lamp and slid open the bolt. He poked his head into the dungeon enclosure. "Howdy, boys. I ain't no angel, but I'm here to set you free."

Allen jumped up. "Dex." He rushed over to hug his friend.

"Mr. Dex, you look as good as an angel to me." Abraham beamed.

"Glad to see you." Dex's grin then dropped. "But we best get going."

Emerging from the cell, they saw Danny holding a pistol to the guard's head. He shoved the man in and bolted the door. All four quickly climbed the stairs.

As they moved carefully toward the entryway, Allen noted a wooden trunk on which was folded a satin banner with a symbol he recognized. He opened the top fold and read in the dim light. *Masonic Temple.* He dropped the fold as he caught Deacon Abraham's attention.

Danny looked up and down the street and waved them forward. They walked to the corner, away from the window where the guard was, turned right, and broke into a run until Dex stopped at the back apartment of the land surveyor's office. Marylou opened the door and hustled them inside. Dawn had broken through, and the darkness of night was gone.

CHAPTER TWENTY-SEVEN

ALLEN'S CHEST HEAVED AS HE caught his breath. He peeked through a curtain to watch for followers, but there was no movement.

"Thank God y'all are safe." Marylou hugged Dex. "I have food for you, and your bags. I hope I got everything."

"Ma, it's good. We'll need to take off right away." Dex shoved the food sack into a satchel and slipped on a pair of low-cut boots.

Marylou hugged each man and paused before Deacon Abraham. "I want you to know that I took to heart the things you said. I asked God to forgive me and make me right. I feel such peace. My heart feels like it's flying. Thank you."

"God bless you, ma'am." Deacon Abraham squeezed her hand.

"We better git." Danny held the door open a crack.

"The Trace can be dangerous, so be careful." Marylou frowned. "And stay away from the Witch Dance. That is a wicked place."

Dex glanced at Allen. "Yes, Ma. We'll steer clear of it."

"But listen." Marylou folded her arms. "Larson was here earlier. He said Sylvester will hold you captive until La Marque gets here, or else they'll hang you all for helping a runaway slave."

"But, Ma, he's a free man," Dex blurted out. "They can't be making lies."

"I know it. But folks around here will put a stop to runaways, and the truth don't matter." She put her hand on Dex's arm.

"We'll be going then, before they find out we escaped." Dex took his mother's hand in his. "Will you be safe?"

"I got places to hide out for a spell. Don't worry on it." She pursed her lips. "Larson said they already had a bounty on you, all four. So once they discover you're on the loose, they'll be recruiting men to hunt you down. They'll be watching the river, the Trace, and every road leading out of town. They intend to tell every farmer to report you and get a reward. The army patrols will be searching for a runaway slave and those assisting him. Even the governor is in on it."

Allen's brow creased. "La Marque, Sylvester, the army, the governor, and any man seeking a bounty. What are we going to do? Seems like all the giants are after us."

"Giants?" Dex pointed his finger at Allen. "If it's only giants surrounding us, then we got them beat. Deacon Abraham is heading home, and we got to get you back to your true love. We can't disappoint little Moon Cloud now, can we?"

"No, I reckon not." Allen smiled with pride at his friend.

"Keep the faith." Dex grinned and led them out the door.

SNEAK PREVIEW

OF

THE RIVER WEST,

THE THIRD BOOK
IN
THE TWO RIVERS TRILOGY

CHAPTER ONE

THE OVERCAST MORNING WARMED QUICKLY with the humidity of the Mississippi River Basin. Two miles northeast of Natchez on the Washington Road, Reverend Allen Hartman peered over the brush from behind a hickory tree. Barely an hour before, he had been rescued from a basement holding cell of the Masonic Temple. The lump on his head had shrunk but was still tender. Now he and his friends were trying to escape from the assassin and his thugs, who would be on their trail soon. He scanned the side pasture of a horse farm, waiting for visual contact of Danny, who finally appeared crouching along the corral fence toward the house. After checking the surroundings, he approached and knocked. A man opened the door, they exchanged words, and then Danny waved Allen, Dex, and Deacon Abraham forward.

Allen trotted across the grassy field toward the house, Dex and Deacon Abraham beside him. Allen kept an eye on the road to their right and the tree line in every direction. It might be safe here, but probably not.

Danny, named *Danuwoa*—warrior—by his Cherokee father and Choctaw mother, introduced Allen and the others to Ben Shirkland, a horse breeder, racer, and trader who owed Danny money. The night before, Danny and Ben had met at the Pharsalia racetrack, where they'd struck a deal for Danny to acquire four retired racehorses, which would clear Ben's debt.

Dex—Dexter Yates—was a young keelboat captain who preferred life on the river and considered Natchez his home port. He had said he had a vague acquaintance with the horse trader and knew his reputation as a decent breeder but a lousy gambler. He nodded but kept surveying the area beyond.

Abraham remained a few steps back. The Negro pastor Deacon Abraham, being falsely accused as a runaway slave, was several inches shorter than Allen, whose elbow he gripped as he whispered, "We need to be careful with this one."

Allen nodded slightly, and they all moved toward the barn. He held back with Deacon Abraham and paused. "Danny will make the deal as fast as possible, and we'll head up the Trace. We'll leave Natchez and the swamp behind us and get you home."

"Are these the nags you promised?" Danny assessed the livestock.

"Yes, and I appreciate the business. You can choose the saddles and pack bags, but it'll cost extra."

"I figured." Danny cleared his throat. "We'll see what you have and settle."

The four horses sniffed the dirt for something to nibble in a corral next to weather-worn barn. In a small pasture beyond were six more tall sorrel thoroughbred racers. Allen noted that the horses they were buying had thoroughbred features but also worn-out countenances. Age and overwork had forced them into retirement.

Allen and the others selected their saddles and rigged up.

Danny took the bill of sale and tucked it into his shirt. He loaded food and camp gear in each saddle pack. "Will fifty cover the saddles?"

"I was thinking a hundred and fifty." Shirkland folded his arms.

"That's steep for used saddles." Danny squinted and shifted on his feet. Clearly there was something about the beleaguered horse trader that bugged Danny.

Dex looked around at the road and the tree lines. "Here's a hundred." He slapped the bills on a barrel head. "Thanks, but we got to get going." He flicked his hand toward Allen and Deacon Abraham, and they mounted.

"Well, no need to rush. My wife baked a ginger cake, and we'll put on the coffee." Shirkland held the reins of Dex's bay.

Dex looked antsy and glanced down the road. "Look." He pointed to a band of horsemen riding fast in their direction.

Danny sidled his horse. "Shirkland, what did you do?"

"Nothing."

"Let go of the reins," Dex shouted.

Danny gigged his horse and raised his foot to kick Shirkland in the head. He knocked the trader to the dirt. "Ride."

The four raced up Washington Road as shots rang out. Allen leaned forward over his horse's neck while looking over his shoulder. He saw smoke dissipate as the riders came in hot pursuit. After a half mile they reached a clearing, and Dex pointed to the right and shouted.

Allen leaned into the turn and galloped over the yard of a farmhouse. A woman and two children were tending chores as the four thundered toward them. Allen veered and jumped a low rail fence to race across the pasture to the south. When he heard enough hooves pounding behind him to know his friends were in the pasture with him, he turned to glance back.

The pursuing riders stopped at the fence and fired wildly at the escaping party.

Dex slowed when they reached the tree line at the far end of the pasture. "They ain't following yet." He caught his breath.

"Who are they?" Allen searched the field behind them.

"I didn't see Sly, but it must be men out for the bounty." Danny spun his horse around once he reached the cover of the trees. "Shirkland must have alerted them."

"Must be why he offered cake, that derned varmint." Dex shook his head. "About a quarter mile through these woods and we'll reach the Trace. We'll have to be careful and quick. They likely have people on the way looking for us."

"We're not well armed." Allen pointed at Danny's musket and pistol.

Dex lifted a single dueling pistol from under his coat.

Danny led, winding through the dense forest until they could see the narrow opening of the road to Nashville. "I'll go on ahead to the Hawthorn stand. Give me ten minutes lead time and come along at a trot."

When they rejoined, Danny explained that word had gone up the Natchez Trace to be looking for them. "Now every Kaintuck and his brother will arrest whoever looks like us. We can't trust anyone, not even the army patrols. Looks like La Marque is putting up serious money. Plus, the Freemasons and slave owners are out for vengeance."

"It will be too slow off the road and too risky at night," Dex put in. "This is a merry fix. How far you going with us, Danny? I ain't figuring you for the whole way to Ohio."

"I was thinking to go as far as Yowani. I have family living there. I'm most worried about this stretch up to Jackson. More people will be hunting us."

Allen rose on his stirrups to see down the road. "Guess we're going to see what these old racers are made of."

Danny nodded and heeled his sorrel to a trot. The Trace was wide enough for large wagons at this stretch. They varied their pace over the next several hours with little contact with people.

"This seem odd to you that we ain't seeing many people?" Dex looked for agreement when they slowed for a walk.

"Let's count it as fortunate. We're making good time." Allen wiped the sweat off his forehead.

"Allen's right. I think we should make the most of it while we got light. After dark we'll make a camp in the trees and rest the horses. Maybe Big Sand Creek." Danny nudged alongside Deacon Abraham. "You've been quiet. You doing well?"

"Yes, sir, Mister Danny. I don't ride much, so when we was back at the Shirkland's farm, I snatched me a sheepskin to sit on for protection." He grinned.

"I should a got me one of those." Dex stood in his stirrups to rub his sores. "I don't get blisters sitting on my boat."

Avoiding Port Gibson and most of the farms, they kept the low profile until sunset, when they came to the Big Sand. Danny angled south off the road and through the woods for a couple hundred yards until they found a clearing by the creek. A small fire heated water, roasted meat, and soaked them in its glow until they were ready to hide within the darkness.

The gray light of dawn barely reached the dirt road when they had put five miles behind them. Over the next few hours, they trotted past farmhouses and shunned conversations with other travelers. Danny allowed them a brief rest just before reaching Clinton. His reasoning was then to ride fast until they were beyond Jackson. Army patrols were dispatched to keep criminal activity to a minimum along the Trace. But now they would be looking for a runaway slave and an abolitionist. Allen shuddered. Vigilante crews made up of slave catchers and opportunists often bullied travelers and unsuspecting farmers in the Jackson vicinity and possibly more at Nashville. Jason Sylvester, the slavecatcher and assassin, posed the darkest threat. He served a vindictive master who utilized his extensive influence to accomplish his devious will—a man Allen and his motley crew had recently rescued Deacon Abraham from.

Danny swallowed the last of a corn biscuit and washed it down from a canteen. "Listen up, fellas. We're about fifteen miles from Jackson. The road skirts the town proper but comes within a few miles, so we have to be wary." He swept his hand across the landscape. "Brush will be thick like this all the way, making it chancy to jump off the road. Past Jackson we'll be along the Pearl River and then the swamps. Staying on the road is the fastest way but could be the most dangerous too." He mounted and reined a circle. "Let's go."

Hooves kicked up dirt for a mile before they slowed to a trot. Passing one group of riders heading the other way caused stares and pointing. They reached the junction of the Canton Road, where five men were lounging. One jumped up upon seeing the riders approaching.

"Hey, come over here. Stop you." The others joined him with guns in hand. "I said stop. Come here now."

Danny waved his men on, prodding his horse to a lope. Allen looked back to see the men scrambling for their horses. After several minutes, they paused in an open grove off the road. "You hide in the brush here. I'm going to ride ahead for a look." Danny's chest heaved.

"What about those other boys coming up behind?" Allen patted the sorrel's neck.

"I don't trust what's beyond the bend before us. Those coming from behind ain't in view yet." Danny kicked the bay and vanished with the curving road.

"I hate hiding in the bushes." Dex stretched out his legs. "And these derned boots are killing my toes."

Several shots sounded in the distance. A half minute later Danny came flying around the bend, pumping his arms and leaning far over the racer's neck.

"Roadblock. This way." He skidded his turn and kept riding into the trees.

The three kicked into action and crashed through the brush and branches. They slowed for the obstacles and leaped into the shallow river, splashing water and mud high into the air. Deep into the green cover, Danny stopped them to listen.

"Hear that?"

"I hears it." Deacon Abraham shivered. "Hound dogs."

Dex strained to hear. "They can't follow us in the water, can they?"

"They ain't coon dogs, brother," Deacon Abraham said. "Them's slave hounds. They won't stop for water. They won't stop at all." He visibly shook.

"Come on. We'll ride when we can and walk when we have to." Danny ducked under a branch. "We're going deeper into the swamp."

"Wait," Dex called out. "You're bleeding."

Danny shifted in his saddle to look at his hip. "One of them blokes hit me with his smoothbore. Must have been goose shot."

"We got to stop the bleeding, or them hounds will catch us for dang sure." Dex slit the tail of his linen shirt with a knife. "It's right above your hip bone. Did it go on through?"

"No. I can feel the ball here, under the skin."

"We best cut it out quick, so it don't slip back in and lodge somewhere," Dex urged.

"No time now. Them hounds is getting louder." Danny took a deep breath. "I'll just have to pinch it here until we can hide away." He packed that cloth against his entry wound and pulled his sash up to hold it in place.

He weaved them through the tupelo and cypress trees in water that was deep enough to wet the horses' cannons. An hour later they stepped the animals onto a pitch of dry ground.

Allen handed his canteen to Danny. "You're looking pale."

The guide gulped water, but his head wobbled and he swayed in the saddle.

"Dex, help me get him down." Allen leaped off his horse.

The two men slid Danny off the horse and to the ground.

The peanut-sized bump protruded above the hip bone. Dex wiped the knife on his shirt. "Abraham, there's a bottle of whiskey in my saddle pack."

Danny took a drink, and then Dex sipped. "I expect this is going to hurt."

"No doubt. Get on with it." Danny grimaced.

Dex pinched the skin under the ball and was setting the edge of the blade against the top, when Deacon Abraham stopped him.

"If I may, Mr. Dex. Cut along the base of the lump, and it will pop out." Deacon Abraham gave a little flick with his fingers.

Dex handed him the knife. Deacon Abraham directed him to stretch out the skin, and he made a quick, smooth slice the width of the lead ball. He tapped Dex's hand, and it burst out with a stream of blood. "Pour whiskey on that cut and let the blood flow for a bit. Then press on there till it stop."

Danny groaned at the sting of the whiskey and breathed deeply while Dex kept pressure on the wound.

"It will be dark in less than an hour." Allen searched the sky light and surroundings. "I don't hear the hounds. Think we should wait out the night right here?"

Dex looked at Danny, who struggled not to give in to his wound. "You need rest, and we can keep watch in turns." Finally, Danny nodded.

Allen tied the horses on a patch of grass about ten yards away, then bunched together with the men in a cluster of tupelo and laurel brush.

"Nobody move," a voice commanded, followed by splashing steps. A man with a rifle aimed at them came forward.

"Now look what we got here." A second man marched forward with two pistols up and ready. "Surprised to see me again, Yates?"

"Finster?" Dex raised his hands. "I am surprised, you scoundrel. I thought they chucked you in the river."

"Ha. They did. But I come back to life just to haunt you." He aimed at Allen. "I want my gold nugget back."

Dex lowered his hands. "Look, I know you ain't no miracle story, but how did you get here?"

The pirate flicked his gun to keep Dex's hands up. "Bennett, go fetch Sylvester, and be quick about it." The rifleman faded into the shadows. "That's right. Sly pulled me out of the river and offered me money to find you. I told him I'd do it for free just so I could see the look on your face."

"Well, I'll be. You got more grit than I give you credit for, Finster." Dex put his hands on his hips. "You should go on back to Cave in Rock and be the big man."

The rogue stood with one foot in the water and the other on a log. He smiled at the flattery and leaned his elbows on his knees. "Yeah, maybe I'll do that. But first I want my gold and the money you cheated off me. Now Sly wants those two alive"—he nodded toward Deacon Abraham and Allen—"but he didn't say anything about you. And your friend's about dead as it is. So maybe I'll cut you up slow like and have myself a good laugh."

"I guess you deserve that. You caught me fair and square."

"That's right. You might be a slick hand at poker, but when I put on the hunt, I catch what I'm after. I'm thinking I'll partner up with Sly and make my living hunting down ... Agh!"

A splash and forceful slap of its tail and the alligator lunged, gripped a leg, and flopped Finster against the log and into the water. He screamed in agony. The fierce teeth dug into his thigh, and the jaws shook him like a rag doll.

Allen froze with his eyes wide and mouths agape.

Danny poked Dex. "Quick. Get me up on a horse—we need to go."

Finster screeched and gulped for air as he was thrashed and dragged.

"Lord have mercy." Deacon Abraham hustled into action.

Dex hoisted Danny up, and the others walked the horses away from the monster and deeper into the swamp. Finster's cries continued until the muffled boom of guns stopped them.

Slogging on for more than a half hour, Allen snapped his fingers twice. Dex stopped and let them catch up.

"Any idea where we're heading?" Allen spoke softly.

Danny was sitting up in the saddle, holding the cloth against the wound. "The swamp goes on for twenty miles or more. As long as we keep clear of the Pearl, we'll be all right."

"I say we take our chances on the road," Dex piped in. "I've had enough of swamps and gators."

"Mr. Danny, the swamp's a good place to hide, but if they turn them hounds on us again, we'd be in a fix. On the road we could outrun them," Deacon Abraham offered.

Danny exhaled. "Let's angle off that way, Dex. Take it slow and quiet."

Once they reached solid ground, the cracking of fallen branches made alarming noises. The forest was black, so they trusted the horses' night vision. When the brush became impassable, Dex risked lighting matches. Finally, they broke into a clearing. Motioning for the others to stay in place, Dex crept forward alone.

"The Trace is right over there. About a mile back down, I can see torches. Nothing up ahead," he said when he returned.

"Don't mean there ain't guards out, so let's be careful." Danny took the lead.

They moved out at a trot. About twelve miles later, they stopped where a small cabin stood at the edge of road, with a two-acre clearing behind.

Danny reined to a halt. "That cabin is too convenient for vigilantes and highwaymen to be watching the road." He dismounted. "I'm thinking we cut through the trees and loop around behind and make a camp at the edge of the farm. That way we can watch and see if Sly's boys are this far out."

"It's well past midnight now. A few hours' sleep will help." Dex rubbed his bay's neck. "Lead the way."

They found a grassy spot with logs to protect them for the night.

At first light no movement stirred around the cabin. They ate corn dodgers and smoked ham as they lay the miles down before the sun shone through the trees. The road was lined with oak, elm, laurel, and a dozen other species of trees. Allen had heard that what had once been Indian trails and a course for bison and elk migrations following salt licks, the Natchez Trace was now the main communication between the cities of the east and Louisiana. Wilderness settlements had grown quickly with the westward movement to become towns—which, to Allen's thinking, attracted the ambitious, the greedy, the corrupt, as well as honest, hard-working people of faith.

Allen and Abraham rode side by side sharing Scripture verses back and forth and praying for their journey. The long stretches of roadway passed by more quickly, and the fellowship cheered their hearts.

"Danny, how are you feeling?" Allen urged the bay up closer.

"I'm fine. Koskiusko is a few miles. We should reach Yowani tomorrow, and I can heal."

"Maybe there's an inn we can have us a steak." Dex looked back over his shoulder and frowned. "Abraham, you hear something?"

He wagged his finger and then patted his chest. "Don't hear them yet, but someone's coming up ahead."

Danny felt for his pistol. Allen reined to fall back in place next to his friend.

"I don't see no one." Dex stood in his stirrups. "You sure?" He looked back but then jumped in his saddle.

"Hold it there." A man stepped out of the brush with a Kentucky long rifle pointed at Danny. "Y'all get down. Slow."

"Yes, sir," Dex said. "We ain't got much money." They dismounted.

"Maybe not, but you're worth some." The man wore patched wool pants and a stained shirt and brown leather vest. His gray hat looked like a cone with a sagging brim. "They's been riders out offering reward for two men, a Injun, and a colored. Y'all fit that description."

"Pa, put the gun down." A girl came to his side leading a mule. "They's the men I told you about. Ones I dreamt on."

She looked like maybe thirteen years old. She wore a sack dress that came below her knees and homemade shoes.

The man squinted, huffed, and lowered the barrel. "Say your piece."

"I saw him in the dream." She pointed at Allen. "And the black man. We was all walking on this road covered by a big chicken wing. Then they was in our house preaching, and Patrick got off the bed. Pa, Patrick is healed—I know it."

He rubbed his whiskered chin. "The Lord done give her the dreaming gift. Sees things what come to pass. I abides by the word of the Lord, so best follow on." The man marched up the road, then turned with the gun at his waist. "Y'all best do what the Lord says if you know what's good for you."

Dumbfounded, Allen looked at each man, then followed.

"Did the Lord say anything about fixing a plate of steaks in that dream?" Dex cocked his head toward the girl.

"How far is your house?" Danny asked, frowning at the delay.

"Trail's up yonder before that bend." The father walked at a brisk pace.

Dex gave Danny a puzzled look. "Sir, what are you doing out here, anyway?"

"Mule wandered off. Usually find her at a salt lick." His cheek twitched under an untrimmed beard. "Suzy here found her in the crick stomping on a cottonmouth. Twern't bit though."

"Suzy? I'm Dex, and this is Danny, Allen, and Abraham. And what do we call you, sir?"

"Call me Tommy." He didn't pause to shake hands.

As they approached the bend, they halted as a crew of seven riders came their way fast. But they thundered by without slowing or even looking at them.

"Them's the fellas what put out the reward for y'all." The man watched them race away. "Wonder where they's going. Like they didn't even see us."

Abraham raised his arm. "He shall cover thee with his feathers, and under his wings shalt thou trust: his truth shall be thy shield and buckler. Psalm 91." He put his hand on the girl's shoulder. "Your dream just come to pass, Miss Suzy. The Lord hid us from the eyes of the enemy."

"Best hurry." Tommy led them down a narrow trail through dense brush to a cabin nestled in the trees. Next to it was a second shed with animal traps and hides hanging on every available space. Suzy tied the mule to a post and followed the men into the cabin.

"My wife's taking care of her sister up to town. Got the croup. Patrick here fell on a log and hurt his hip and back." Tommy lit a candle.

Danny shifted his feet. "Go ahead, Abraham. Get to preaching or praying or whatever you need to do."

Deacon Abraham took the lad's hand. "Patrick, do you believe in the Lord? And that he died on the cross and rose again?"

Patrick nodded.

"That's fine, fine. Let me ask the Lord Jesus how he's going to bring the healing."

Deacon Abraham then spread his arms out above the bed. "Lord, you bring the healing." He quoted Scripture of healing the lame by the faith of friends. "Does you feel pain while you're just laying there? Can you sit up?"

Patrick shook his head. "Hurts too bad."

Abraham continued praying, until Allen interrupted. "Patrick, do you need to forgive someone who hurt you?"

After several more minutes of quiet, he burst into tears. "Yes. My heart's going to bust." He gasped for air. "A man in town cheated me out of some furs. We needed the money, but there was nothing I could do. I was fixing to burn down his store, but Pa came, and we left."

Abraham leaned in. "You got to forgive him. Let God have the vengeance."

"That was the week before he fell," Tommy recalled.

"Let go of the hate. Tell the Lord you forgive him."

"I do—I forgive him. I forgive him for cheating me." He cried.

Deacon Abraham continued speaking over the young man, who finally caught his breath. Taking both hands, the pastor pulled slowly to raise him to a sitting position. "Now, does that hurt?"

Patrick's eyes widened, and he breathed deeply. He shook his head.

"Lord Jesus, you are the healer." Deacon Abraham pulled again and gently raised the wounded lad to his feet. "Has you got the pain?"

"Little." Patrick looked at the father and sister, who wiped her eyes.

"We thanks you, Lord, for healing your son here. We thanks your great love and power." Deacon Abraham took Patrick's right arm, and Allen the left. "Try a small step."

Patrick grimaced as he moved his foot forward. His face relaxed, and he took another step, and another. He moved his arms out of the supporting hands and walked around a table. He circled again and hugged Suzy.

"I abide in the word of the Lord." Tommy embraced his son. "Thank you, sir. Thank all of you." He shook each man's hand.

A few minutes later, Suzy came in with her hands full of a meat. "We done butchered a calf yesterday. We can fry steaks if you got the time."

Dex spoke for the group. "Well, praise the Lord—we got time."

After their bellies were full of steak and roasted turnips, they said their farewells, gathered the horses, and made their way toward Koskiusko.

Danny permitted a small fire while they settled down to rest.

"Abraham, how do you figure that troop of men rode by without seeing us? I mean, we was right there in the open." Dex dropped a handful of twigs on the fire.

"Mr. Dex, all I can do is give God the glory. He's protecting us as we walk in faith. I got no other explanation."

"And that girl had a dream about it. How'd that happen?"

Allen sat cross-legged across from Dex. "I went to seminary, and they never explained those things. Only agreed that they are mentioned in the Bible. I don't understand how it works, but I'm living to see it. I have to take it in faith."

"Well, how'd you know he needed to forgive somebody?"

Allen swiped his hand from his belly to his throat. "The

thought came to me like it was rising up from within me. I'm not sure how it works, only that it always seems to fit."

"That's how the Holy Ghost work, different ways for different people." Deacon Abraham yawned. "It's a lot to think on, Mister Dex."

By noon the next day, Danny veered north off the Trace heading for the Big Black River. "My mother's family lived in this area until the relocation. I still have uncles and cousins that hunt and trap. Used to be a big Choctaw village, but they're all spread out now. More white farmers moving in and taking over the land. I fear that soon I will have no homeland."

The trail merged with the river, and Danny slid off his horse and kneeled to look at tracks. "This way." He remounted. A half hour later, he pointed. "See them chukkas?" The round huts were clustered along the bank, some made of small logs and some of grass bundles.

Danny was welcomed by his cousins, and a large meal was provided for them. Since the horses were spent, he traded for three fresh ones.

"Allen, Abraham, I don't know if our paths will cross again, but it's been good to know you." Danny held out his hand.

"Danuwoa, the warrior." Allen gripped his hand. "I would not have found Abraham without you, and we wouldn't be this far along without you as our guide. I have no doubt that God brought us together because you were uniquely skilled to help. I pray that you heal quickly and return to prosperous hunting and trapping."

Abraham shook Danny's hand and nodded in agreement. "Danny, I trusted you from the first moment when you came into that barn to set me free. God used you for this special purpose, and I believe he will use you again."

"Dex, take care." They shook hands.

"I'll be seeing you, Danny." Dex heeled the new dapple-gray mount and led the way back to the Trace.